invisible REPUBLIC

CREATED BY GABRIEL HARDMAN & CORINNA BECHKO

WRITTEN BY	GABRIEL HARDMAN & CORINNA BECHKO
ART BY	GABRIEL HARDMAN
COLORS BY	JORDAN BOYD
DESIGN BY	DYLAN TODD
EDITORIAL ASSISTANCE BY	BRENDA SCOTT ROYCE

INVISIBLE REPUBLIC, VOLUME 01.

COPYRIGHT 2015 GABRIEL HARDMAN & CORINNA BECHKO.

FIRST PRINTING. AUGUST 2015.

ISBN : 978-1-63215-408-8

Published by Image Comics, Inc. Office of publication: 2001 Center Street, 6th Floor, Berkeley, CA 94704.
© 2015 Gabriel Hardman & Corinna Bechko. Image Comics® and its logos are registered trademarks of
Image Comics, Inc.

Originally published in single magazine form as INVISIBLE REPUBLIC #1-5.

Printed in the USA.

For information regarding the CPSIA on this printed material call:
203-595-3636 and provide reference # RICH – 632037

For International Rights, contact: foreignlicensing@imagecomics.com

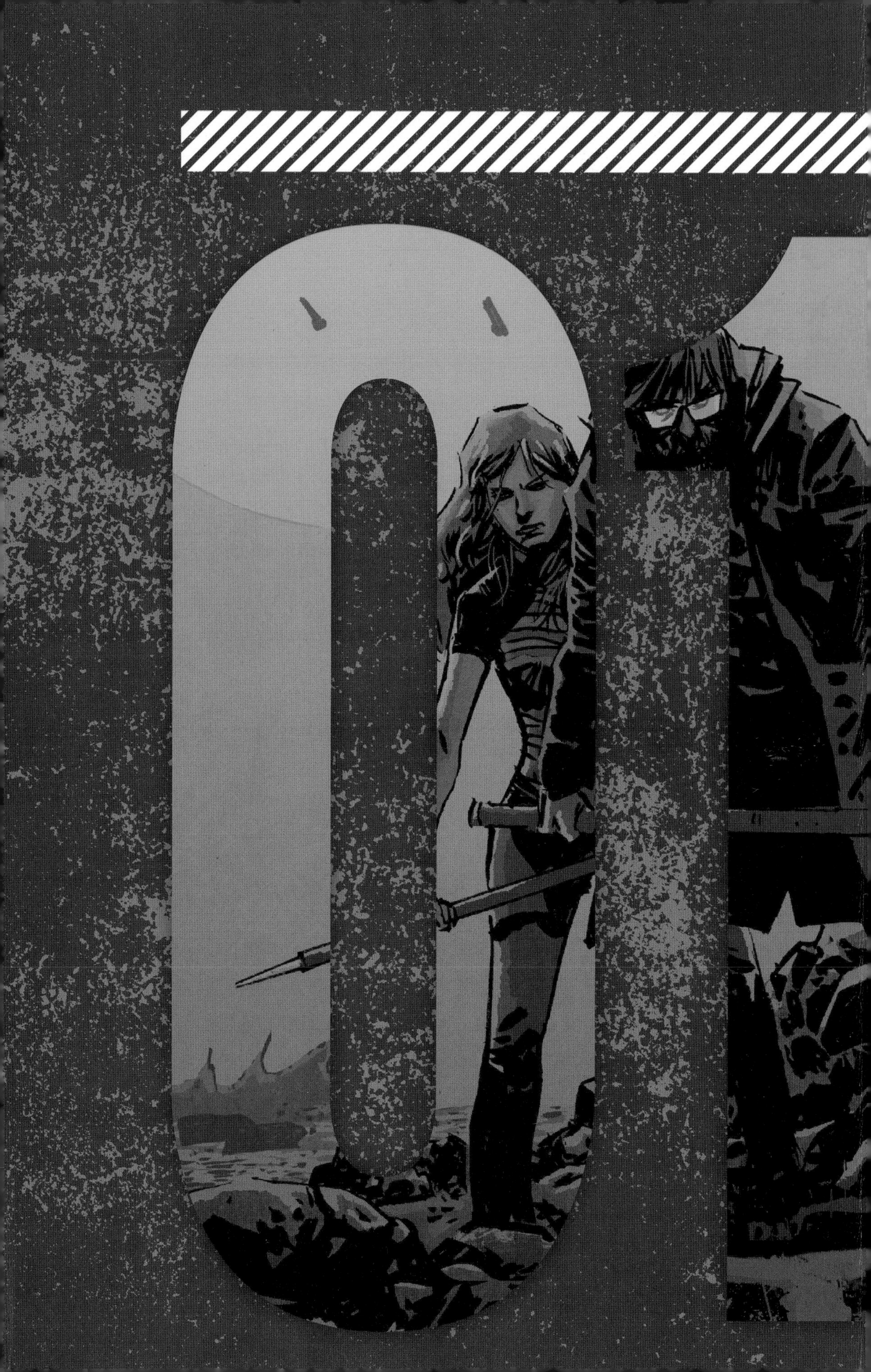

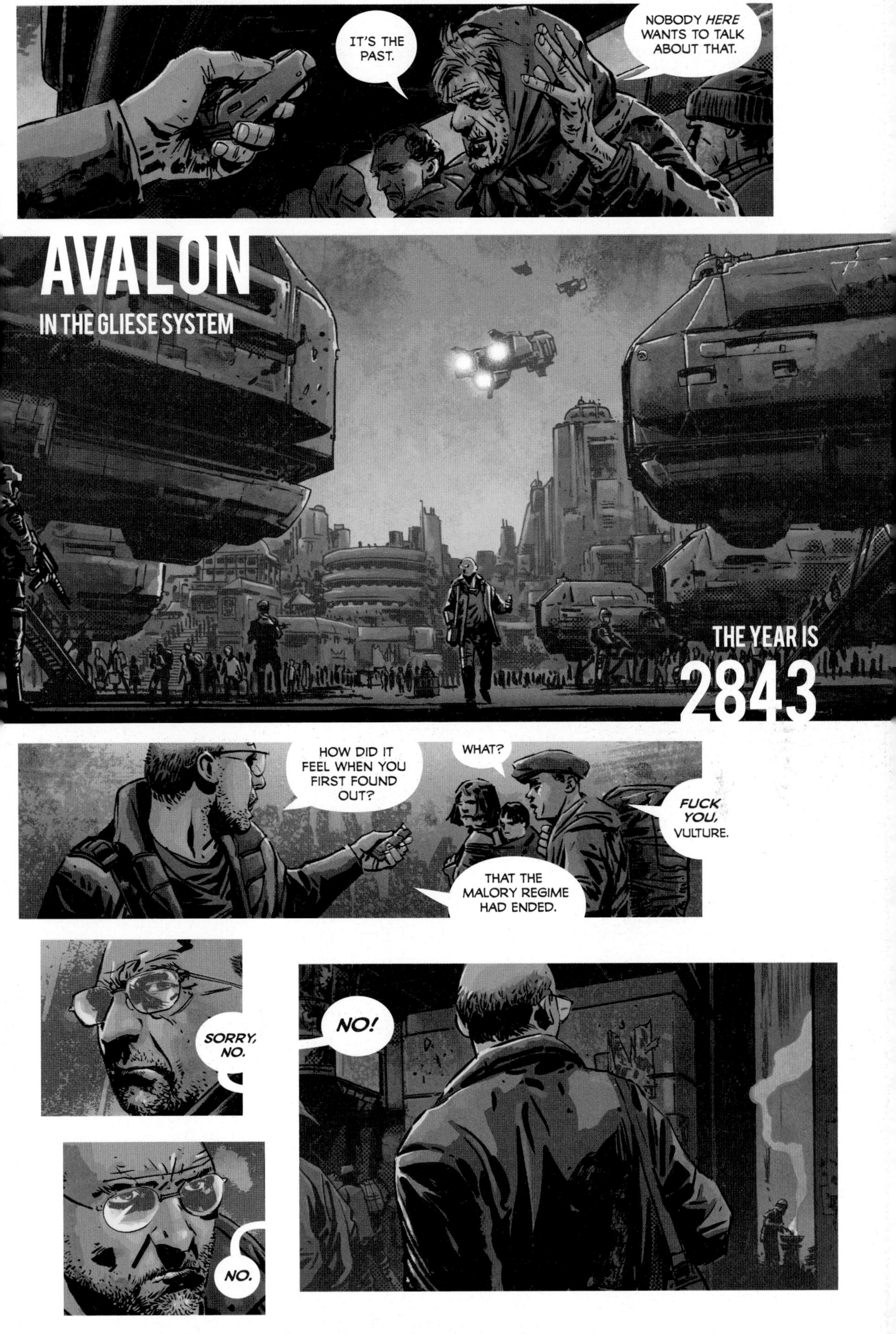
IT'S THE PAST.
NOBODY *HERE* WANTS TO TALK ABOUT THAT.
AVALON
IN THE GLIESE SYSTEM
THE YEAR IS
2843
HOW DID IT FEEL WHEN YOU FIRST FOUND OUT?
WHAT?
THAT THE MALORY REGIME HAD ENDED.
FUCK YOU, VULTURE.
SORRY, NO.
NO.
NO!

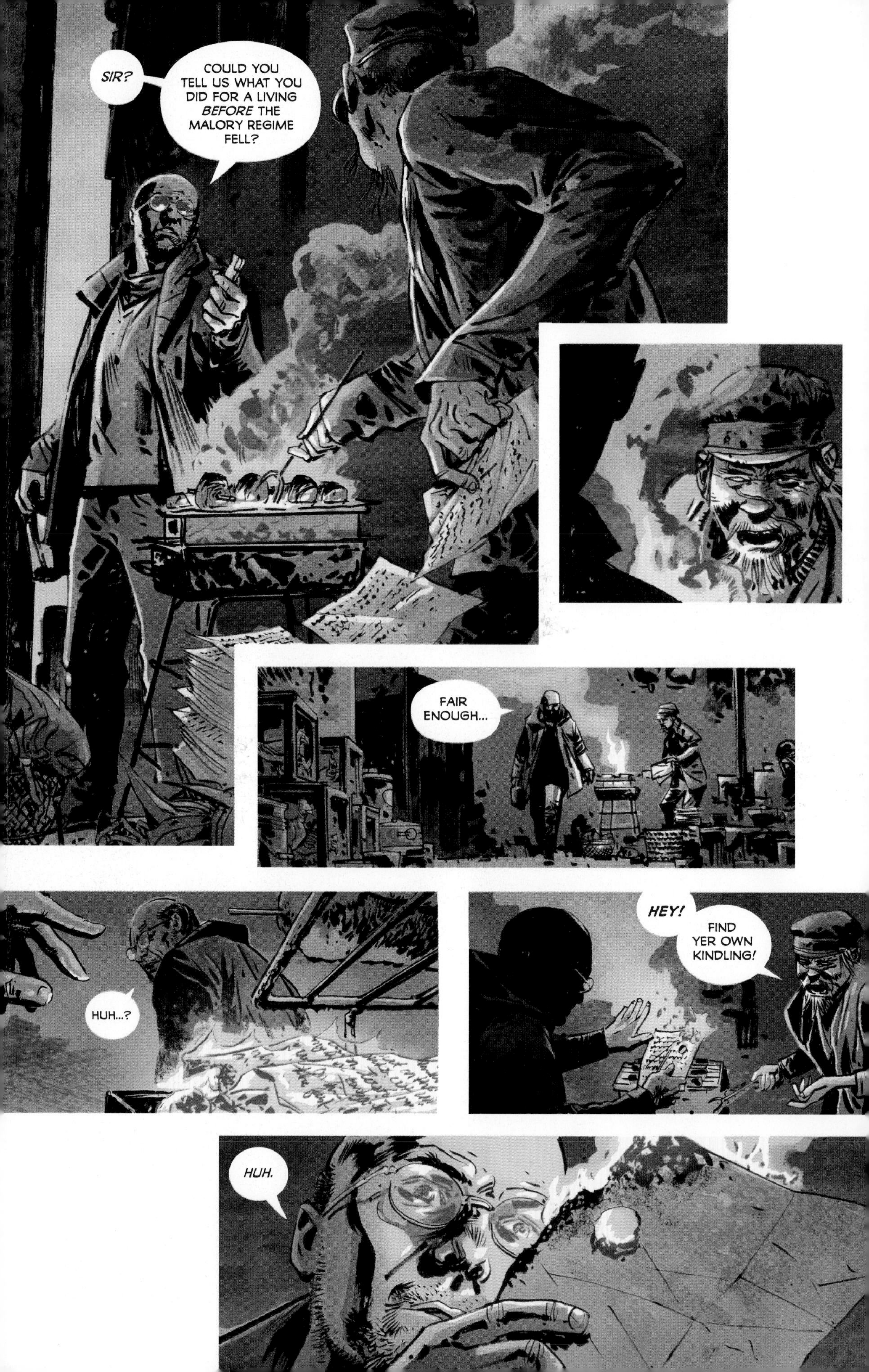

SIR?
COULD YOU TELL US WHAT YOU DID FOR A LIVING *BEFORE* THE MALORY REGIME FELL?
FAIR ENOUGH...
HUH...?
HEY!
FIND YER OWN KINDLING!
HUH.

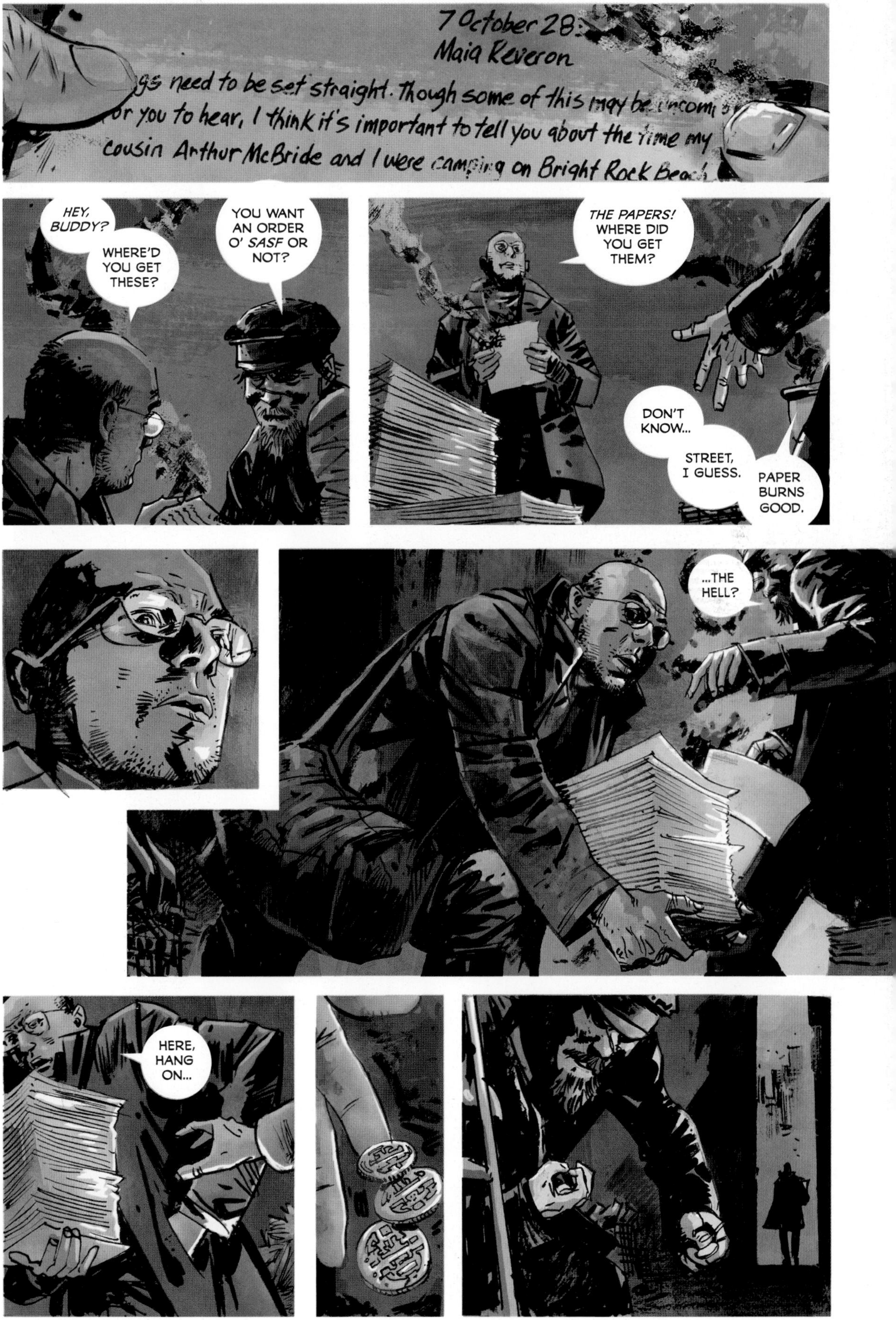
7 October 28:
Maia Keveron
gs need to be set straight. Though some of this may be uncom
or you to hear, I think it's important to tell you about the time my
cousin Arthur McBride and I were camping on Bright Rock Beach
HEY, BUDDY?
WHERE'D YOU GET THESE?
YOU WANT AN ORDER O' SASF OR NOT?
THE PAPERS! WHERE DID YOU GET THEM?
DON'T KNOW...
STREET, I GUESS.
PAPER BURNS GOOD.
...THE HELL?
HERE, HANG ON...

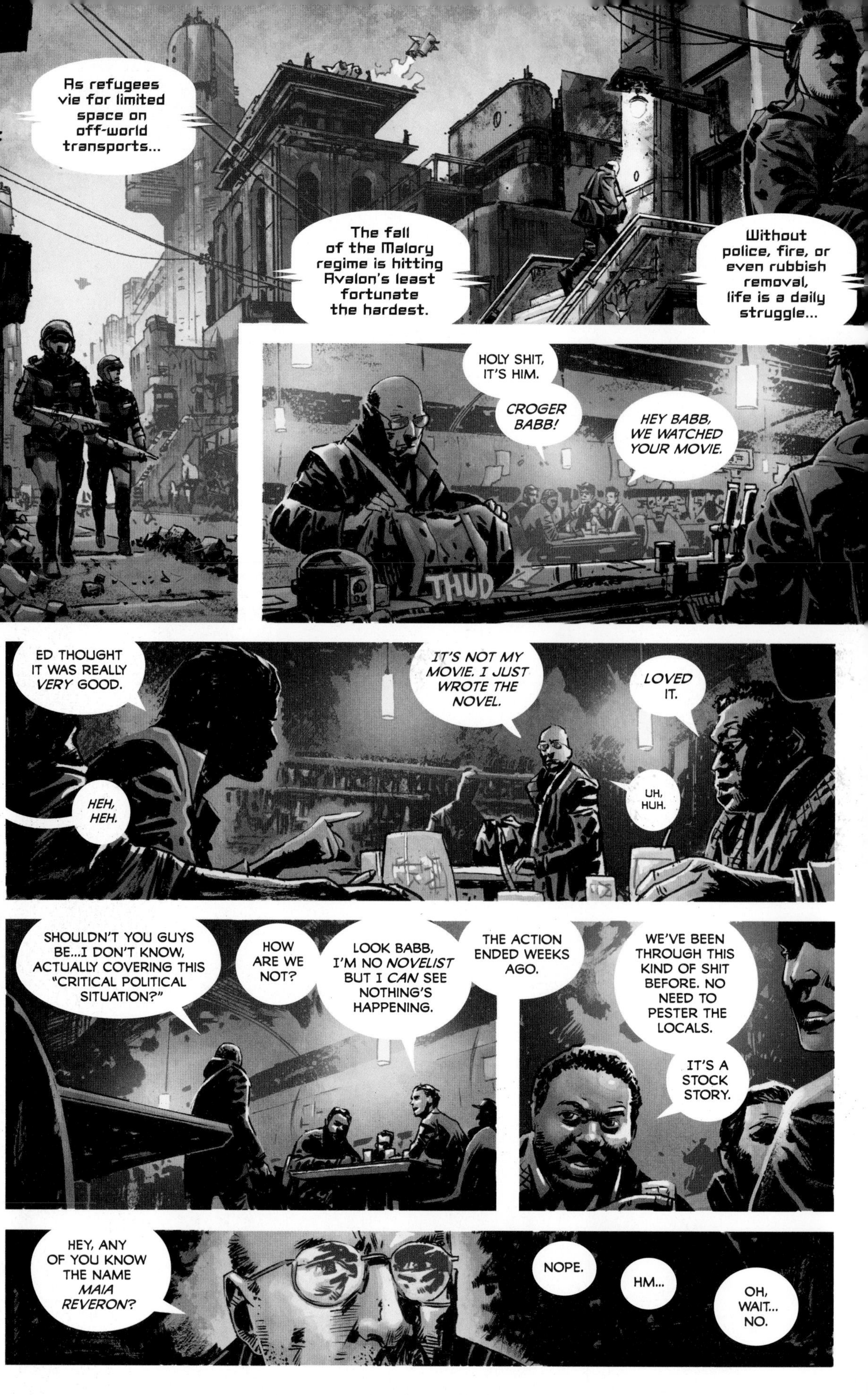
As refugees vie for limited space on off-world transports...
The fall of the Malory regime is hitting Avalon's least fortunate the hardest.
Without police, fire, or even rubbish removal, life is a daily struggle...
HOLY SHIT, IT'S HIM.
CROGER BABB!
HEY BABB, WE WATCHED YOUR MOVIE.
THUD
ED THOUGHT IT WAS REALLY VERY GOOD.
HEH, HEH.
IT'S NOT MY MOVIE. I JUST WROTE THE NOVEL.
LOVED IT.
UH, HUH.
SHOULDN'T YOU GUYS BE...I DON'T KNOW, ACTUALLY COVERING THIS "CRITICAL POLITICAL SITUATION?"
HOW ARE WE NOT?
LOOK BABB, I'M NO NOVELIST BUT I CAN SEE NOTHING'S HAPPENING.
THE ACTION ENDED WEEKS AGO.
WE'VE BEEN THROUGH THIS KIND OF SHIT BEFORE. NO NEED TO PESTER THE LOCALS.
IT'S A STOCK STORY.
HEY, ANY OF YOU KNOW THE NAME MAIA REVERON?
NOPE.
HM...
OH, WAIT... NO.

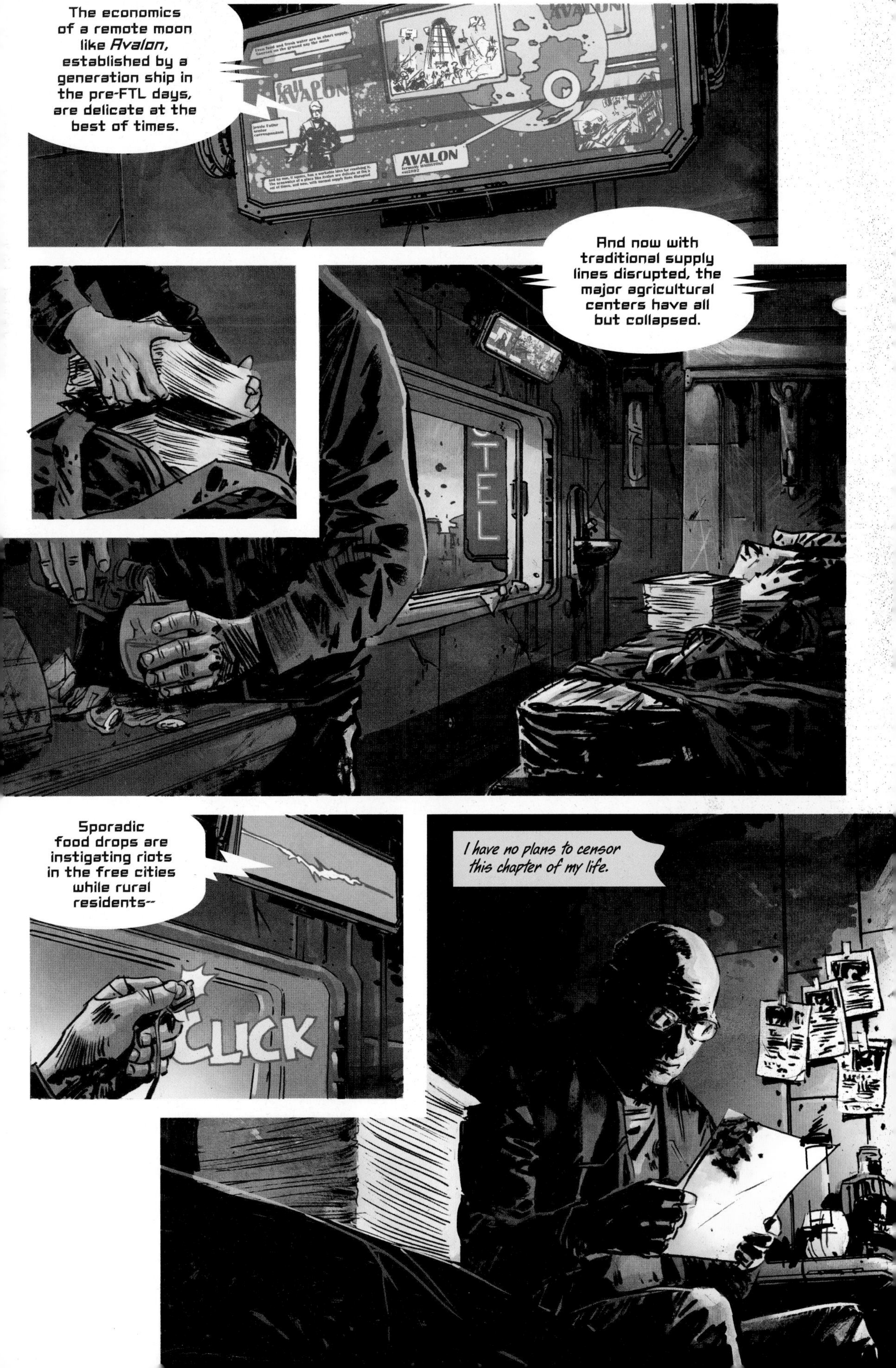

The economics of a remote moon like *Avalon*, established by a generation ship in the pre-FTL days, are delicate at the best of times.
fall of AVALON
AVALON
And now with traditional supply lines disrupted, the major agricultural centers have all but collapsed.
Sporadic food drops are instigating riots in the free cities while rural residents--
CLICK
I have no plans to censor this chapter of my life.

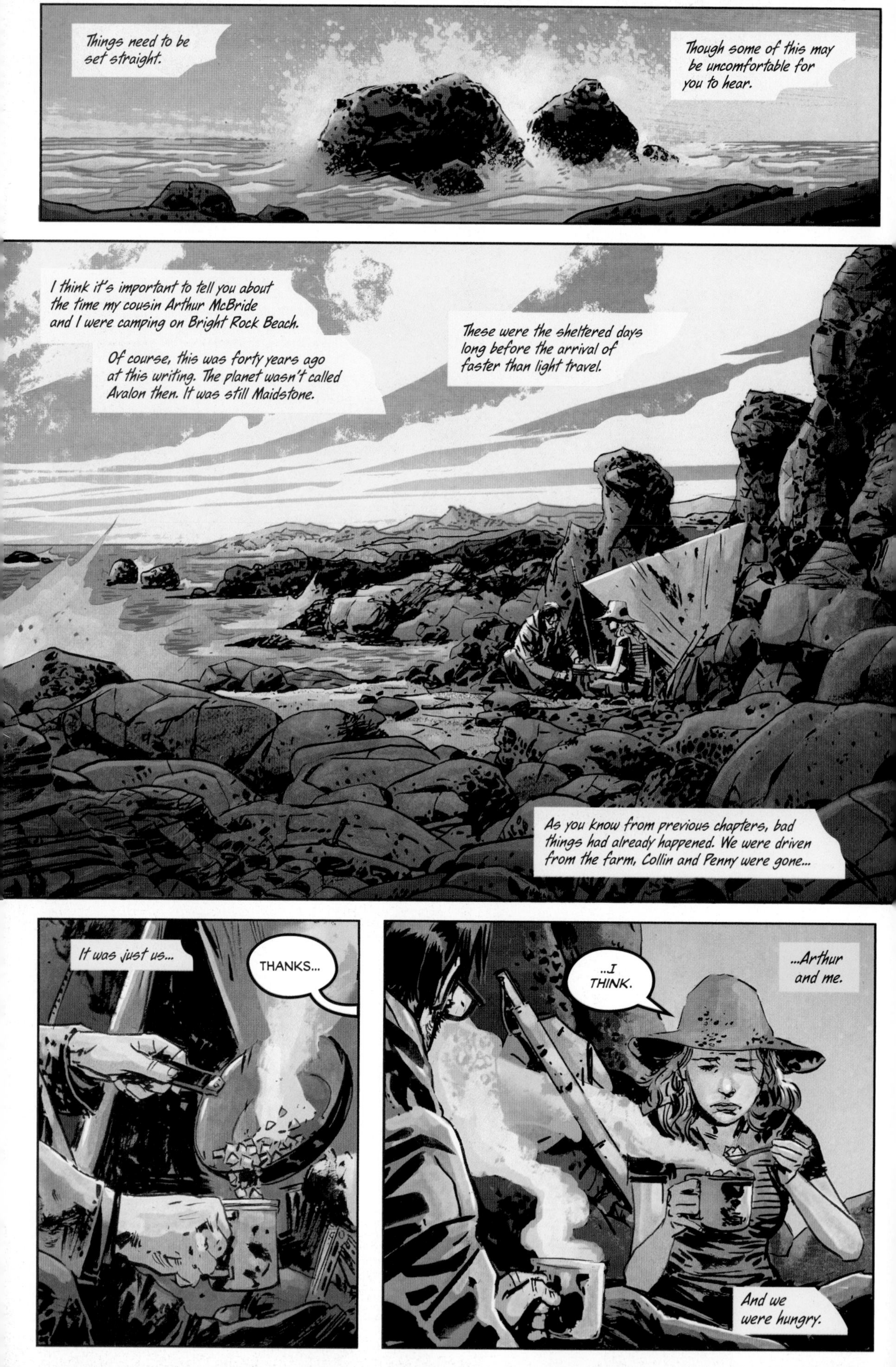
Things need to be set straight.
Though some of this may be uncomfortable for you to hear.
I think it's important to tell you about the time my cousin Arthur McBride and I were camping on Bright Rock Beach.
Of course, this was forty years ago at this writing. The planet wasn't called Avalon then. It was still Maidstone.
These were the sheltered days long before the arrival of faster than light travel.
As you know from previous chapters, bad things had already happened. We were driven from the farm, Collin and Penny were gone...
It was just us...
THANKS...
...I THINK.
...Arthur and me.
And we were hungry.

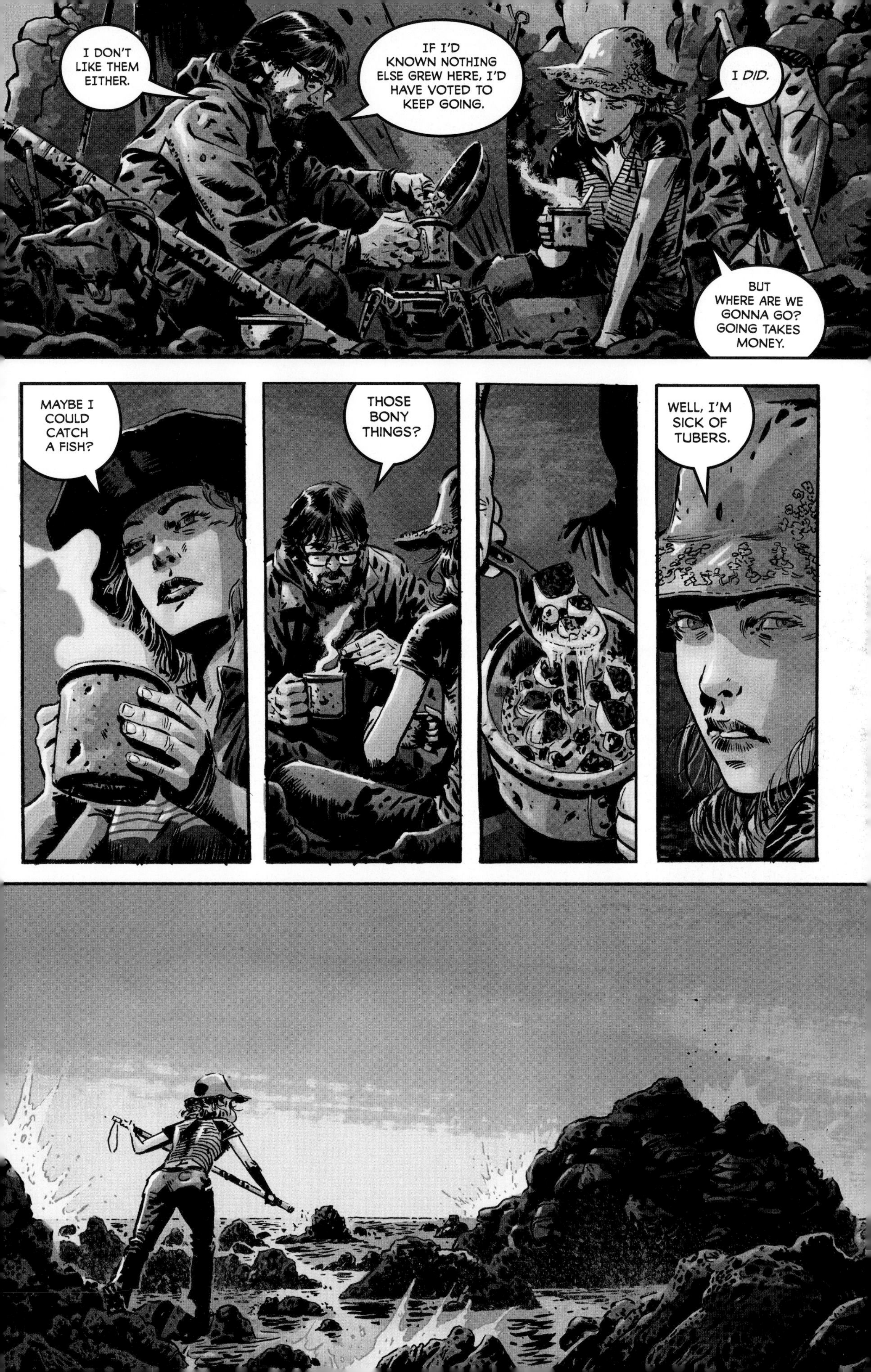
I DON'T LIKE THEM EITHER.
IF I'D KNOWN NOTHING ELSE GREW HERE, I'D HAVE VOTED TO KEEP GOING.
I *DID.*
BUT WHERE ARE WE GONNA GO? GOING TAKES MONEY.
MAYBE I COULD CATCH A FISH?
THOSE BONY THINGS?
WELL, I'M SICK OF TUBERS.

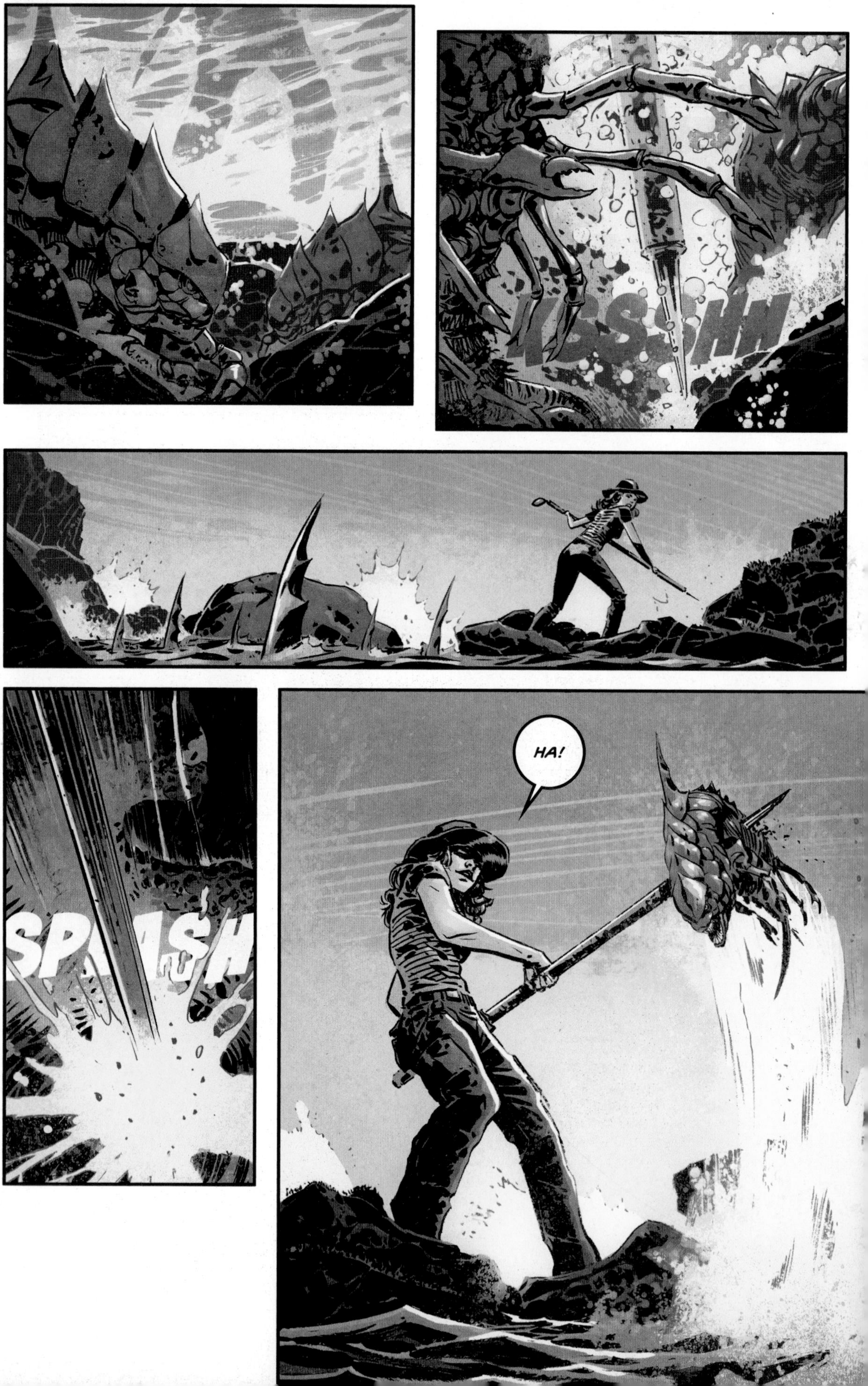
KSSSHH
SPLASH
HA!

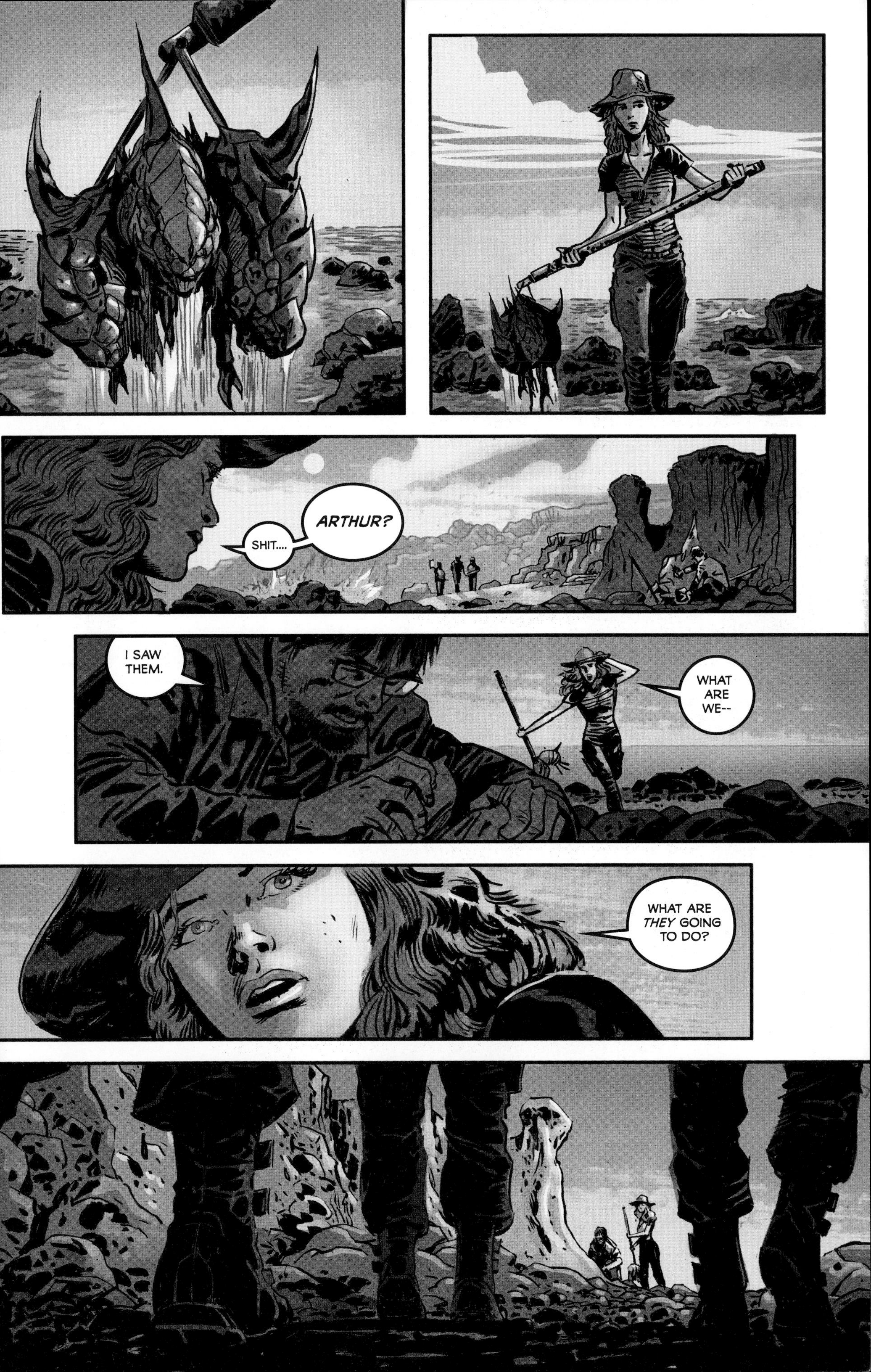
SHIT....
ARTHUR?
I SAW THEM.
WHAT ARE WE--
WHAT ARE *THEY* GOING TO DO?

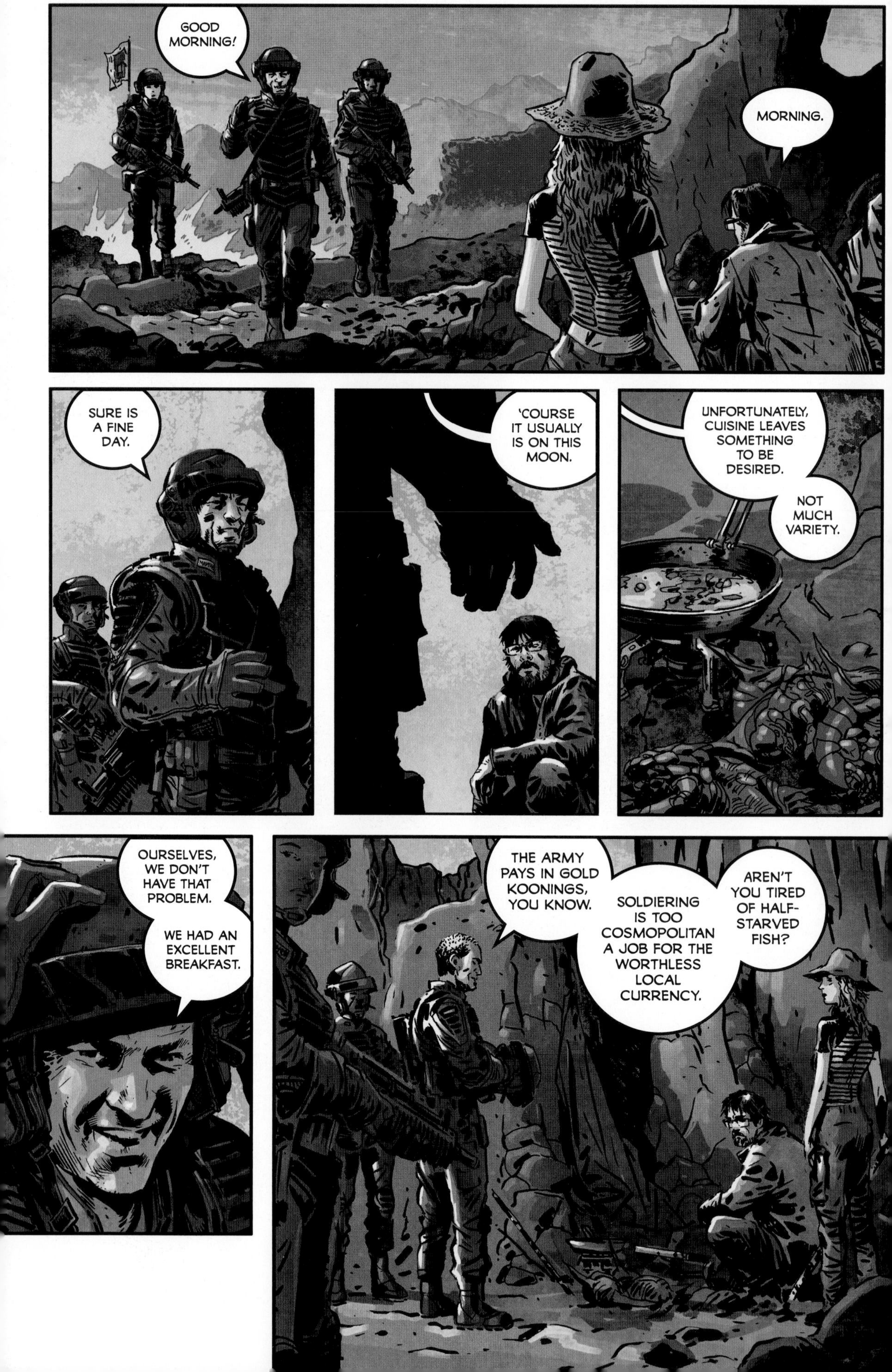
GOOD MORNING!
MORNING.
SURE IS A FINE DAY.
'COURSE IT USUALLY IS ON THIS MOON.
UNFORTUNATELY, CUISINE LEAVES SOMETHING TO BE DESIRED.
NOT MUCH VARIETY.
OURSELVES, WE DON'T HAVE THAT PROBLEM.
WE HAD AN EXCELLENT BREAKFAST.
THE ARMY PAYS IN GOLD KOONINGS, YOU KNOW.
SOLDIERING IS TOO COSMOPOLITAN A JOB FOR THE WORTHLESS LOCAL CURRENCY.
AREN'T YOU TIRED OF HALF-STARVED FISH?

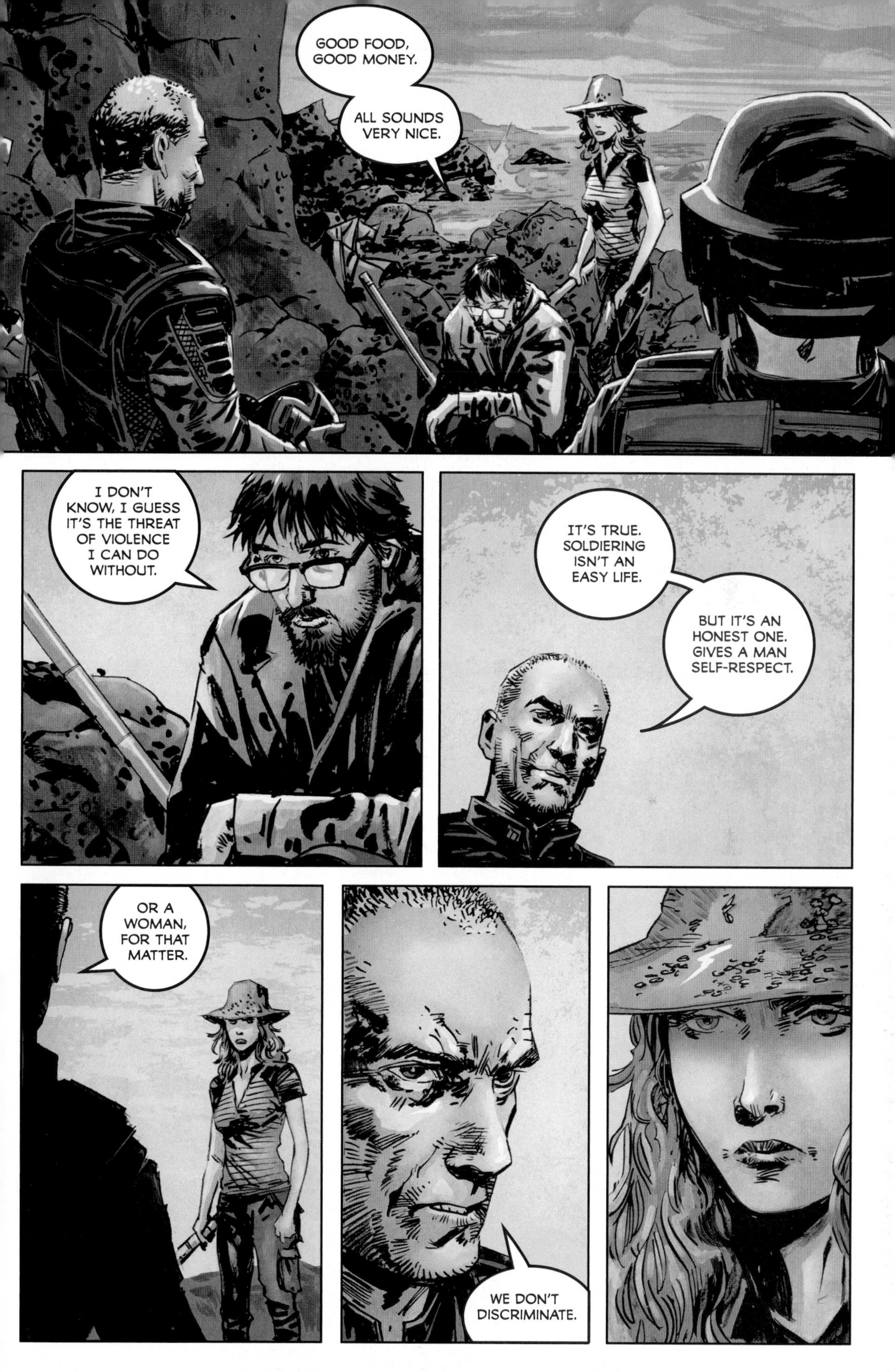
GOOD FOOD, GOOD MONEY.
ALL SOUNDS VERY NICE.
I DON'T KNOW, I GUESS IT'S THE THREAT OF VIOLENCE I CAN DO WITHOUT.
IT'S TRUE. SOLDIERING ISN'T AN EASY LIFE.
BUT IT'S AN HONEST ONE. GIVES A MAN SELF-RESPECT.
OR A WOMAN, FOR THAT MATTER.
WE DON'T DISCRIMINATE.

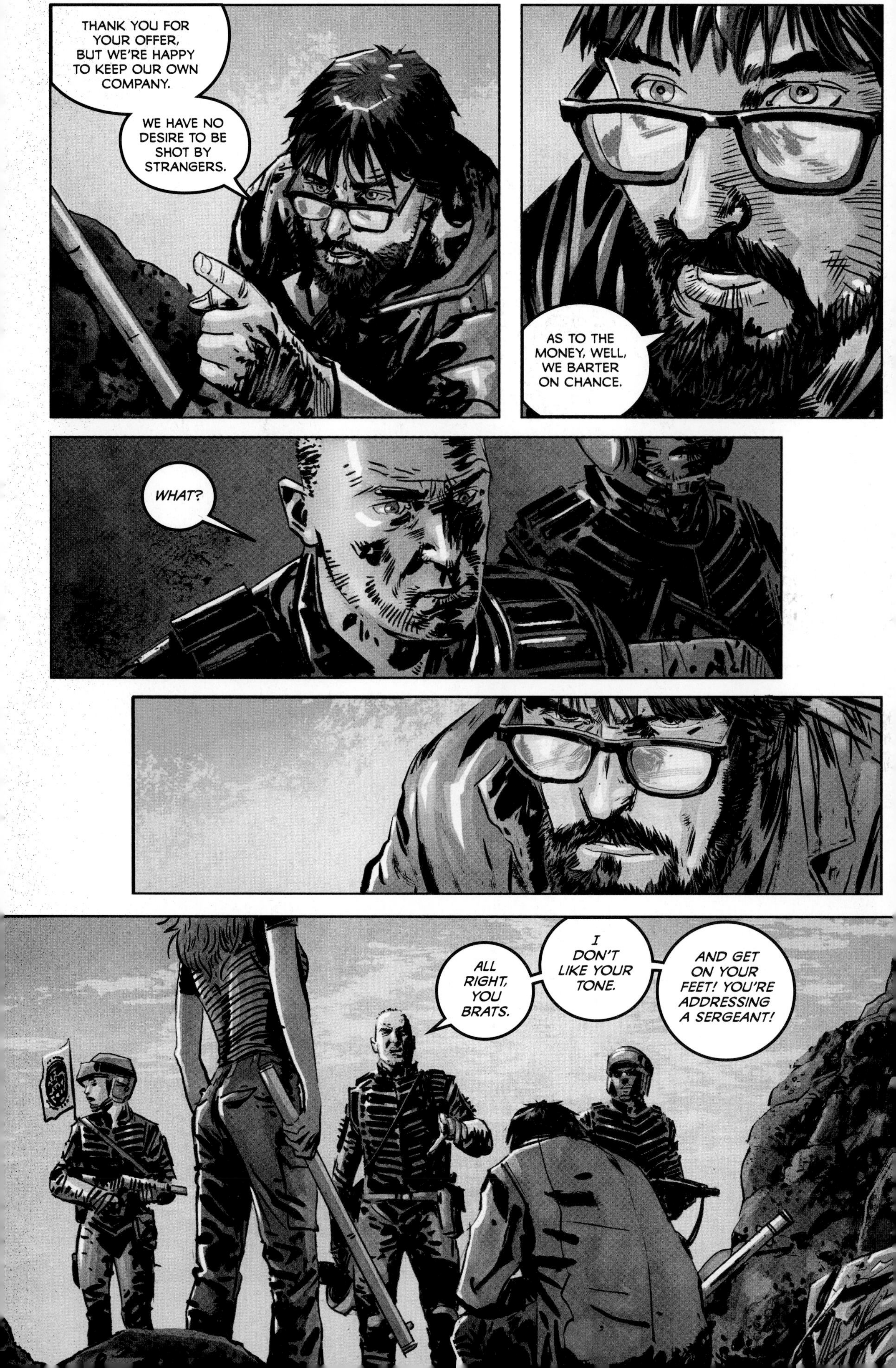
THANK YOU FOR YOUR OFFER, BUT WE'RE HAPPY TO KEEP OUR OWN COMPANY.
WE HAVE NO DESIRE TO BE SHOT BY STRANGERS.
AS TO THE MONEY, WELL, WE BARTER ON CHANCE.
WHAT?
ALL RIGHT, YOU BRATS.
I DON'T LIKE YOUR TONE.
AND GET ON YOUR FEET! YOU'RE ADDRESSING A SERGEANT!

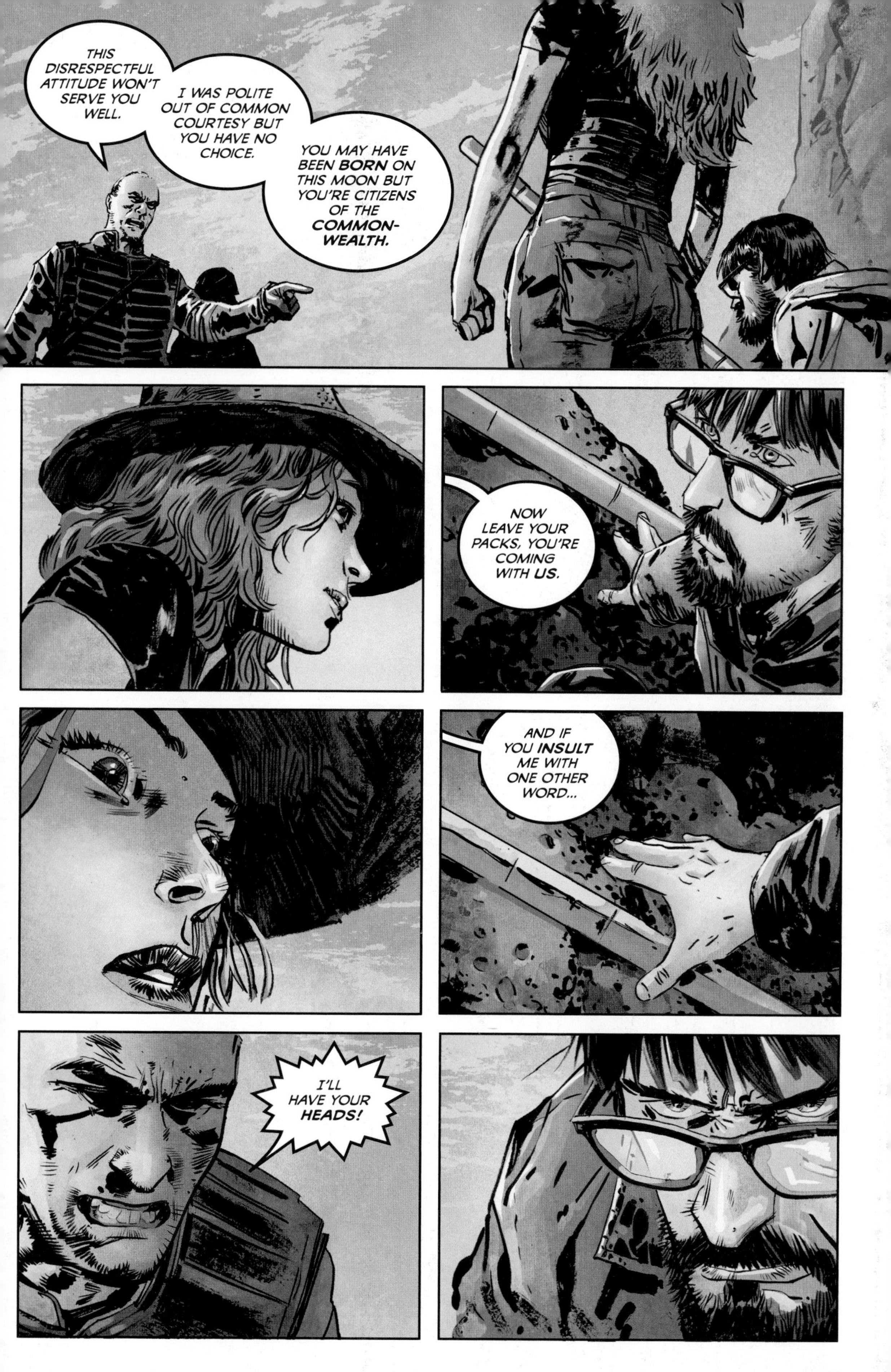
THIS DISRESPECTFUL ATTITUDE WON'T SERVE YOU WELL.
I WAS POLITE OUT OF COMMON COURTESY BUT YOU HAVE NO CHOICE.
YOU MAY HAVE BEEN BORN ON THIS MOON BUT YOU'RE CITIZENS OF THE COMMON-WEALTH.
NOW LEAVE YOUR PACKS, YOU'RE COMING WITH US.
AND IF YOU INSULT ME WITH ONE OTHER WORD...
I'LL HAVE YOUR HEADS!

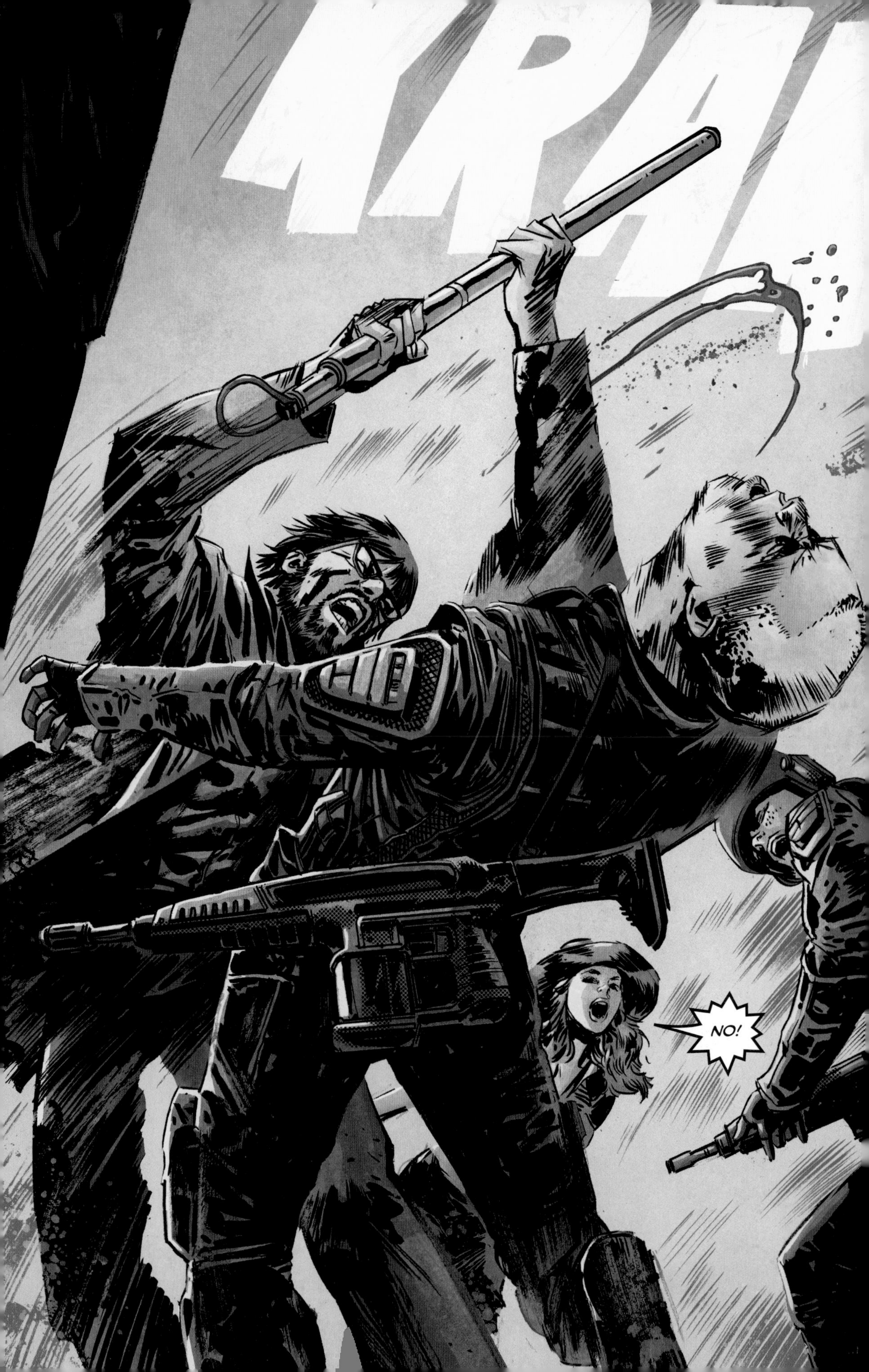
KRA
NO!

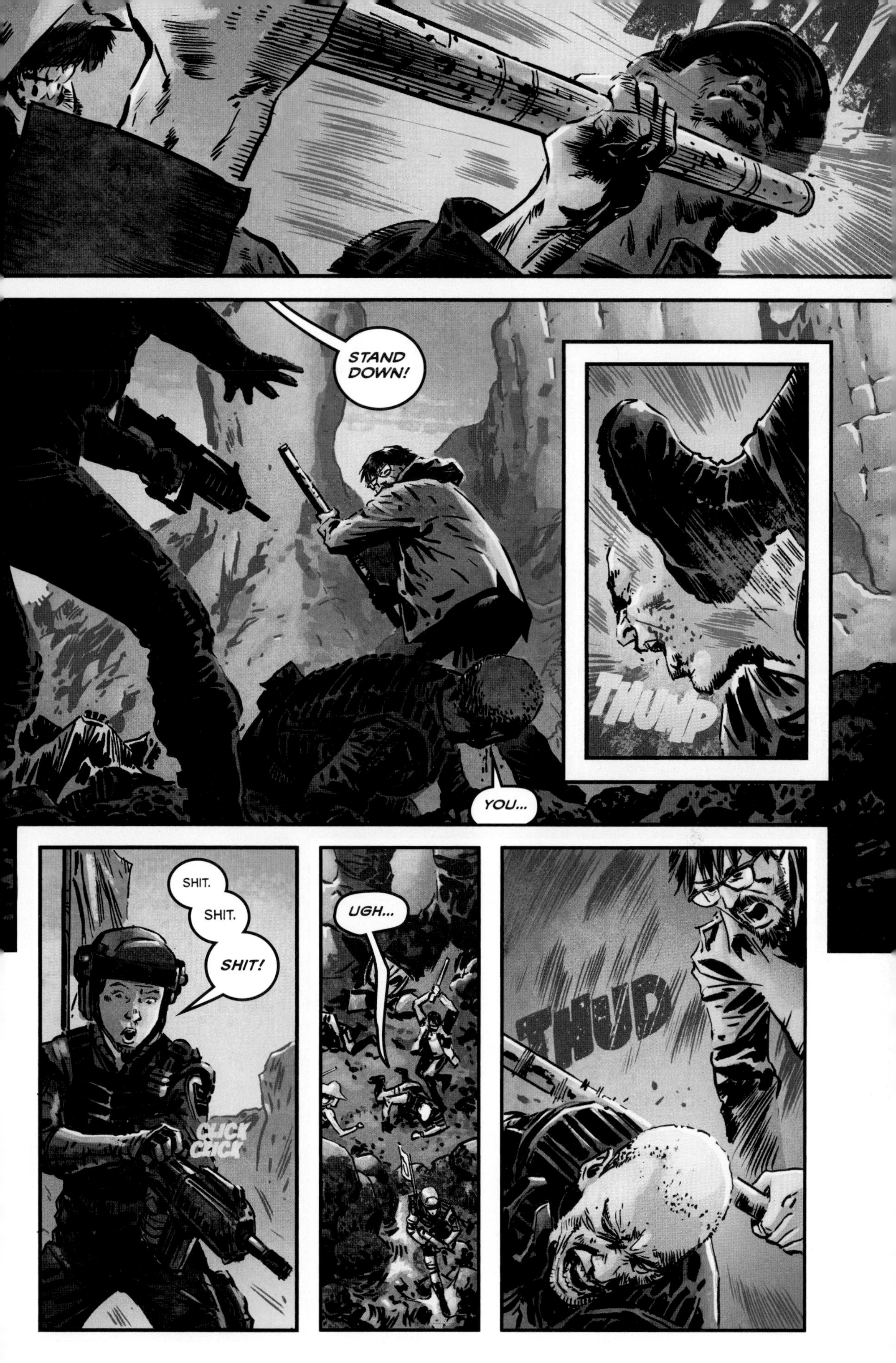
STAND DOWN!
THUMP
YOU...
SHIT.
SHIT.
SHIT!
CLICK CLICK
UGH...
THUD

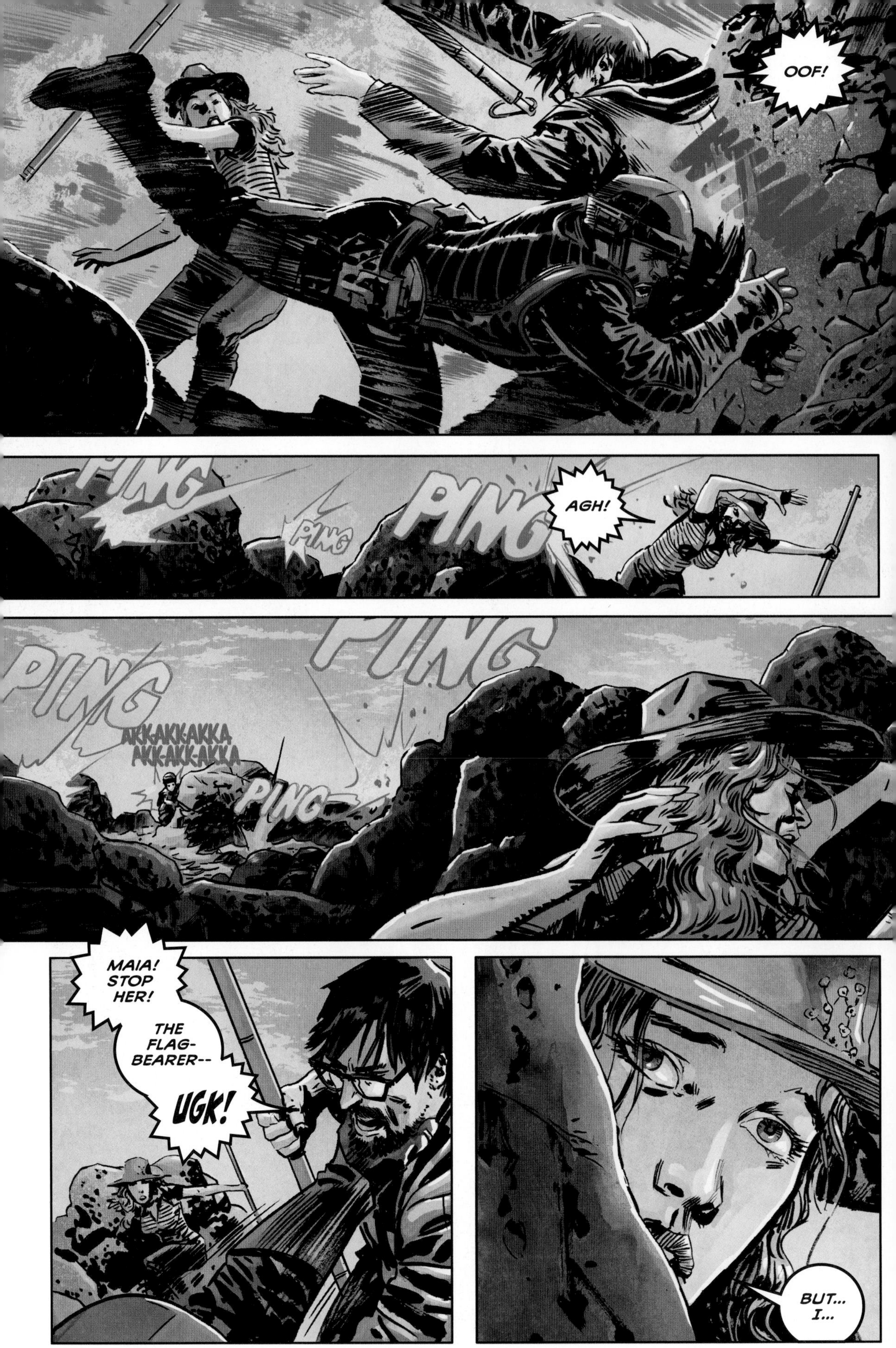
OOF!
PING
PING
PING
AGH!
PING
PING
AKK-AKK-AKKA
AKK-AKK-AKKA
PING
MAIA! STOP HER!
THE FLAG-BEARER--
UGK!
BUT... I...

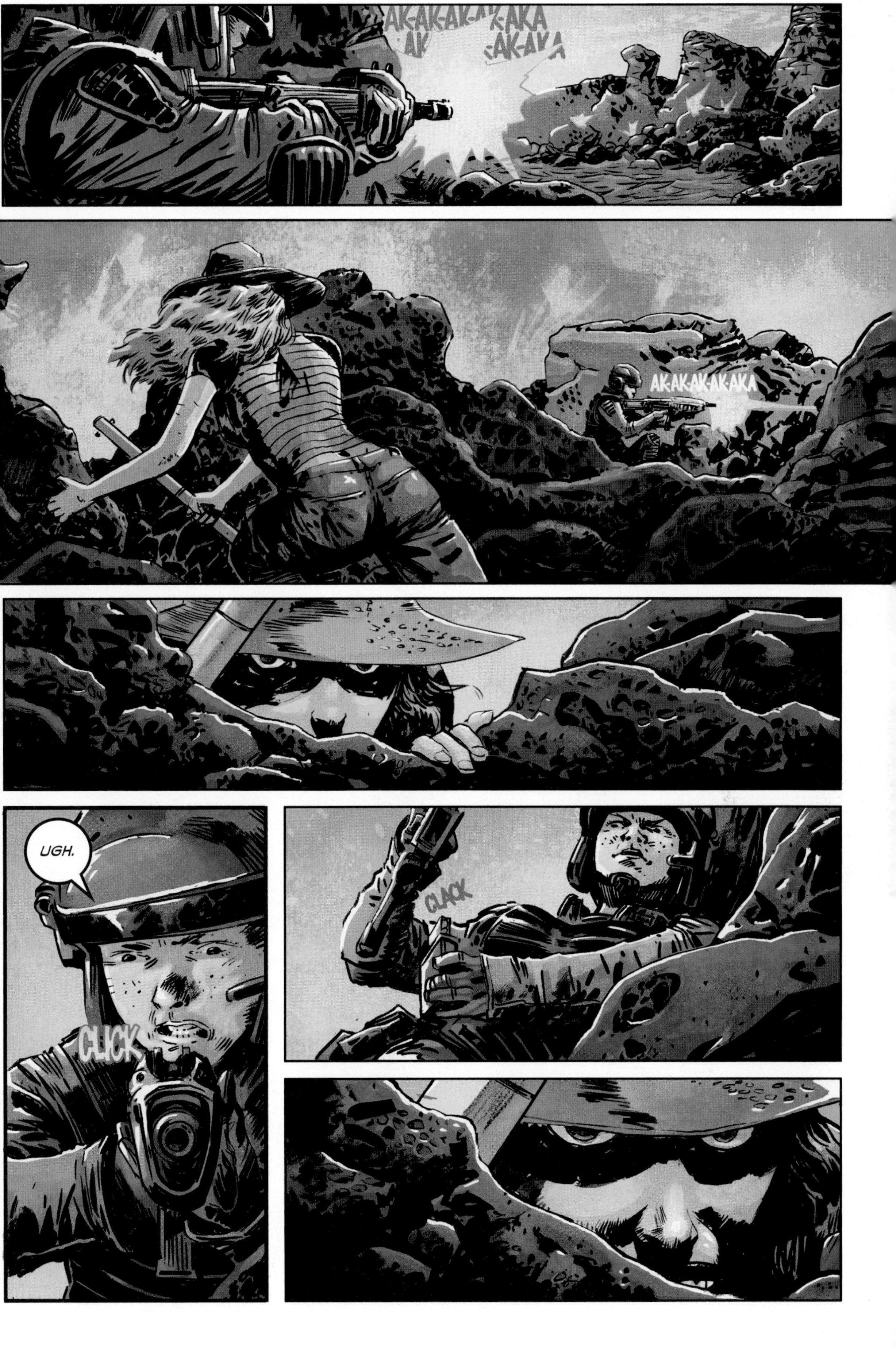
AK-AK-AK-AK-AK
AK
K-AKA
AK-AKA
AK-AK-AK-AK-AKA
UGH.
CLICK
CLACK

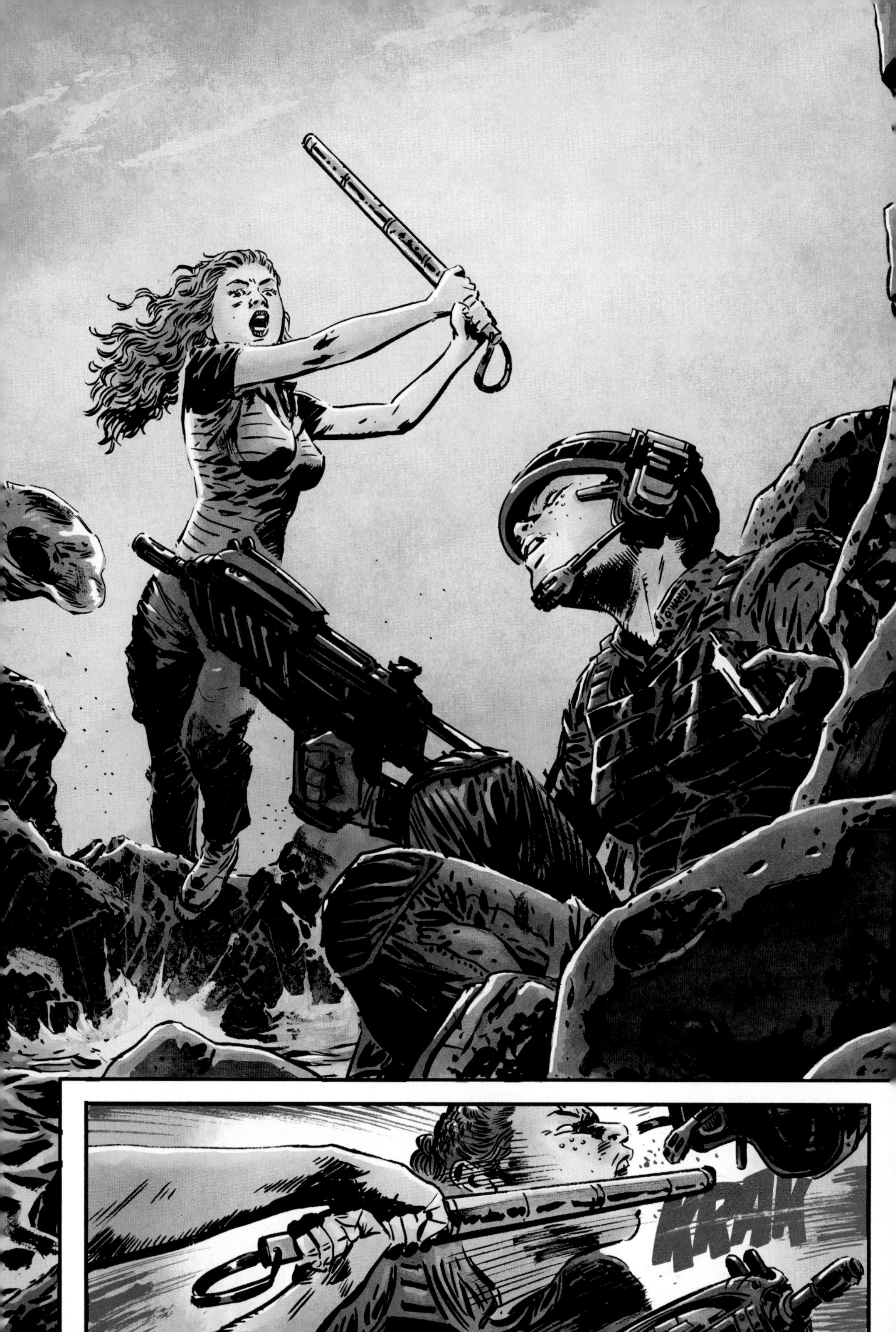
KRAK

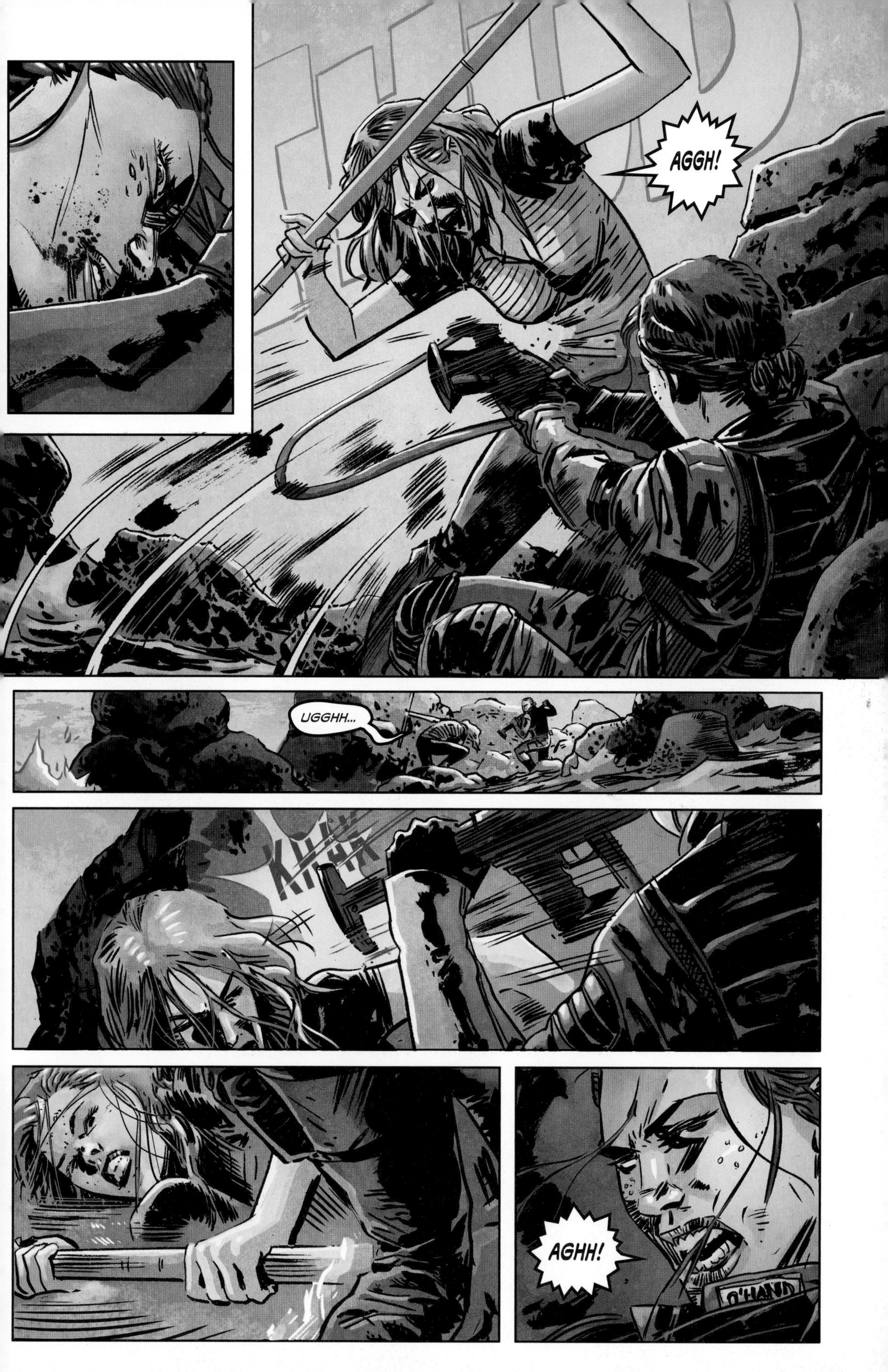
AGGH!
UGGHH...
KHHK
AGHH!
O'HAND

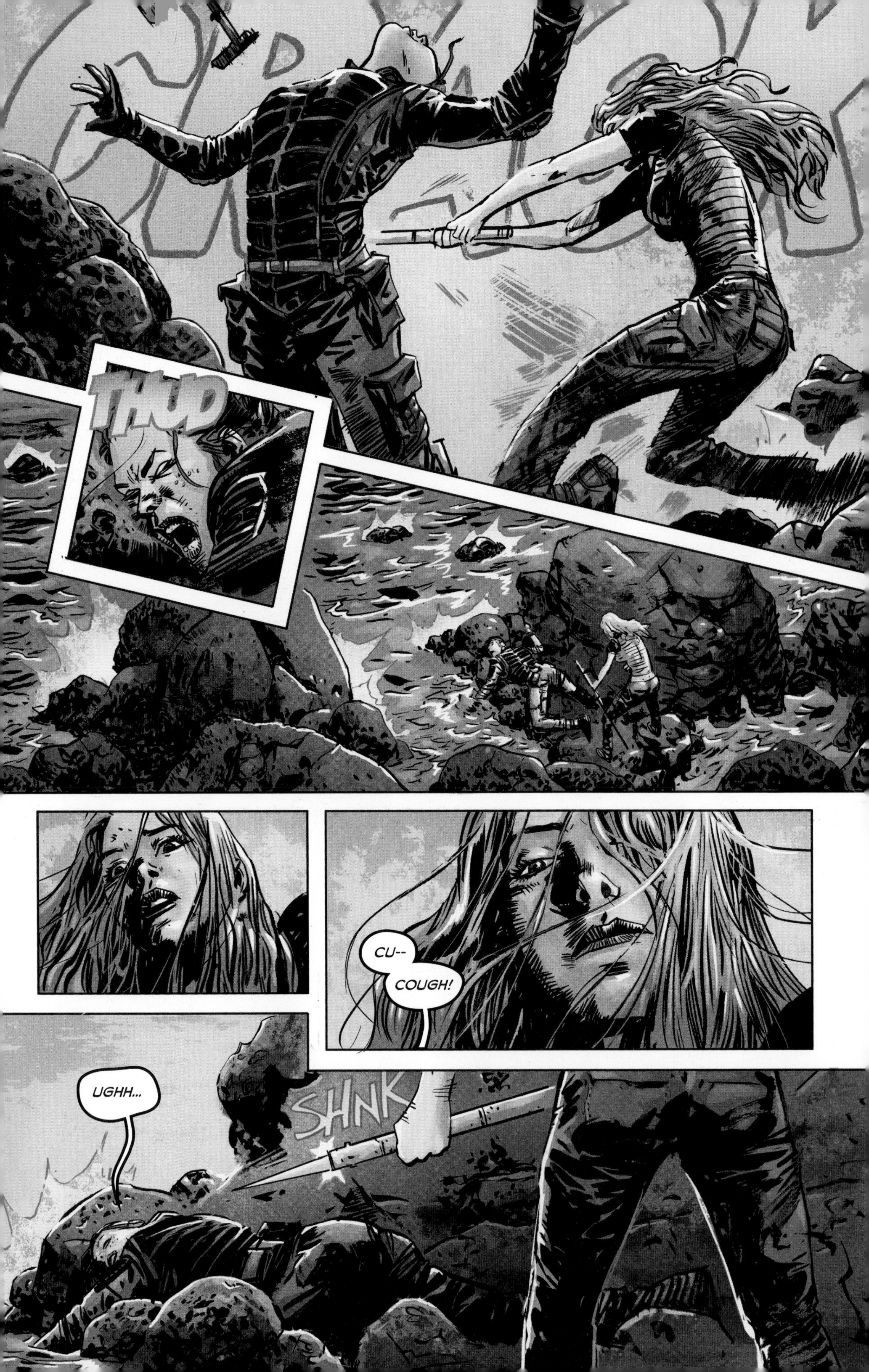
THUD
CU--
COUGH!
UGHH...
SHNK

CLACK
CLACK

CLACK
CLAC.
CLA.

CLACK

CLACK
CLACK

CYCK

LAJCK

UGHH...

DID YOU GET HER?

WHA-- WHAT?

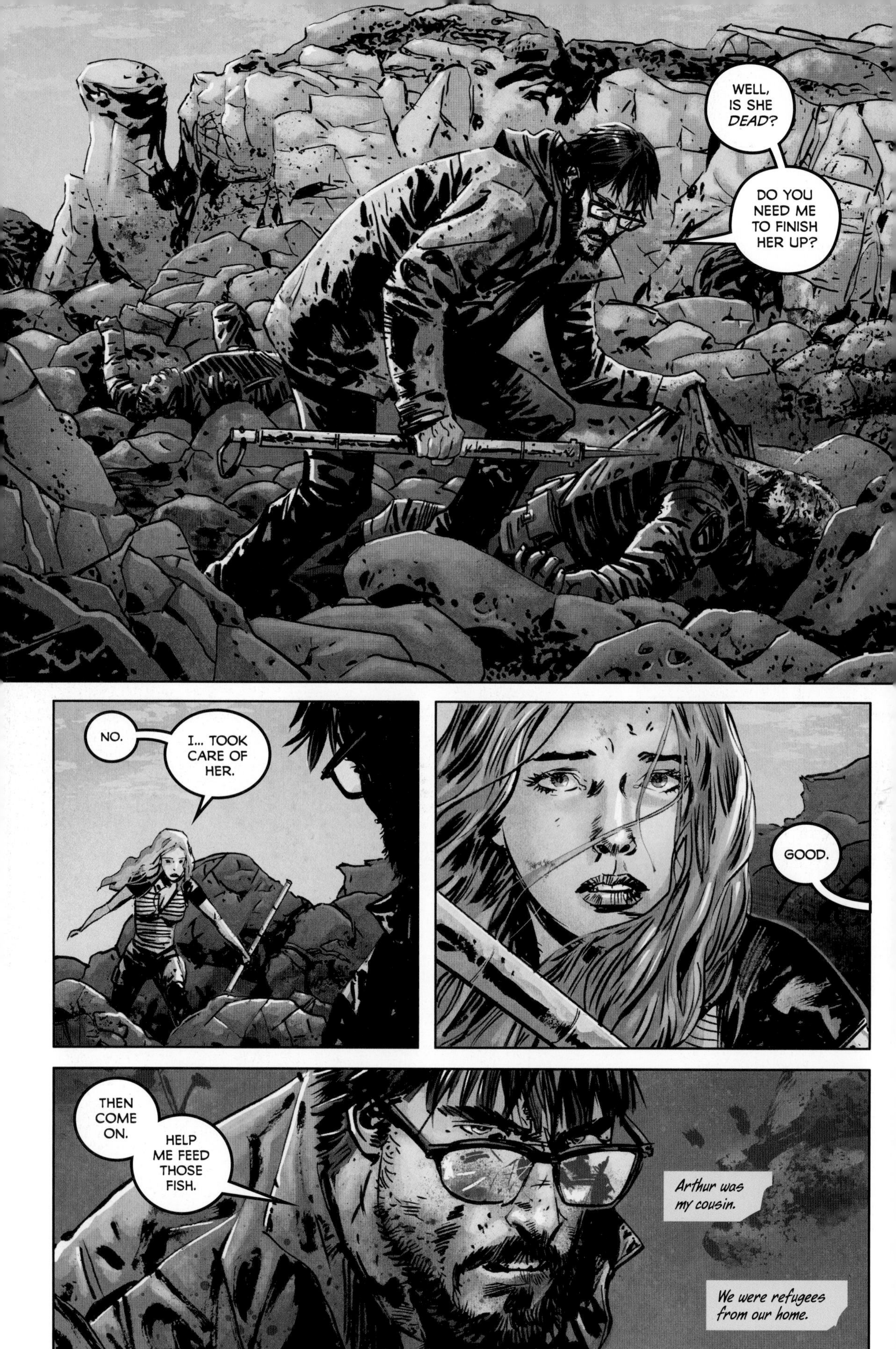
WELL, IS SHE *DEAD*?
DO YOU NEED ME TO FINISH HER UP?
NO.
I... TOOK CARE OF HER.
GOOD.
THEN COME ON.
HELP ME FEED THOSE FISH.
Arthur was my cousin.
We were refugees from our home.

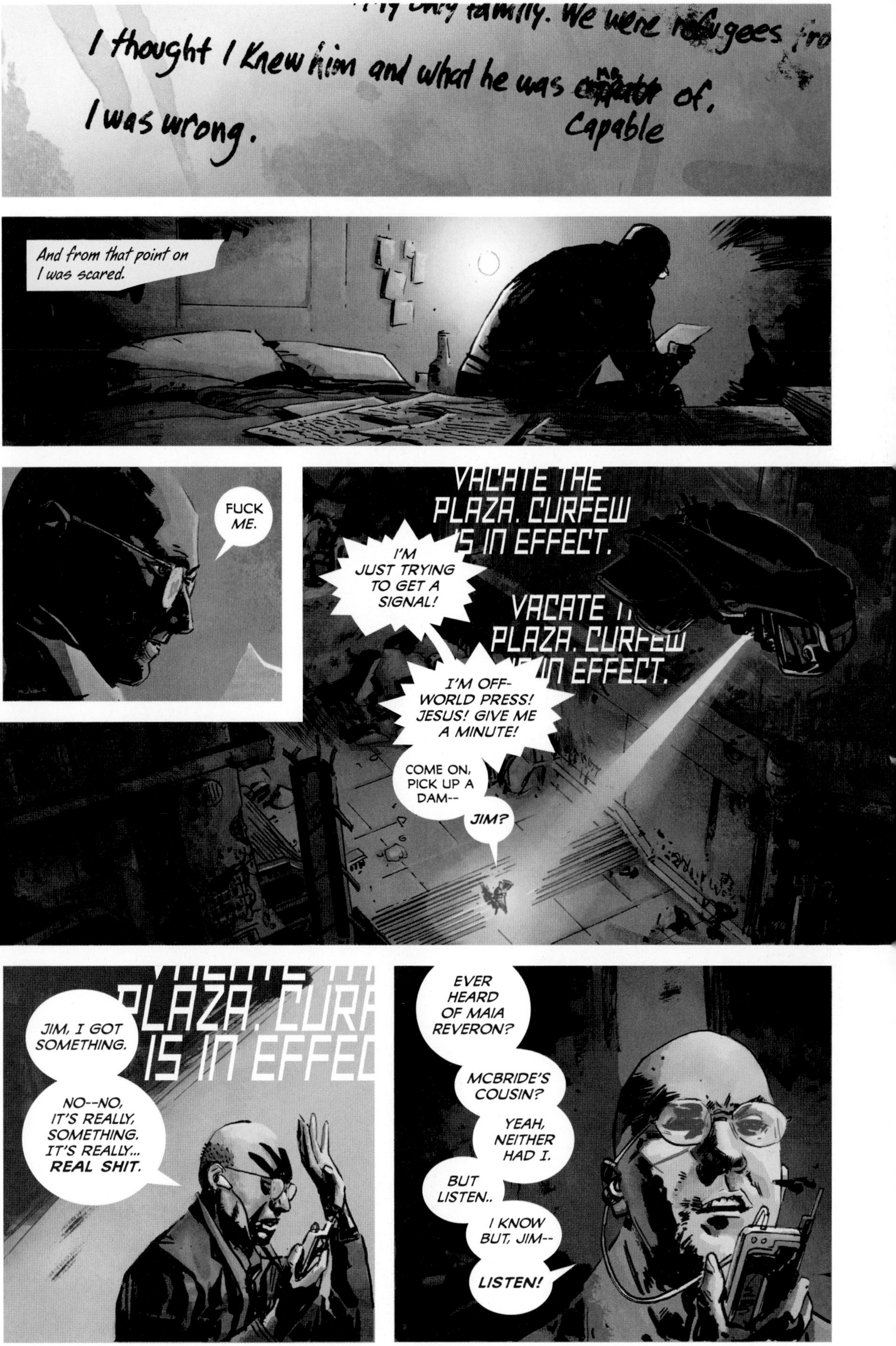
family. We were refugees
I thought I Knew him and what he was capable of.
I was wrong.
And from that point on I was scared.
FUCK ME.
VACATE THE PLAZA. CURFEW IS IN EFFECT.
I'M JUST TRYING TO GET A SIGNAL!
VACATE THE PLAZA. CURFEW IN EFFECT.
I'M OFF-WORLD PRESS! JESUS! GIVE ME A MINUTE!
COME ON, PICK UP A DAM--
JIM?
PLAZA. CUR IS IN EFFE
JIM, I GOT SOMETHING.
NO--NO, IT'S REALLY, SOMETHING. IT'S REALLY... REAL SHIT.
EVER HEARD OF MAIA REVERON?
MCBRIDE'S COUSIN?
YEAH, NEITHER HAD I.
BUT LISTEN..
I KNOW BUT, JIM--
LISTEN!

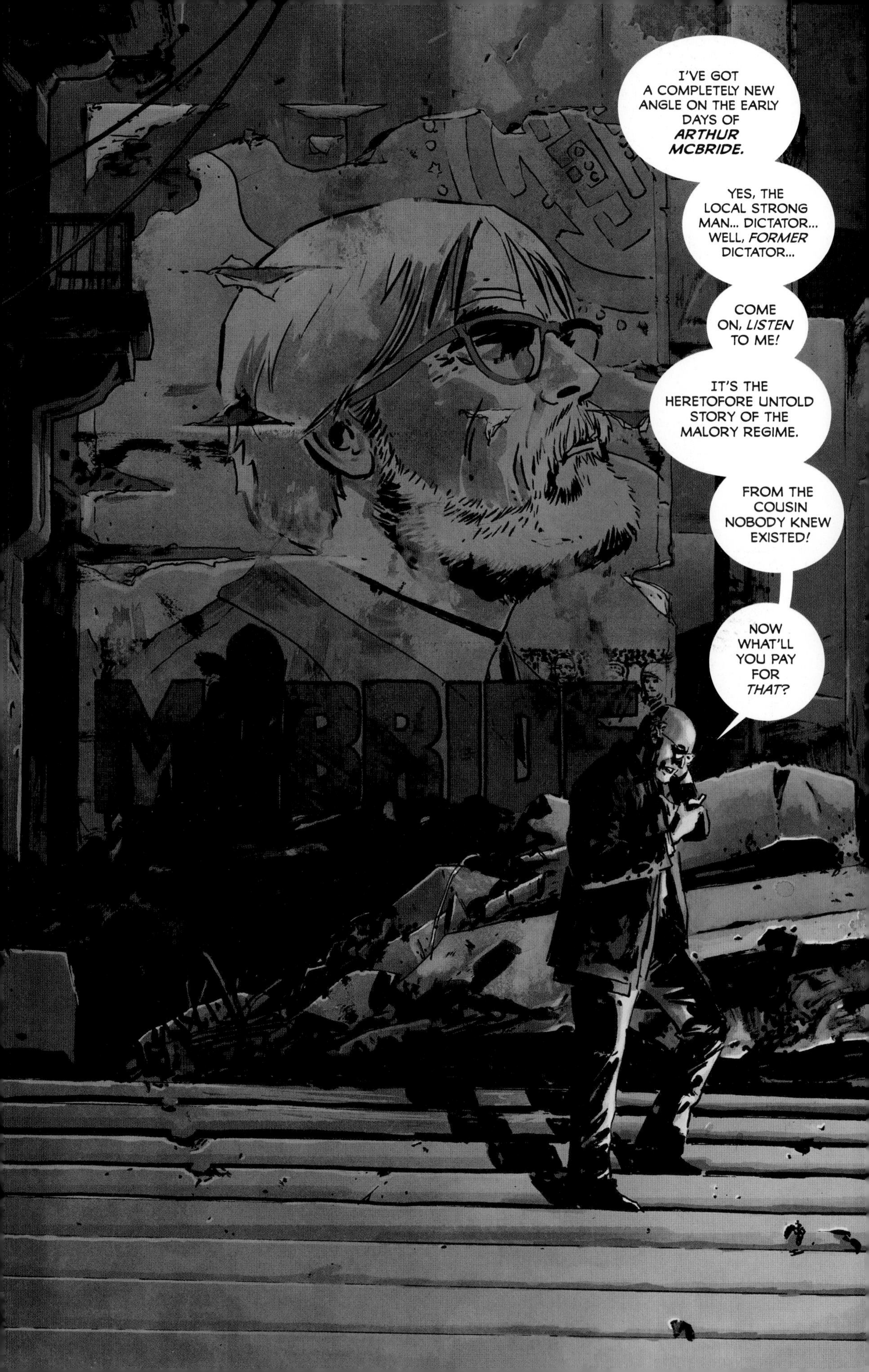
I'VE GOT A COMPLETELY NEW ANGLE ON THE EARLY DAYS OF ARTHUR MCBRIDE.
YES, THE LOCAL STRONG MAN... DICTATOR... WELL, FORMER DICTATOR...
COME ON, LISTEN TO ME!
IT'S THE HERETOFORE UNTOLD STORY OF THE MALORY REGIME.
FROM THE COUSIN NOBODY KNEW EXISTED!
NOW WHAT'LL YOU PAY FOR THAT?

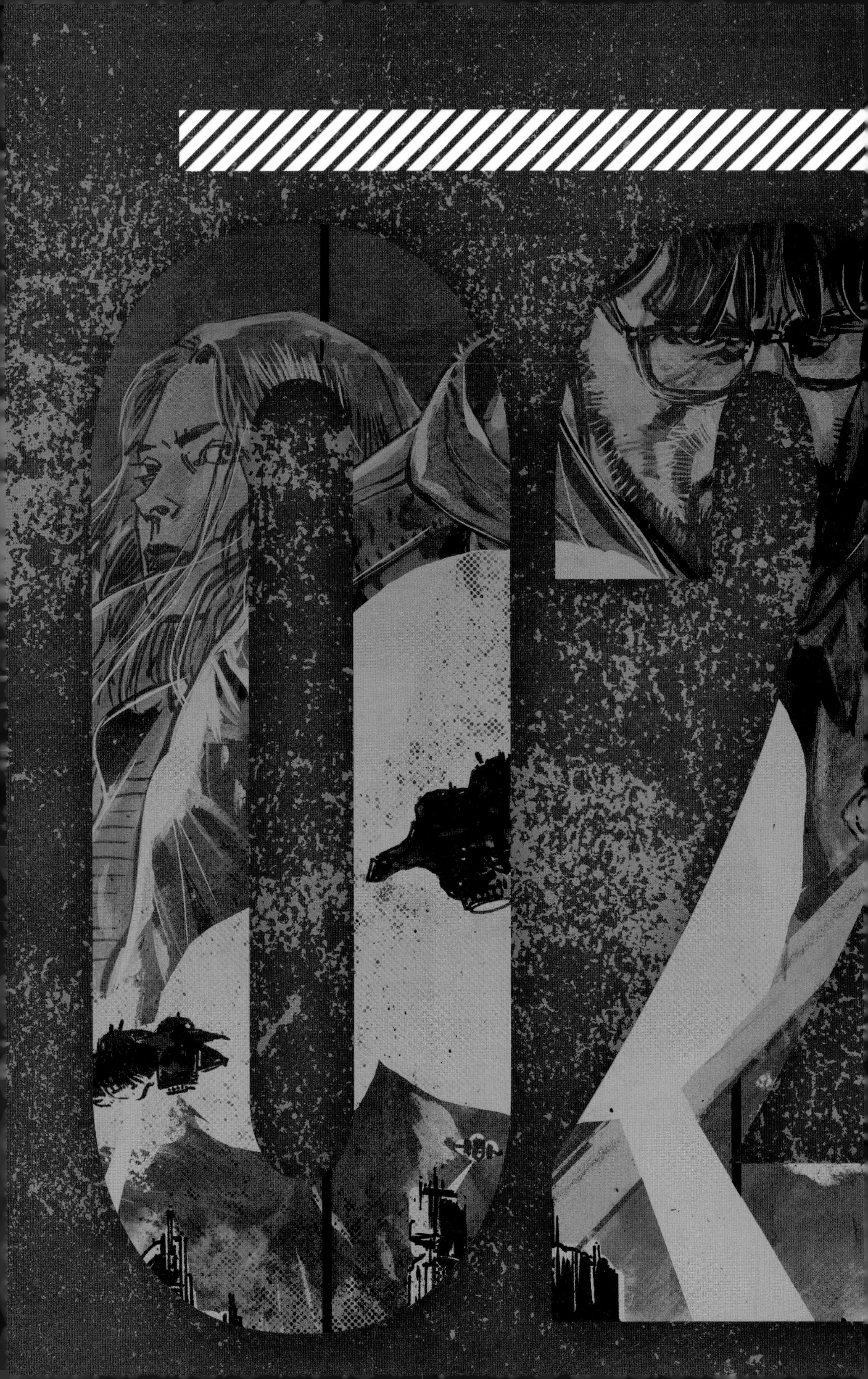

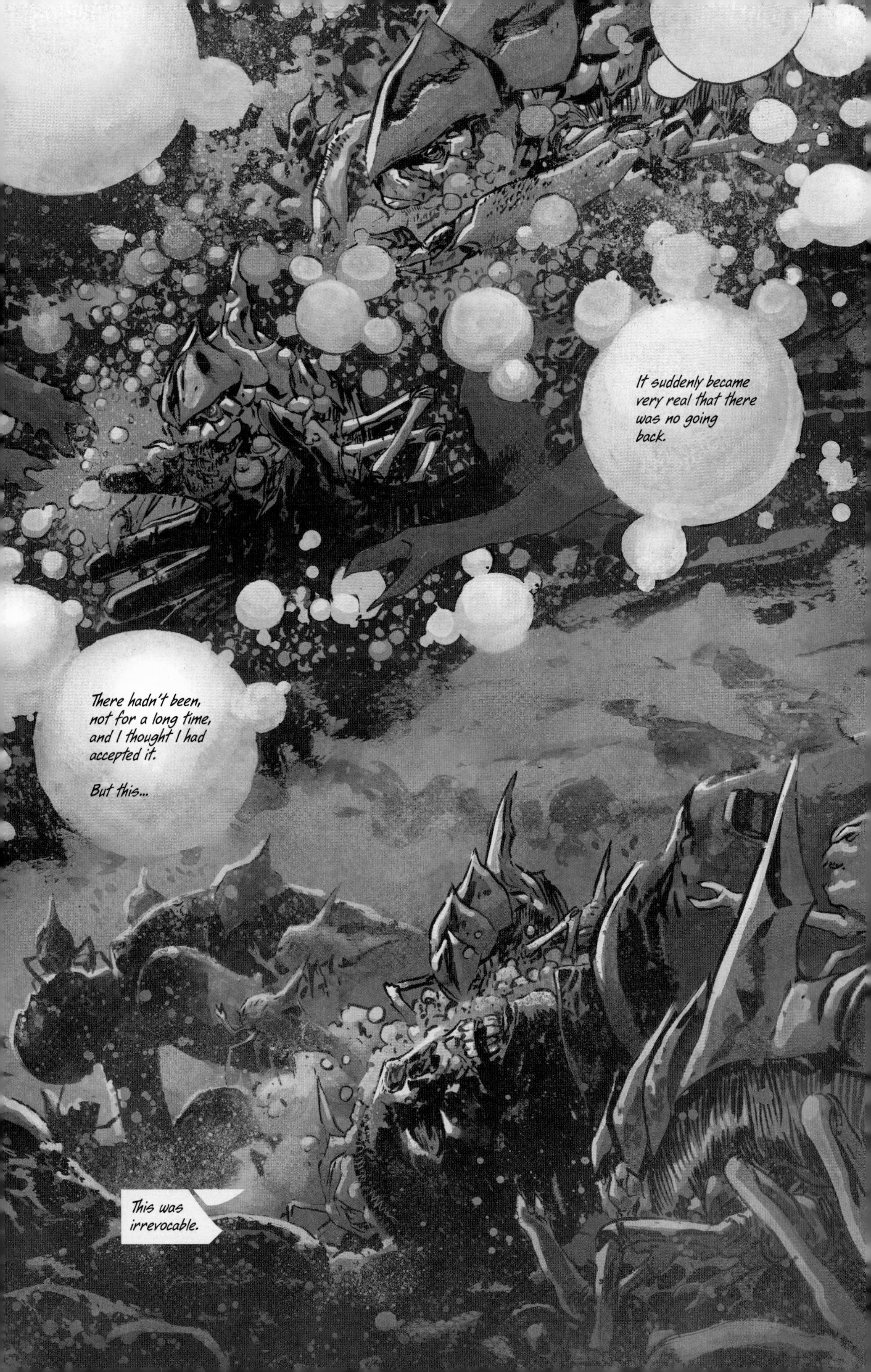
It suddenly became very real that there was no going back.
There hadn't been, not for a long time, and I thought I had accepted it.
But this...
This was irrevocable.

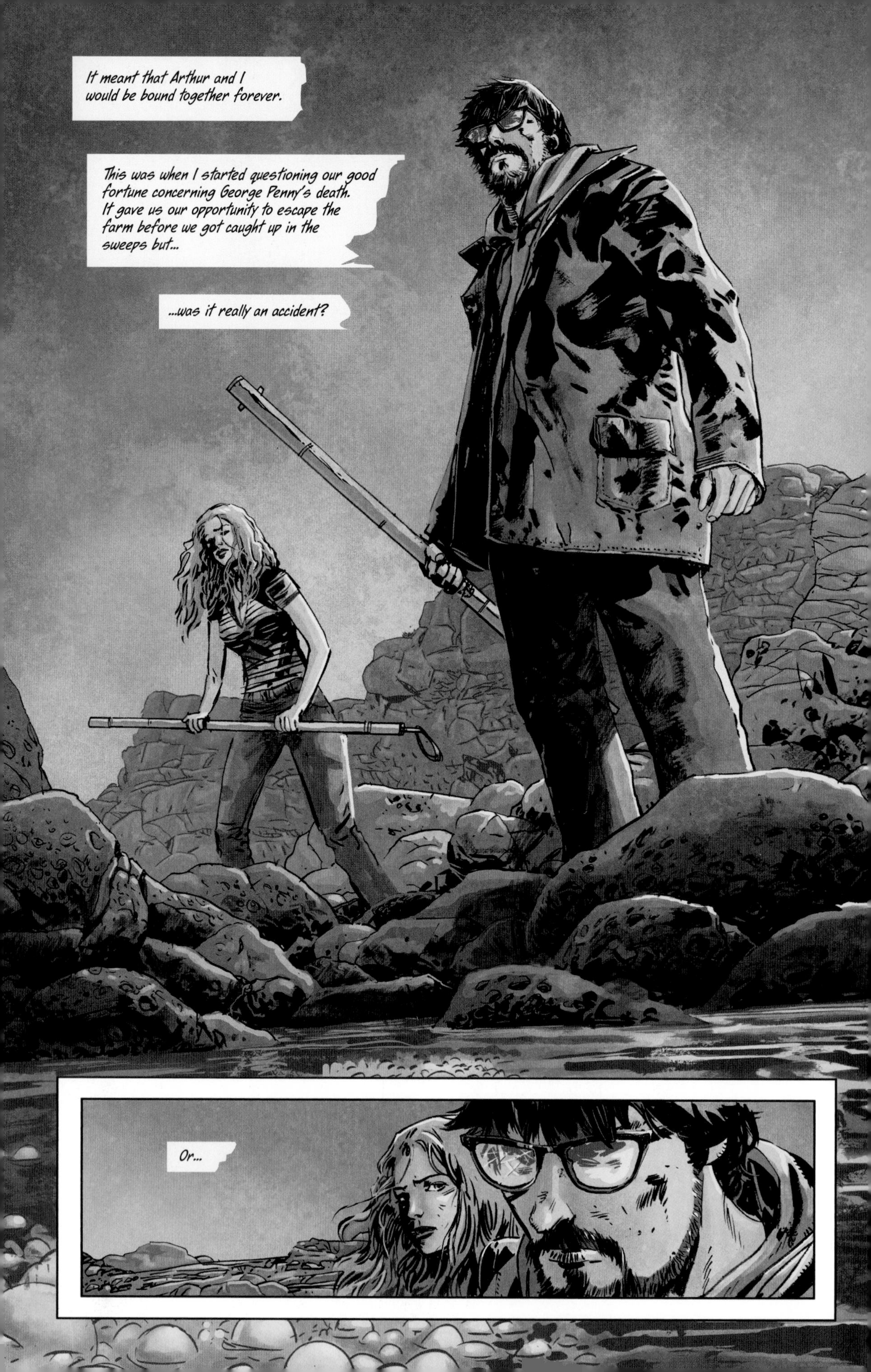
It meant that Arthur and I would be bound together forever.
This was when I started questioning our good fortune concerning George Penny's death. It gave us our opportunity to escape the farm before we got caught up in the sweeps but...
...was it really an accident?
Or...

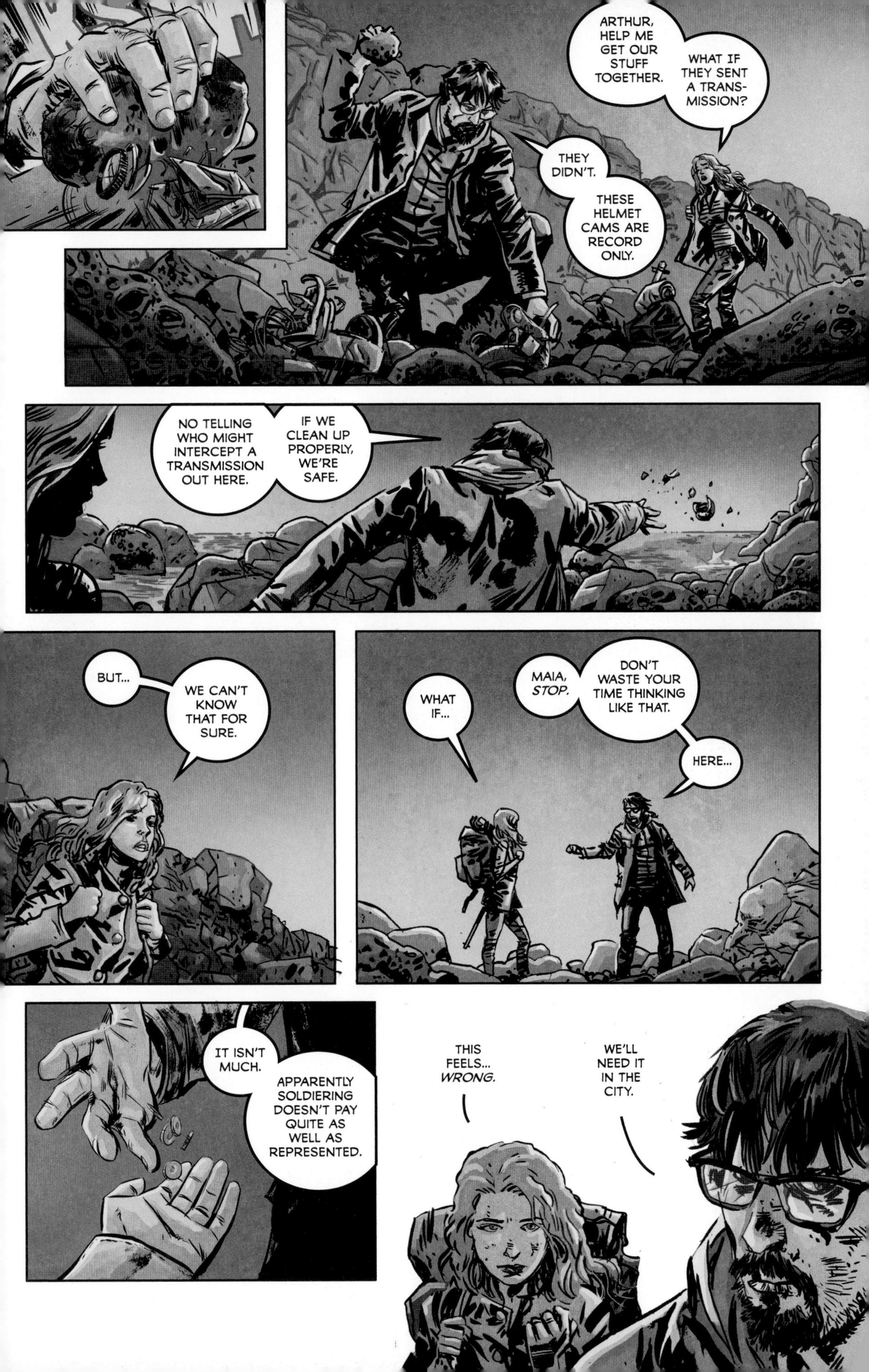
ARTHUR, HELP ME GET OUR STUFF TOGETHER.
WHAT IF THEY SENT A TRANS-MISSION?
THEY DIDN'T.
THESE HELMET CAMS ARE RECORD ONLY.
NO TELLING WHO MIGHT INTERCEPT A TRANSMISSION OUT HERE.
IF WE CLEAN UP PROPERLY, WE'RE SAFE.
BUT...
WE CAN'T KNOW THAT FOR SURE.
WHAT IF...
MAIA, *STOP.*
DON'T WASTE YOUR TIME THINKING LIKE THAT.
HERE...
IT ISN'T MUCH.
APPARENTLY SOLDIERING DOESN'T PAY QUITE AS WELL AS REPRESENTED.
THIS FEELS... *WRONG.*
WE'LL NEED IT IN THE CITY.

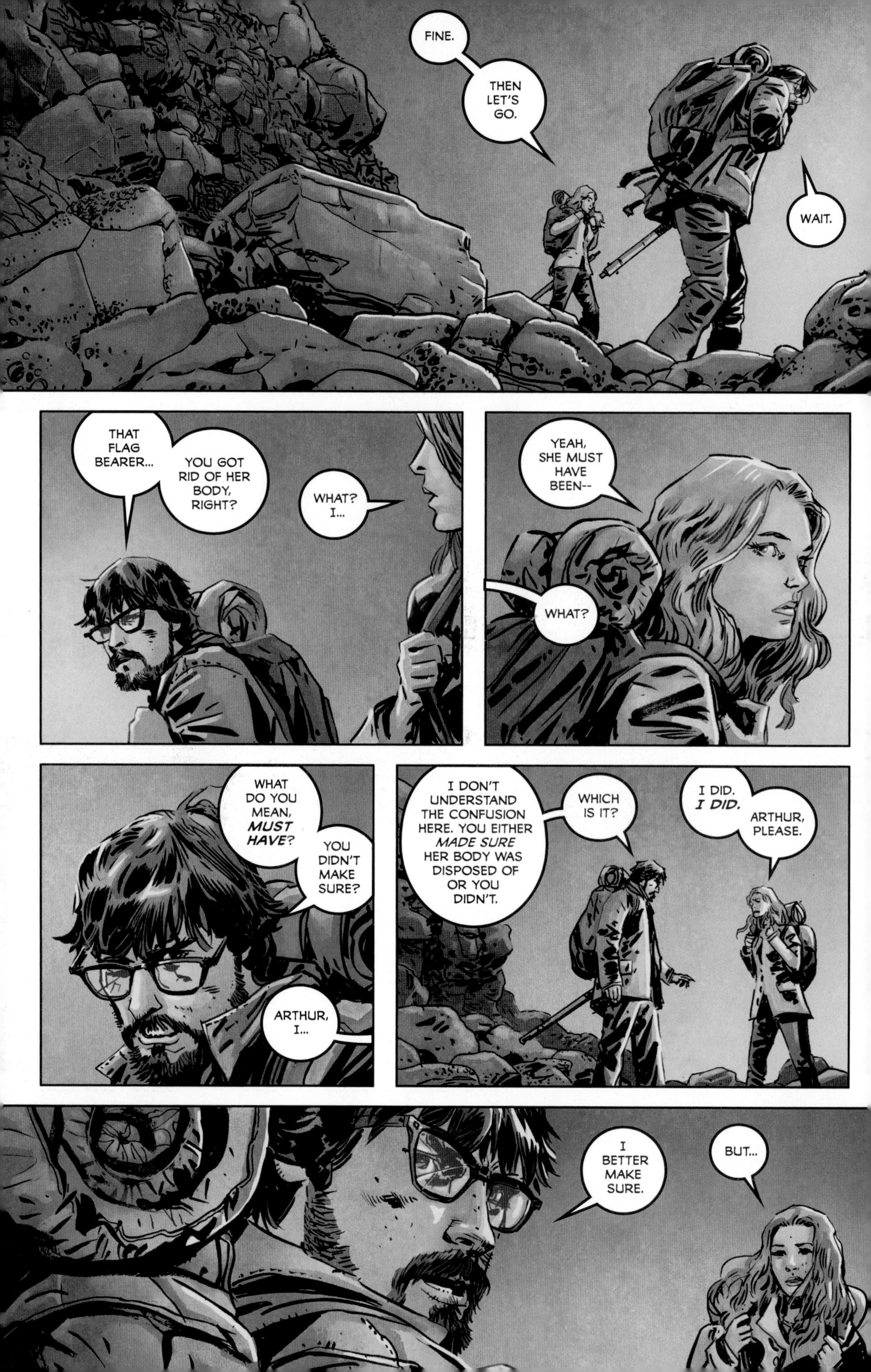
FINE.
THEN LET'S GO.
WAIT.
THAT FLAG BEARER...
YOU GOT RID OF HER BODY, RIGHT?
WHAT? I...
YEAH, SHE MUST HAVE BEEN--
WHAT?
WHAT DO YOU MEAN, *MUST HAVE*?
YOU DIDN'T MAKE SURE?
ARTHUR, I...
I DON'T UNDERSTAND THE CONFUSION HERE. YOU EITHER *MADE SURE* HER BODY WAS DISPOSED OF OR YOU DIDN'T.
WHICH IS IT?
I DID. *I DID.*
ARTHUR, PLEASE.
I BETTER MAKE SURE.
BUT...

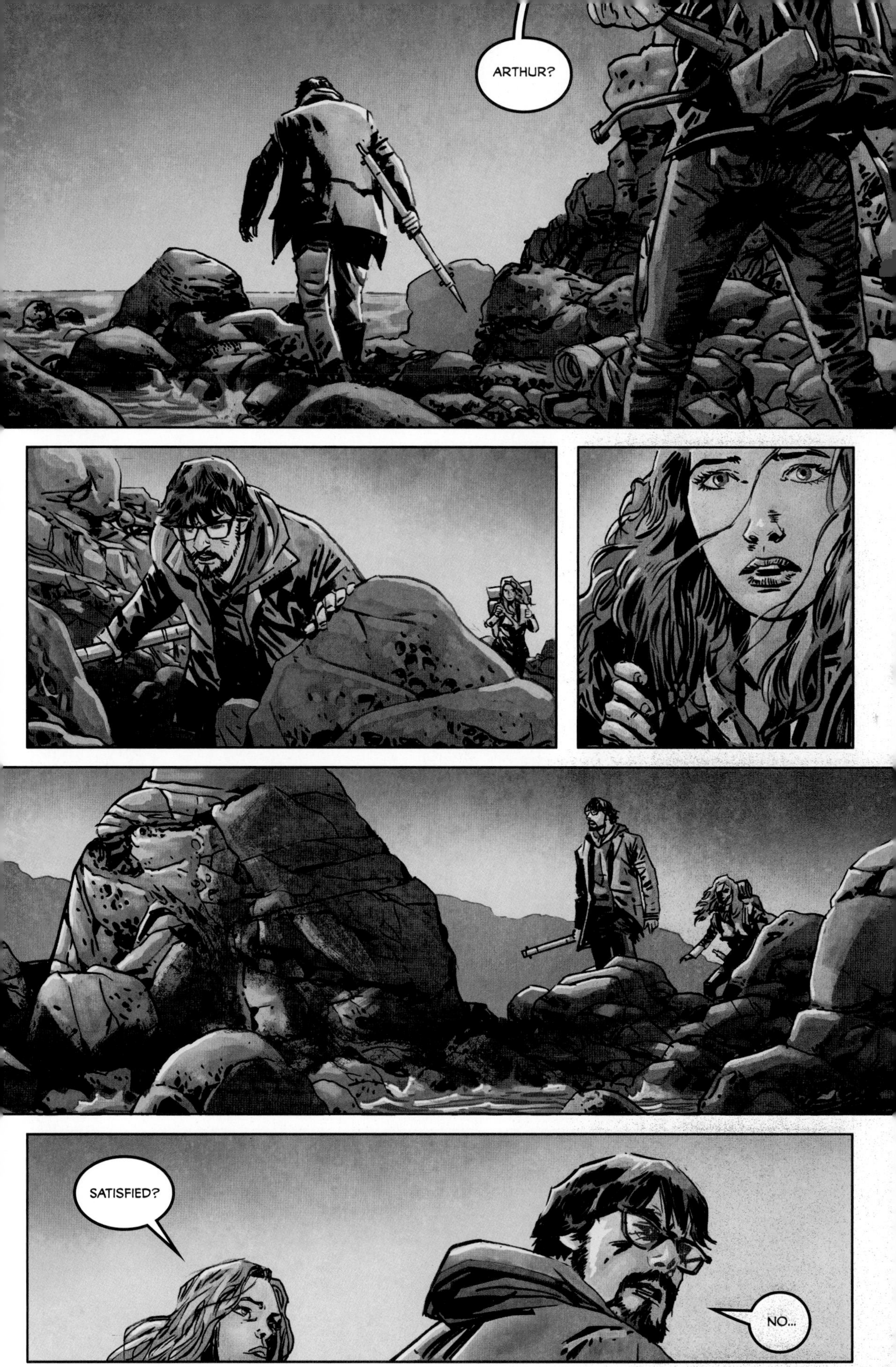
ARTHUR?
SATISFIED?
NO...

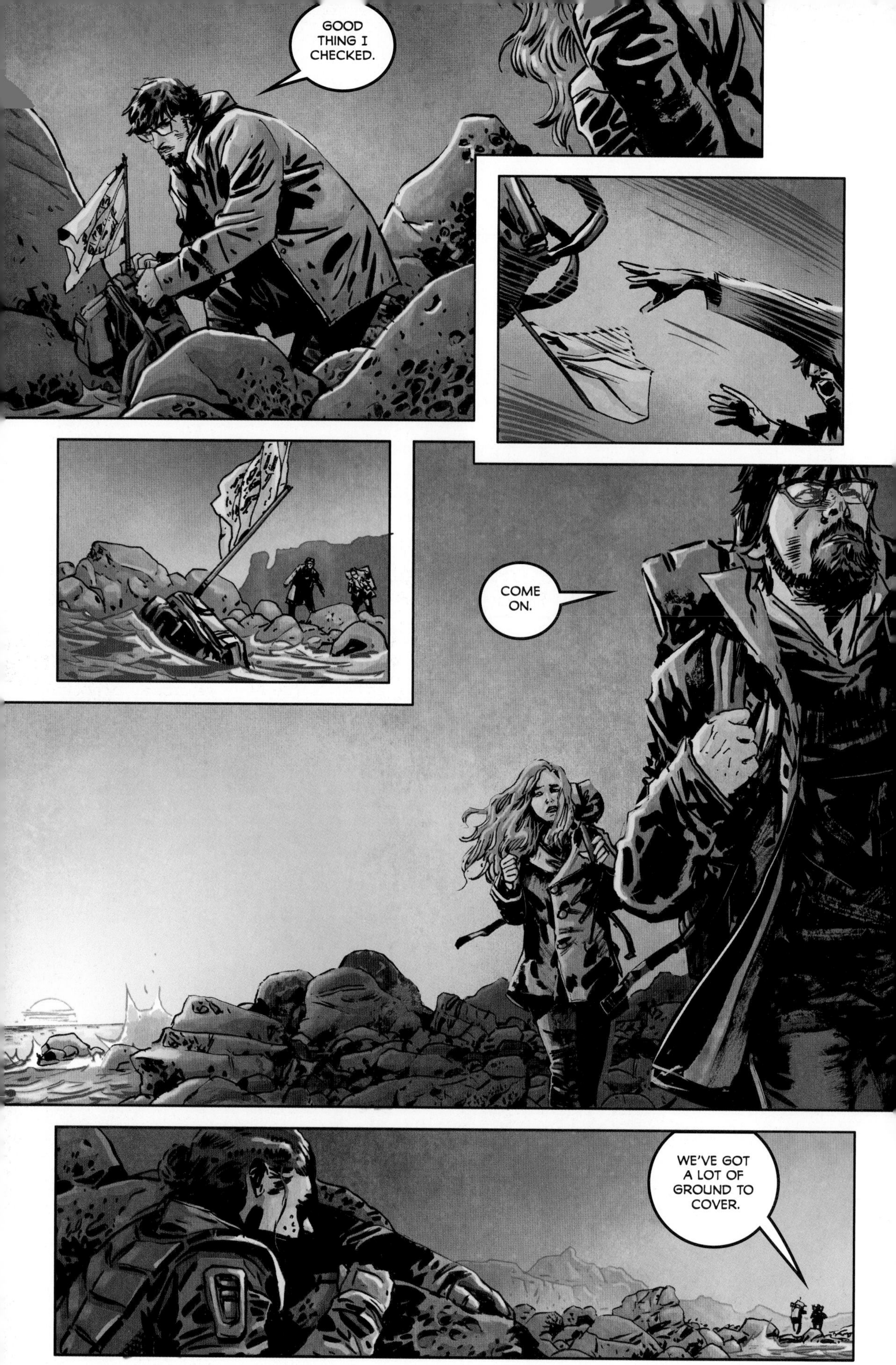
GOOD THING I CHECKED.
COME ON.
WE'VE GOT A LOT OF GROUND TO COVER.

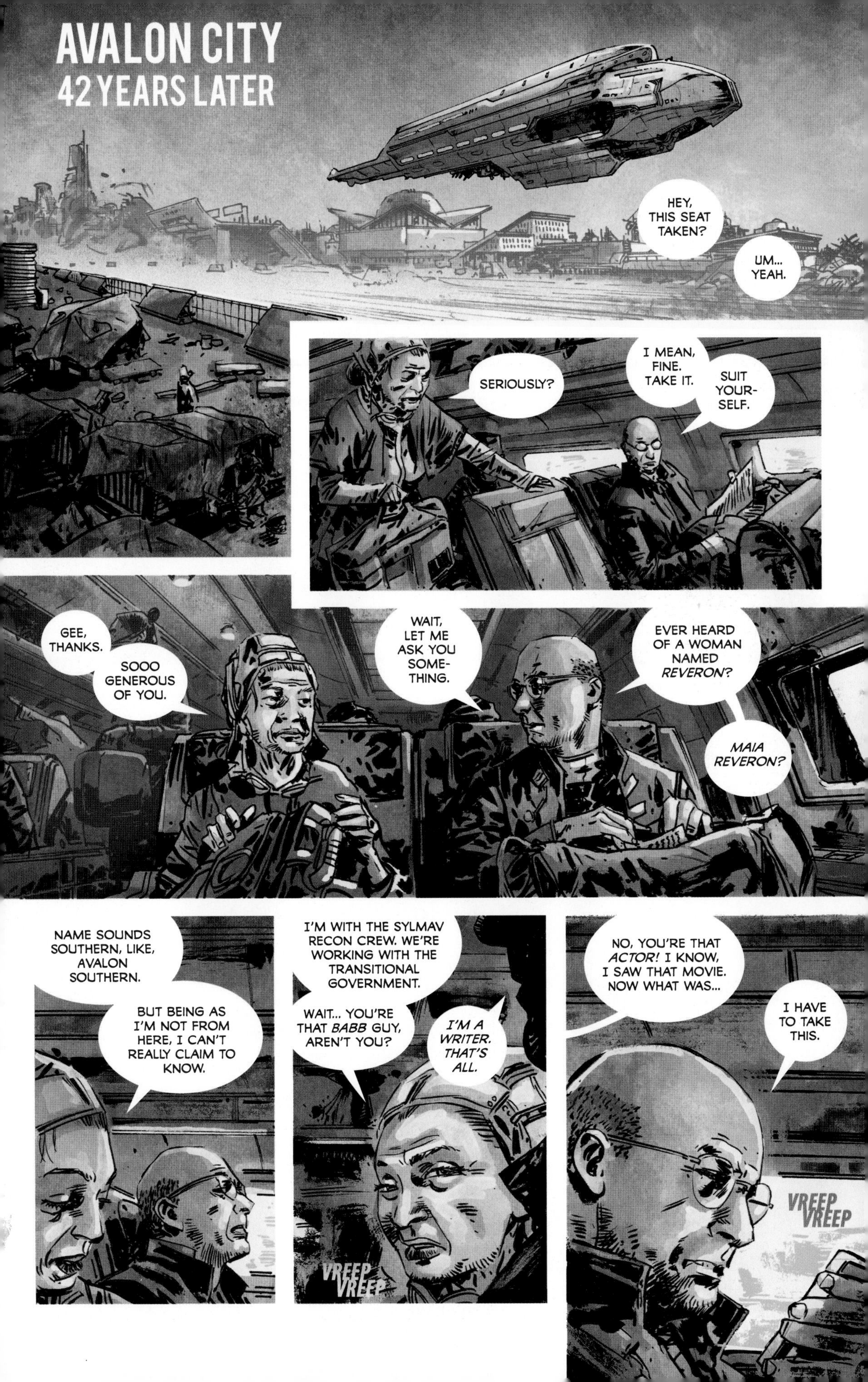
AVALON CITY
42 YEARS LATER
HEY, THIS SEAT TAKEN?
UM... YEAH.
SERIOUSLY?
I MEAN, FINE. TAKE IT.
SUIT YOURSELF.
GEE, THANKS.
SOOO GENEROUS OF YOU.
WAIT, LET ME ASK YOU SOMETHING.
EVER HEARD OF A WOMAN NAMED *REVERON?*
MAIA REVERON?
NAME SOUNDS SOUTHERN, LIKE, AVALON SOUTHERN.
BUT BEING AS I'M NOT FROM HERE, I CAN'T REALLY CLAIM TO KNOW.
I'M WITH THE SYLMAV RECON CREW. WE'RE WORKING WITH THE TRANSITIONAL GOVERNMENT.
WAIT... YOU'RE THAT *BABB* GUY, AREN'T YOU?
I'M A WRITER. THAT'S ALL.
VREEP VREEP
NO, YOU'RE THAT *ACTOR!* I KNOW, I SAW THAT MOVIE. NOW WHAT WAS...
I HAVE TO TAKE THIS.
VREEP VREEP

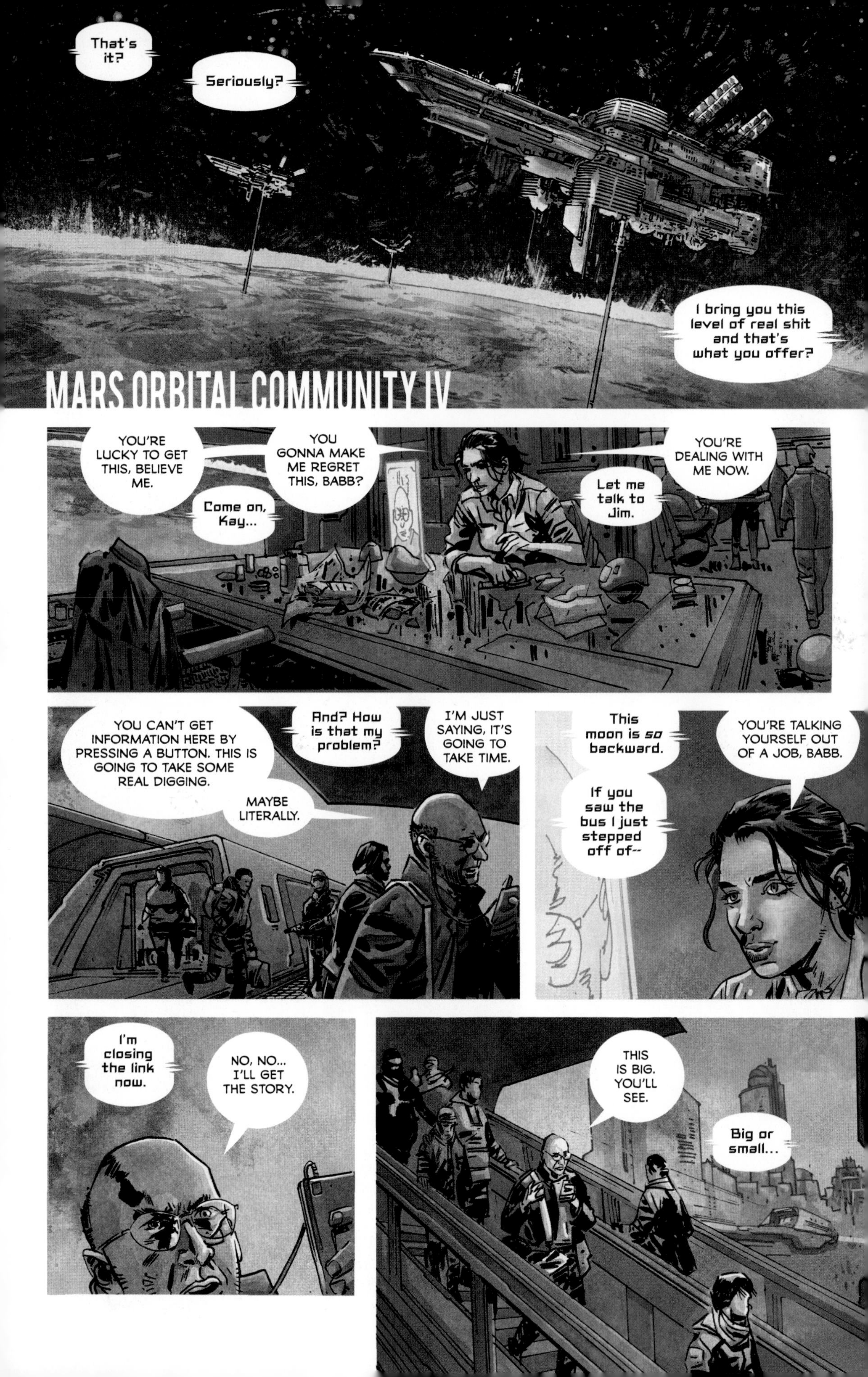
That's it?
Seriously?
I bring you this level of real shit and that's what you offer?
MARS ORBITAL COMMUNITY IV
YOU'RE LUCKY TO GET THIS, BELIEVE ME.
Come on, Kay...
YOU GONNA MAKE ME REGRET THIS, BABB?
Let me talk to Jim.
YOU'RE DEALING WITH ME NOW.
YOU CAN'T GET INFORMATION HERE BY PRESSING A BUTTON. THIS IS GOING TO TAKE SOME REAL DIGGING.
MAYBE LITERALLY.
And? How is that my problem?
I'M JUST SAYING, IT'S GOING TO TAKE TIME.
This moon is *so* backward.
If you saw the bus I just stepped off of--
YOU'RE TALKING YOURSELF OUT OF A JOB, BABB.
I'm closing the link now.
NO, NO... I'LL GET THE STORY.
THIS IS BIG. YOU'LL SEE.
Big or small...

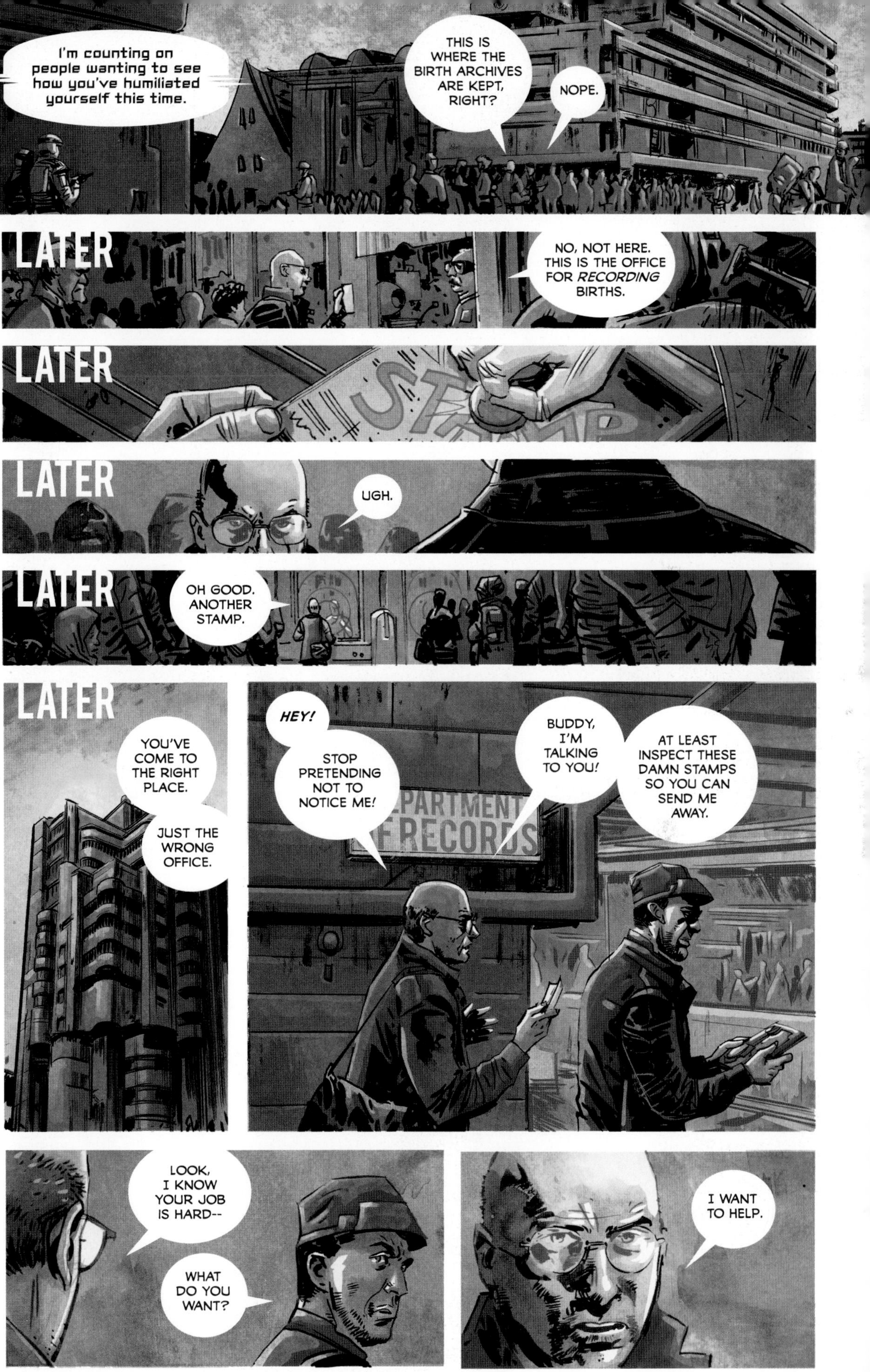
I'm counting on people wanting to see how you've humiliated yourself this time.
THIS IS WHERE THE BIRTH ARCHIVES ARE KEPT, RIGHT?
NOPE.
LATER
NO, NOT HERE. THIS IS THE OFFICE FOR *RECORDING* BIRTHS.
LATER
STAMP
LATER
UGH.
LATER
OH GOOD. ANOTHER STAMP.
LATER
YOU'VE COME TO THE RIGHT PLACE.
JUST THE WRONG OFFICE.
HEY!
STOP PRETENDING NOT TO NOTICE ME!
BUDDY, I'M TALKING TO YOU!
AT LEAST INSPECT THESE DAMN STAMPS SO YOU CAN SEND ME AWAY.
LOOK, I KNOW YOUR JOB IS HARD--
WHAT DO YOU WANT?
I WANT TO HELP.

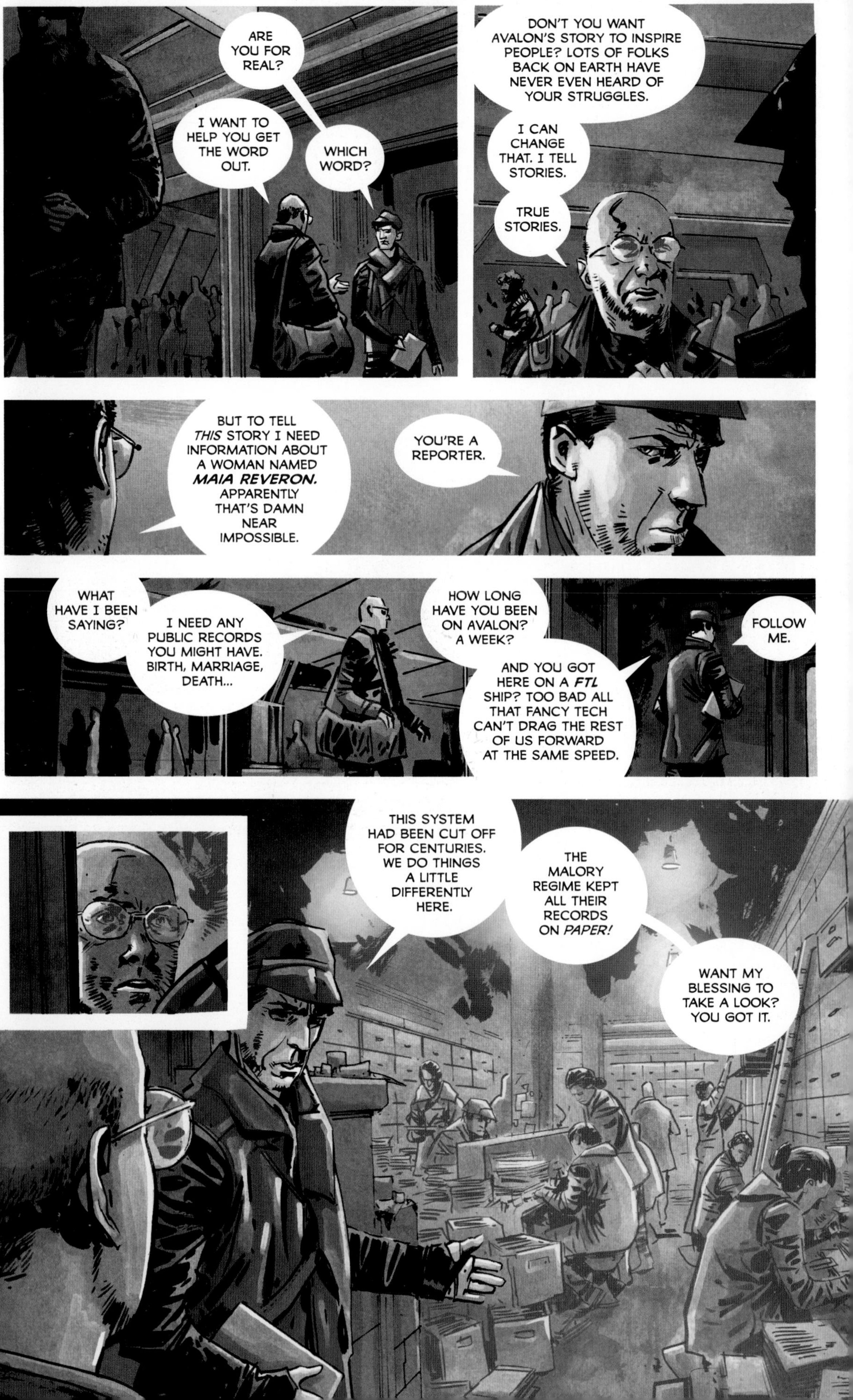

ARE YOU FOR REAL?
I WANT TO HELP YOU GET THE WORD OUT.
WHICH WORD?
DON'T YOU WANT AVALON'S STORY TO INSPIRE PEOPLE? LOTS OF FOLKS BACK ON EARTH HAVE NEVER EVEN HEARD OF YOUR STRUGGLES.
I CAN CHANGE THAT. I TELL STORIES.
TRUE STORIES.
BUT TO TELL *THIS* STORY I NEED INFORMATION ABOUT A WOMAN NAMED ***MAIA REVERON.*** APPARENTLY THAT'S DAMN NEAR IMPOSSIBLE.
YOU'RE A REPORTER.
WHAT HAVE I BEEN SAYING?
I NEED ANY PUBLIC RECORDS YOU MIGHT HAVE. BIRTH, MARRIAGE, DEATH...
HOW LONG HAVE YOU BEEN ON AVALON? A WEEK?
AND YOU GOT HERE ON A ***FTL*** SHIP? TOO BAD ALL THAT FANCY TECH CAN'T DRAG THE REST OF US FORWARD AT THE SAME SPEED.
FOLLOW ME.
THIS SYSTEM HAD BEEN CUT OFF FOR CENTURIES. WE DO THINGS A LITTLE DIFFERENTLY HERE.
THE MALORY REGIME KEPT ALL THEIR RECORDS ON *PAPER!*
WANT MY BLESSING TO TAKE A LOOK? YOU GOT IT.

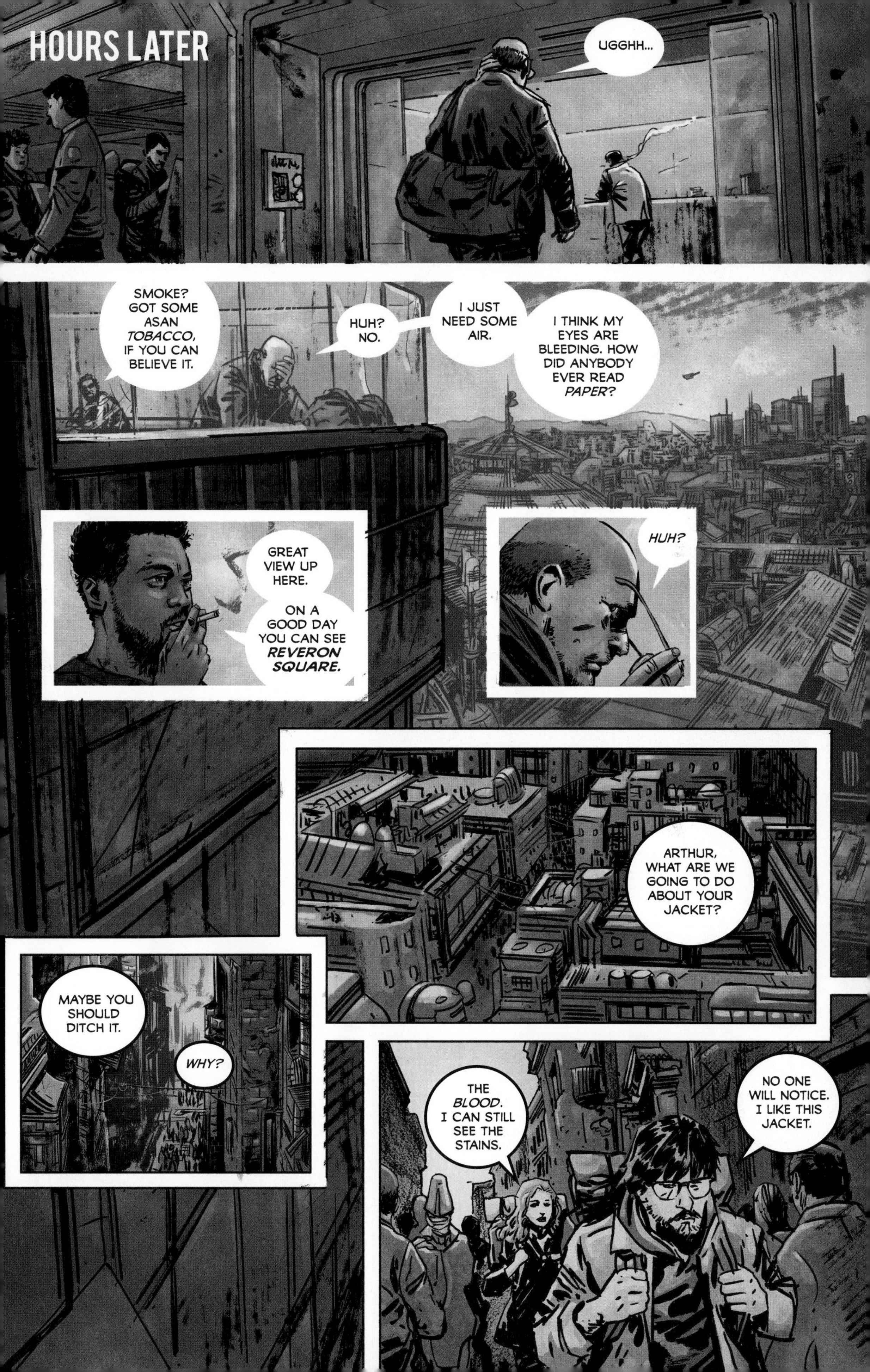
HOURS LATER
UGGHH...
SMOKE? GOT SOME ASAN *TOBACCO*, IF YOU CAN BELIEVE IT.
HUH? NO.
I JUST NEED SOME AIR.
I THINK MY EYES ARE BLEEDING. HOW DID ANYBODY EVER READ *PAPER*?
GREAT VIEW UP HERE.
ON A GOOD DAY YOU CAN SEE ***REVERON SQUARE.***
HUH?
ARTHUR, WHAT ARE WE GOING TO DO ABOUT YOUR JACKET?
MAYBE YOU SHOULD DITCH IT.
WHY?
THE *BLOOD*. I CAN STILL SEE THE STAINS.
NO ONE WILL NOTICE. I LIKE THIS JACKET.

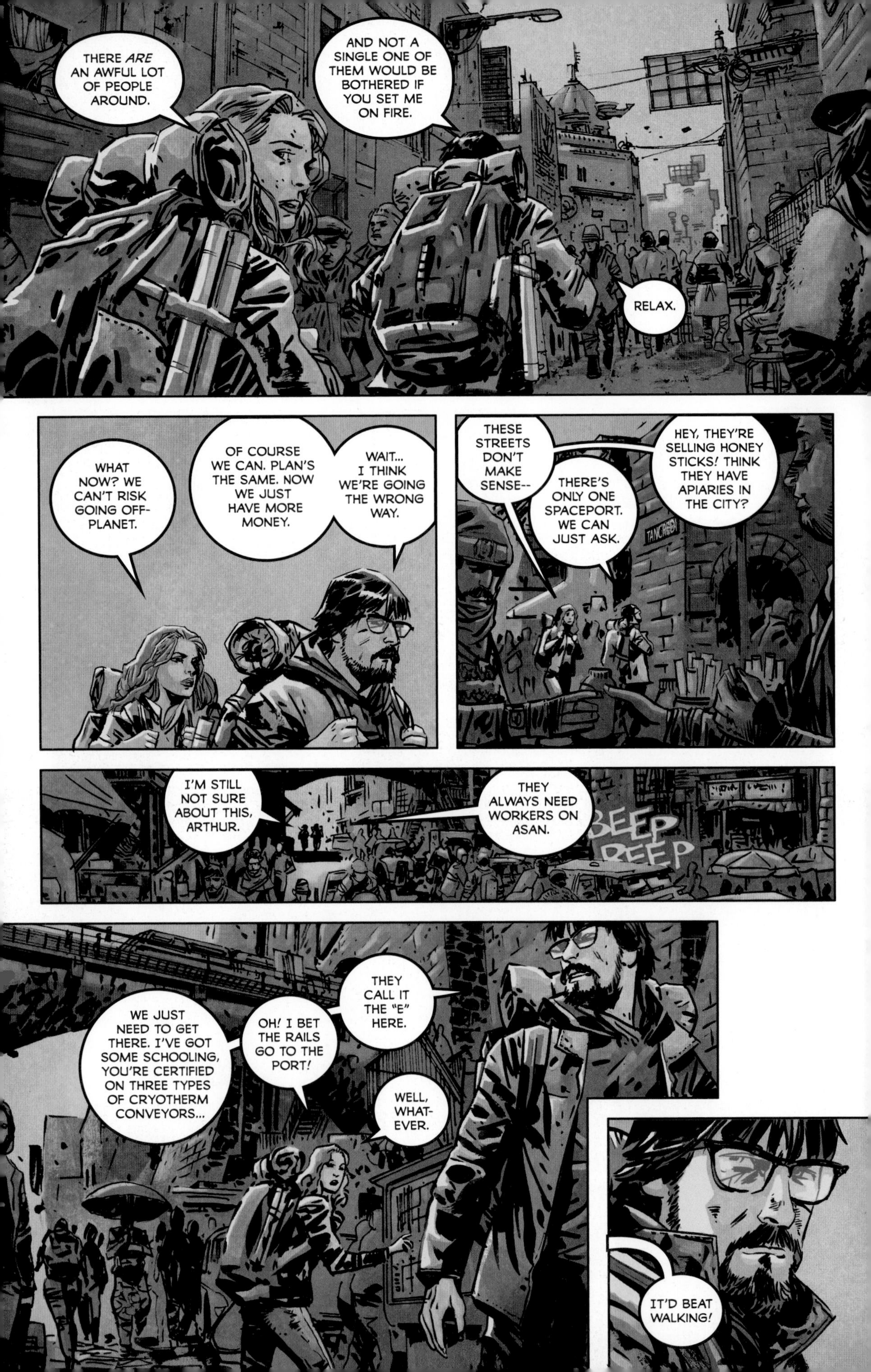

THERE *ARE* AN AWFUL LOT OF PEOPLE AROUND.
AND NOT A SINGLE ONE OF THEM WOULD BE BOTHERED IF YOU SET ME ON FIRE.
RELAX.
WHAT NOW? WE CAN'T RISK GOING OFF-PLANET.
OF COURSE WE CAN. PLAN'S THE SAME. NOW WE JUST HAVE MORE MONEY.
WAIT... I THINK WE'RE GOING THE WRONG WAY.
THESE STREETS DON'T MAKE SENSE--
THERE'S ONLY ONE SPACEPORT. WE CAN JUST ASK.
HEY, THEY'RE SELLING HONEY STICKS! THINK THEY HAVE APIARIES IN THE CITY?
I'M STILL NOT SURE ABOUT THIS, ARTHUR.
THEY ALWAYS NEED WORKERS ON ASAN.
BEEP BEEP
WE JUST NEED TO GET THERE. I'VE GOT SOME SCHOOLING, YOU'RE CERTIFIED ON THREE TYPES OF CRYOTHERM CONVEYORS...
OH! I BET THE RAILS GO TO THE PORT!
THEY CALL IT THE "E" HERE.
WELL, WHAT-EVER.
IT'D BEAT WALKING!

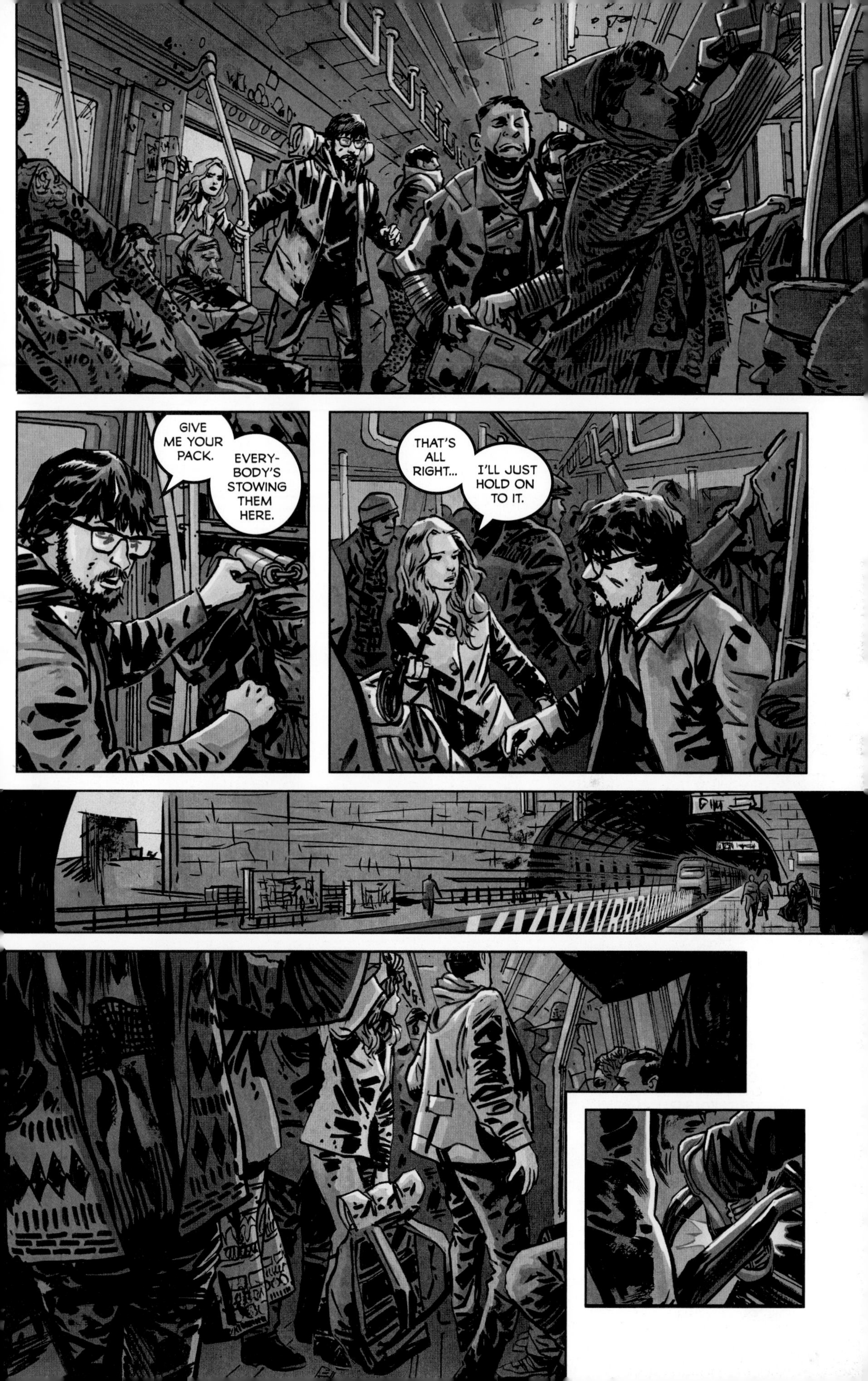
GIVE ME YOUR PACK.
EVERY-BODY'S STOWING THEM HERE.
THAT'S ALL RIGHT...
I'LL JUST HOLD ON TO IT.

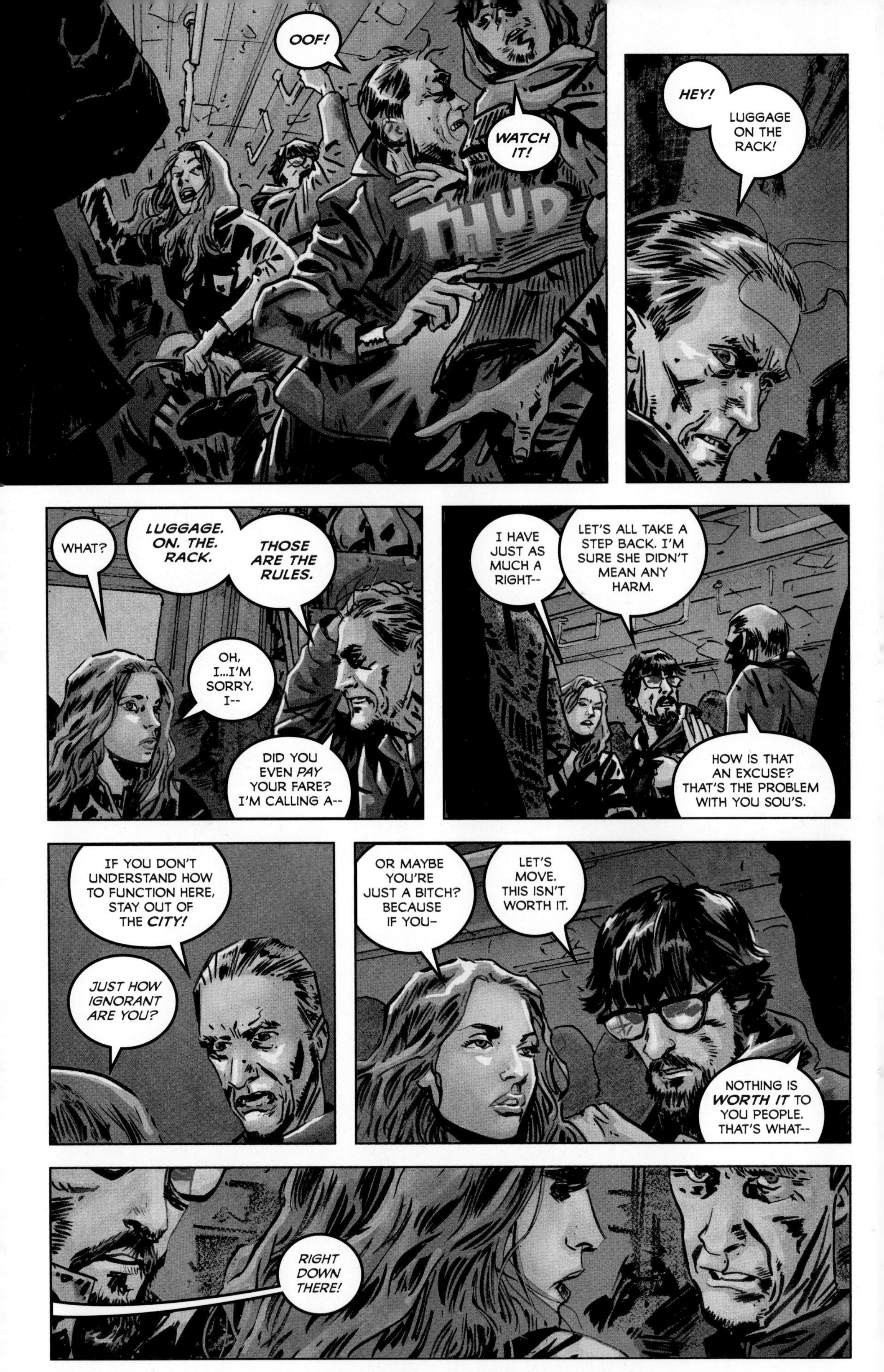
OOF!
WATCH IT!
THUD
HEY!
LUGGAGE ON THE RACK!
WHAT?
LUGGAGE. ON. THE. RACK.
THOSE ARE THE RULES.
OH, I...I'M SORRY. I--
DID YOU EVEN PAY YOUR FARE? I'M CALLING A--
I HAVE JUST AS MUCH A RIGHT--
LET'S ALL TAKE A STEP BACK. I'M SURE SHE DIDN'T MEAN ANY HARM.
HOW IS THAT AN EXCUSE? THAT'S THE PROBLEM WITH YOU SOU'S.
IF YOU DON'T UNDERSTAND HOW TO FUNCTION HERE, STAY OUT OF THE CITY!
JUST HOW IGNORANT ARE YOU?
OR MAYBE YOU'RE JUST A BITCH? BECAUSE IF YOU-
LET'S MOVE. THIS ISN'T WORTH IT.
NOTHING IS WORTH IT TO YOU PEOPLE. THAT'S WHAT--
RIGHT DOWN THERE!

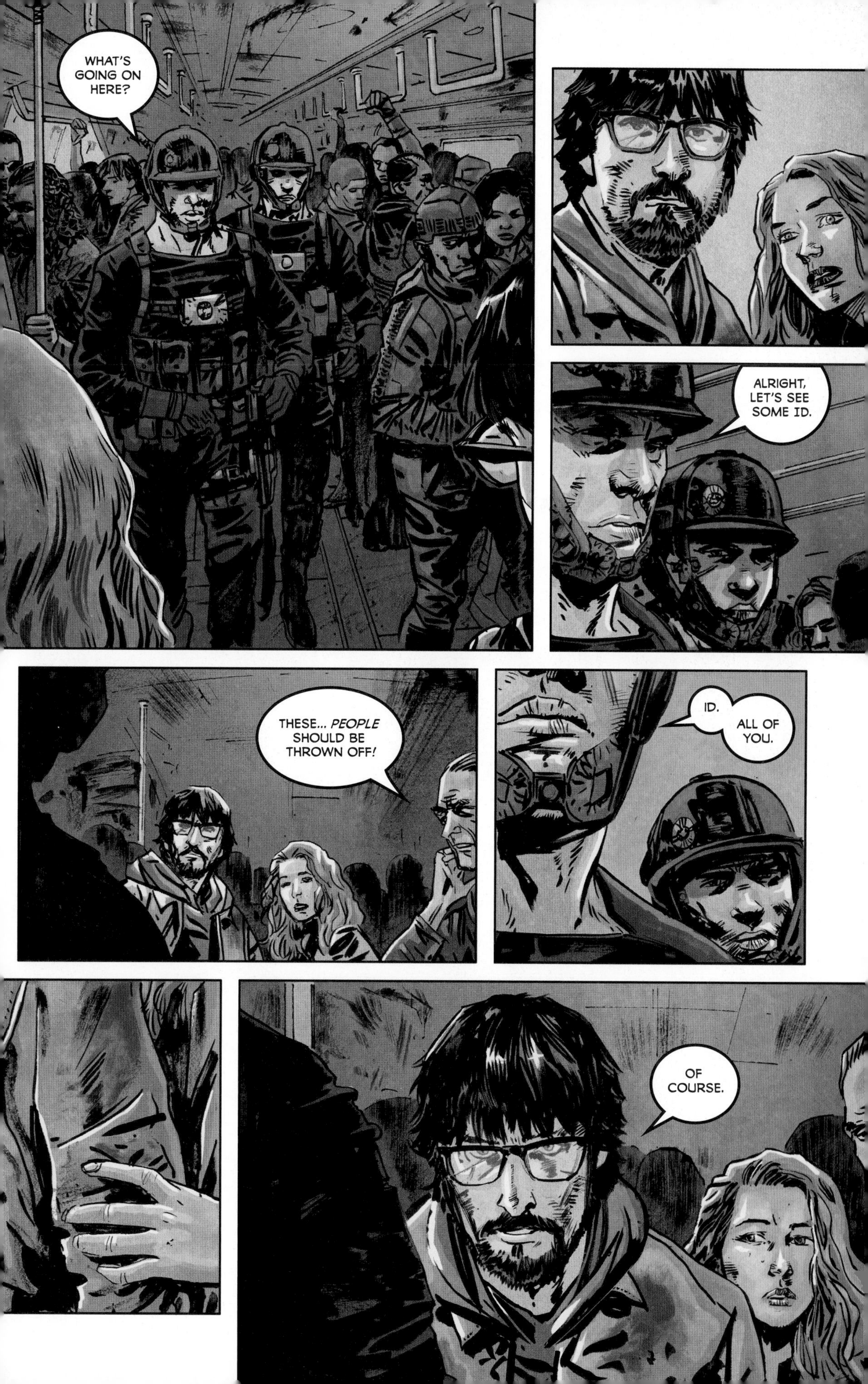
WHAT'S GOING ON HERE?
ALRIGHT, LET'S SEE SOME ID.
THESE... *PEOPLE* SHOULD BE THROWN OFF!
ID.
ALL OF YOU.
OF COURSE.

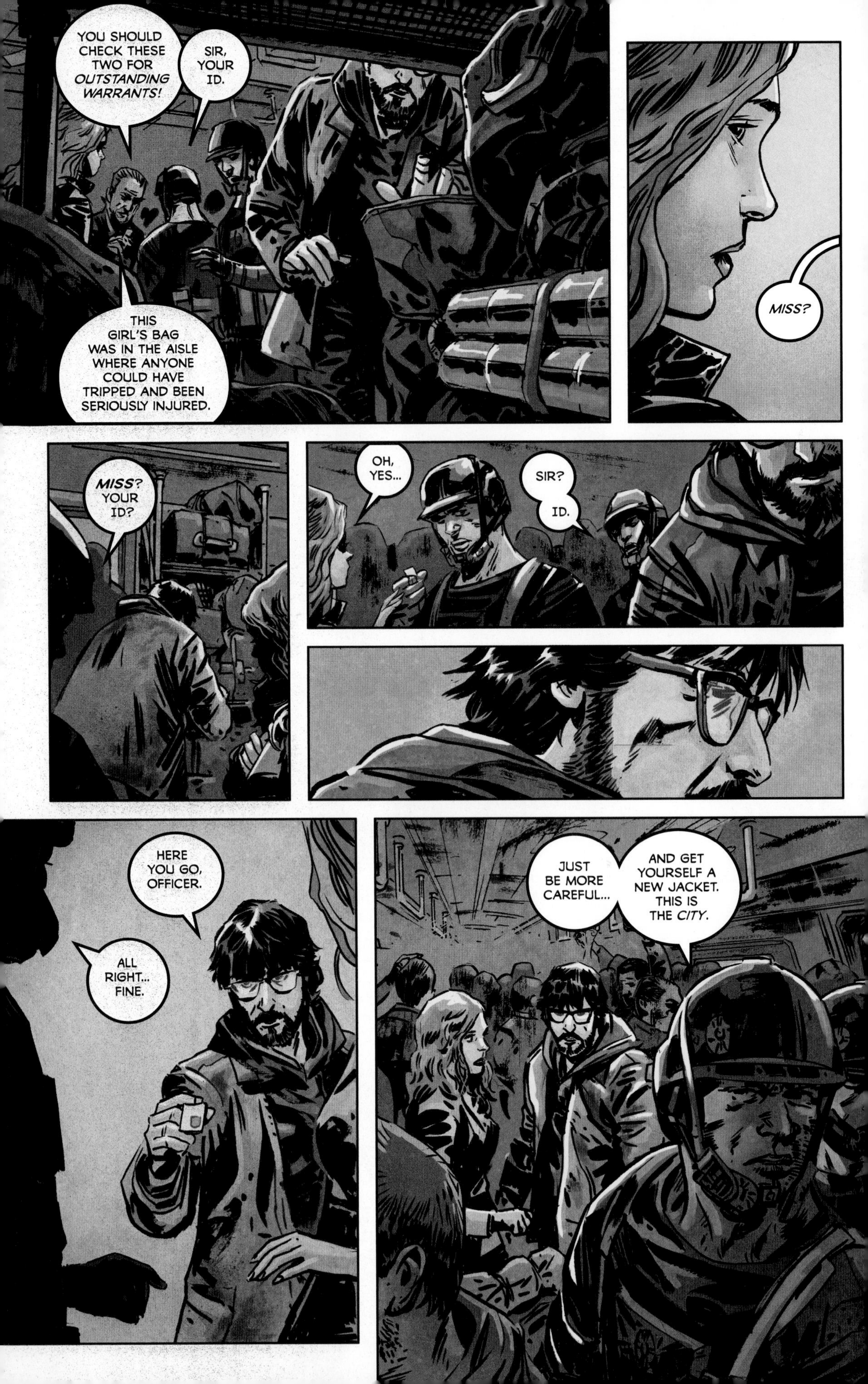
YOU SHOULD CHECK THESE TWO FOR *OUTSTANDING WARRANTS!*
SIR, YOUR ID.
THIS GIRL'S BAG WAS IN THE AISLE WHERE ANYONE COULD HAVE TRIPPED AND BEEN SERIOUSLY INJURED.
MISS?
MISS? YOUR ID?
OH, YES...
SIR?
ID.
HERE YOU GO, OFFICER.
ALL RIGHT... FINE.
JUST BE MORE CAREFUL...
AND GET YOURSELF A NEW JACKET. THIS IS THE *CITY*.

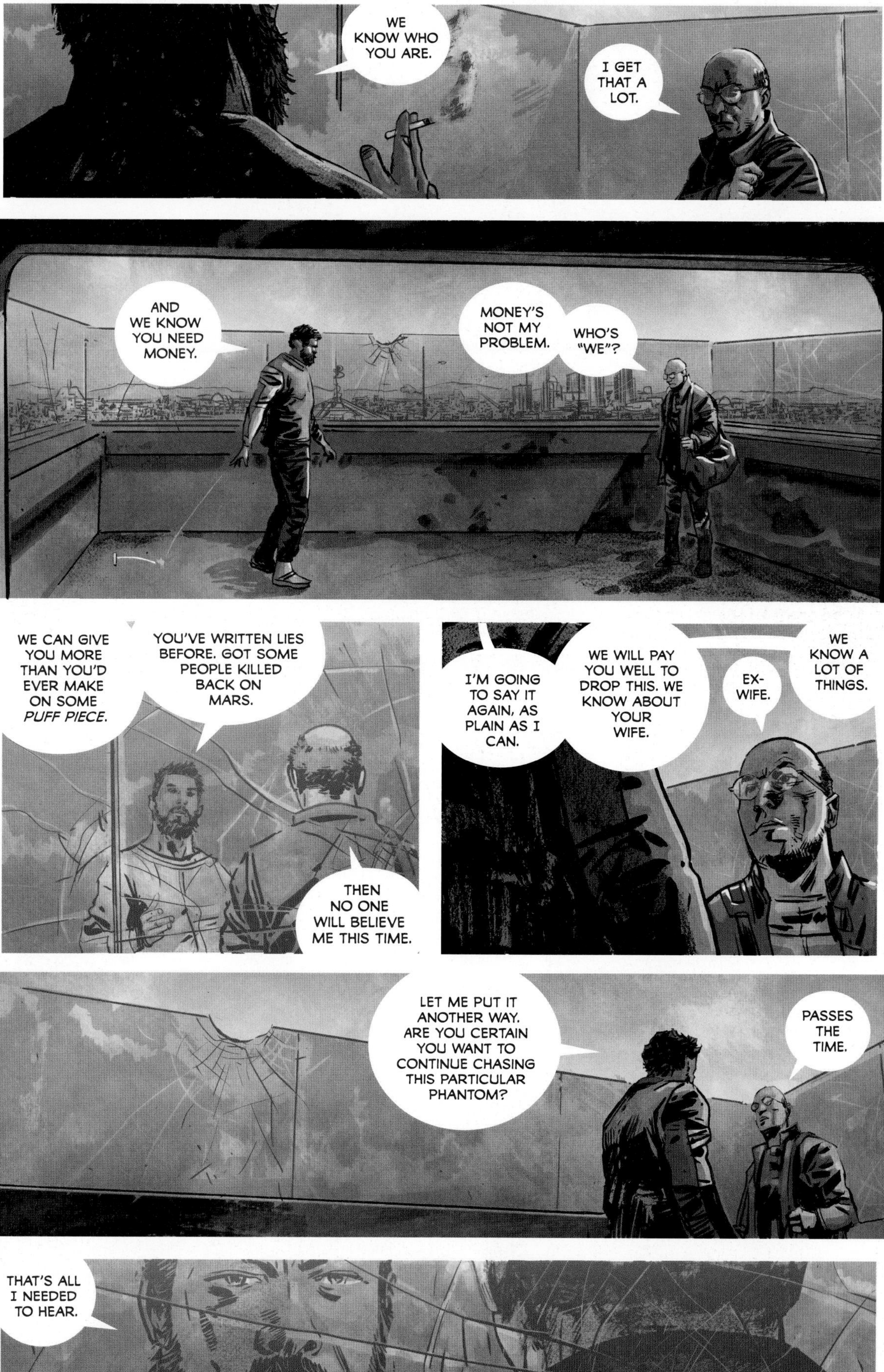
WE KNOW WHO YOU ARE.
I GET THAT A LOT.
AND WE KNOW YOU NEED MONEY.
MONEY'S NOT MY PROBLEM.
WHO'S "WE"?
WE CAN GIVE YOU MORE THAN YOU'D EVER MAKE ON SOME *PUFF PIECE*.
YOU'VE WRITTEN LIES BEFORE. GOT SOME PEOPLE KILLED BACK ON MARS.
THEN NO ONE WILL BELIEVE ME THIS TIME.
I'M GOING TO SAY IT AGAIN, AS PLAIN AS I CAN.
WE WILL PAY YOU WELL TO DROP THIS. WE KNOW ABOUT YOUR WIFE.
EX-WIFE.
WE KNOW A LOT OF THINGS.
LET ME PUT IT ANOTHER WAY. ARE YOU CERTAIN YOU WANT TO CONTINUE CHASING THIS PARTICULAR PHANTOM?
PASSES THE TIME.
THAT'S ALL I NEEDED TO HEAR.

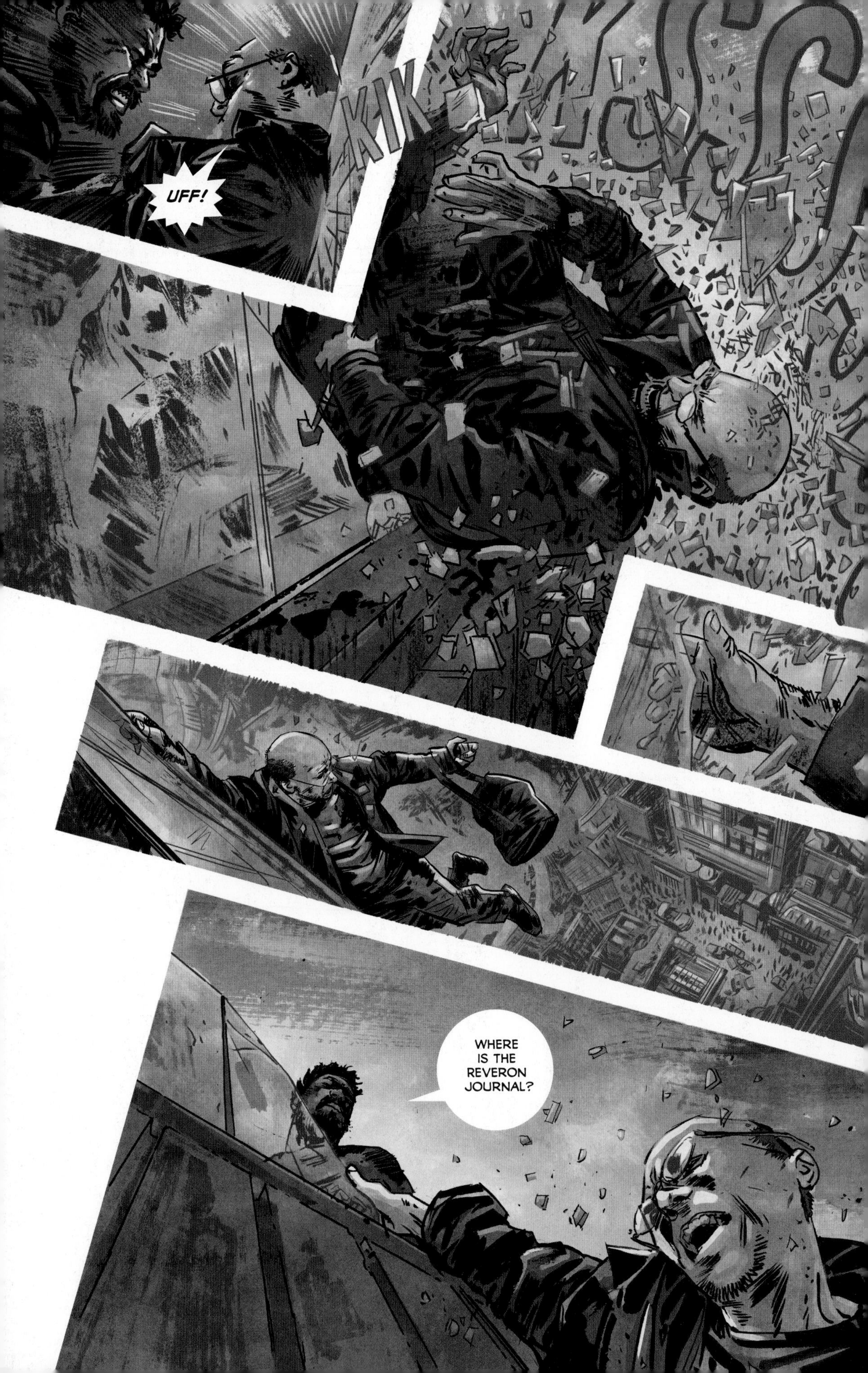
UFF!
KIKSSSH
WHERE IS THE REVERON JOURNAL?

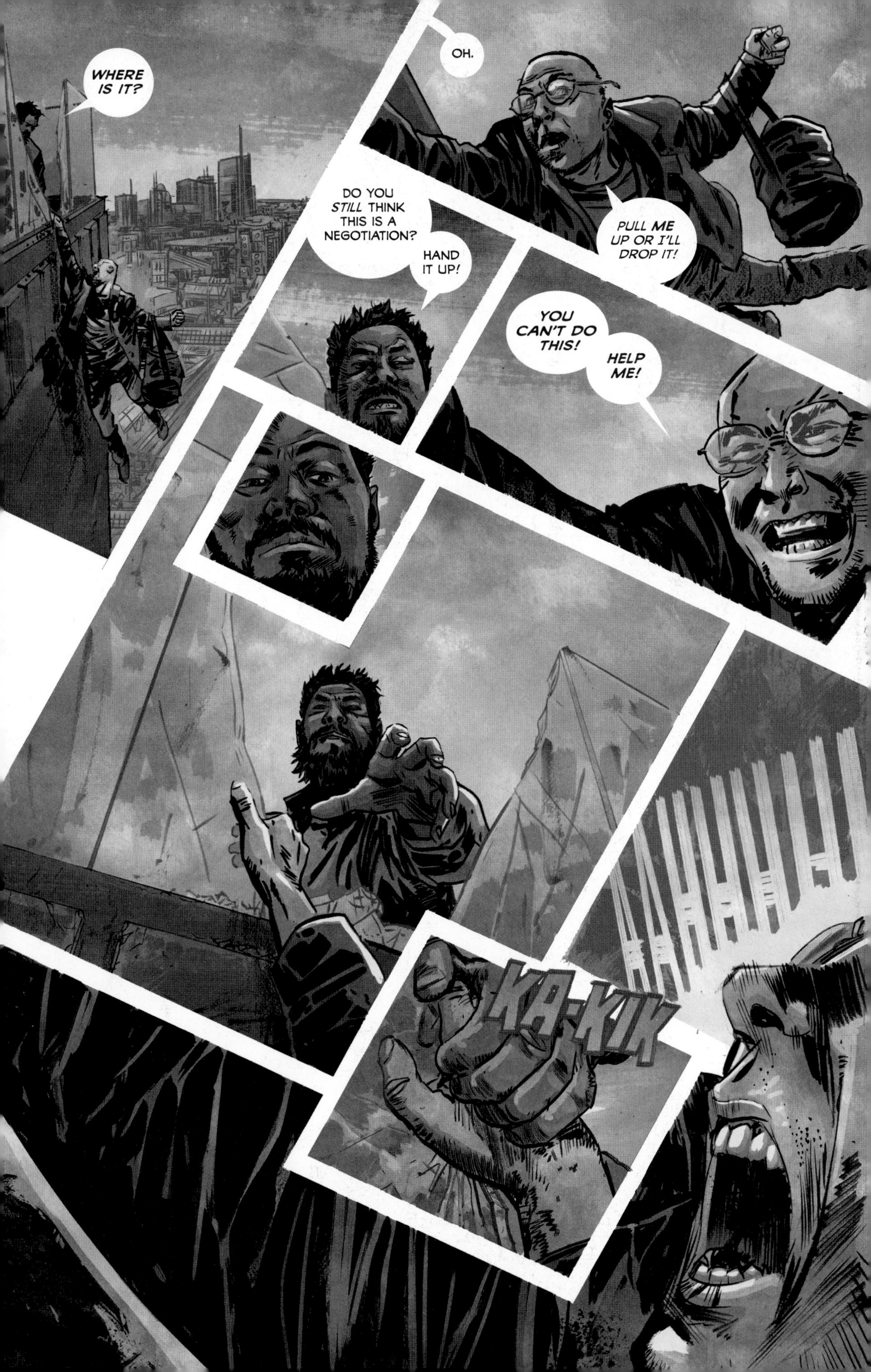
WHERE IS IT?
OH.
PULL ME UP OR I'LL DROP IT!
DO YOU *STILL* THINK THIS IS A NEGOTIATION?
HAND IT UP!
YOU CAN'T DO THIS!
HELP ME!
KA-KIK

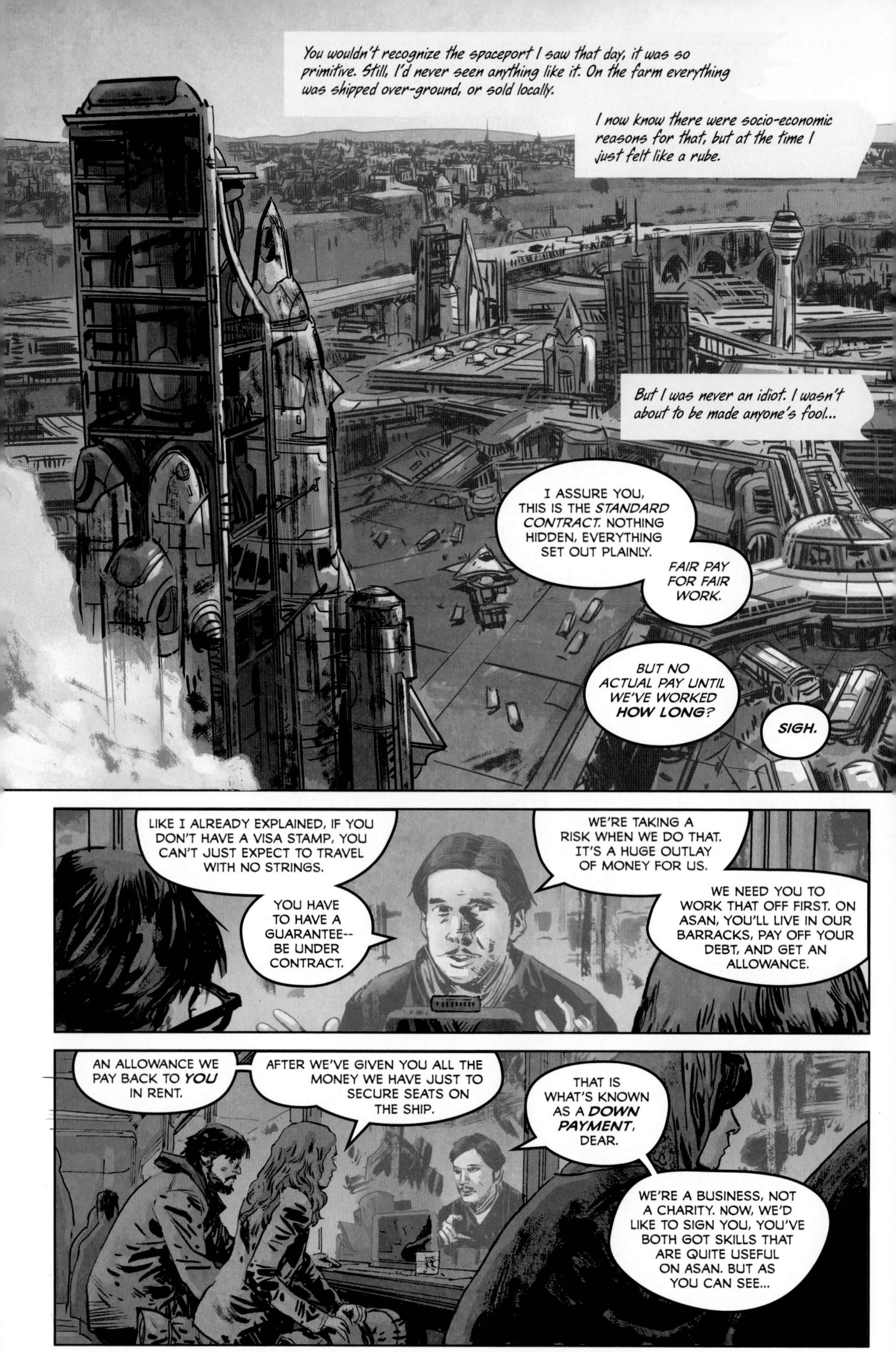

You wouldn't recognize the spaceport I saw that day, it was so primitive. Still, I'd never seen anything like it. On the farm everything was shipped over-ground, or sold locally.
I now know there were socio-economic reasons for that, but at the time I just felt like a rube.
But I was never an idiot. I wasn't about to be made anyone's fool...
I ASSURE YOU, THIS IS THE *STANDARD CONTRACT.* NOTHING HIDDEN, EVERYTHING SET OUT PLAINLY.
FAIR PAY FOR FAIR WORK.
BUT NO ACTUAL PAY UNTIL WE'VE WORKED **HOW LONG?**
SIGH.
LIKE I ALREADY EXPLAINED, IF YOU DON'T HAVE A VISA STAMP, YOU CAN'T JUST EXPECT TO TRAVEL WITH NO STRINGS.
YOU HAVE TO HAVE A GUARANTEE-- BE UNDER CONTRACT.
WE'RE TAKING A RISK WHEN WE DO THAT. IT'S A HUGE OUTLAY OF MONEY FOR US.
WE NEED YOU TO WORK THAT OFF FIRST. ON ASAN, YOU'LL LIVE IN OUR BARRACKS, PAY OFF YOUR DEBT, AND GET AN ALLOWANCE.
AN ALLOWANCE WE PAY BACK TO ***YOU*** IN RENT.
AFTER WE'VE GIVEN YOU ALL THE MONEY WE HAVE JUST TO SECURE SEATS ON THE SHIP.
THAT IS WHAT'S KNOWN AS A ***DOWN PAYMENT***, DEAR.
WE'RE A BUSINESS, NOT A CHARITY. NOW, WE'D LIKE TO SIGN YOU, YOU'VE BOTH GOT SKILLS THAT ARE QUITE USEFUL ON ASAN. BUT AS YOU CAN SEE...

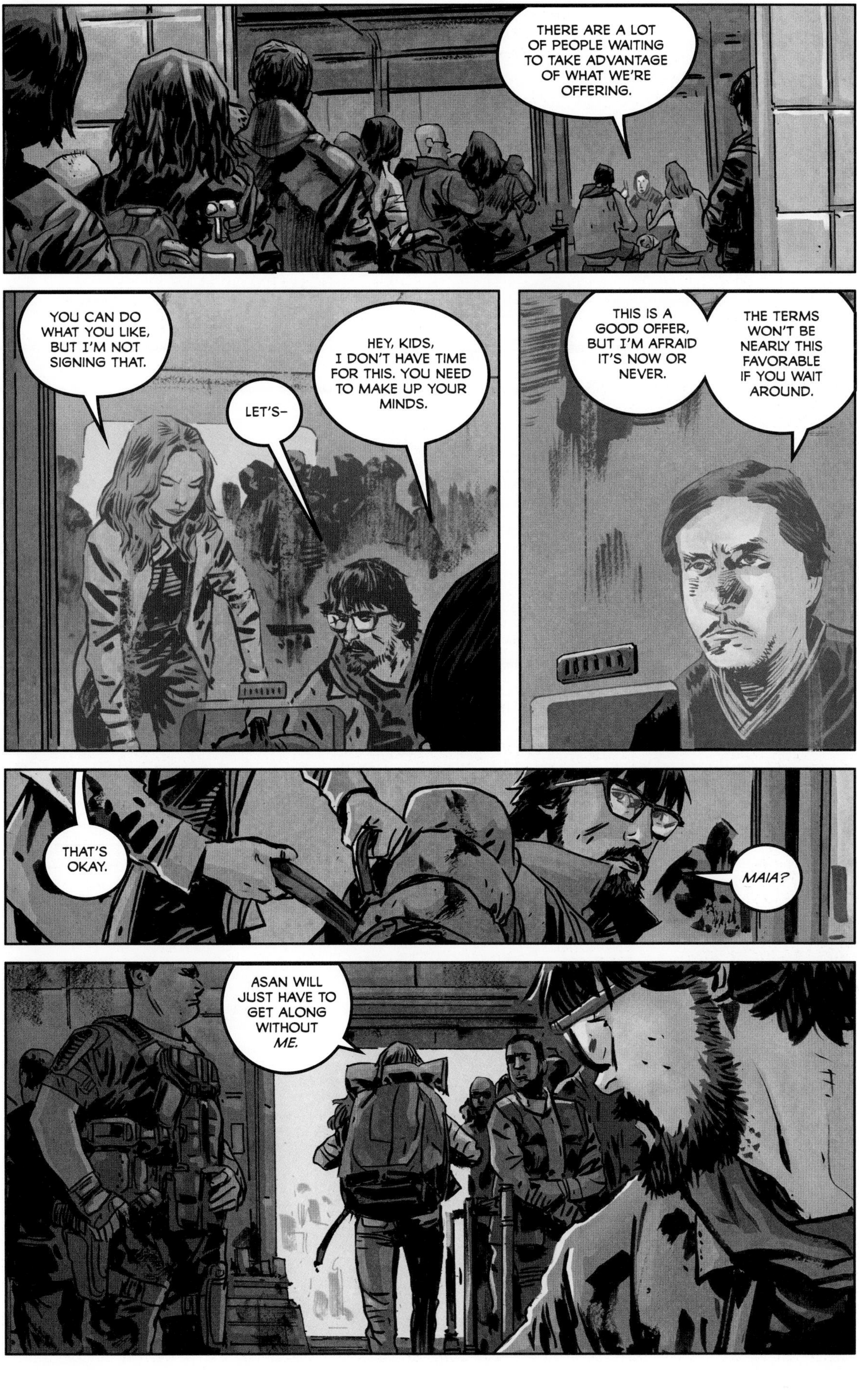
THERE ARE A LOT OF PEOPLE WAITING TO TAKE ADVANTAGE OF WHAT WE'RE OFFERING.
YOU CAN DO WHAT YOU LIKE, BUT I'M NOT SIGNING THAT.
LET'S–
HEY, KIDS, I DON'T HAVE TIME FOR THIS. YOU NEED TO MAKE UP YOUR MINDS.
THIS IS A GOOD OFFER, BUT I'M AFRAID IT'S NOW OR NEVER.
THE TERMS WON'T BE NEARLY THIS FAVORABLE IF YOU WAIT AROUND.
THAT'S OKAY.
MAIA?
ASAN WILL JUST HAVE TO GET ALONG WITHOUT *ME.*

MAIA, WAIT.

ARTHUR, AREN'T YOU TIRED OF BEING A... A SLAVE? DO YOU REALLY WANT TO GO BACK TO THAT?

SLAVES? WE WERE INDENTURED.

IF THE SWEEPS HAD STAYED TO THE NORTH FOR ANOTHER YEAR, WE WOULD HAVE BEEN OUT.

YOU REALLY THINK SO?

BECAUSE I'M PRETTY SURE PENNY HAD A WAY FIGURED AROUND THAT.

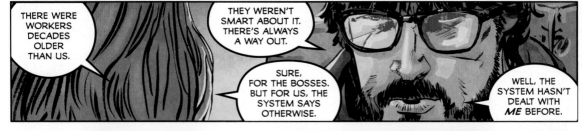

THERE WERE WORKERS DECADES OLDER THAN US.

THEY WEREN'T SMART ABOUT IT. THERE'S ALWAYS A WAY OUT.

SURE, FOR THE BOSSES. BUT FOR US, THE SYSTEM SAYS OTHERWISE.

WELL, THE SYSTEM HASN'T DEALT WITH ME BEFORE.

HOW CAN YOU KEEP ON LIKE THIS?

ARTHUR, YOU KILLED THOSE PEOPLE!

WE KILLED THOSE SOLDIERS.

THEY WERE PEOPLE! DOING THEIR JOB. THEY DIDN'T HAVE TO DIE!

WE GOT FREE OF THE FARM, FOR WHAT?

TO END UP HERE, WITHOUT ENOUGH MONEY TO FORGE A TRAVEL VISA, AND...

AND... OH, SHIT.

JUST SHIT.

I...I'M JUST SO TIRED. AND HUNGRY.

WELL, THAT WE CAN FIX.

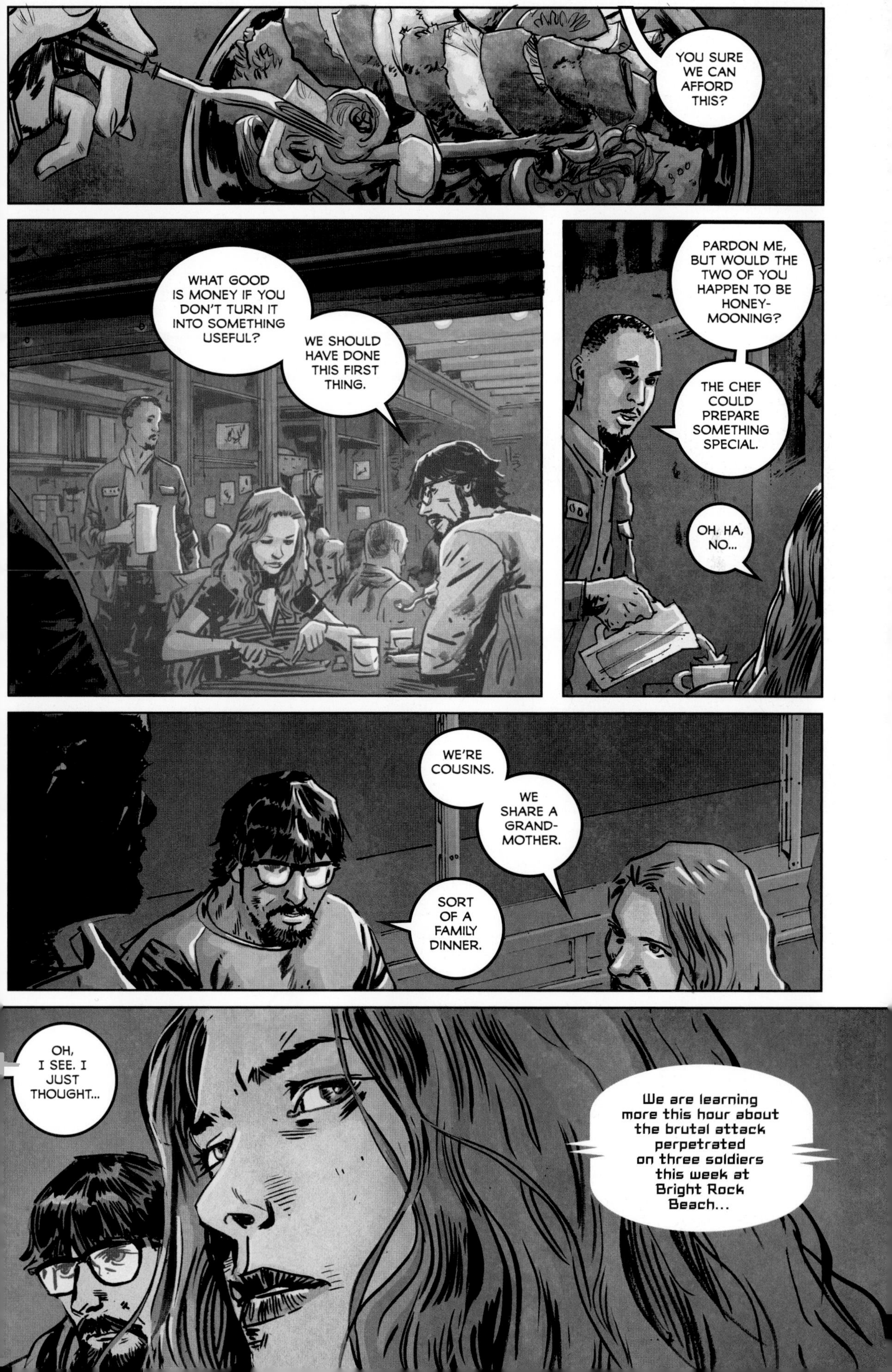
YOU SURE WE CAN AFFORD THIS?
WHAT GOOD IS MONEY IF YOU DON'T TURN IT INTO SOMETHING USEFUL?
WE SHOULD HAVE DONE THIS FIRST THING.
PARDON ME, BUT WOULD THE TWO OF YOU HAPPEN TO BE HONEY-MOONING?
THE CHEF COULD PREPARE SOMETHING SPECIAL.
OH. HA, NO...
WE'RE COUSINS.
WE SHARE A GRAND-MOTHER.
SORT OF A FAMILY DINNER.
OH, I SEE. I JUST THOUGHT...
We are learning more this hour about the brutal attack perpetrated on three soldiers this week at Bright Rock Beach...

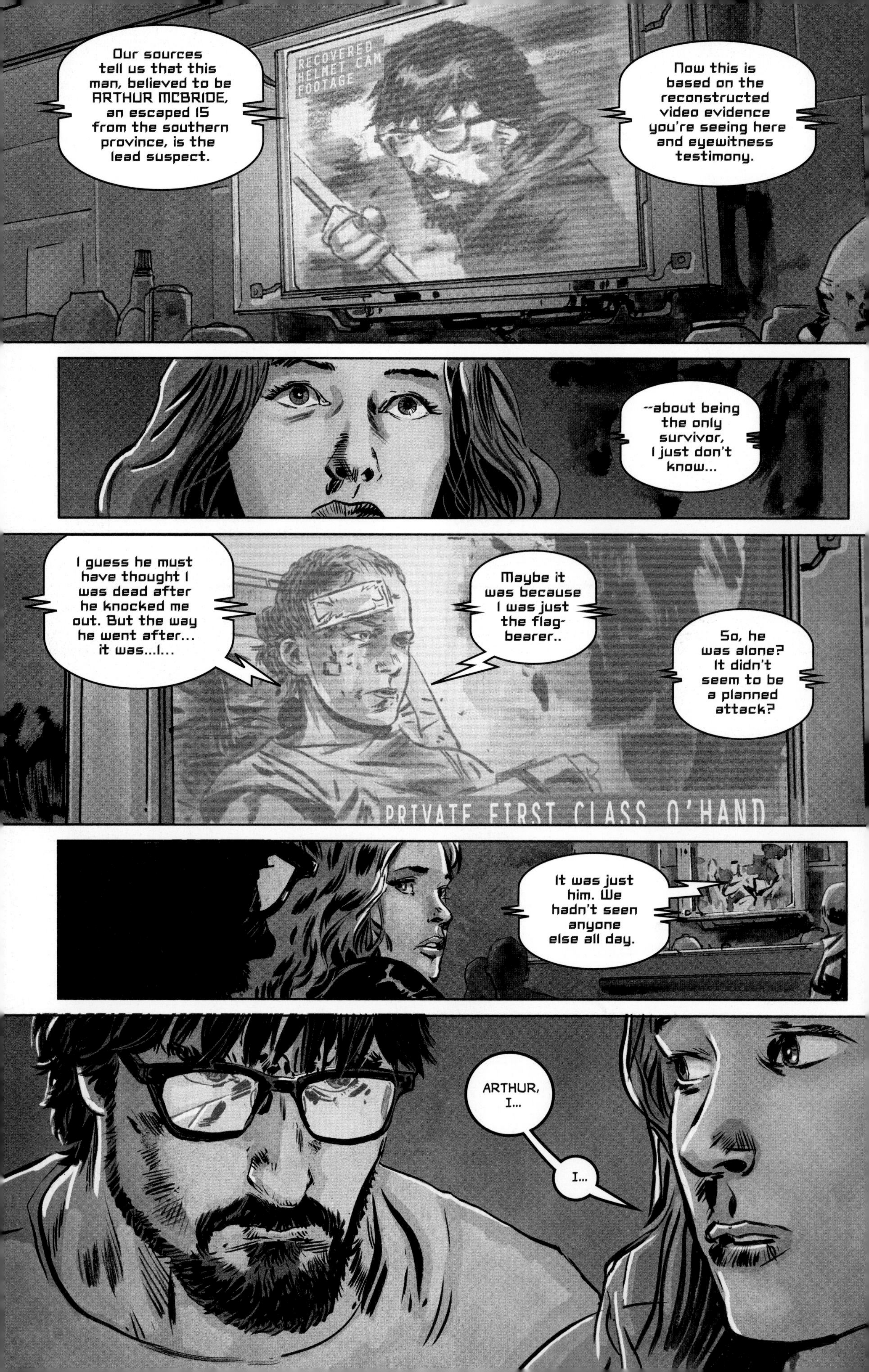
RECOVERED HELMET CAM FOOTAGE
Our sources tell us that this man, believed to be ARTHUR MCBRIDE, an escaped 15 from the southern province, is the lead suspect.
Now this is based on the reconstructed video evidence you're seeing here and eyewitness testimony.
--about being the only survivor, I just don't know...
I guess he must have thought I was dead after he knocked me out. But the way he went after... it was...I...
Maybe it was because I was just the flag-bearer..
So, he was alone? It didn't seem to be a planned attack?
PRIVATE FIRST CLASS O'HAND
It was just him. We hadn't seen anyone else all day.
ARTHUR, I...
I...

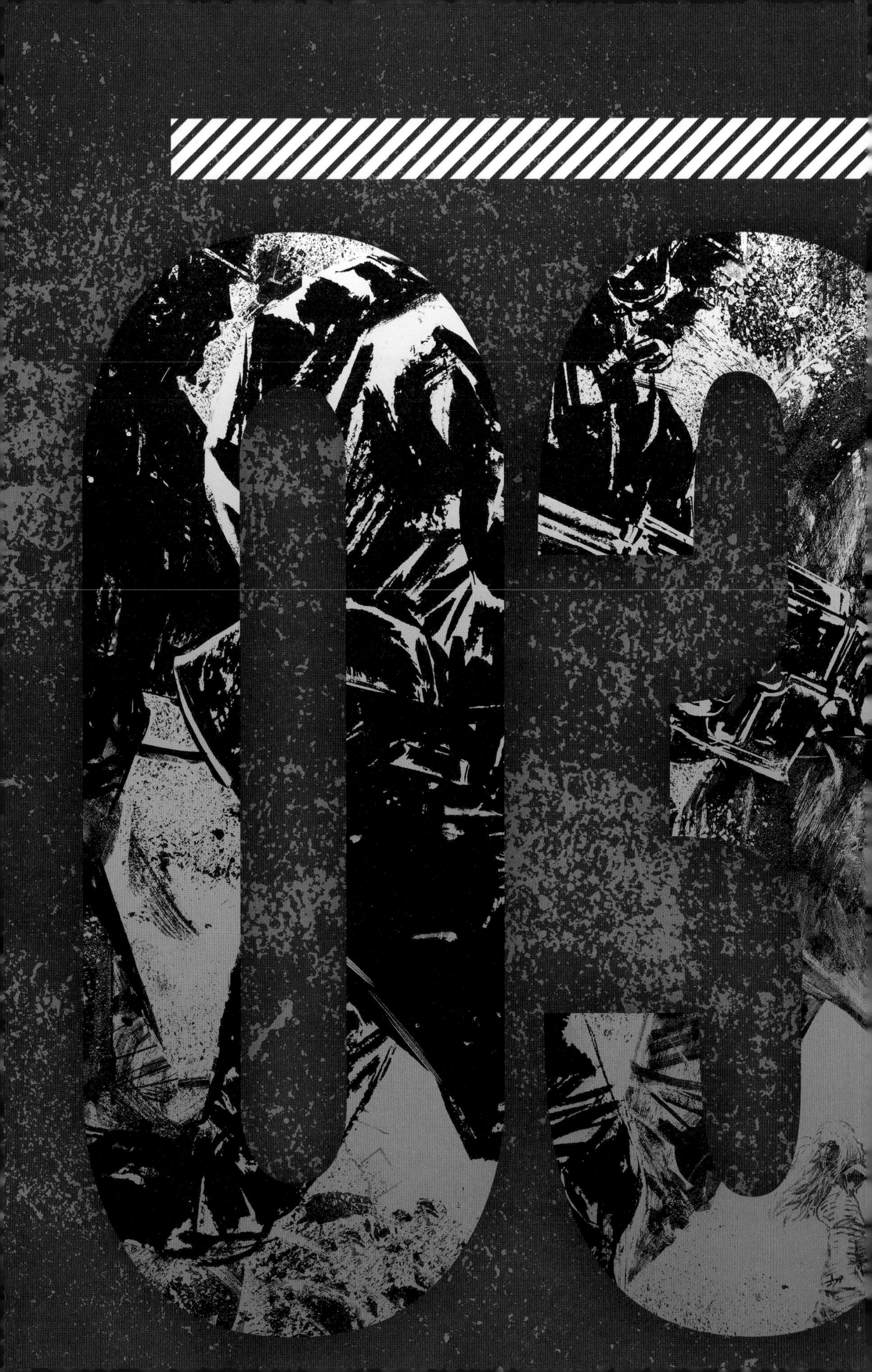
03

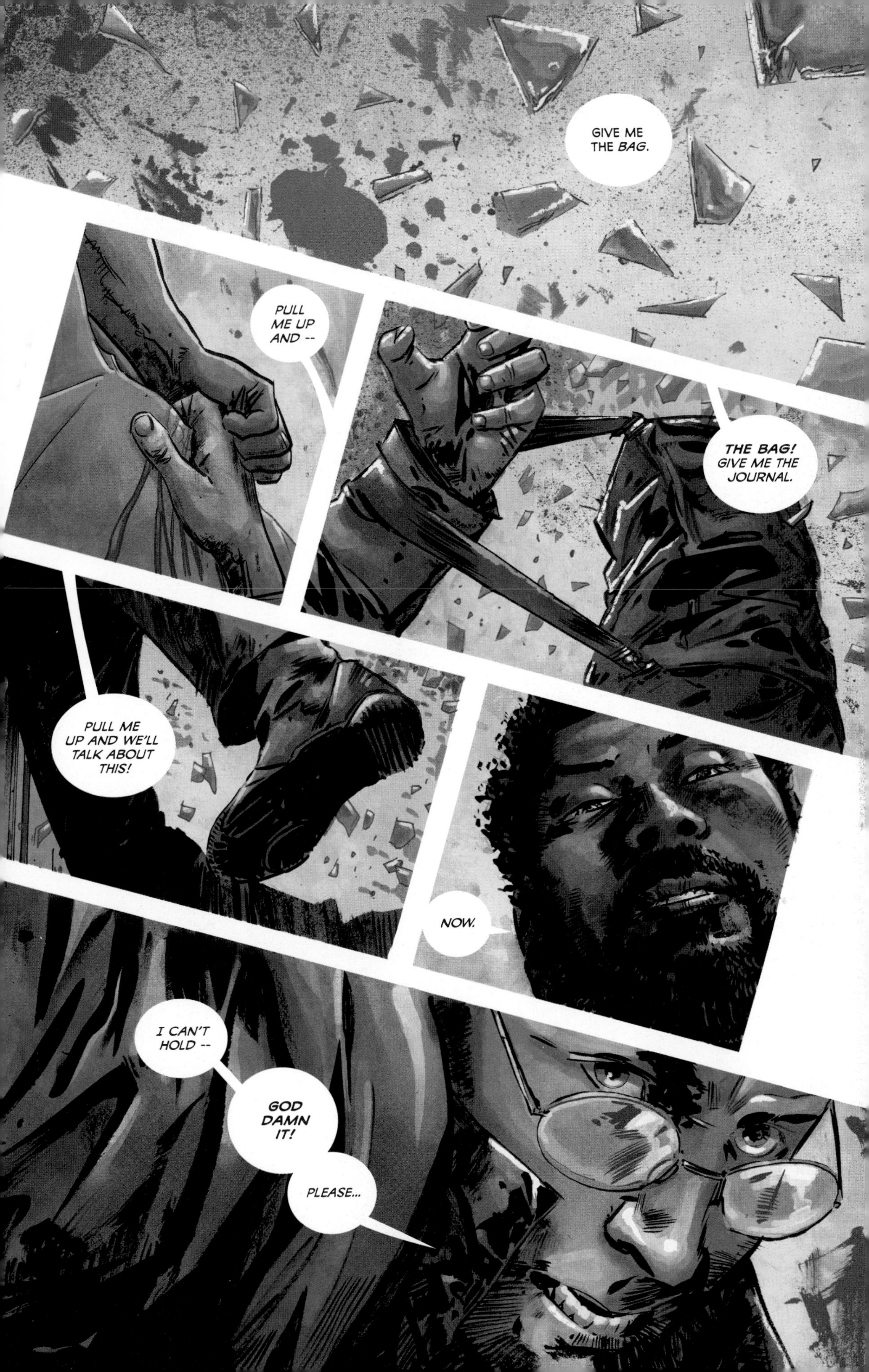
GIVE ME THE BAG.
PULL ME UP AND --
THE BAG! GIVE ME THE JOURNAL.
PULL ME UP AND WE'LL TALK ABOUT THIS!
NOW.
I CAN'T HOLD --
GOD DAMN IT!
PLEASE...

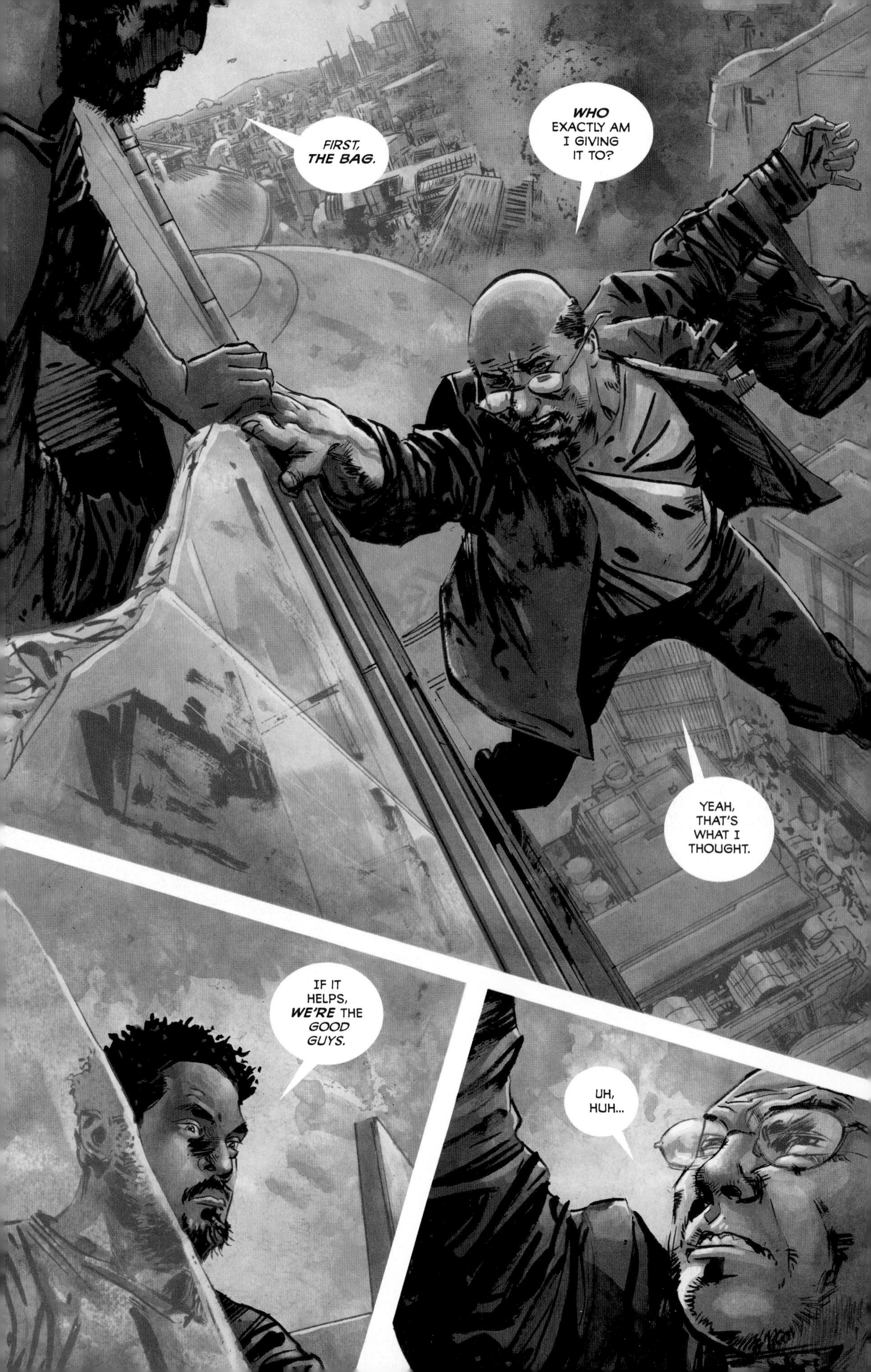
FIRST, *THE BAG*.
WHO EXACTLY AM I GIVING IT TO?
YEAH, THAT'S WHAT I THOUGHT.
IF IT HELPS, *WE'RE* THE *GOOD GUYS*.
UH, HUH...

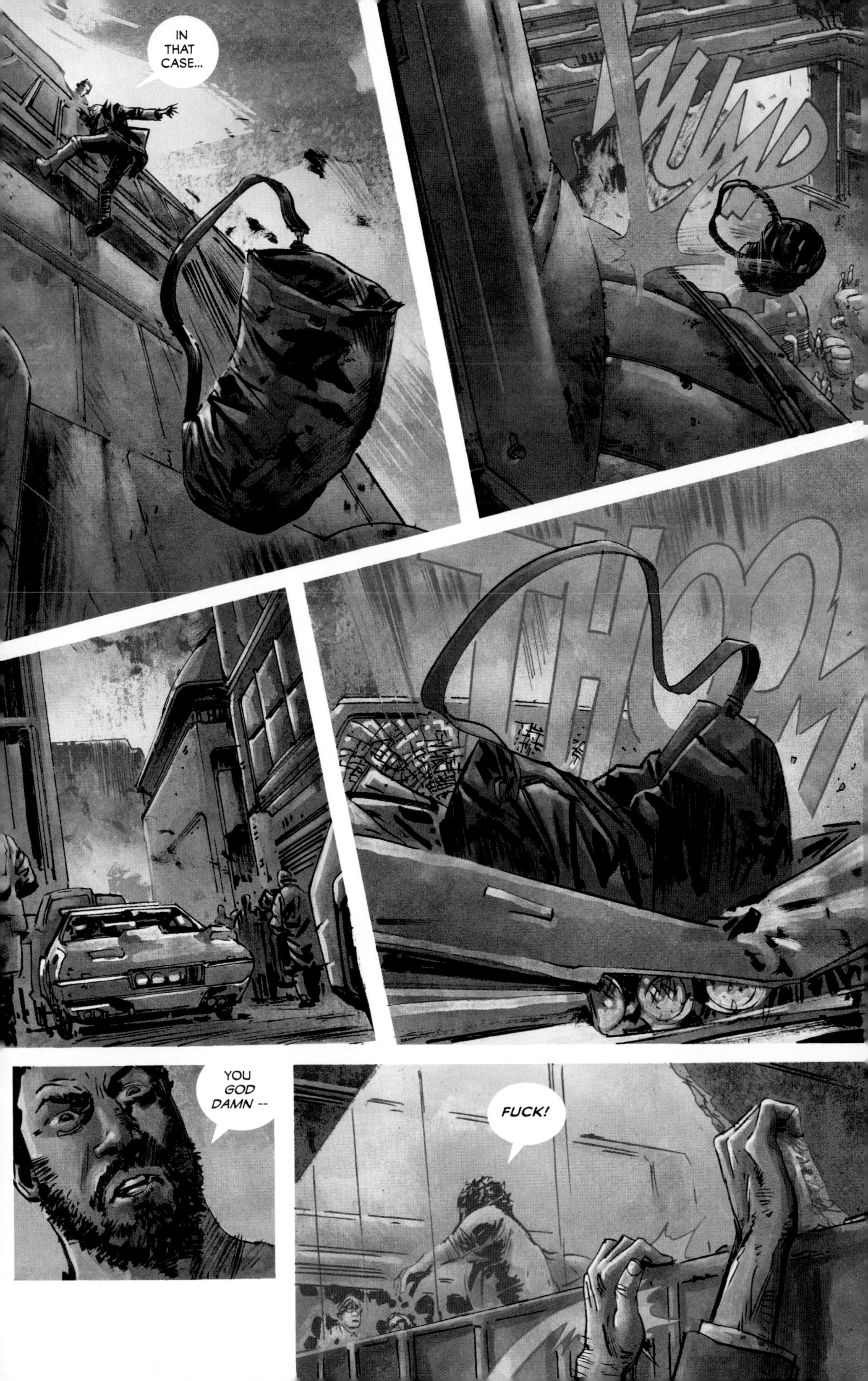
IN THAT CASE...
YOU *GOD DAMN* --
FUCK!

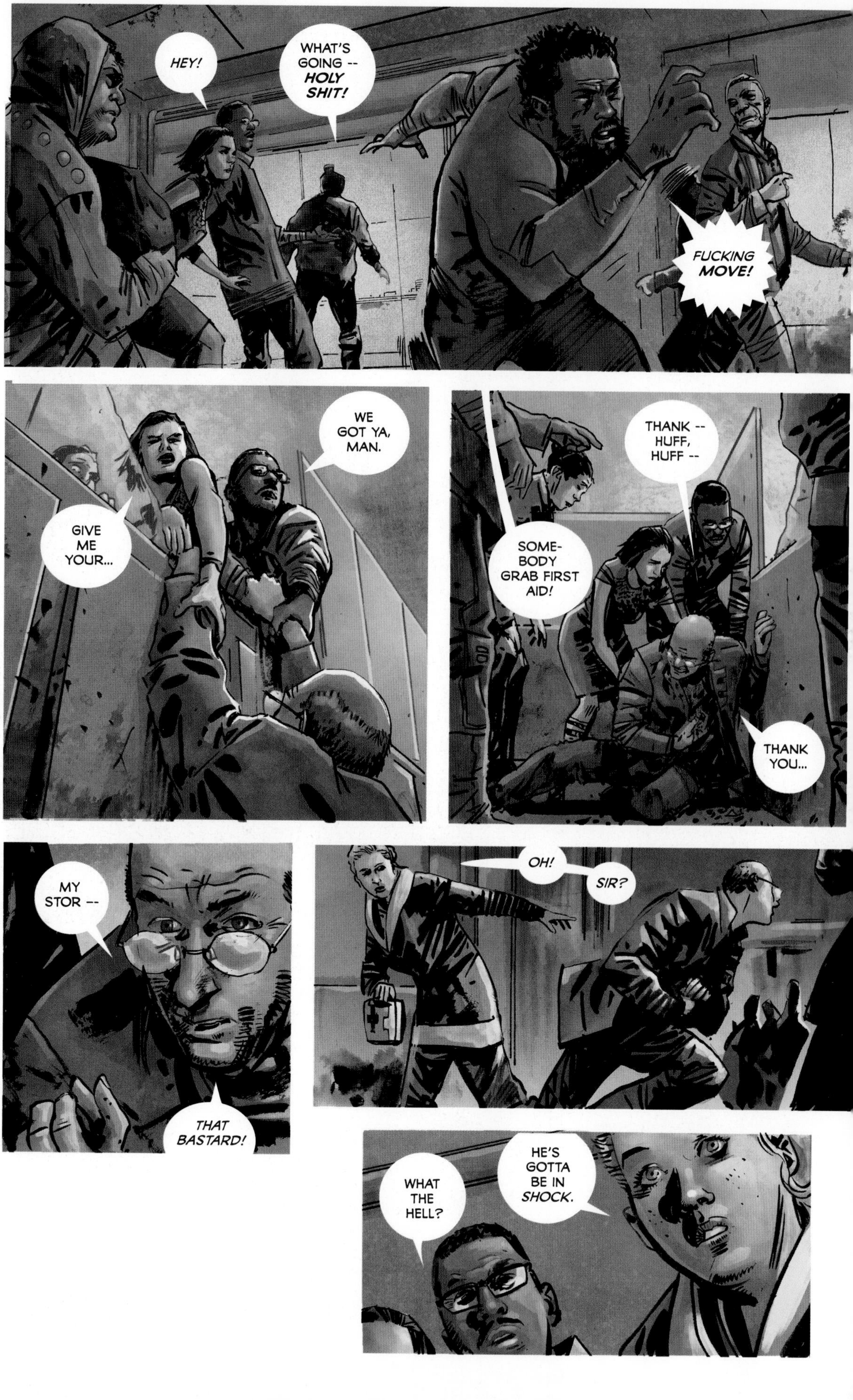
HEY!
WHAT'S GOING -- HOLY SHIT!
FUCKING MOVE!
GIVE ME YOUR...
WE GOT YA, MAN.
SOME-BODY GRAB FIRST AID!
THANK -- HUFF, HUFF --
THANK YOU...
MY STOR --
THAT BASTARD!
OH!
SIR?
WHAT THE HELL?
HE'S GOTTA BE IN SHOCK.

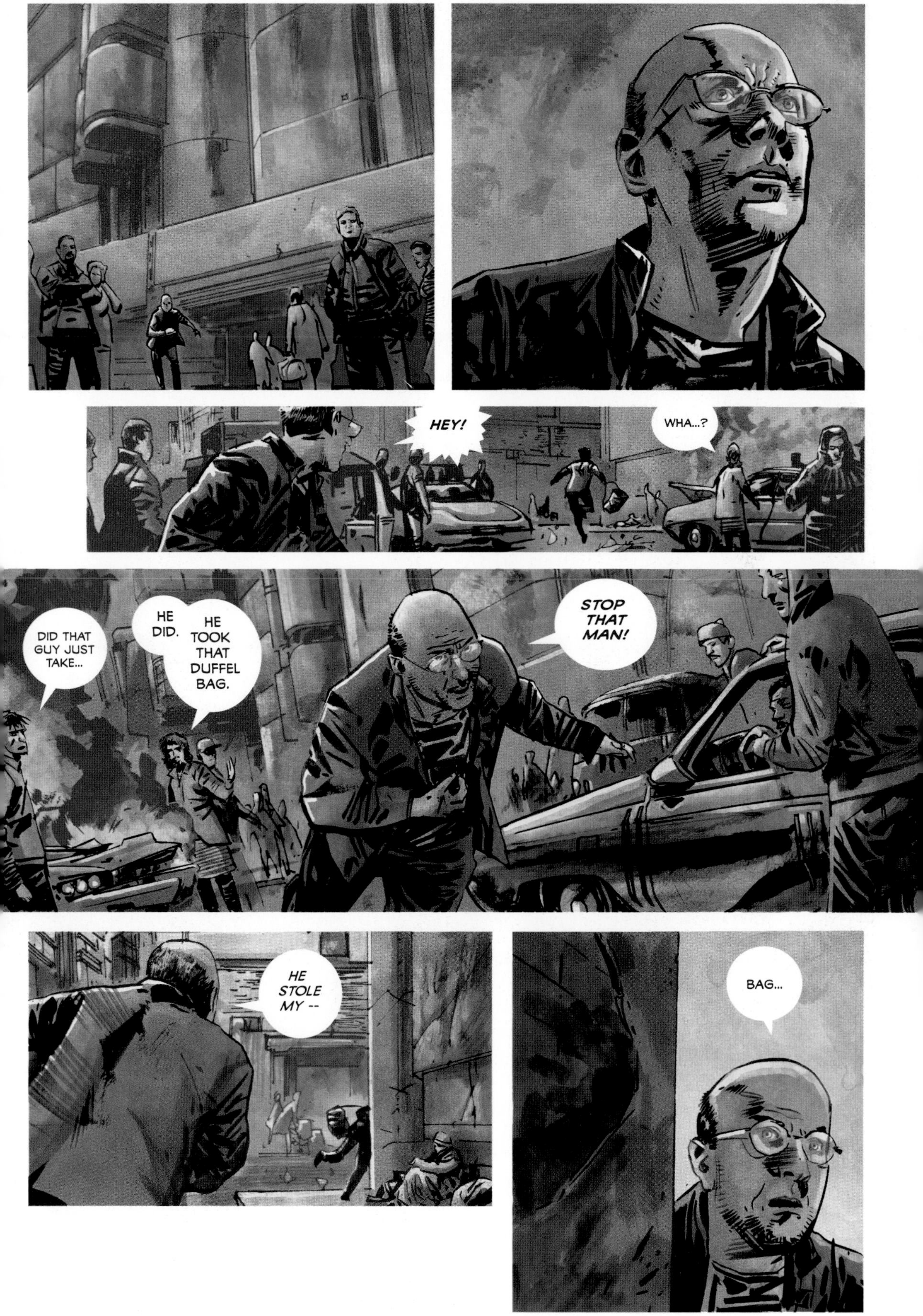
HEY!
WHA...?
DID THAT GUY JUST TAKE...
HE DID.
HE TOOK THAT DUFFEL BAG.
STOP THAT MAN!
HE STOLE MY --
BAG...

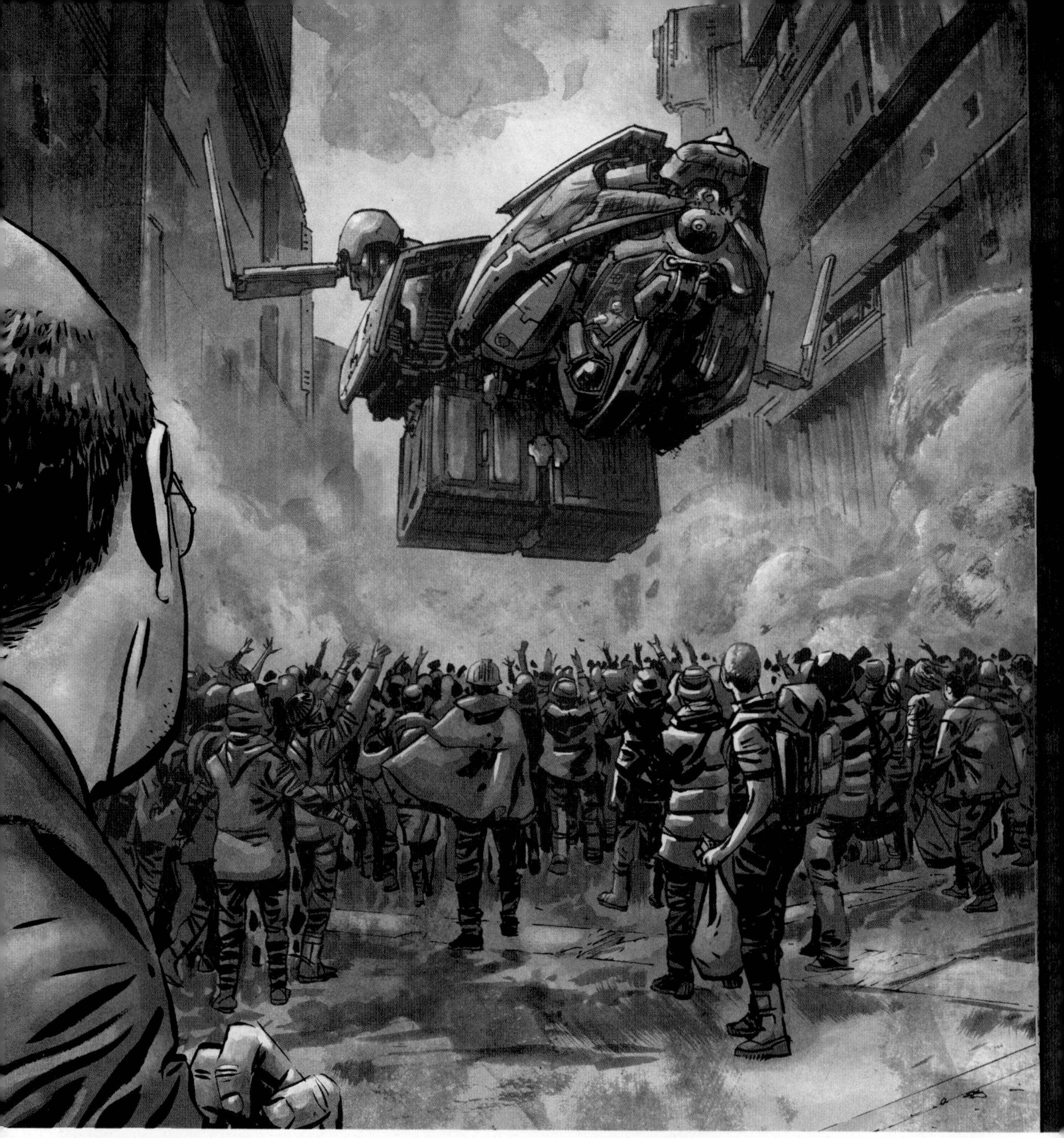

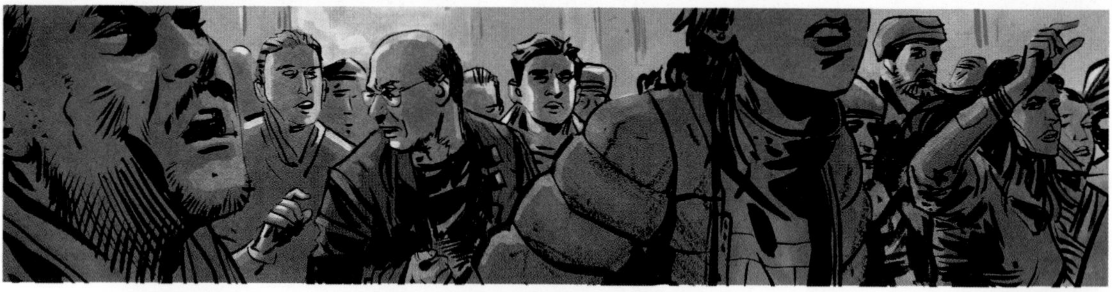

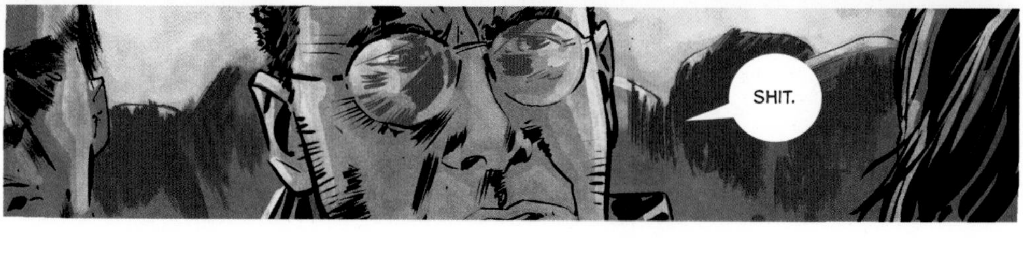
SHIT.

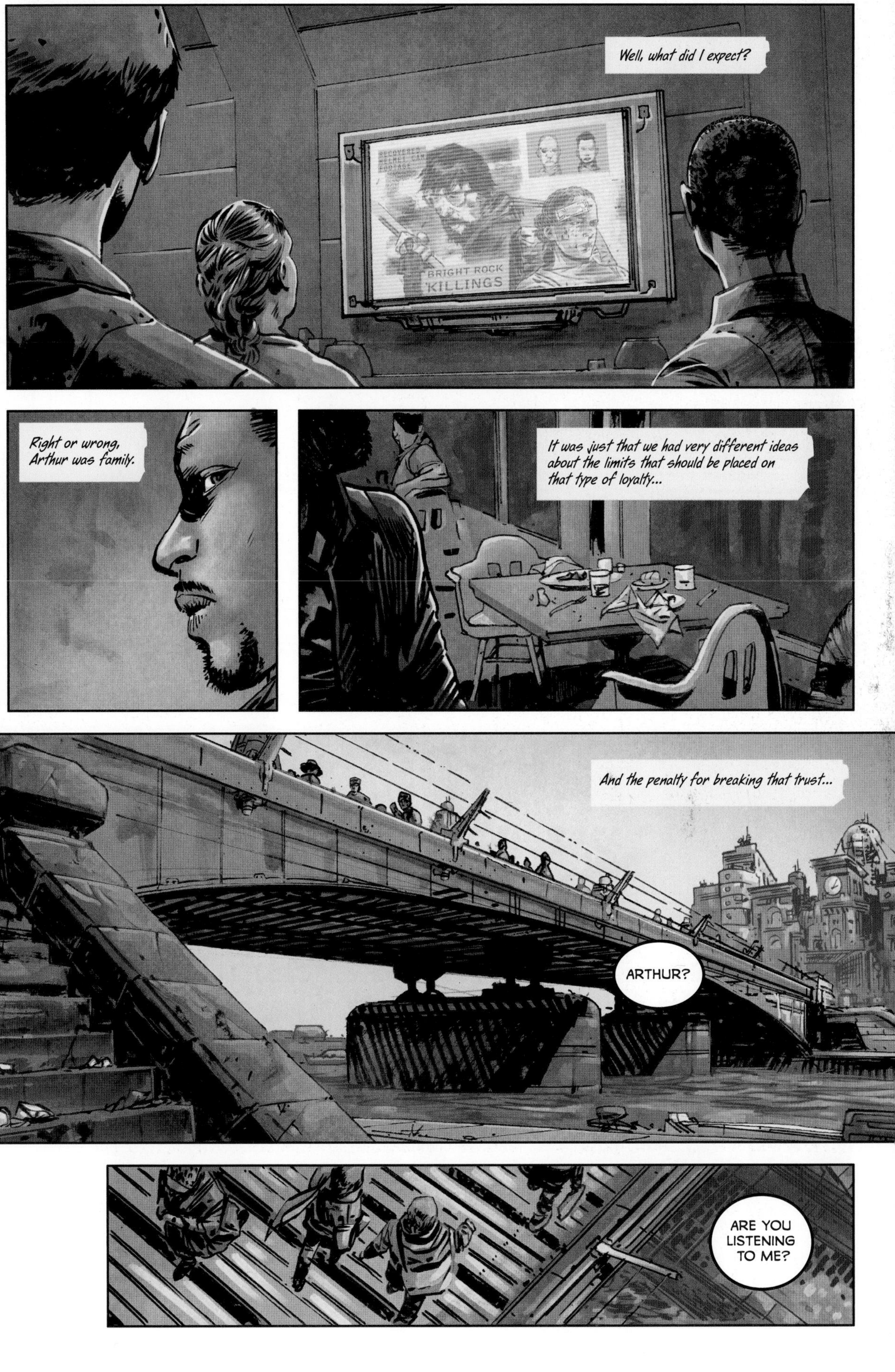
Well, what did I expect?
BRIGHT ROCK
KILLINGS
Right or wrong, Arthur was family.
It was just that we had very different ideas about the limits that should be placed on that type of loyalty...
And the penalty for breaking that trust...
ARTHUR?
ARE YOU LISTENING TO ME?

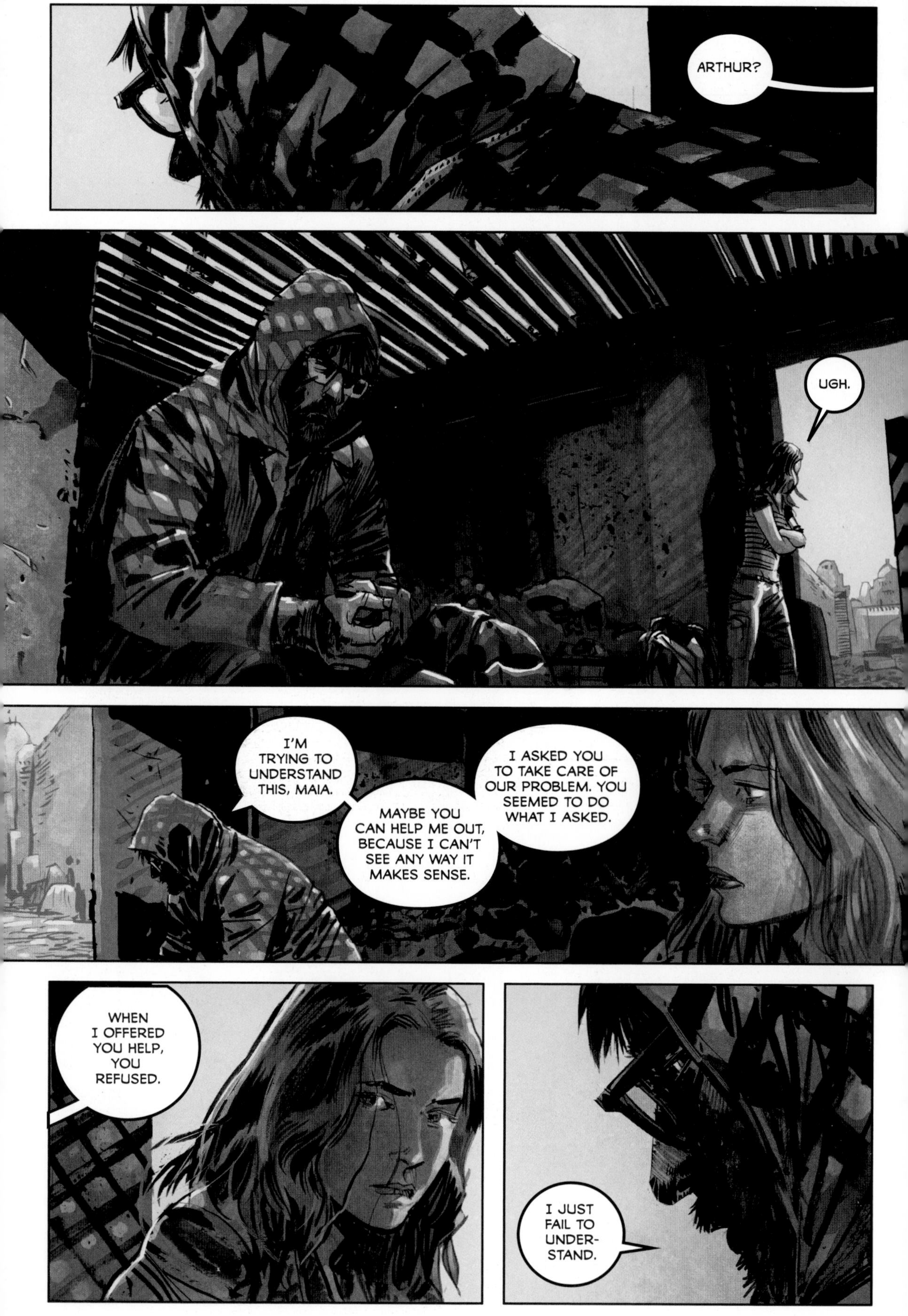
ARTHUR?
UGH.
I'M TRYING TO UNDERSTAND THIS, MAIA.
MAYBE YOU CAN HELP ME OUT, BECAUSE I CAN'T SEE ANY WAY IT MAKES SENSE.
I ASKED YOU TO TAKE CARE OF OUR PROBLEM. YOU SEEMED TO DO WHAT I ASKED.
WHEN I OFFERED YOU HELP, YOU REFUSED.
I JUST FAIL TO UNDER-STAND.

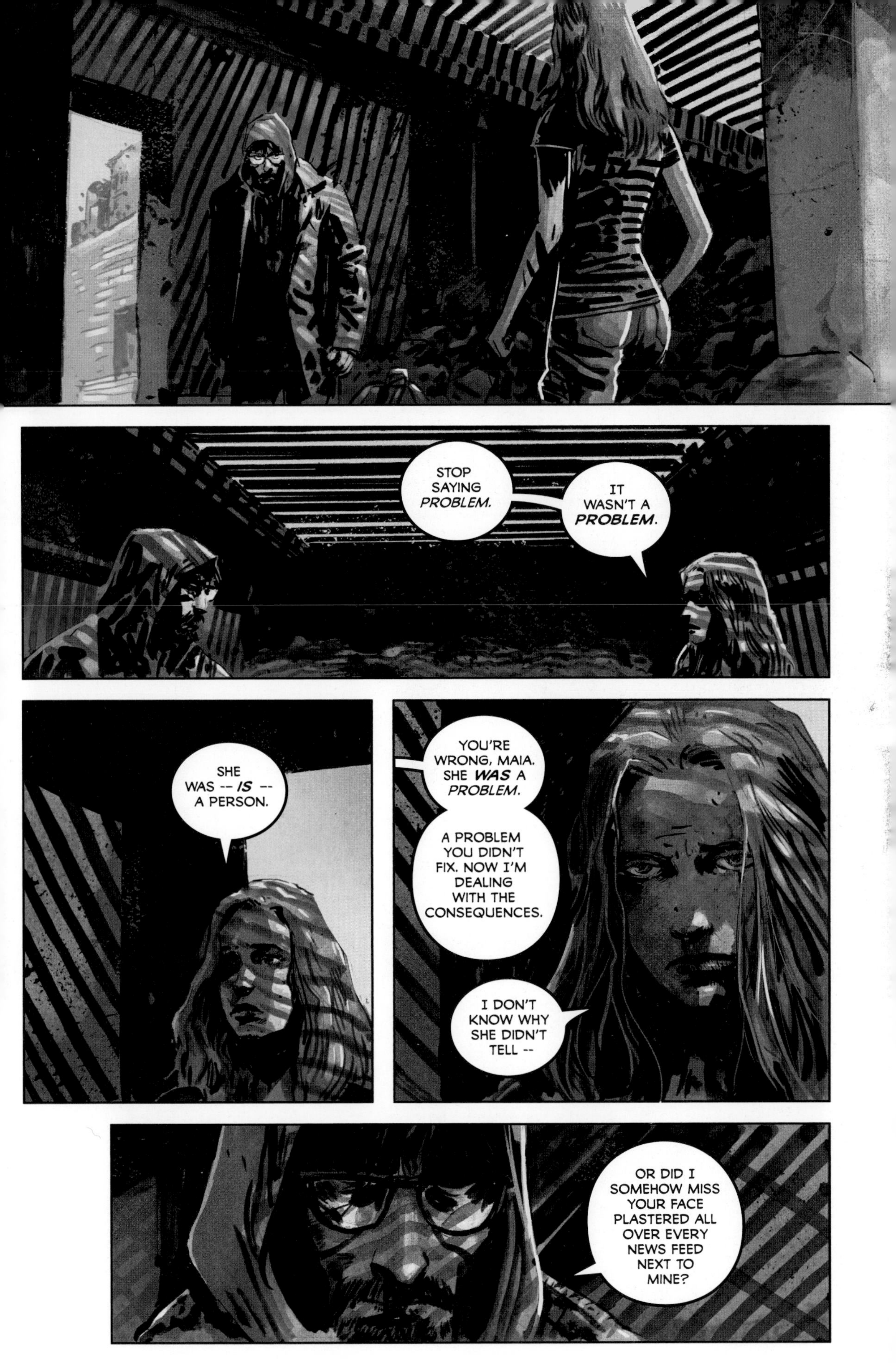
STOP SAYING *PROBLEM.*
IT WASN'T A ***PROBLEM***.
SHE WAS -- ***IS*** -- A PERSON.
YOU'RE WRONG, MAIA. SHE ***WAS*** A *PROBLEM.*
A PROBLEM YOU DIDN'T FIX. NOW I'M DEALING WITH THE CONSEQUENCES.
I DON'T KNOW WHY SHE DIDN'T TELL --
OR DID I SOMEHOW MISS YOUR FACE PLASTERED ALL OVER EVERY NEWS FEED NEXT TO MINE?

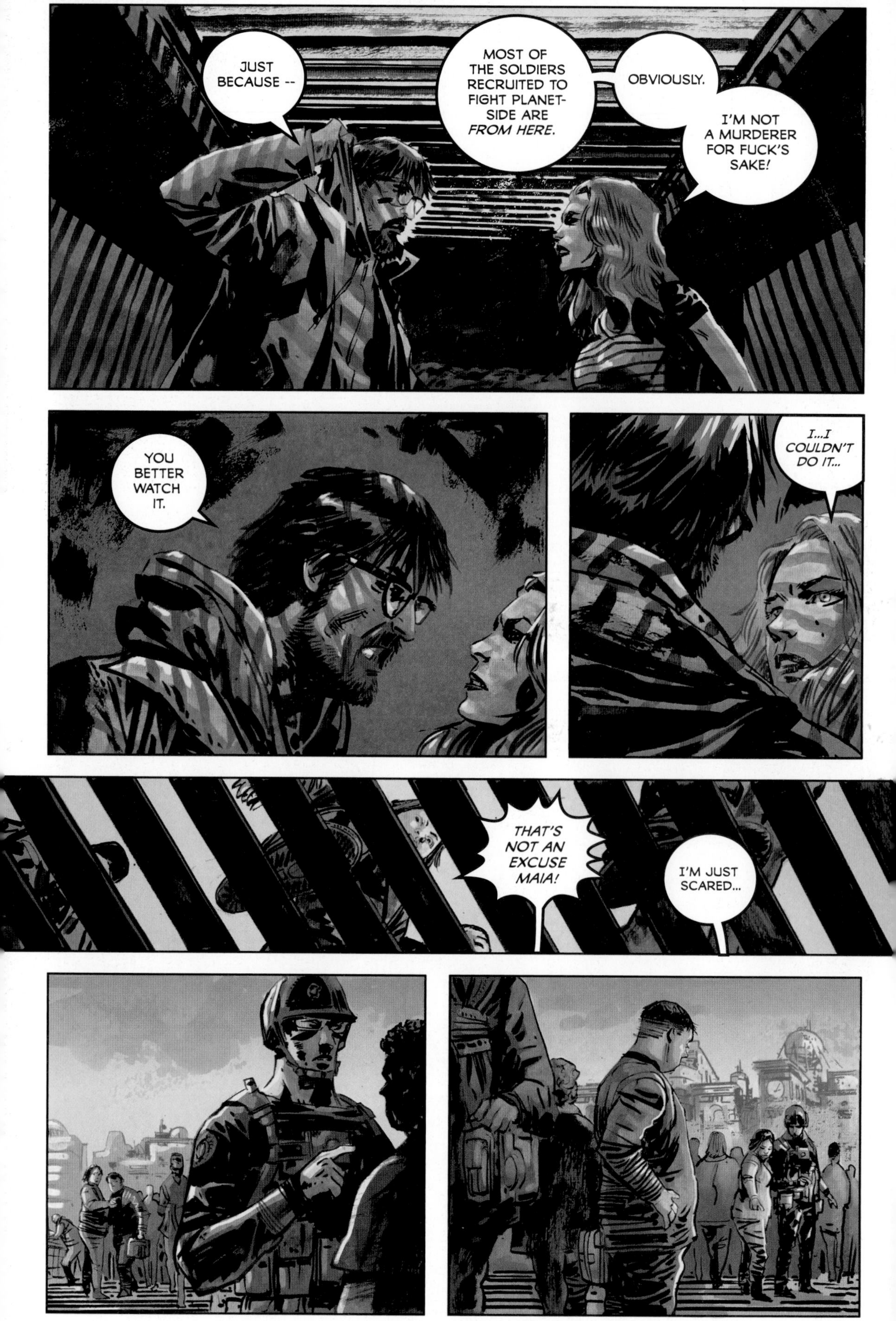
JUST BECAUSE --
MOST OF THE SOLDIERS RECRUITED TO FIGHT PLANET-SIDE ARE *FROM HERE.*
OBVIOUSLY.
I'M NOT A MURDERER FOR FUCK'S SAKE!
YOU BETTER WATCH IT.
I...I COULDN'T DO IT...
THAT'S NOT AN EXCUSE MAIA!
I'M JUST SCARED...

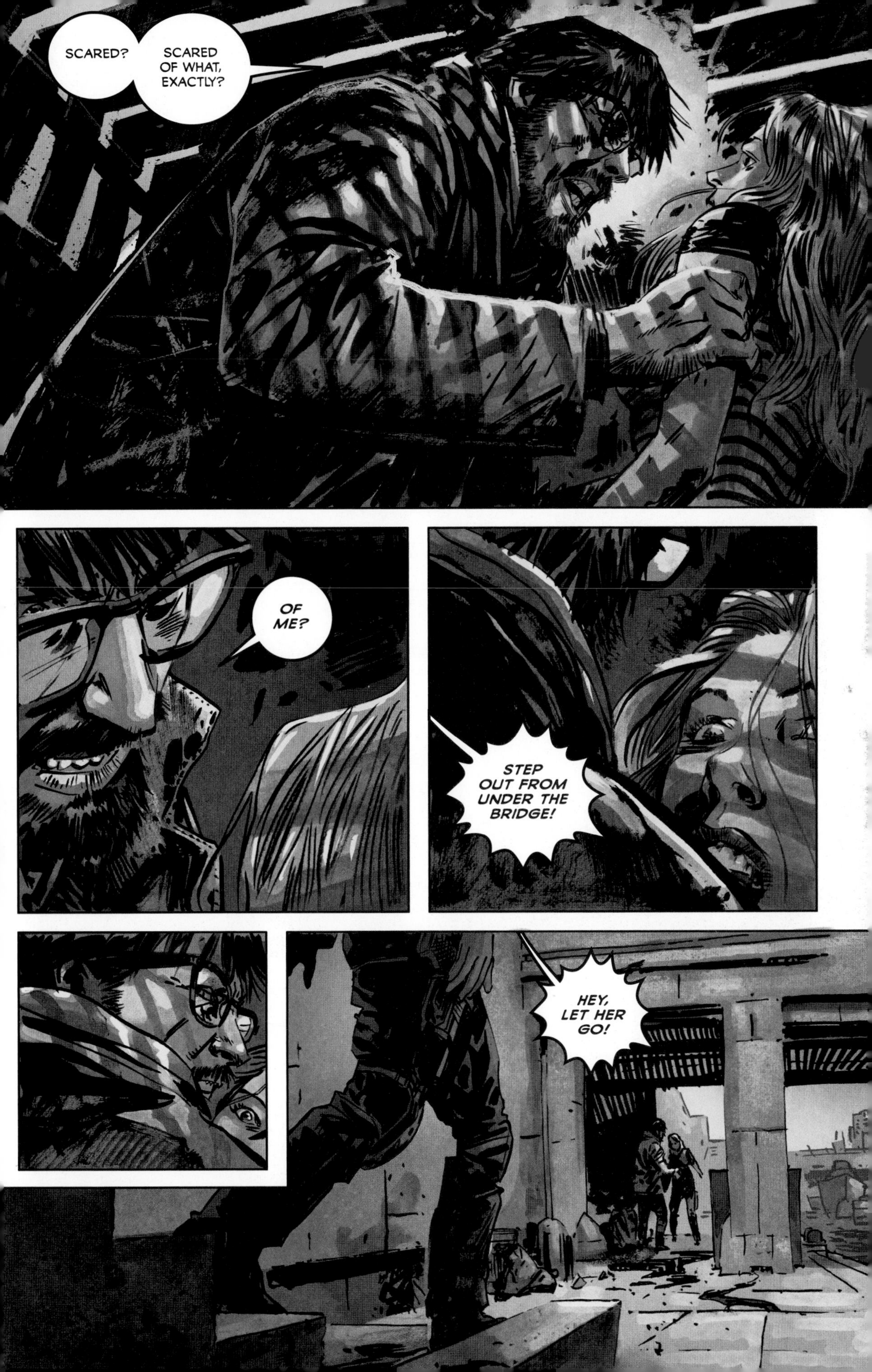
SCARED?
SCARED OF WHAT, EXACTLY?
OF ME?
STEP OUT FROM UNDER THE BRIDGE!
HEY, LET HER GO!

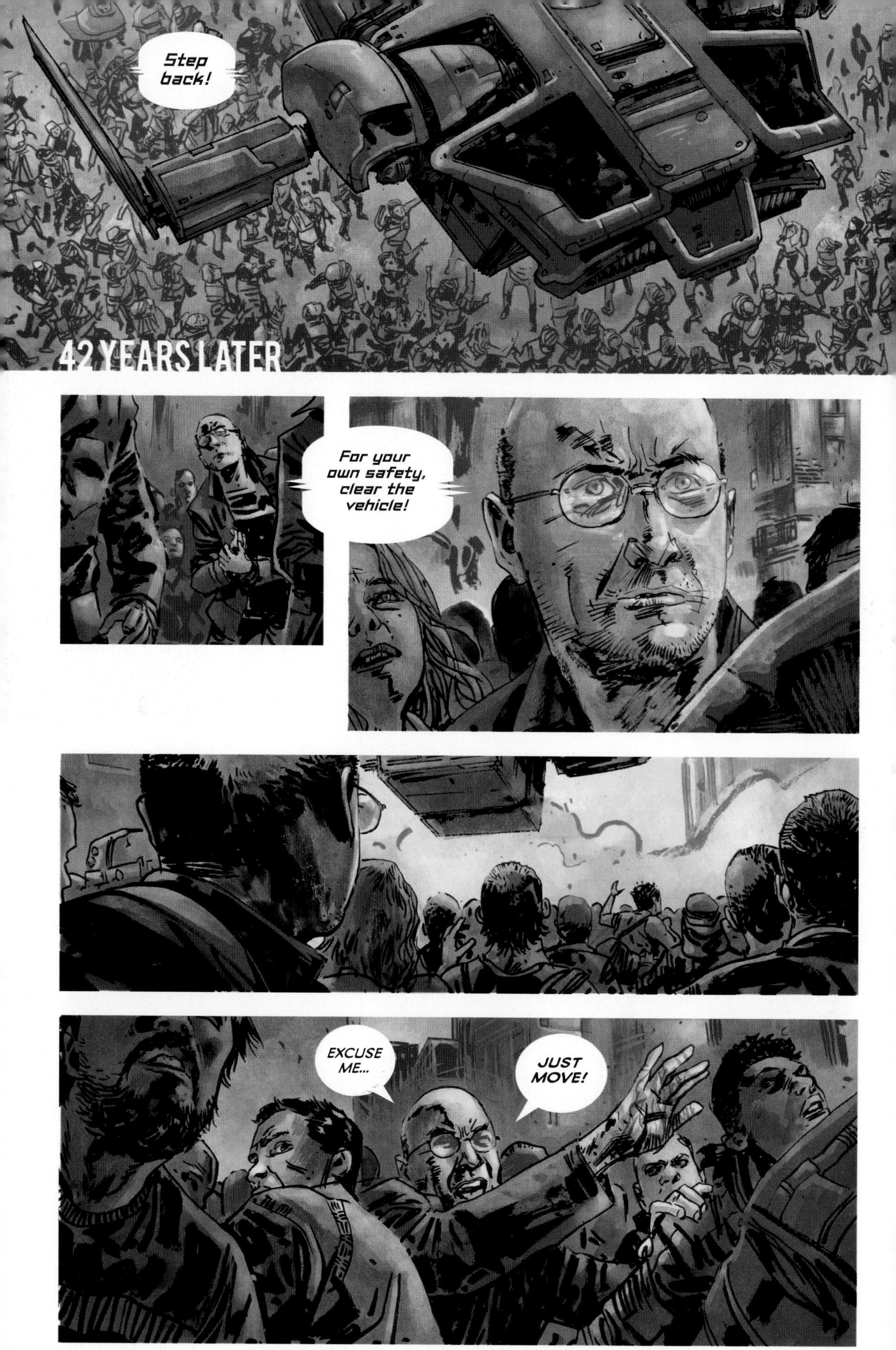
Step back!
42 YEARS LATER
For your own safety, clear the vehicle!
EXCUSE ME...
JUST MOVE!

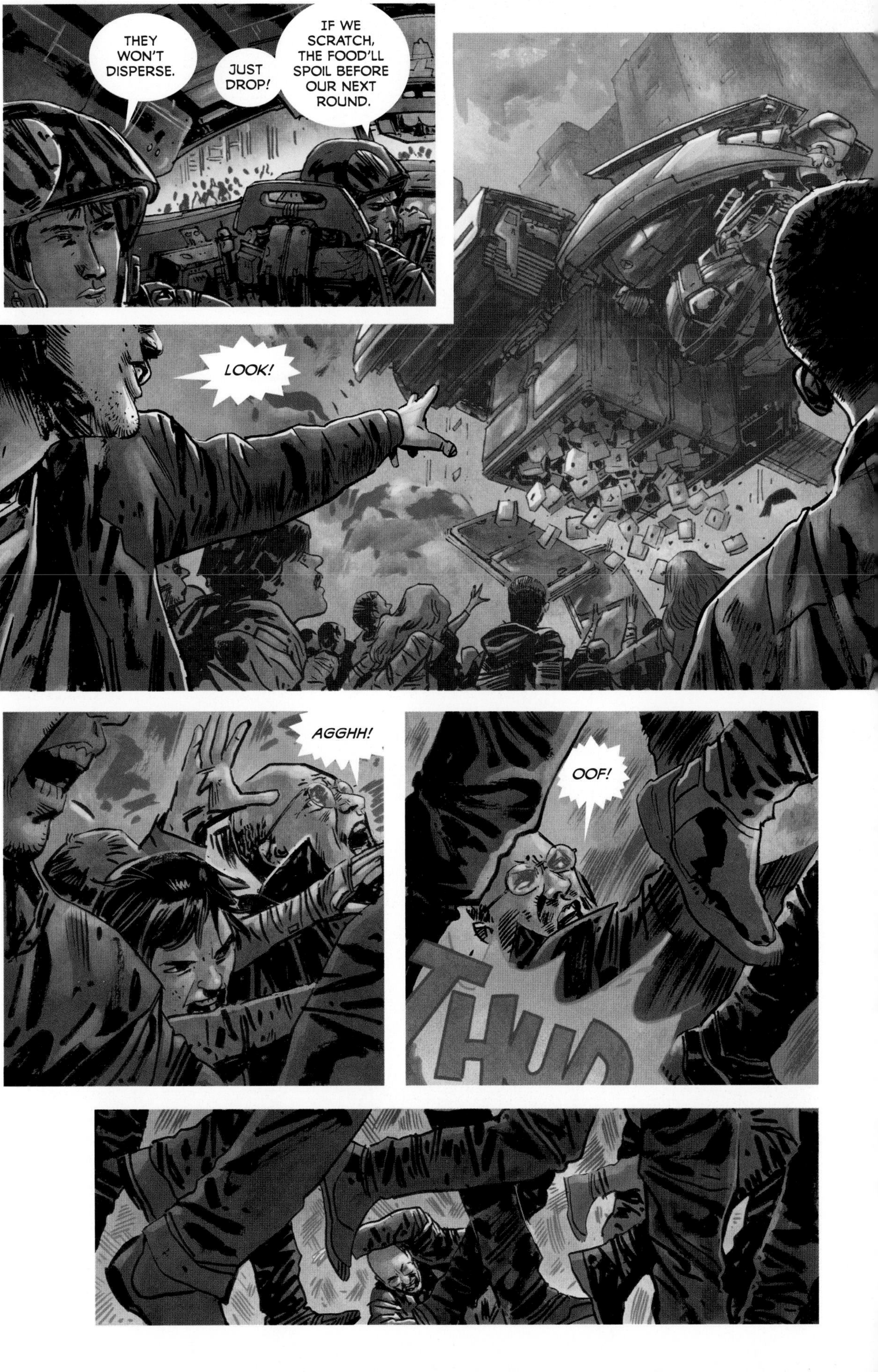
THEY WON'T DISPERSE.
JUST DROP!
IF WE SCRATCH, THE FOOD'LL SPOIL BEFORE OUR NEXT ROUND.
LOOK!
AGGHH!
OOF!

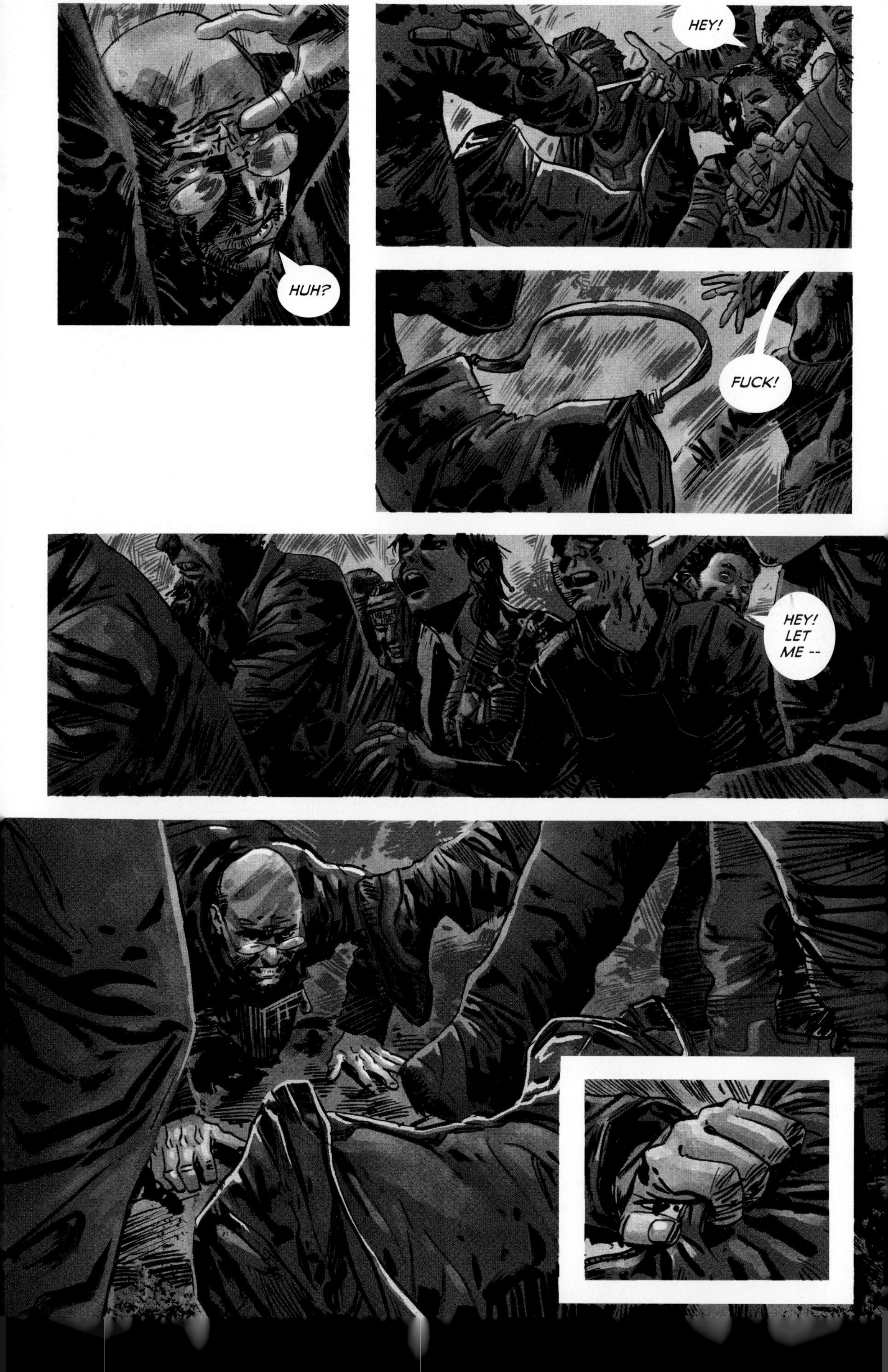
HUH?
HEY!
FUCK!
HEY! LET ME --

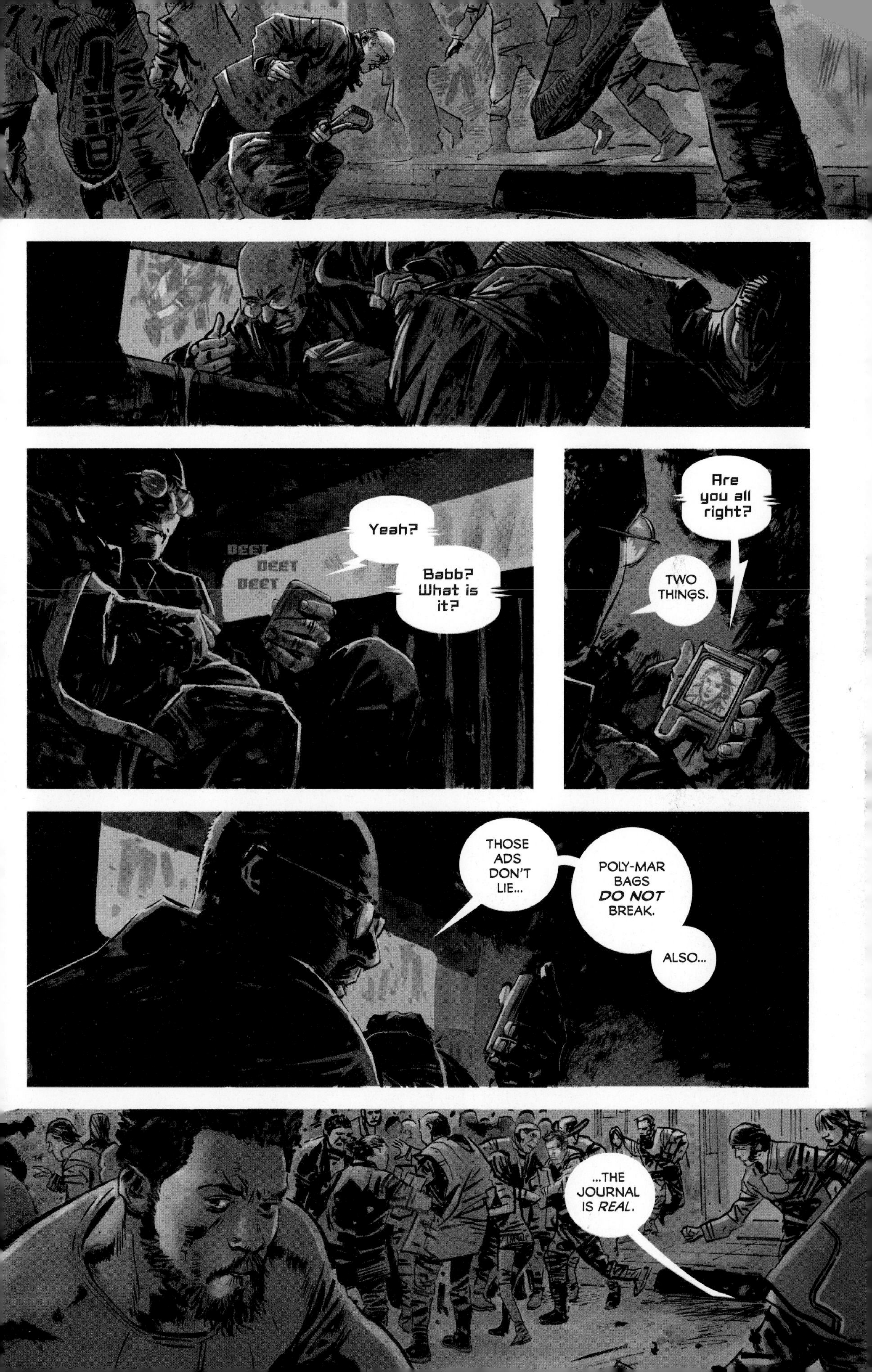
DEET DEET DEET
Yeah?
Babb? What is it?
Are you all right?
TWO THINGS.
THOSE ADS DON'T LIE...
POLY-MAR BAGS *DO NOT* BREAK.
ALSO...
...THE JOURNAL IS *REAL*.

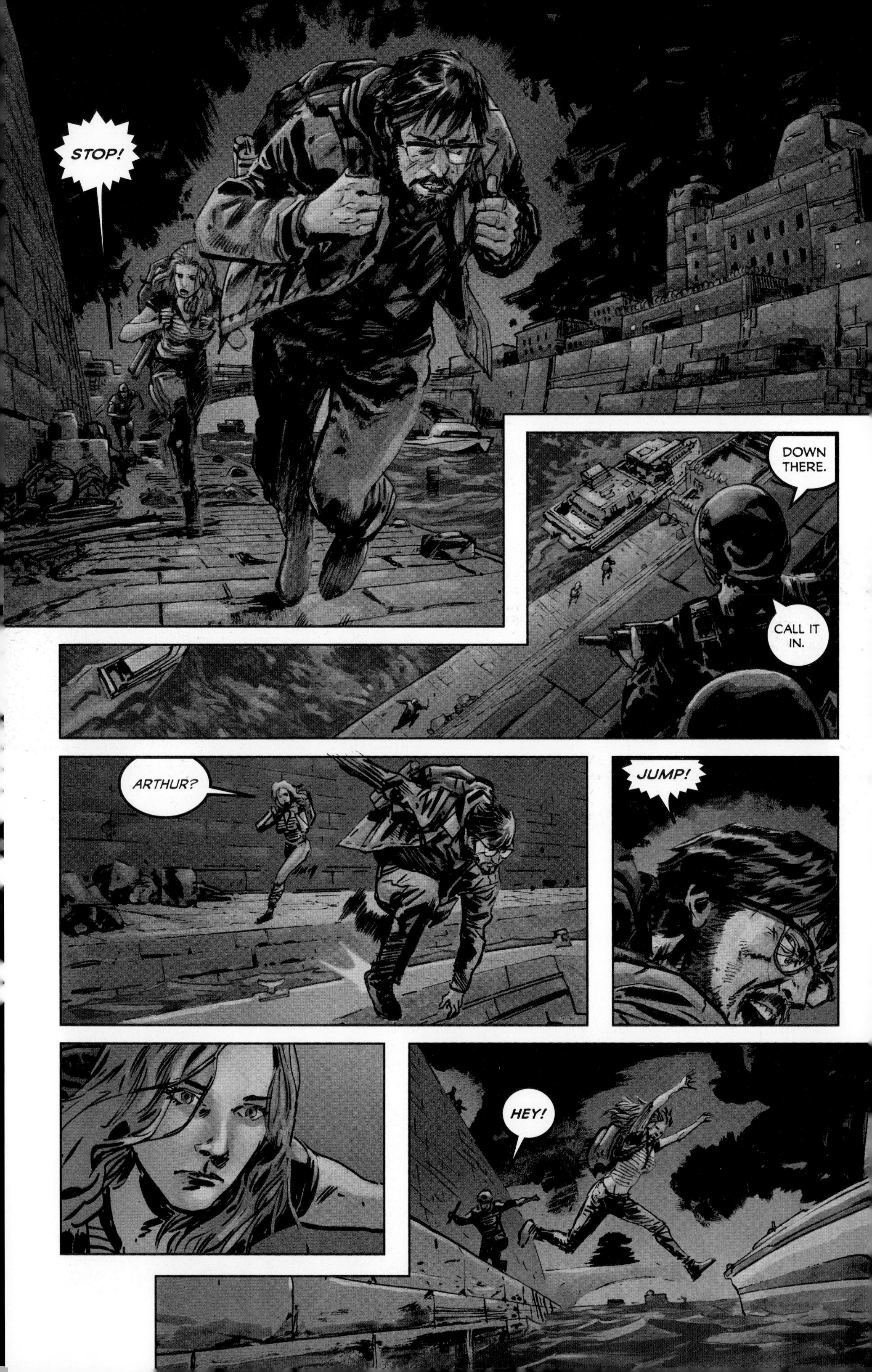
STOP!
DOWN THERE.
CALL IT IN.
ARTHUR?
JUMP!
HEY!

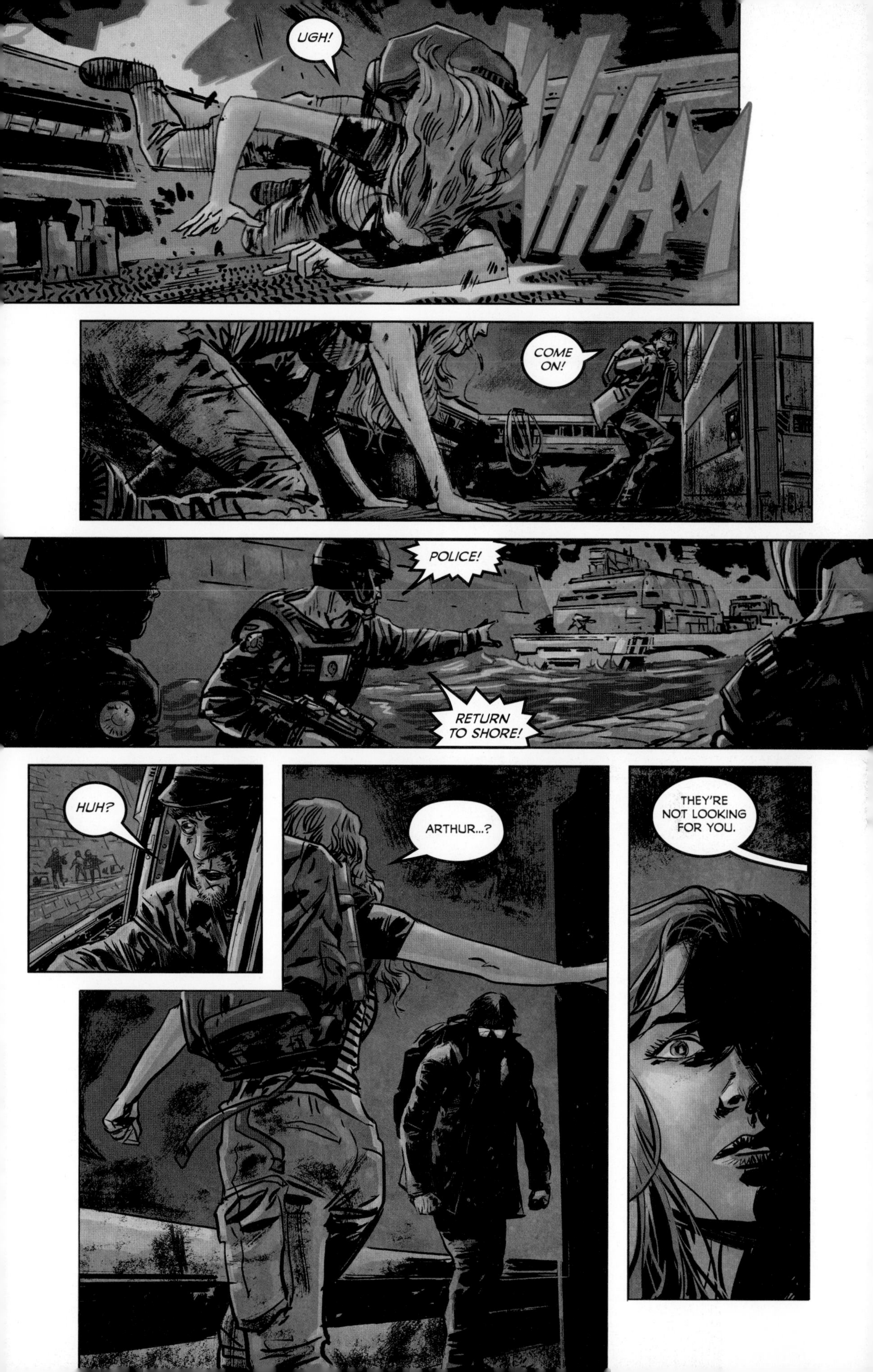
UGH!
WHAM
COME ON!
POLICE!
RETURN TO SHORE!
HUH?
ARTHUR...?
THEY'RE NOT LOOKING FOR YOU.

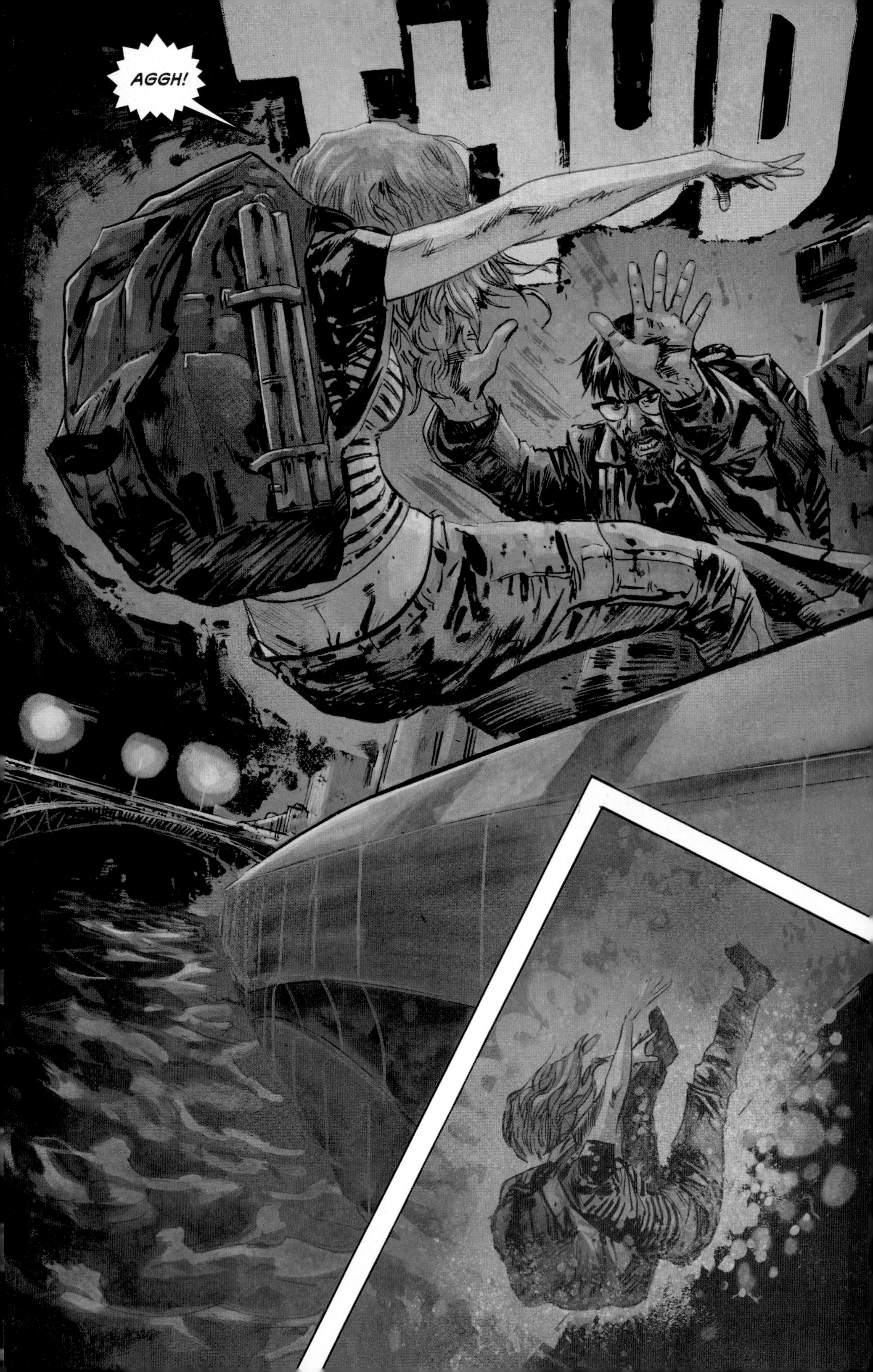
AGGH!

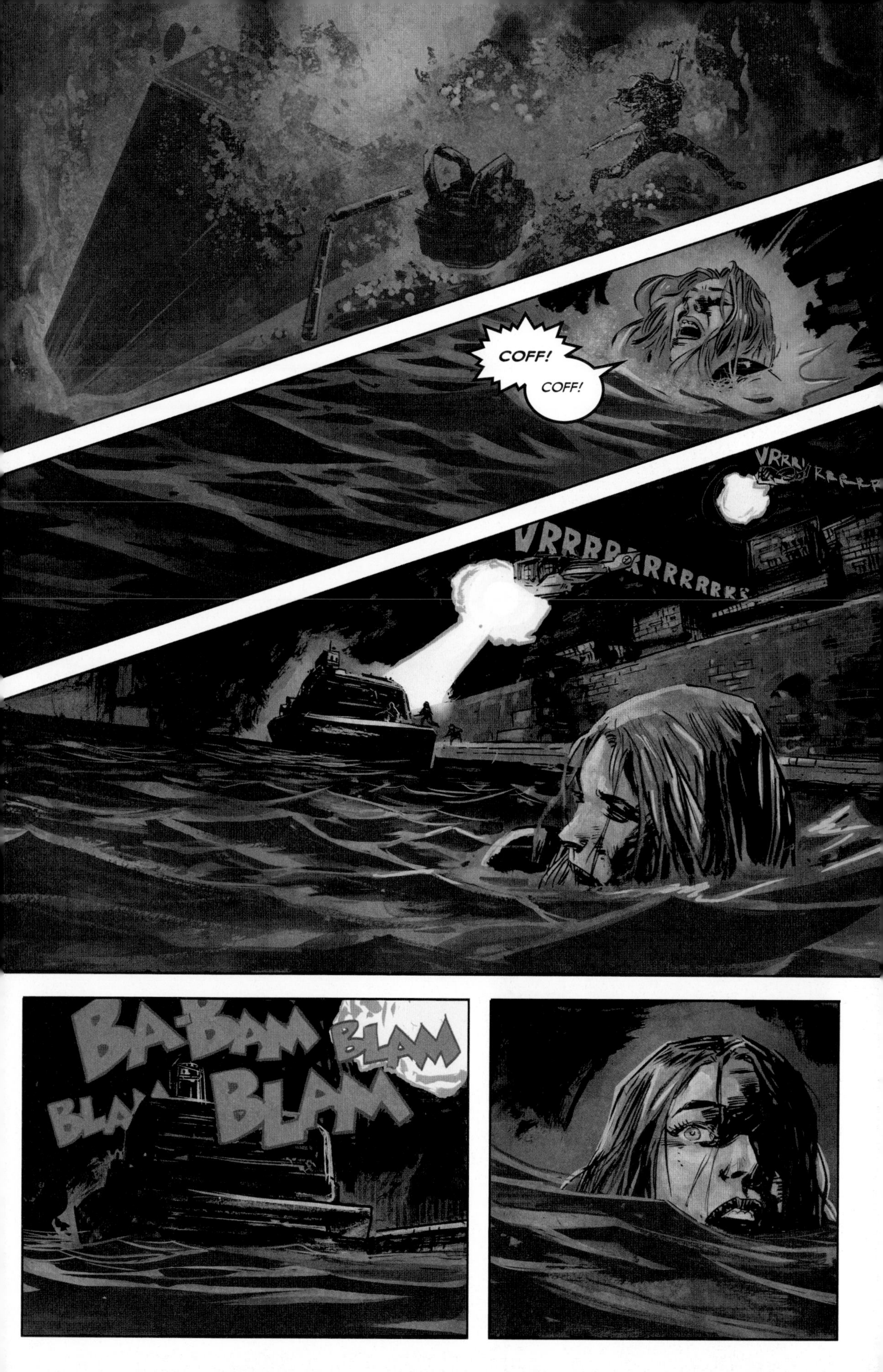
COFF!
COFF!
BA-BAM
BLAM
BLAM
BLAM

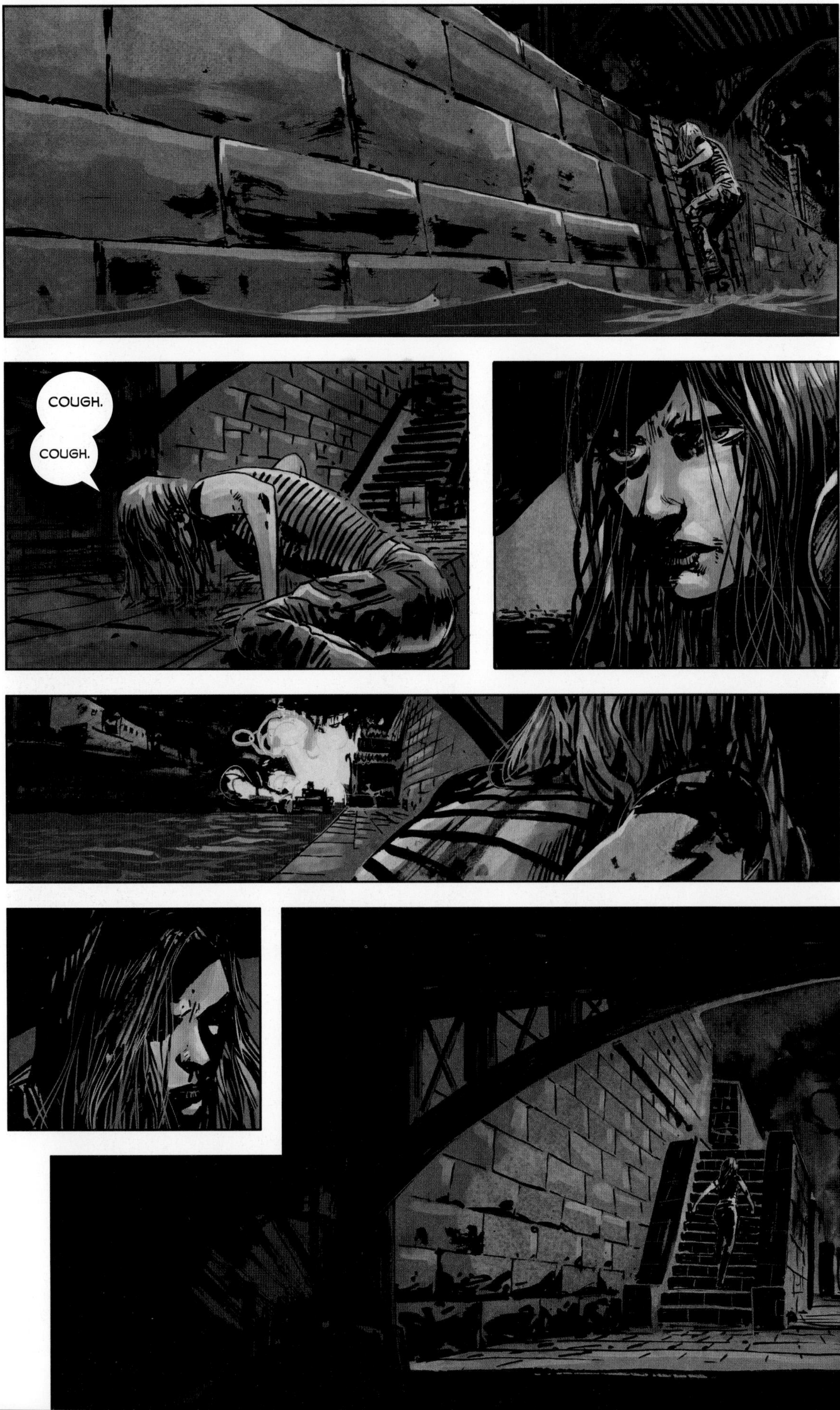
COUGH.
COUGH.

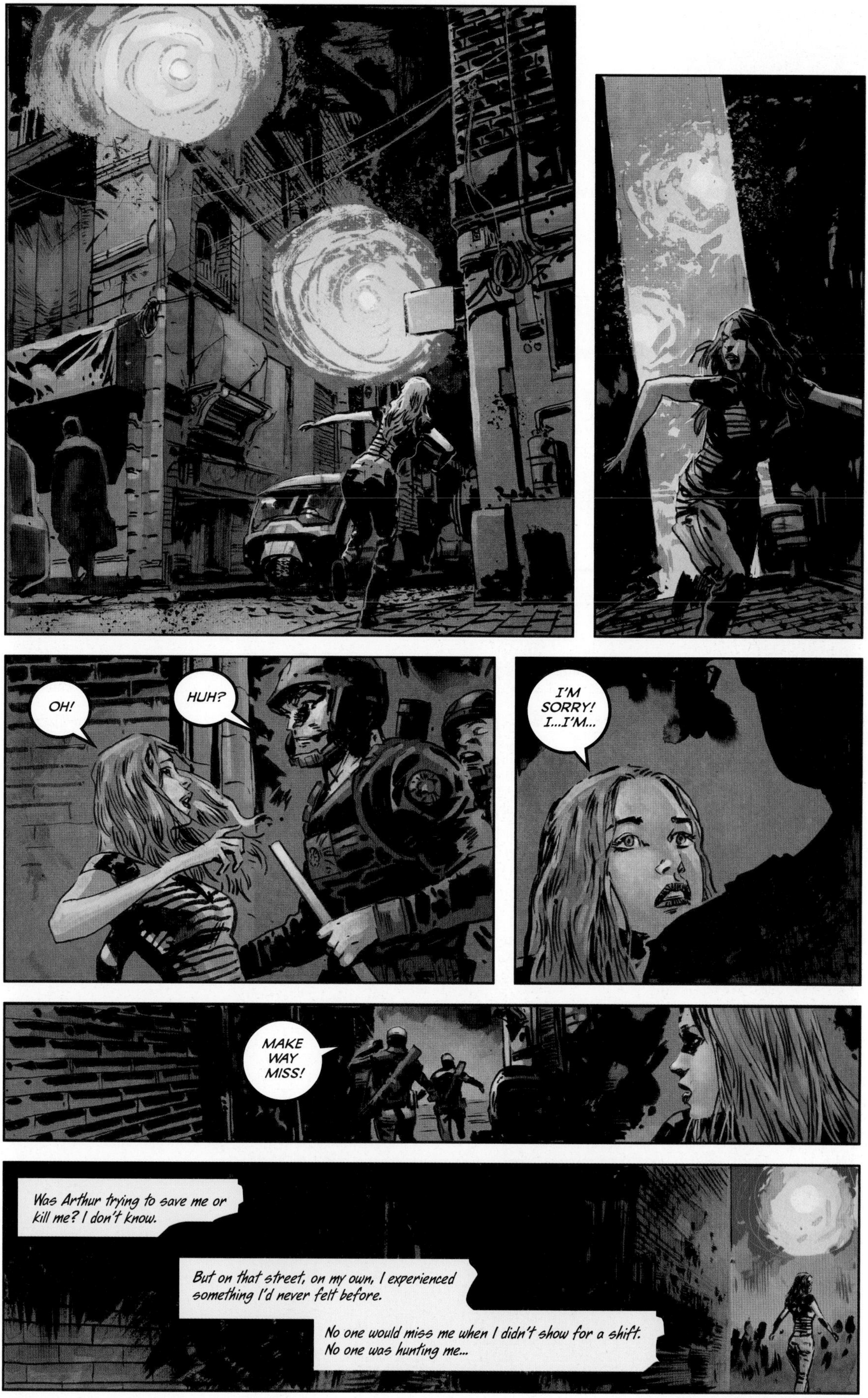
OH!
HUH?
I'M SORRY! I...I'M...
MAKE WAY MISS!
Was Arthur trying to save me or kill me? I don't know.
But on that street, on my own, I experienced something I'd never felt before.
No one would miss me when I didn't show for a shift. No one was hunting me...

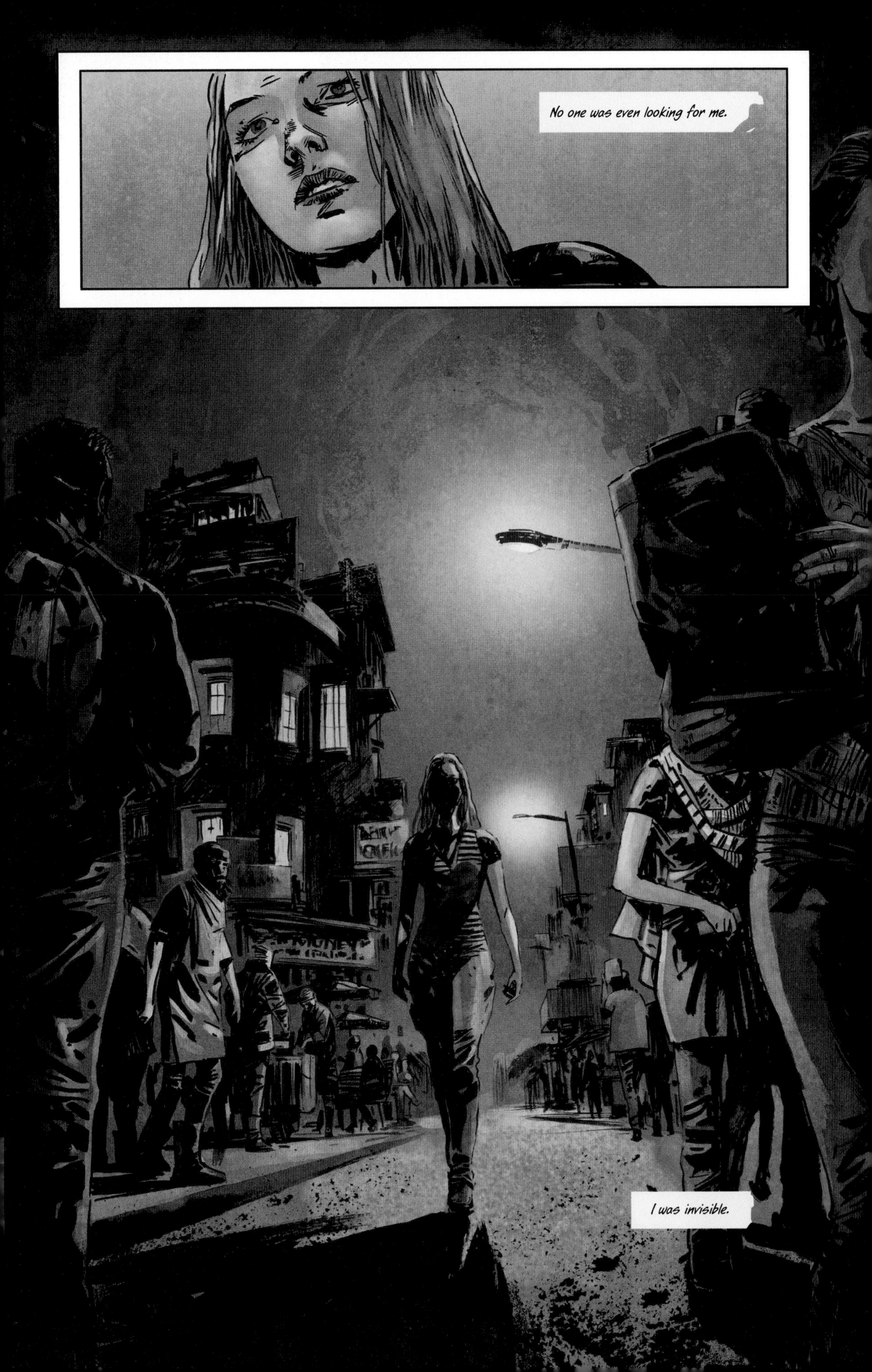
No one was even looking for me.
I was invisible.

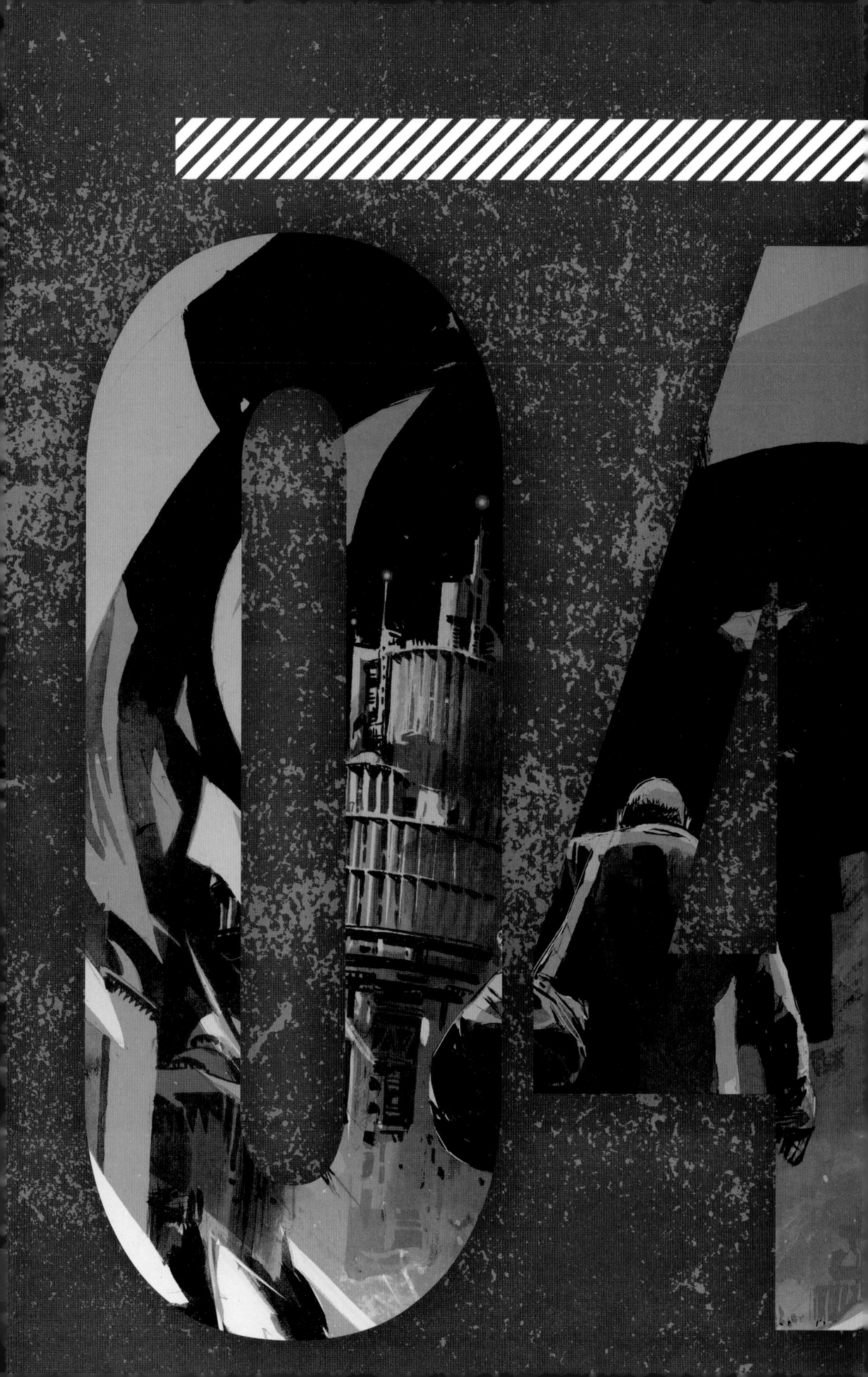
04

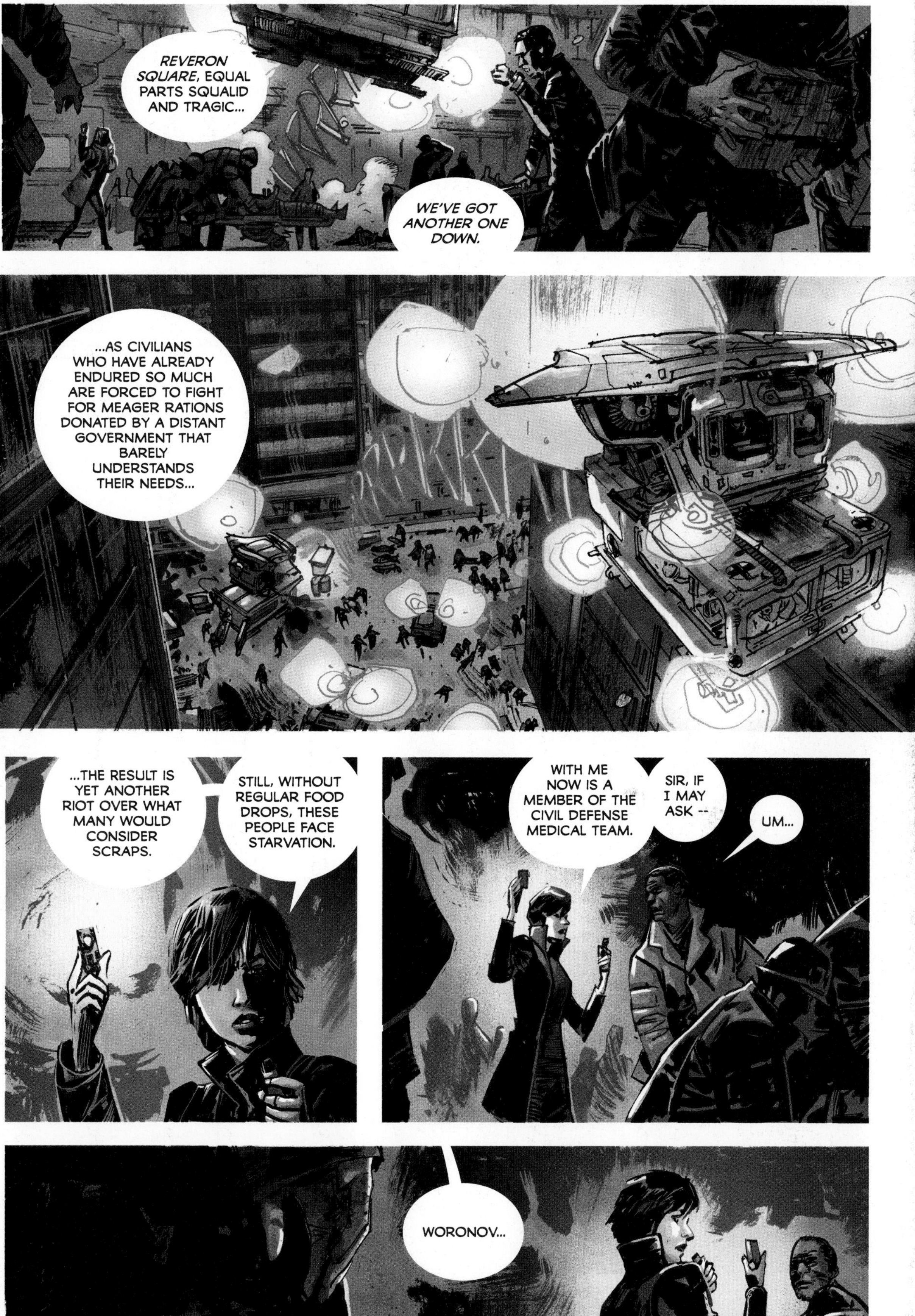
REVERON SQUARE, EQUAL PARTS SQUALID AND TRAGIC...
WE'VE GOT ANOTHER ONE DOWN.
...AS CIVILIANS WHO HAVE ALREADY ENDURED SO MUCH ARE FORCED TO FIGHT FOR MEAGER RATIONS DONATED BY A DISTANT GOVERNMENT THAT BARELY UNDERSTANDS THEIR NEEDS...
...THE RESULT IS YET ANOTHER RIOT OVER WHAT MANY WOULD CONSIDER SCRAPS.
STILL, WITHOUT REGULAR FOOD DROPS, THESE PEOPLE FACE STARVATION.
WITH ME NOW IS A MEMBER OF THE CIVIL DEFENSE MEDICAL TEAM.
SIR, IF I MAY ASK --
UM...
WORONOV...

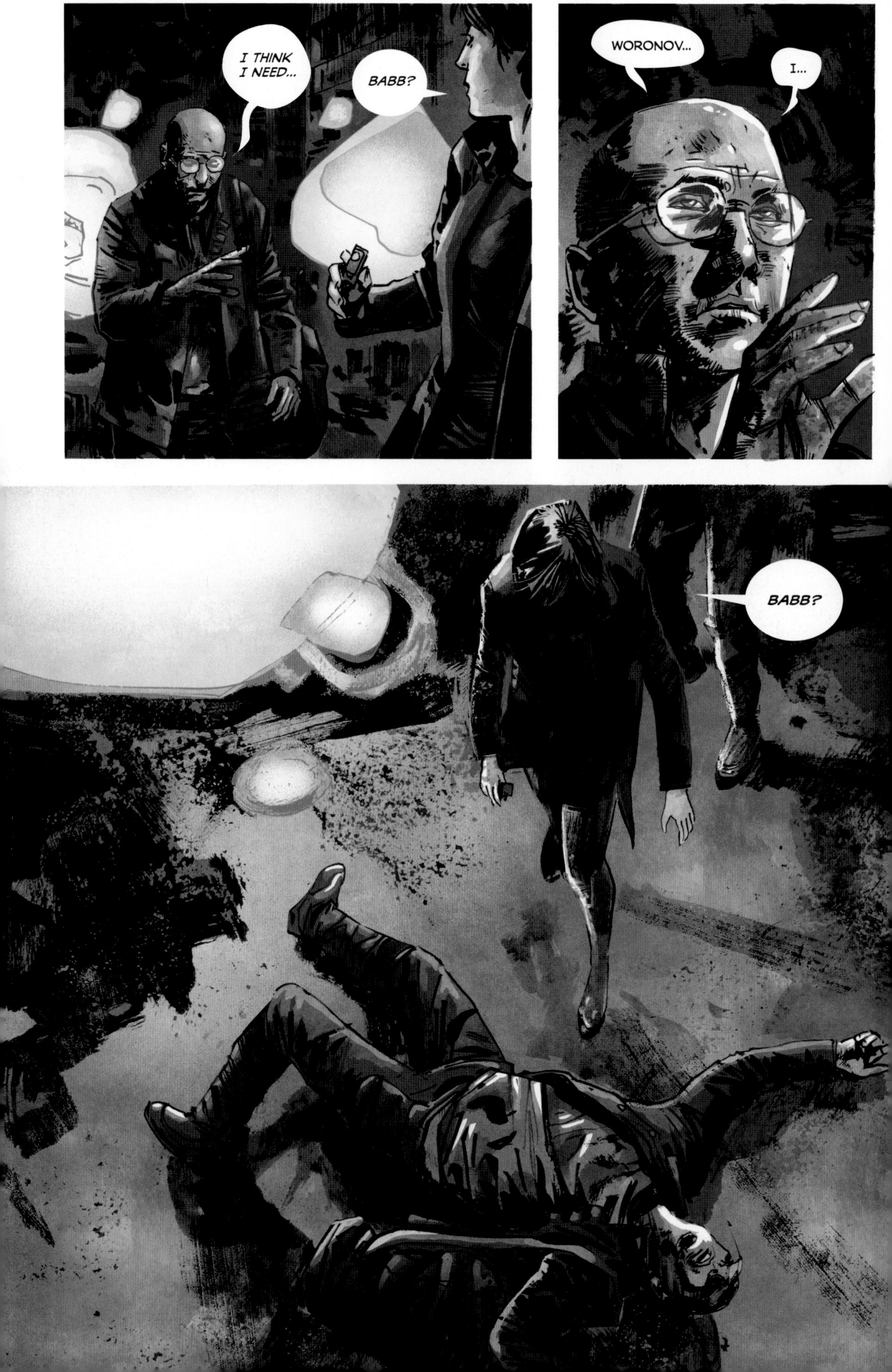
I THINK I NEED...
BABB?
WORONOV...
I...
BABB?

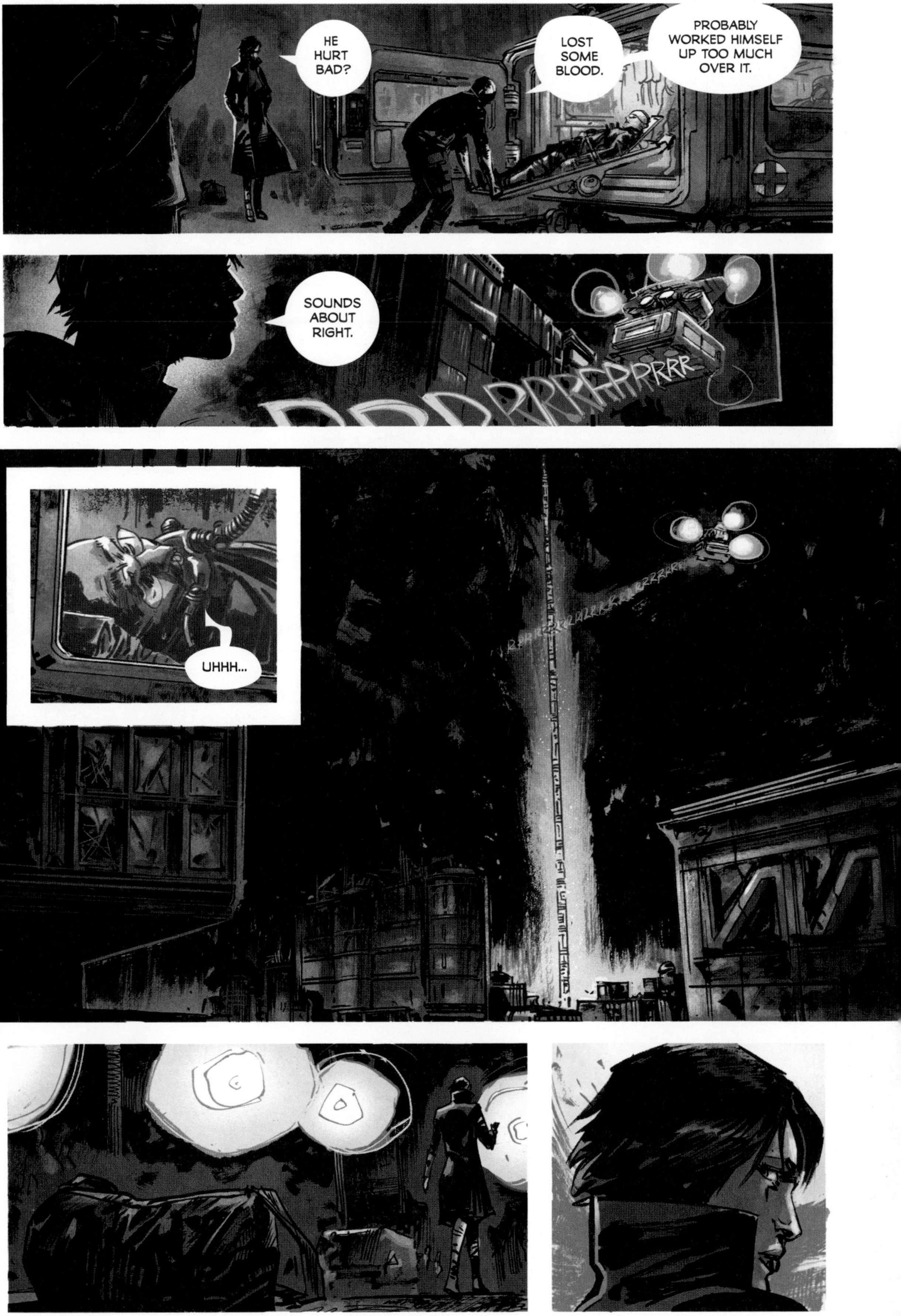
HE HURT BAD?
LOST SOME BLOOD.
PROBABLY WORKED HIMSELF UP TOO MUCH OVER IT.
SOUNDS ABOUT RIGHT.
UHHH...

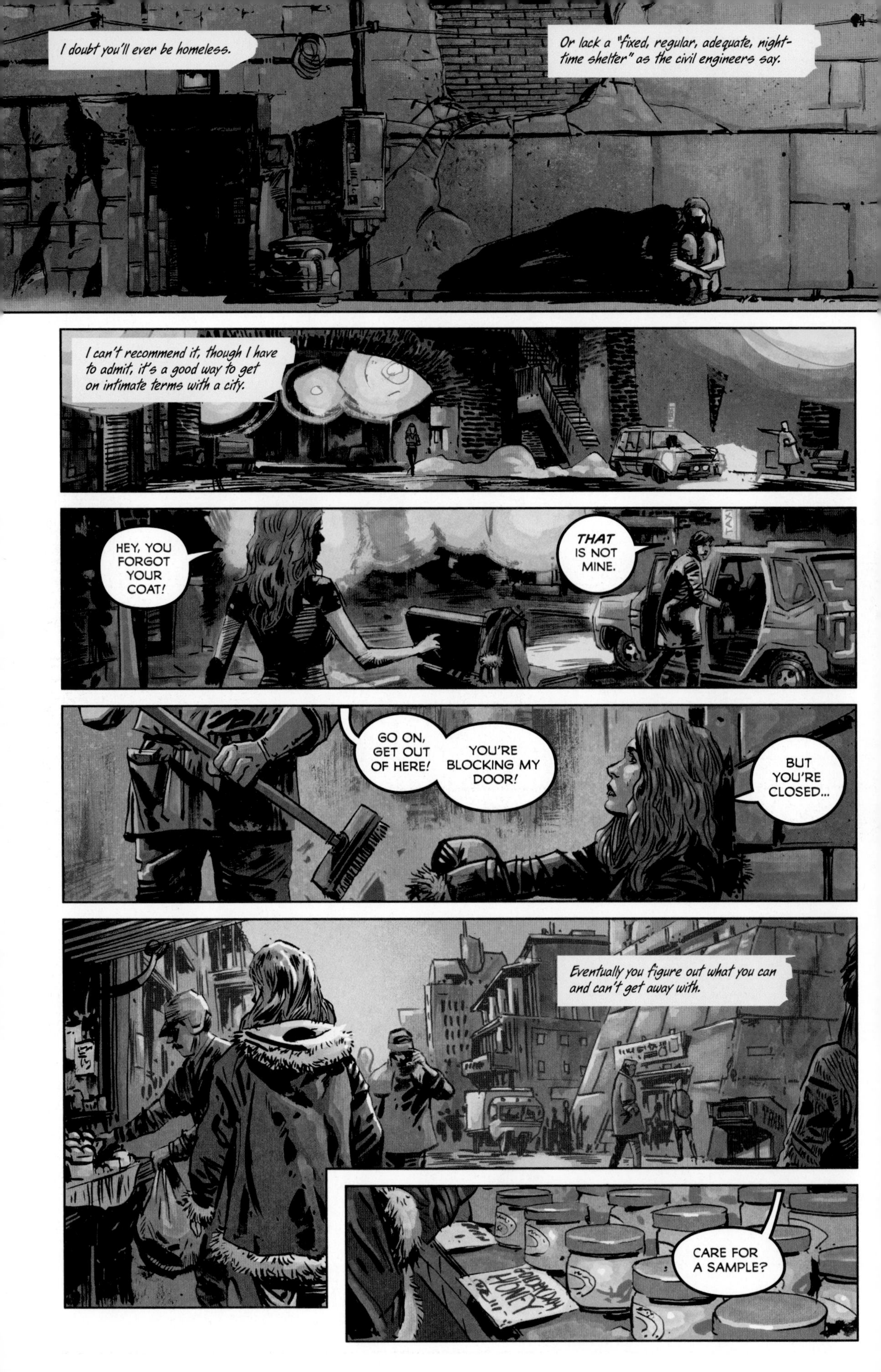
I doubt you'll ever be homeless.
Or lack a "fixed, regular, adequate, night-time shelter" as the civil engineers say.
I can't recommend it, though I have to admit, it's a good way to get on intimate terms with a city.
HEY, YOU FORGOT YOUR COAT!
THAT IS NOT MINE.
GO ON, GET OUT OF HERE!
YOU'RE BLOCKING MY DOOR!
BUT YOU'RE CLOSED...
Eventually you figure out what you can and can't get away with.
CARE FOR A SAMPLE?

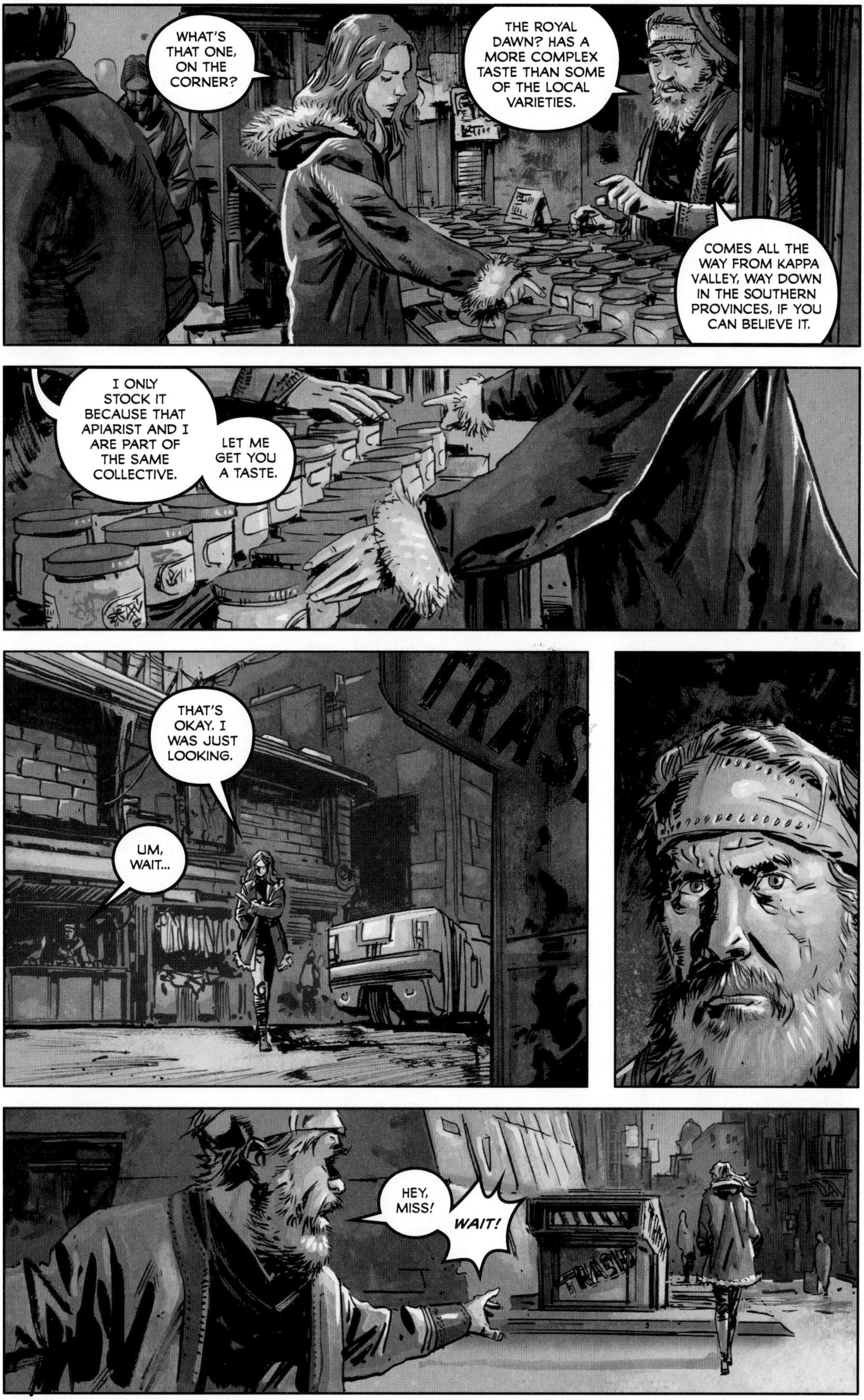
WHAT'S THAT ONE, ON THE CORNER?
THE ROYAL DAWN? HAS A MORE COMPLEX TASTE THAN SOME OF THE LOCAL VARIETIES.
COMES ALL THE WAY FROM KAPPA VALLEY, WAY DOWN IN THE SOUTHERN PROVINCES, IF YOU CAN BELIEVE IT.
I ONLY STOCK IT BECAUSE THAT APIARIST AND I ARE PART OF THE SAME COLLECTIVE.
LET ME GET YOU A TASTE.
THAT'S OKAY. I WAS JUST LOOKING.
UM, WAIT...
HEY, MISS!
WAIT!

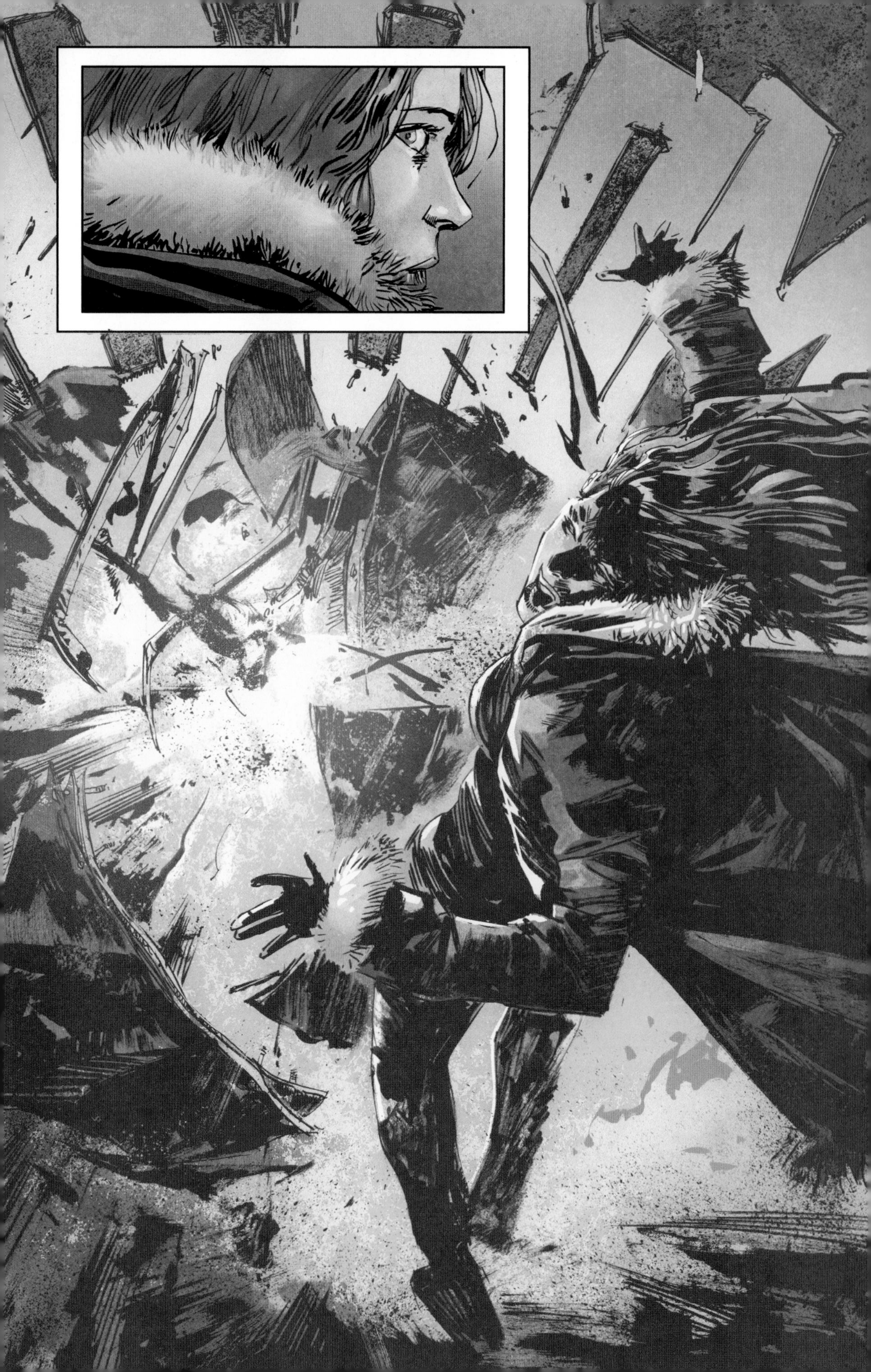

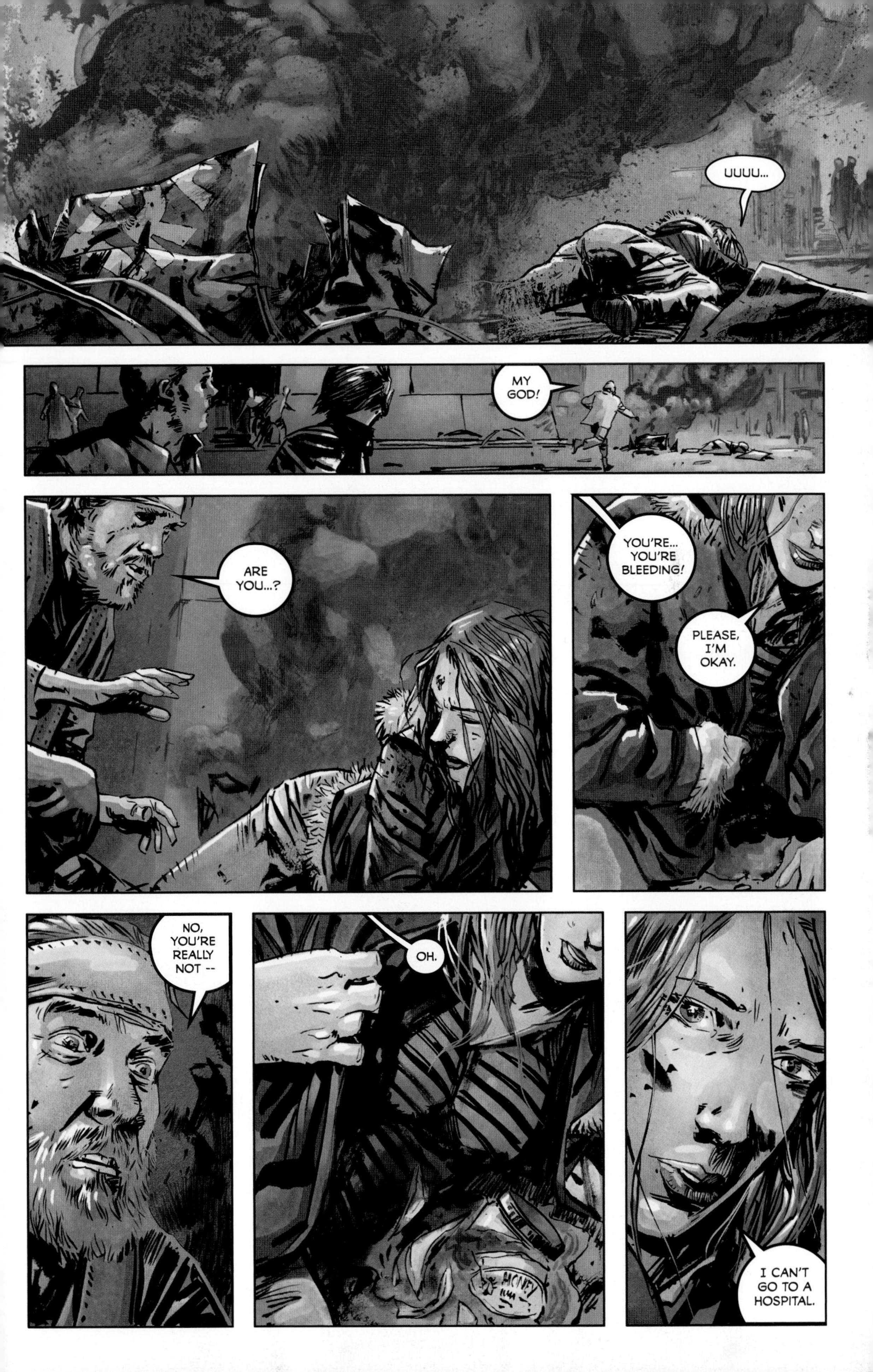
UUUU...
MY GOD!
ARE YOU...?
YOU'RE... YOU'RE BLEEDING!
PLEASE, I'M OKAY.
NO, YOU'RE REALLY NOT --
OH.
I CAN'T GO TO A HOSPITAL.

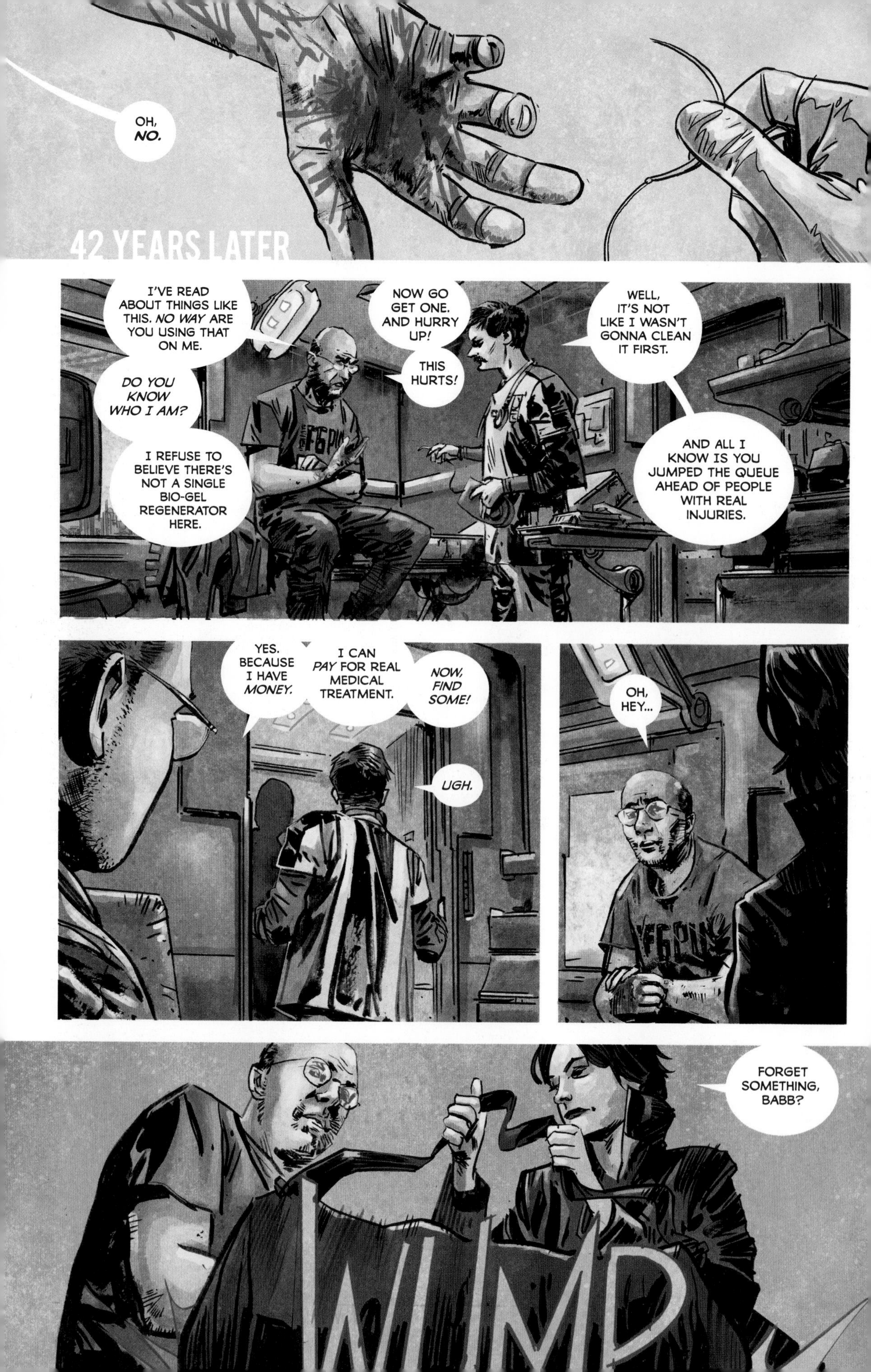
OH, *NO.*
42 YEARS LATER
I'VE READ ABOUT THINGS LIKE THIS. *NO WAY* ARE YOU USING THAT ON ME.
DO YOU KNOW WHO I AM?
I REFUSE TO BELIEVE THERE'S NOT A SINGLE BIO-GEL REGENERATOR HERE.
NOW GO GET ONE. AND HURRY UP*!*
THIS HURTS*!*
WELL, IT'S NOT LIKE I WASN'T GONNA CLEAN IT FIRST.
AND ALL I KNOW IS YOU JUMPED THE QUEUE AHEAD OF PEOPLE WITH REAL INJURIES.
YES. BECAUSE I HAVE *MONEY.*
I CAN *PAY* FOR REAL MEDICAL TREATMENT.
NOW, FIND SOME!
UGH.
OH, HEY...
FORGET SOMETHING, BABB?
WMD

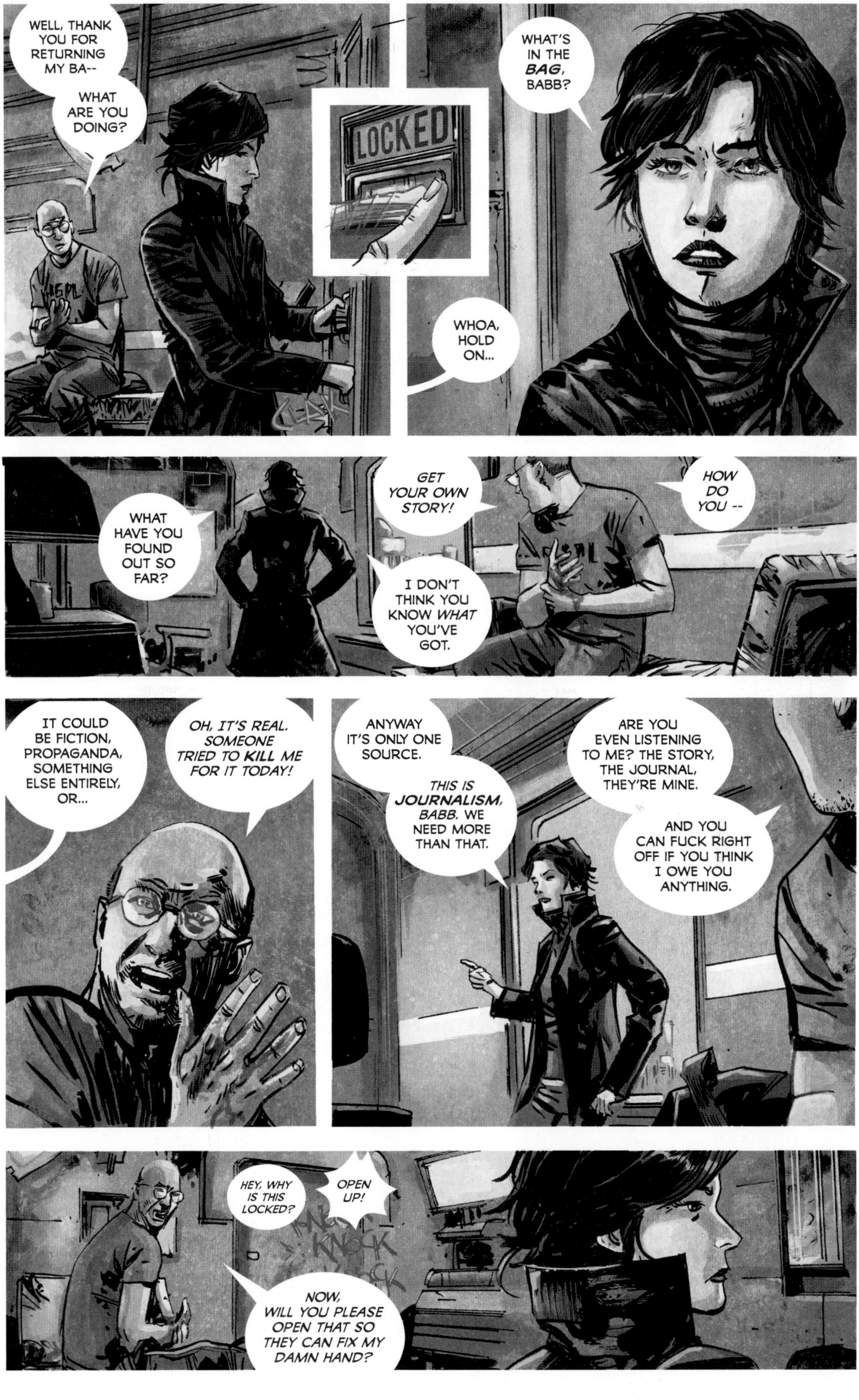
WELL, THANK YOU FOR RETURNING MY BA--
WHAT ARE YOU DOING?
LOCKED
WHAT'S IN THE ***BAG***, BABB?
WHOA, HOLD ON...
WHAT HAVE YOU FOUND OUT SO FAR?
GET YOUR OWN STORY!
I DON'T THINK YOU KNOW *WHAT* YOU'VE GOT.
HOW DO YOU --
IT COULD BE FICTION, PROPAGANDA, SOMETHING ELSE ENTIRELY, OR...
*OH, IT'S REAL. SOMEONE TRIED TO **KILL** ME FOR IT TODAY!*
ANYWAY IT'S ONLY ONE SOURCE.
*THIS IS **JOURNALISM**, BABB.* WE NEED MORE THAN THAT.
ARE YOU EVEN LISTENING TO ME? THE STORY, THE JOURNAL, THEY'RE MINE.
AND YOU CAN FUCK RIGHT OFF IF YOU THINK I OWE YOU ANYTHING.
HEY, WHY IS THIS LOCKED?
OPEN UP!
KNOCK
NOW, WILL YOU PLEASE OPEN THAT SO THEY CAN FIX MY DAMN HAND?

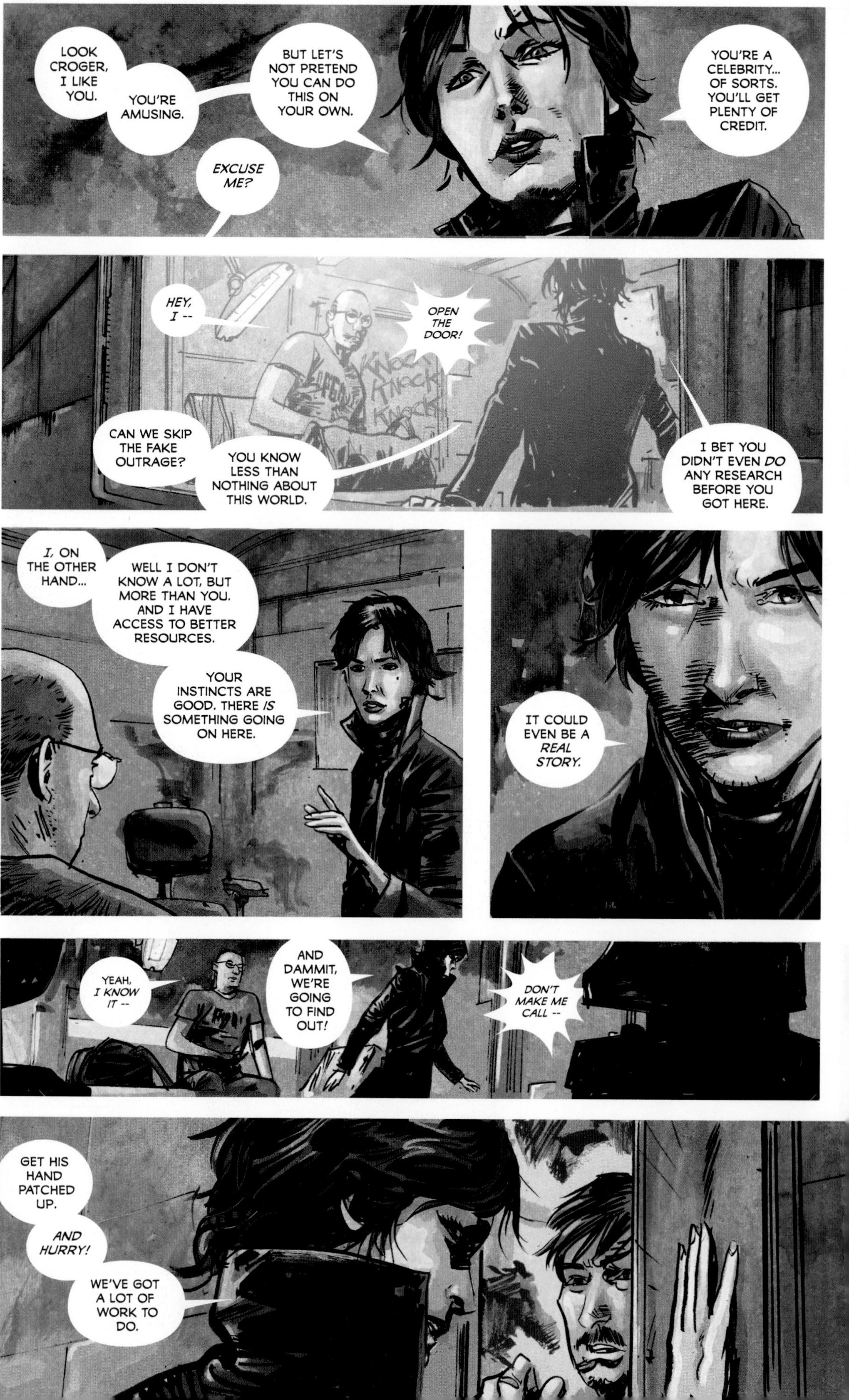
LOOK CROGER, I LIKE YOU.
YOU'RE AMUSING.
BUT LET'S NOT PRETEND YOU CAN DO THIS ON YOUR OWN.
EXCUSE ME?
YOU'RE A CELEBRITY... OF SORTS. YOU'LL GET PLENTY OF CREDIT.
HEY, I --
OPEN THE DOOR!
KNOCK KNOCK KNOCK
CAN WE SKIP THE FAKE OUTRAGE?
YOU KNOW LESS THAN NOTHING ABOUT THIS WORLD.
I BET YOU DIDN'T EVEN DO ANY RESEARCH BEFORE YOU GOT HERE.
I, ON THE OTHER HAND...
WELL I DON'T KNOW A LOT, BUT MORE THAN YOU. AND I HAVE ACCESS TO BETTER RESOURCES.
YOUR INSTINCTS ARE GOOD. THERE IS SOMETHING GOING ON HERE.
IT COULD EVEN BE A REAL STORY.
YEAH, I KNOW IT --
AND DAMMIT, WE'RE GOING TO FIND OUT!
DON'T MAKE ME CALL --
GET HIS HAND PATCHED UP.
AND HURRY!
WE'VE GOT A LOT OF WORK TO DO.

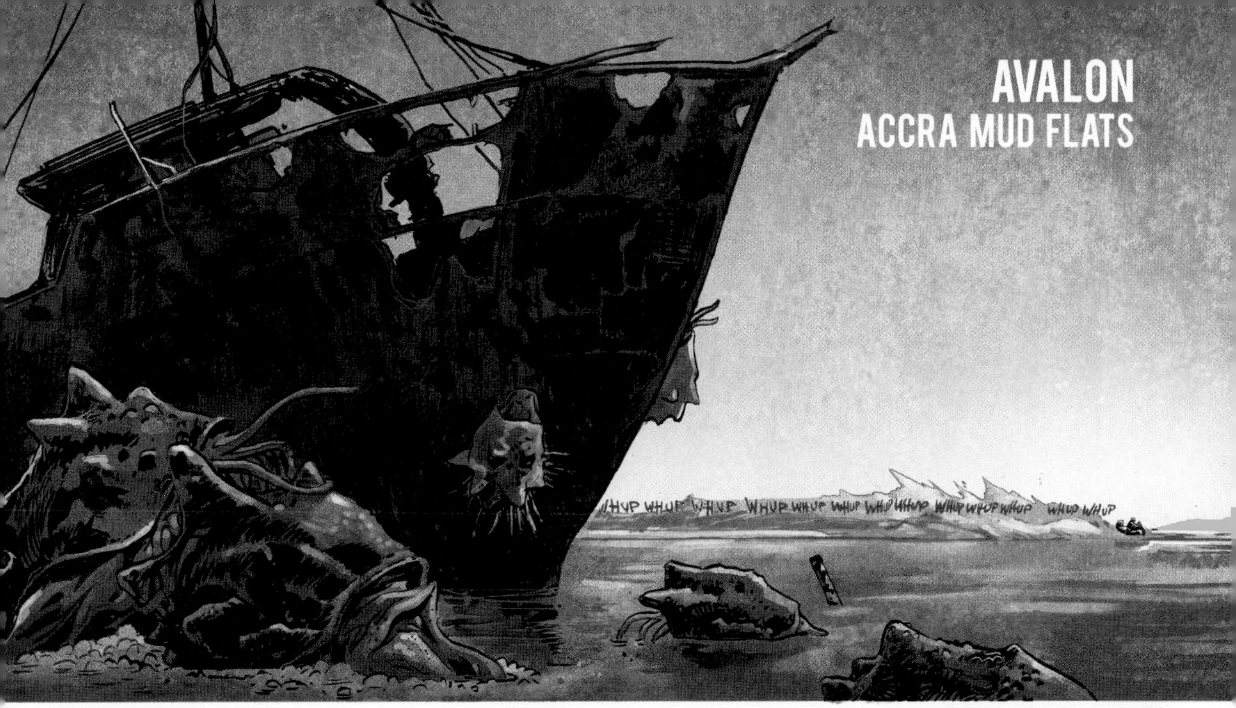
AVALON
ACCRA MUD FLATS
WHUP WHUP WHUP WHUP WHUP WHUP WHUP WHUP WHUP WHUP WHUP
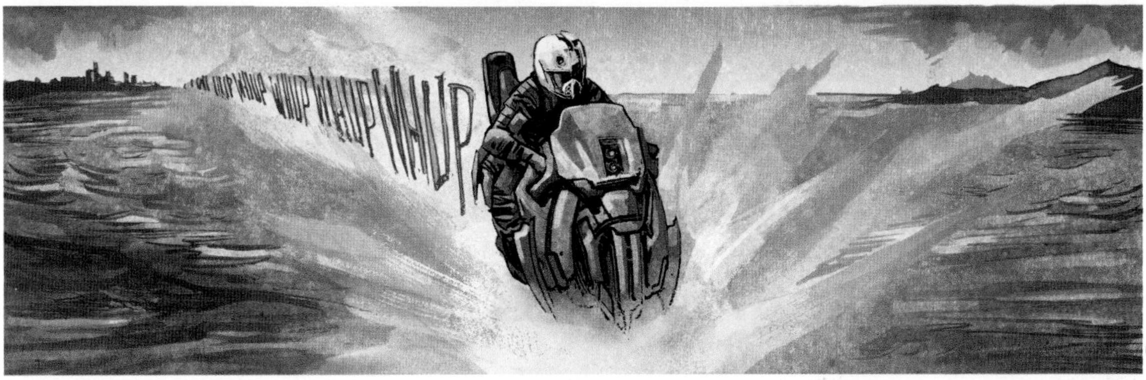
WHUP WHUP WHUP WHUP
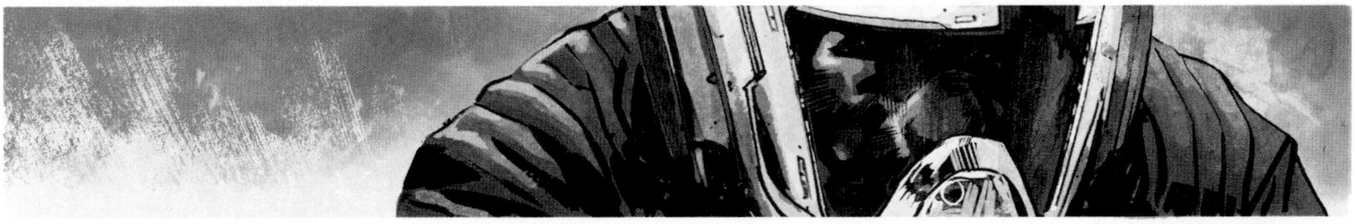
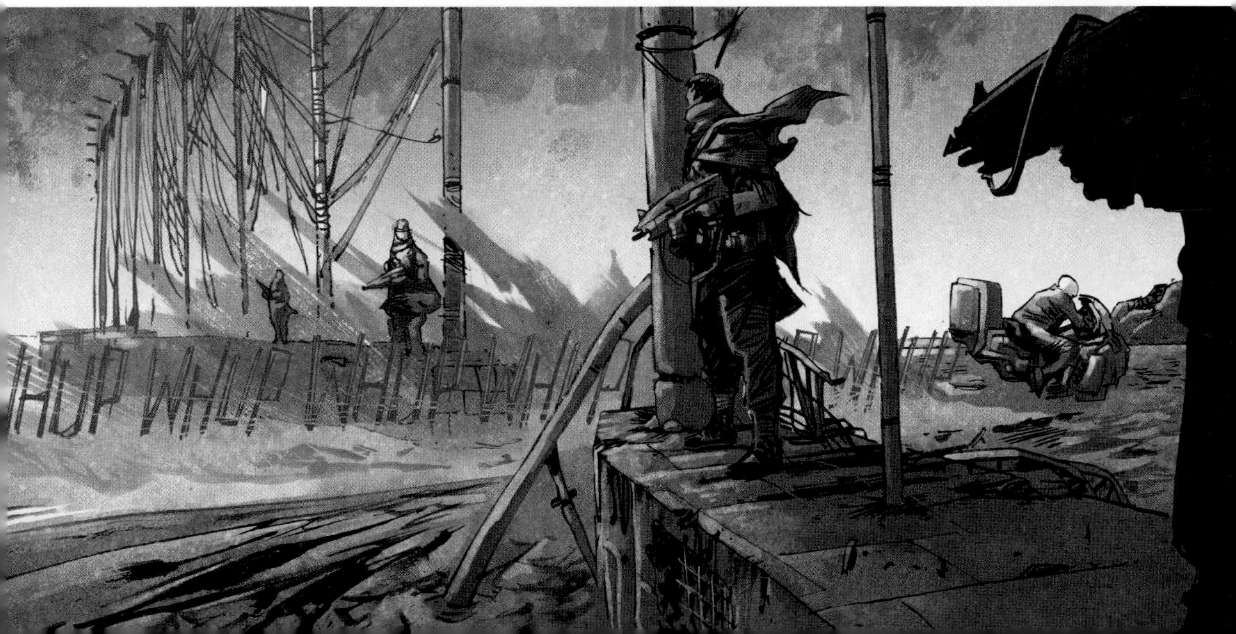
WHUP WHUP

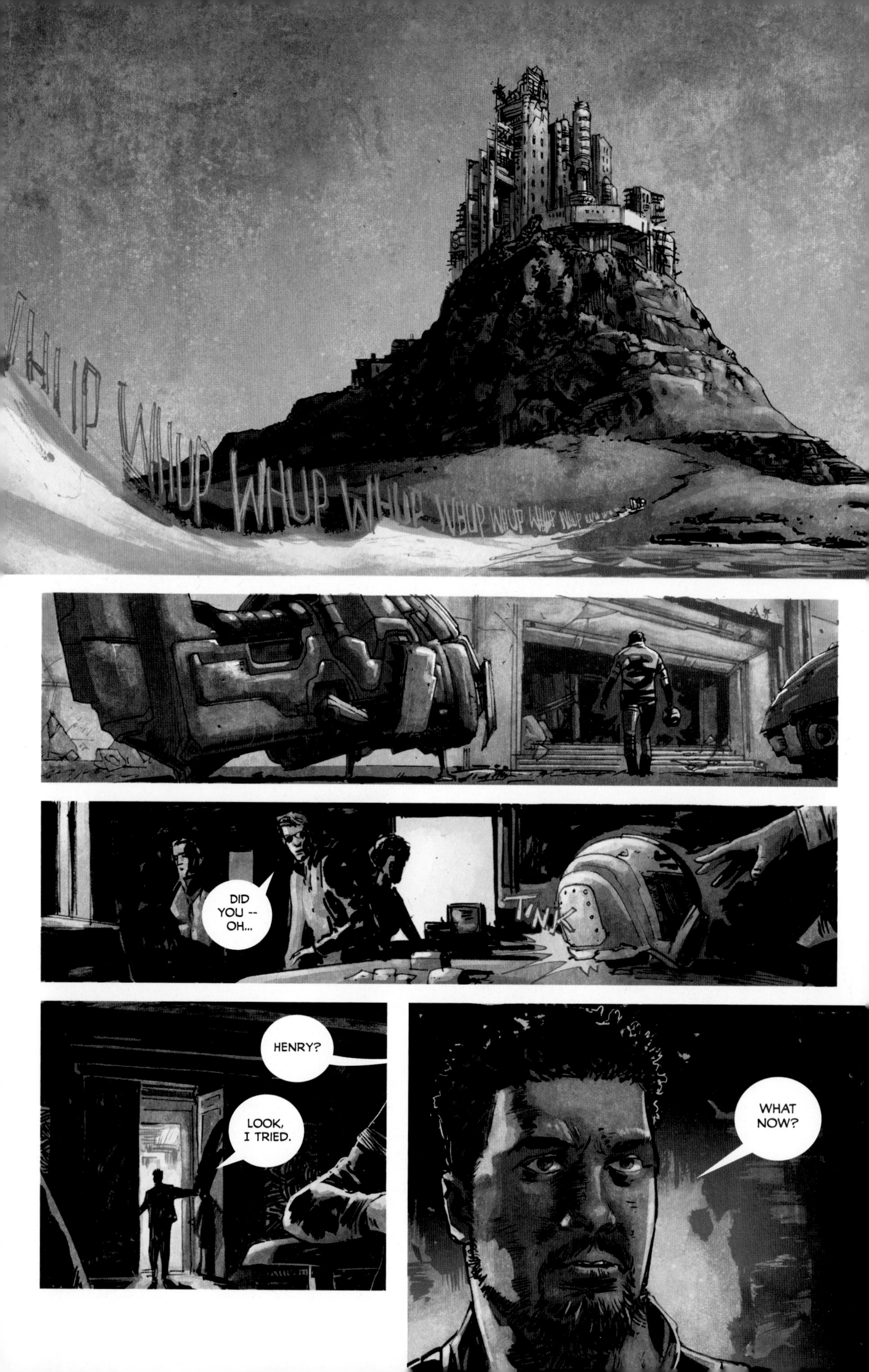
WHUP WHUP WHUP WHUP WHUP
DID YOU -- OH...
TINK
HENRY?
LOOK, I TRIED.
WHAT NOW?

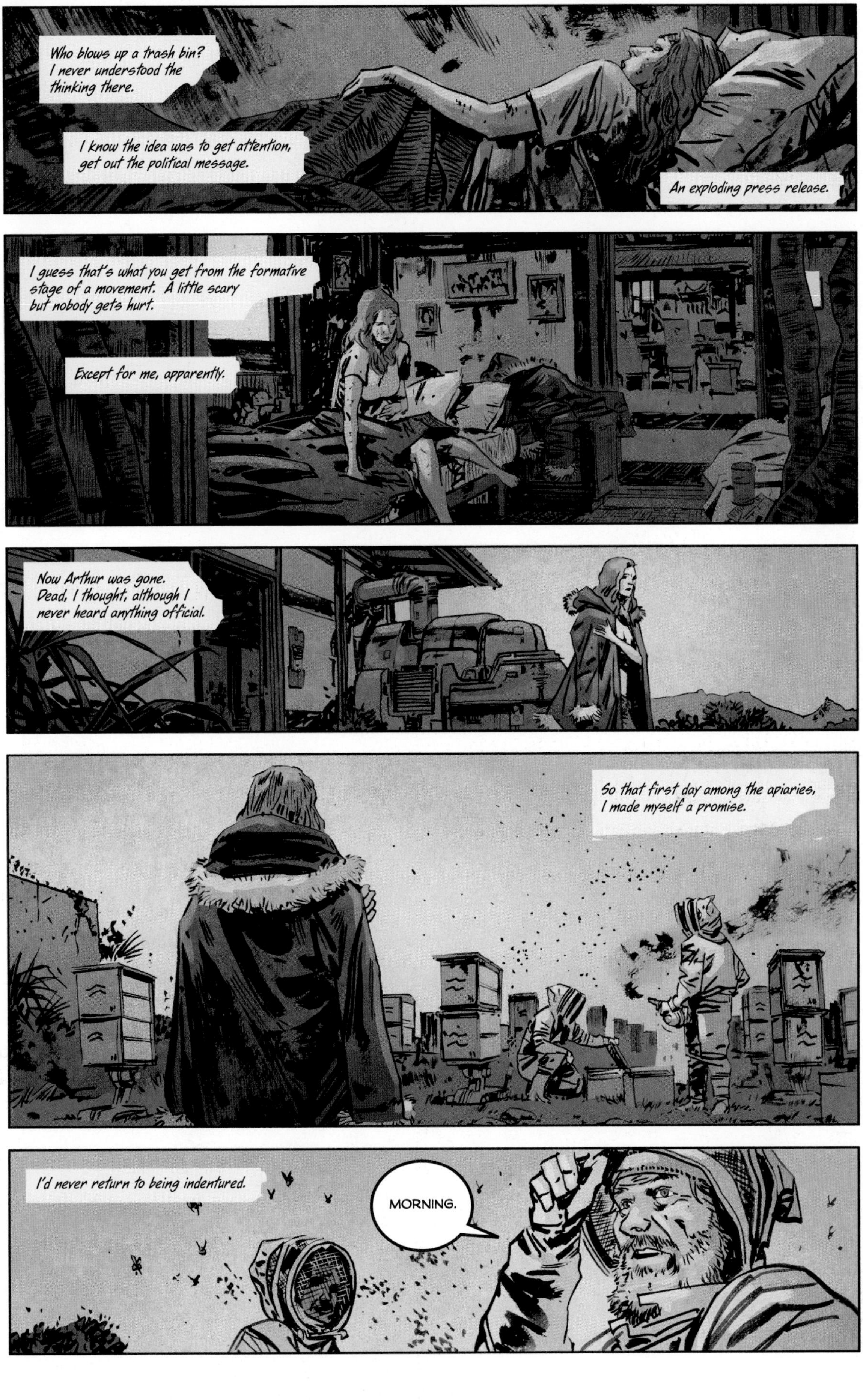
Who blows up a trash bin? I never understood the thinking there.
I know the idea was to get attention, get out the political message.
An exploding press release.
I guess that's what you get from the formative stage of a movement. A little scary but nobody gets hurt.
Except for me, apparently.
Now Arthur was gone. Dead, I thought, although I never heard anything official.
So that first day among the apiaries, I made myself a promise.
I'd never return to being indentured.
MORNING.

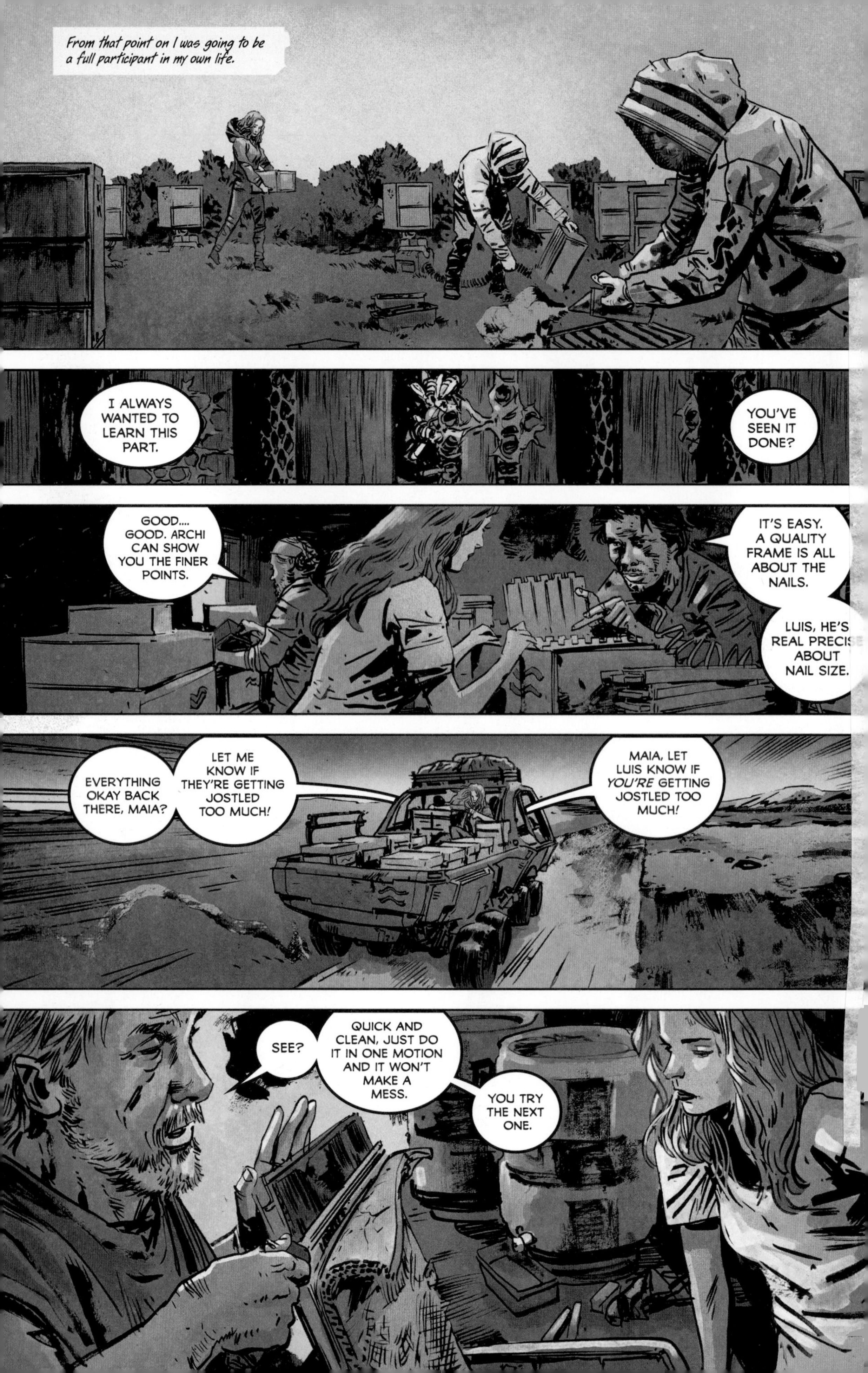
From that point on I was going to be a full participant in my own life.
I ALWAYS WANTED TO LEARN THIS PART.
YOU'VE SEEN IT DONE?
GOOD.... GOOD. ARCHI CAN SHOW YOU THE FINER POINTS.
IT'S EASY. A QUALITY FRAME IS ALL ABOUT THE NAILS.
LUIS, HE'S REAL PRECIS ABOUT NAIL SIZE.
EVERYTHING OKAY BACK THERE, MAIA?
LET ME KNOW IF THEY'RE GETTING JOSTLED TOO MUCH!
MAIA, LET LUIS KNOW IF *YOU'RE* GETTING JOSTLED TOO MUCH!
SEE?
QUICK AND CLEAN, JUST DO IT IN ONE MOTION AND IT WON'T MAKE A MESS.
YOU TRY THE NEXT ONE.

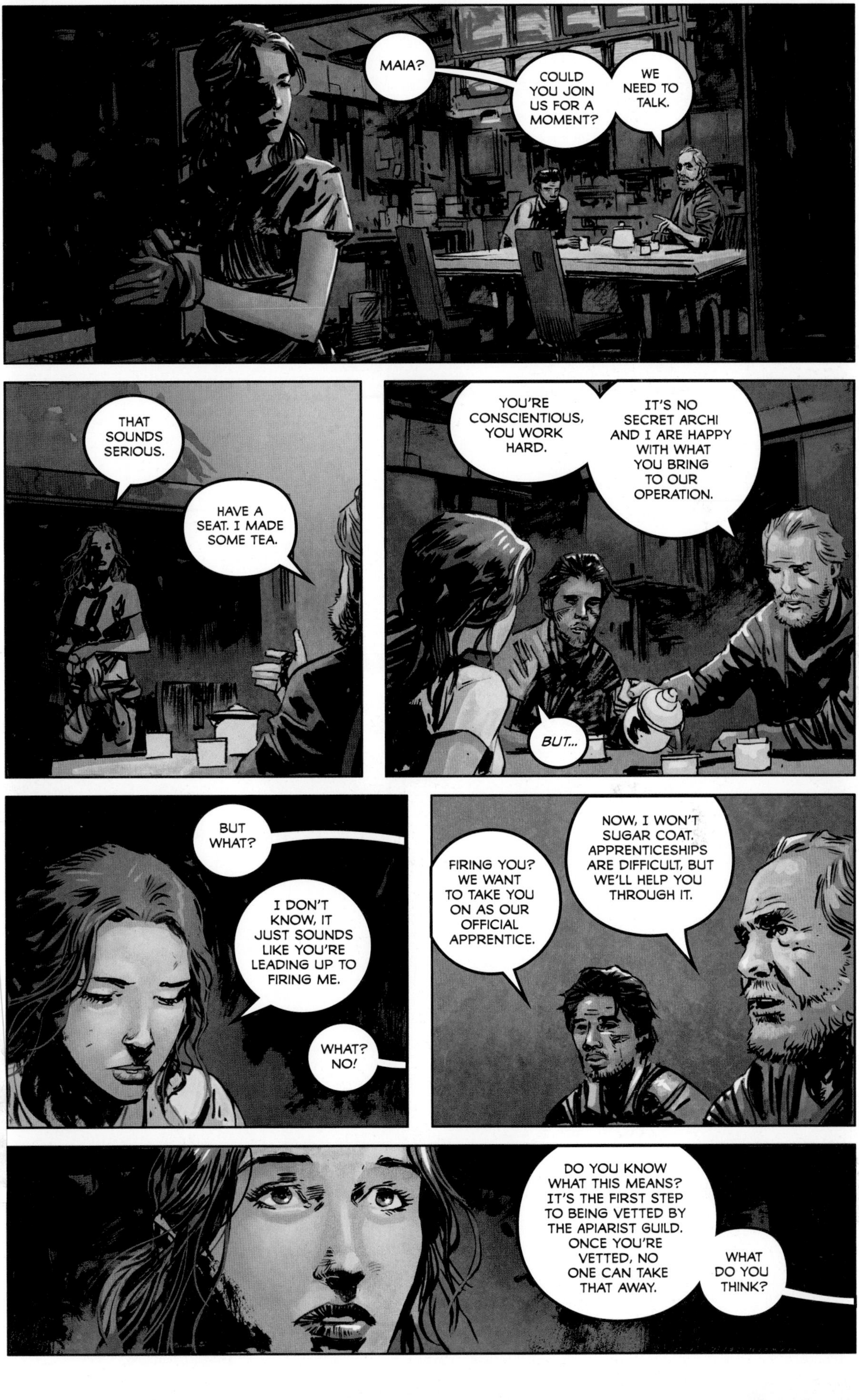
MAIA?
COULD YOU JOIN US FOR A MOMENT?
WE NEED TO TALK.
THAT SOUNDS SERIOUS.
HAVE A SEAT. I MADE SOME TEA.
YOU'RE CONSCIENTIOUS, YOU WORK HARD.
IT'S NO SECRET ARCHI AND I ARE HAPPY WITH WHAT YOU BRING TO OUR OPERATION.
BUT...
BUT WHAT?
I DON'T KNOW, IT JUST SOUNDS LIKE YOU'RE LEADING UP TO FIRING ME.
WHAT? NO!
FIRING YOU? WE WANT TO TAKE YOU ON AS OUR OFFICIAL APPRENTICE.
NOW, I WON'T SUGAR COAT. APPRENTICESHIPS ARE DIFFICULT, BUT WE'LL HELP YOU THROUGH IT.
DO YOU KNOW WHAT THIS MEANS? IT'S THE FIRST STEP TO BEING VETTED BY THE APIARIST GUILD. ONCE YOU'RE VETTED, NO ONE CAN TAKE THAT AWAY.
WHAT DO YOU THINK?

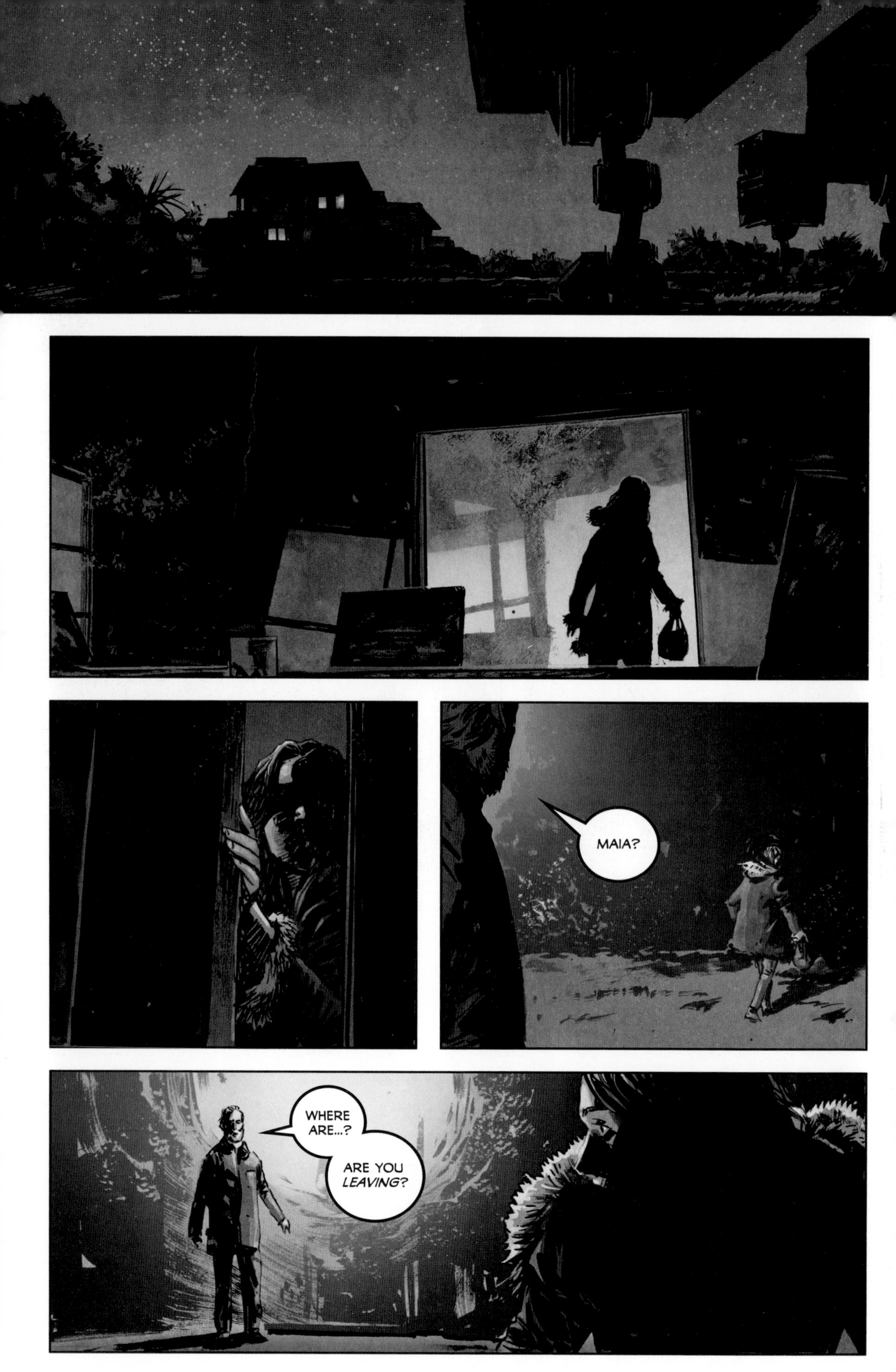
MAIA?
WHERE ARE...?
ARE YOU *LEAVING*?

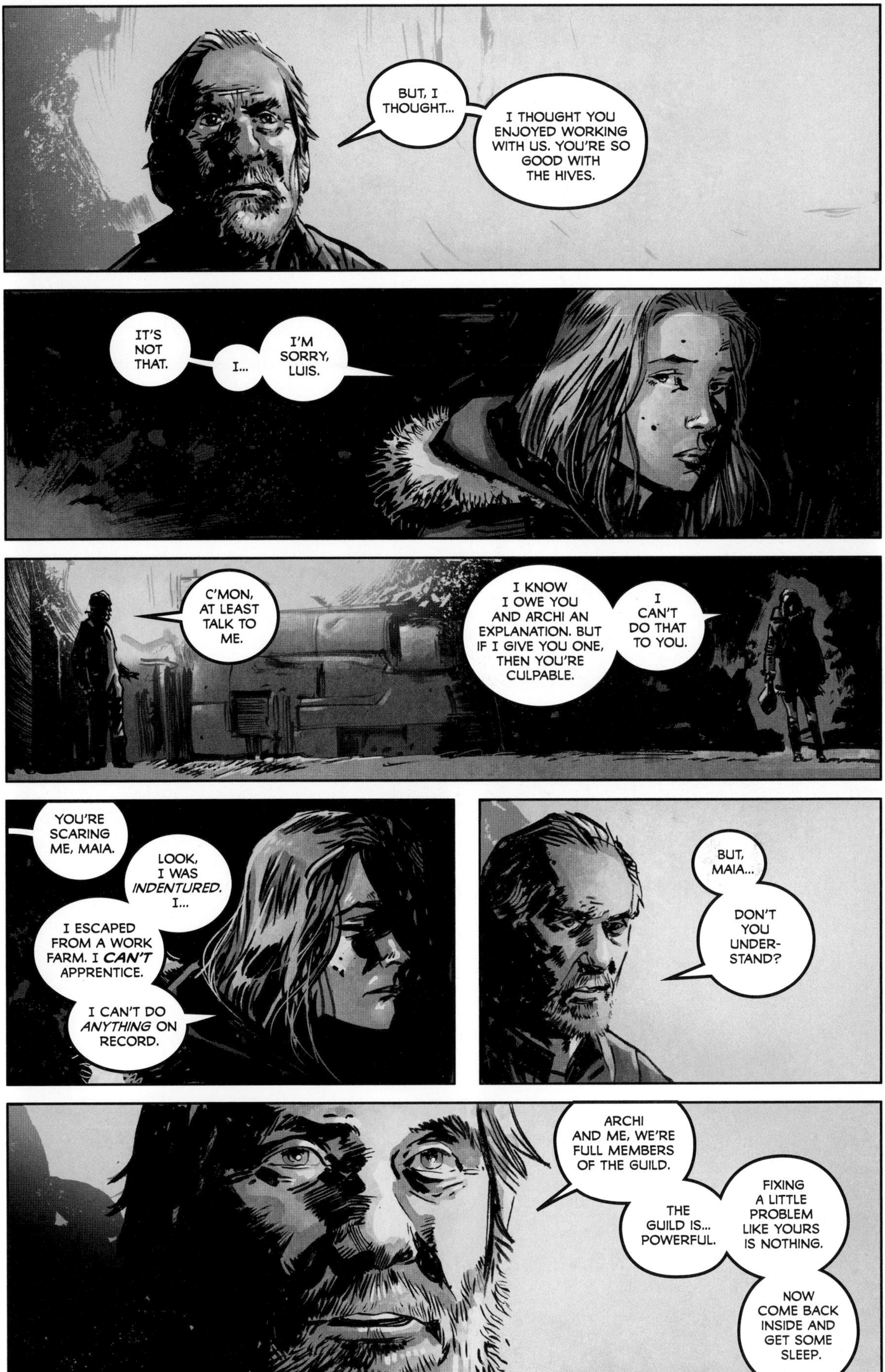
BUT, I THOUGHT...
I THOUGHT YOU ENJOYED WORKING WITH US. YOU'RE SO GOOD WITH THE HIVES.
IT'S NOT THAT.
I...
I'M SORRY, LUIS.
C'MON, AT LEAST TALK TO ME.
I KNOW I OWE YOU AND ARCHI AN EXPLANATION. BUT IF I GIVE YOU ONE, THEN YOU'RE CULPABLE.
I CAN'T DO THAT TO YOU.
YOU'RE SCARING ME, MAIA.
LOOK, I WAS *INDENTURED*. I...
I ESCAPED FROM A WORK FARM. I ***CAN'T*** APPRENTICE.
I CAN'T DO *ANYTHING* ON RECORD.
BUT, MAIA...
DON'T YOU UNDER-STAND?
ARCHI AND ME, WE'RE FULL MEMBERS OF THE GUILD.
THE GUILD IS... POWERFUL.
FIXING A LITTLE PROBLEM LIKE YOURS IS NOTHING.
NOW COME BACK INSIDE AND GET SOME SLEEP.

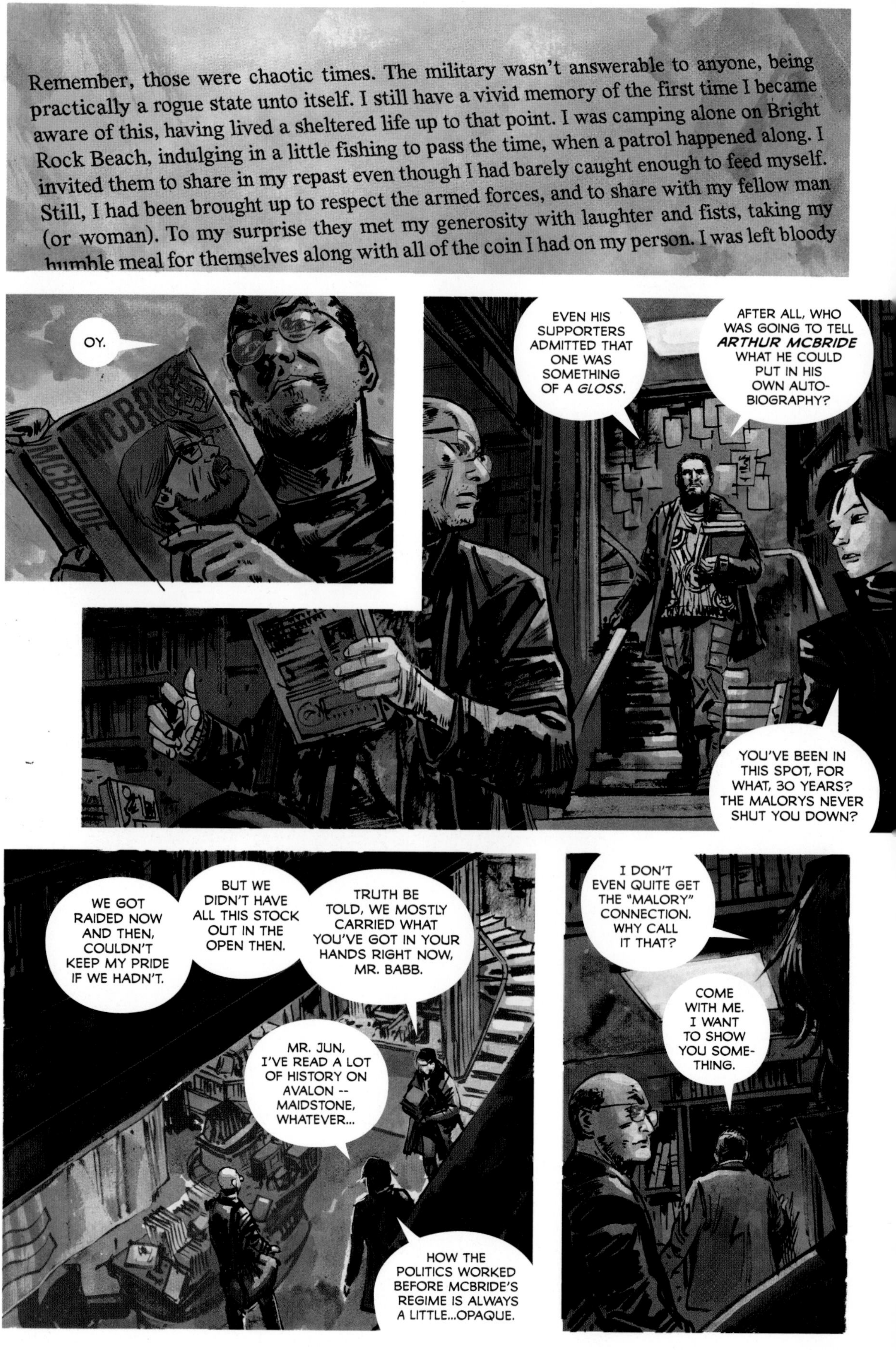
Remember, those were chaotic times. The military wasn't answerable to anyone, being practically a rogue state unto itself. I still have a vivid memory of the first time I became aware of this, having lived a sheltered life up to that point. I was camping alone on Bright Rock Beach, indulging in a little fishing to pass the time, when a patrol happened along. I invited them to share in my repast even though I had barely caught enough to feed myself. Still, I had been brought up to respect the armed forces, and to share with my fellow man (or woman). To my surprise they met my generosity with laughter and fists, taking my humble meal for themselves along with all of the coin I had on my person. I was left bloody
OY.
MCBRIDE
EVEN HIS SUPPORTERS ADMITTED THAT ONE WAS SOMETHING OF A *GLOSS*.
AFTER ALL, WHO WAS GOING TO TELL ***ARTHUR MCBRIDE*** WHAT HE COULD PUT IN HIS OWN AUTO-BIOGRAPHY?
YOU'VE BEEN IN THIS SPOT, FOR WHAT, 30 YEARS? THE MALORYS NEVER SHUT YOU DOWN?
WE GOT RAIDED NOW AND THEN, COULDN'T KEEP MY PRIDE IF WE HADN'T.
BUT WE DIDN'T HAVE ALL THIS STOCK OUT IN THE OPEN THEN.
TRUTH BE TOLD, WE MOSTLY CARRIED WHAT YOU'VE GOT IN YOUR HANDS RIGHT NOW, MR. BABB.
MR. JUN, I'VE READ A LOT OF HISTORY ON AVALON -- MAIDSTONE, WHATEVER...
HOW THE POLITICS WORKED BEFORE MCBRIDE'S REGIME IS ALWAYS A LITTLE...OPAQUE.
I DON'T EVEN QUITE GET THE "MALORY" CONNECTION. WHY CALL IT THAT?
COME WITH ME. I WANT TO SHOW YOU SOME-THING.

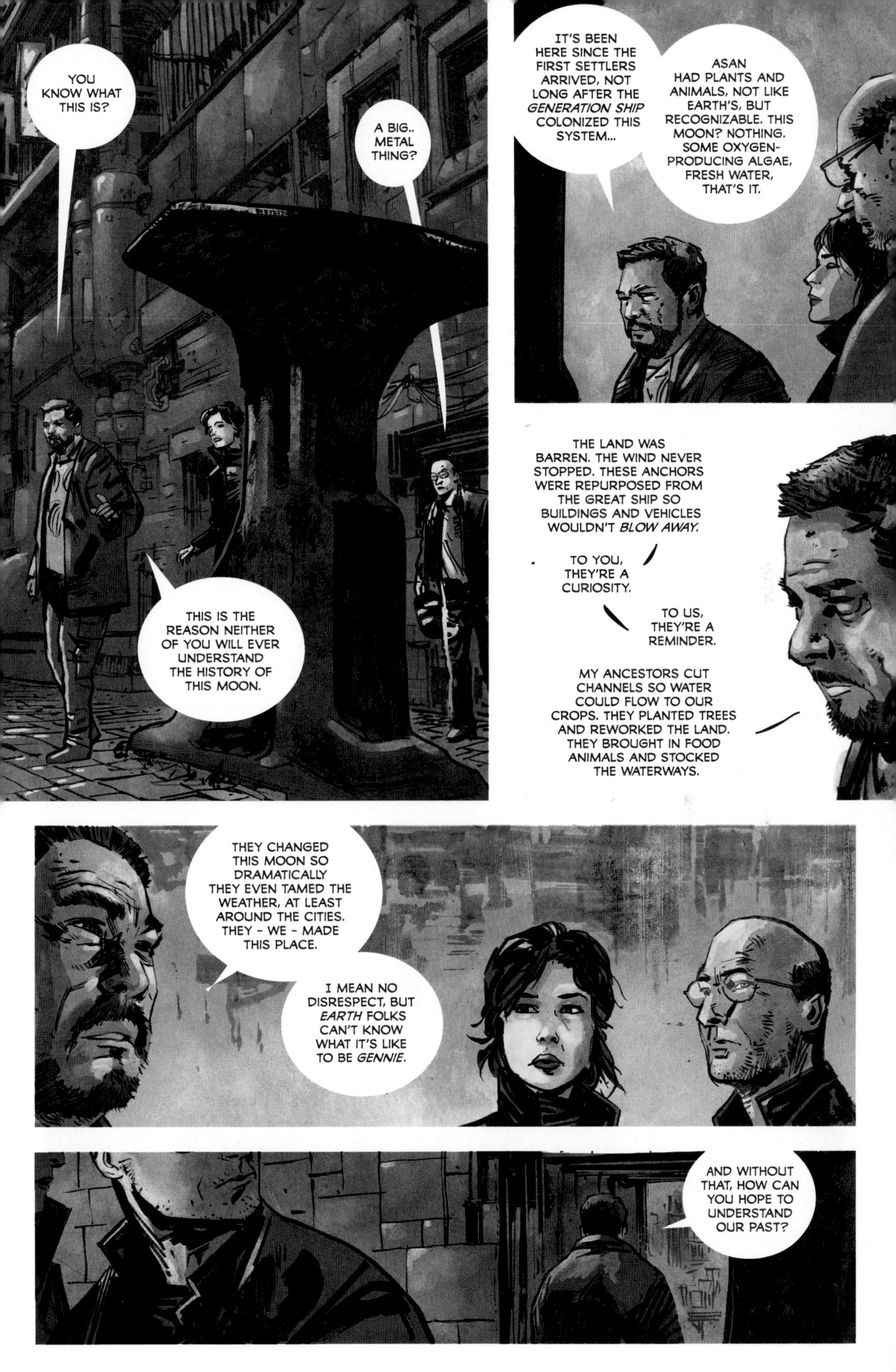
YOU KNOW WHAT THIS IS?
A BIG.. METAL THING?
THIS IS THE REASON NEITHER OF YOU WILL EVER UNDERSTAND THE HISTORY OF THIS MOON.
IT'S BEEN HERE SINCE THE FIRST SETTLERS ARRIVED, NOT LONG AFTER THE *GENERATION SHIP* COLONIZED THIS SYSTEM...
ASAN HAD PLANTS AND ANIMALS, NOT LIKE EARTH'S, BUT RECOGNIZABLE. THIS MOON? NOTHING. SOME OXYGEN-PRODUCING ALGAE, FRESH WATER, THAT'S IT.
THE LAND WAS BARREN. THE WIND NEVER STOPPED. THESE ANCHORS WERE REPURPOSED FROM THE GREAT SHIP SO BUILDINGS AND VEHICLES WOULDN'T *BLOW AWAY.*
TO YOU, THEY'RE A CURIOSITY.
TO US, THEY'RE A REMINDER.
MY ANCESTORS CUT CHANNELS SO WATER COULD FLOW TO OUR CROPS. THEY PLANTED TREES AND REWORKED THE LAND. THEY BROUGHT IN FOOD ANIMALS AND STOCKED THE WATERWAYS.
THEY CHANGED THIS MOON SO DRAMATICALLY THEY EVEN TAMED THE WEATHER, AT LEAST AROUND THE CITIES. THEY - WE - MADE THIS PLACE.
I MEAN NO DISRESPECT, BUT *EARTH* FOLKS CAN'T KNOW WHAT IT'S LIKE TO BE *GENNIE.*
AND WITHOUT THAT, HOW CAN YOU HOPE TO UNDERSTAND OUR PAST?

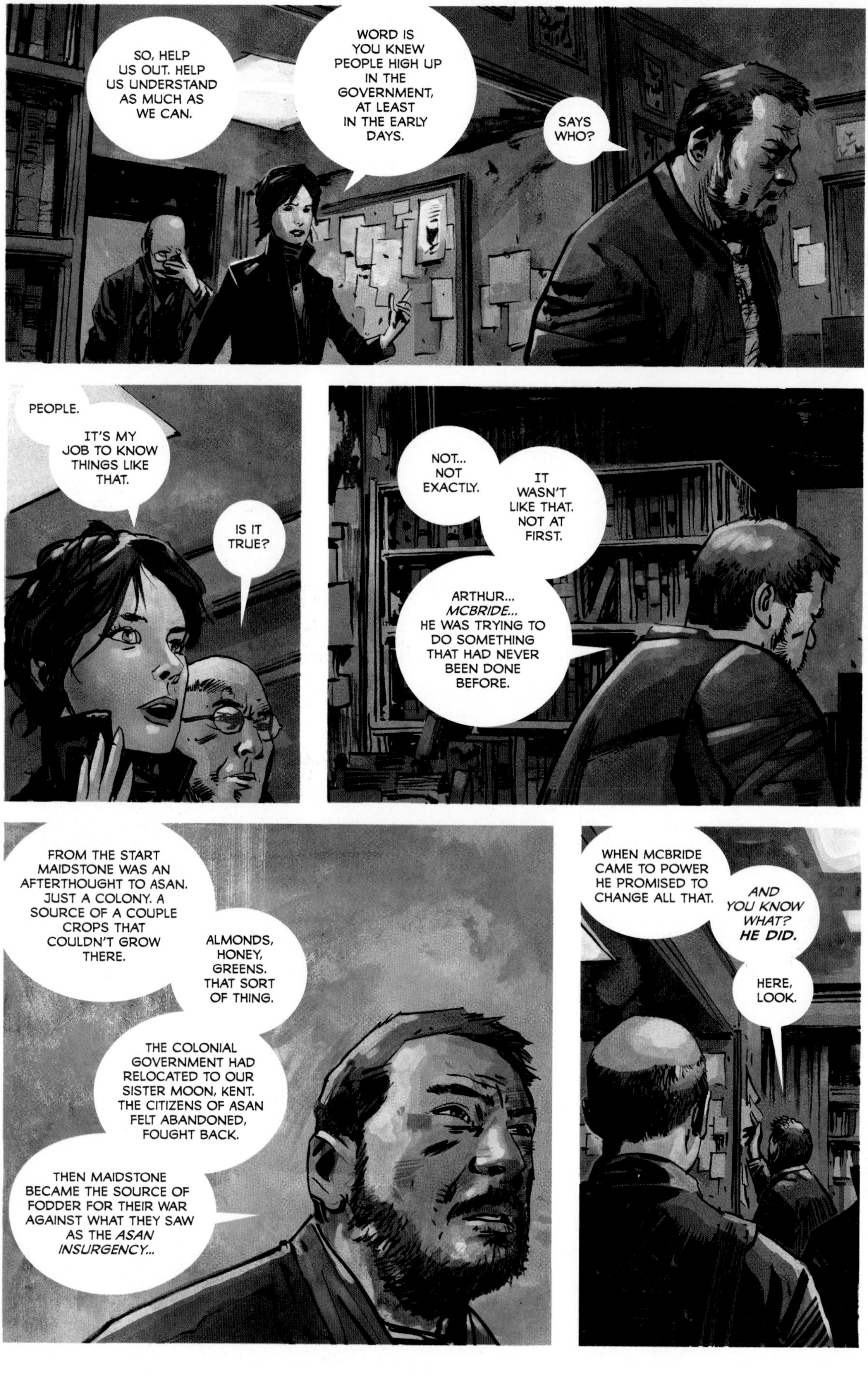
SO, HELP US OUT. HELP US UNDERSTAND AS MUCH AS WE CAN.
WORD IS YOU KNEW PEOPLE HIGH UP IN THE GOVERNMENT, AT LEAST IN THE EARLY DAYS.
SAYS WHO?
PEOPLE.
IT'S MY JOB TO KNOW THINGS LIKE THAT.
IS IT TRUE?
NOT... NOT EXACTLY.
IT WASN'T LIKE THAT. NOT AT FIRST.
ARTHUR... *MCBRIDE...* HE WAS TRYING TO DO SOMETHING THAT HAD NEVER BEEN DONE BEFORE.
FROM THE START MAIDSTONE WAS AN AFTERTHOUGHT TO ASAN. JUST A COLONY. A SOURCE OF A COUPLE CROPS THAT COULDN'T GROW THERE.
ALMONDS, HONEY, GREENS. THAT SORT OF THING.
THE COLONIAL GOVERNMENT HAD RELOCATED TO OUR SISTER MOON, KENT. THE CITIZENS OF ASAN FELT ABANDONED, FOUGHT BACK.
THEN MAIDSTONE BECAME THE SOURCE OF FODDER FOR THEIR WAR AGAINST WHAT THEY SAW AS THE *ASAN INSURGENCY...*
WHEN MCBRIDE CAME TO POWER HE PROMISED TO CHANGE ALL THAT.
AND YOU KNOW WHAT? ***HE DID.***
HERE, LOOK.

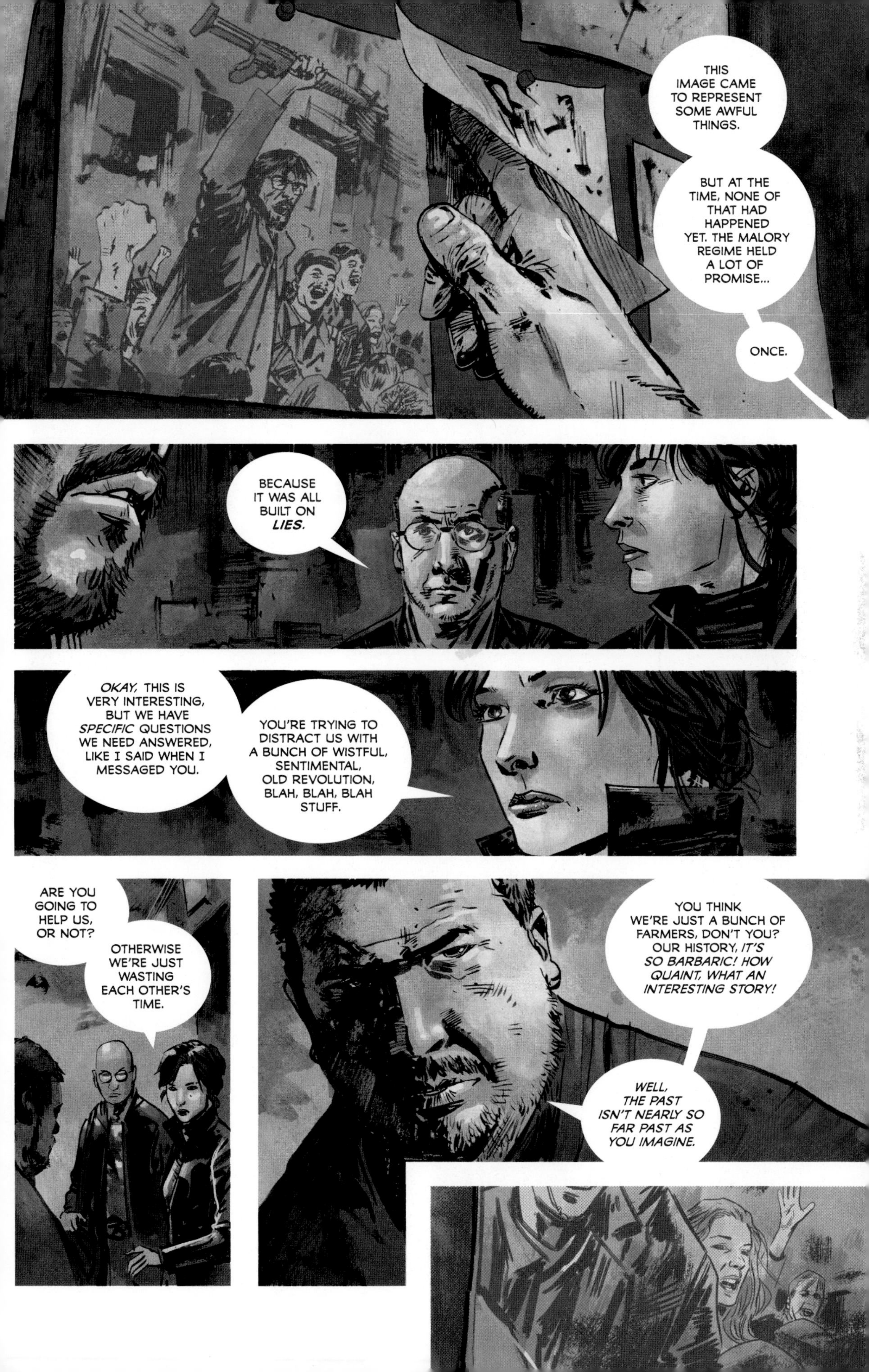
THIS IMAGE CAME TO REPRESENT SOME AWFUL THINGS.
BUT AT THE TIME, NONE OF THAT HAD HAPPENED YET. THE MALORY REGIME HELD A LOT OF PROMISE...
ONCE.
BECAUSE IT WAS ALL BUILT ON *LIES.*
OKAY, THIS IS VERY INTERESTING, BUT WE HAVE *SPECIFIC* QUESTIONS WE NEED ANSWERED, LIKE I SAID WHEN I MESSAGED YOU.
YOU'RE TRYING TO DISTRACT US WITH A BUNCH OF WISTFUL, SENTIMENTAL, OLD REVOLUTION, BLAH, BLAH, BLAH STUFF.
ARE YOU GOING TO HELP US, OR NOT?
OTHERWISE WE'RE JUST WASTING EACH OTHER'S TIME.
YOU THINK WE'RE JUST A BUNCH OF FARMERS, DON'T YOU? OUR HISTORY, *IT'S SO BARBARIC! HOW QUAINT, WHAT AN INTERESTING STORY!*
WELL, THE PAST ISN'T NEARLY SO FAR PAST AS YOU IMAGINE.

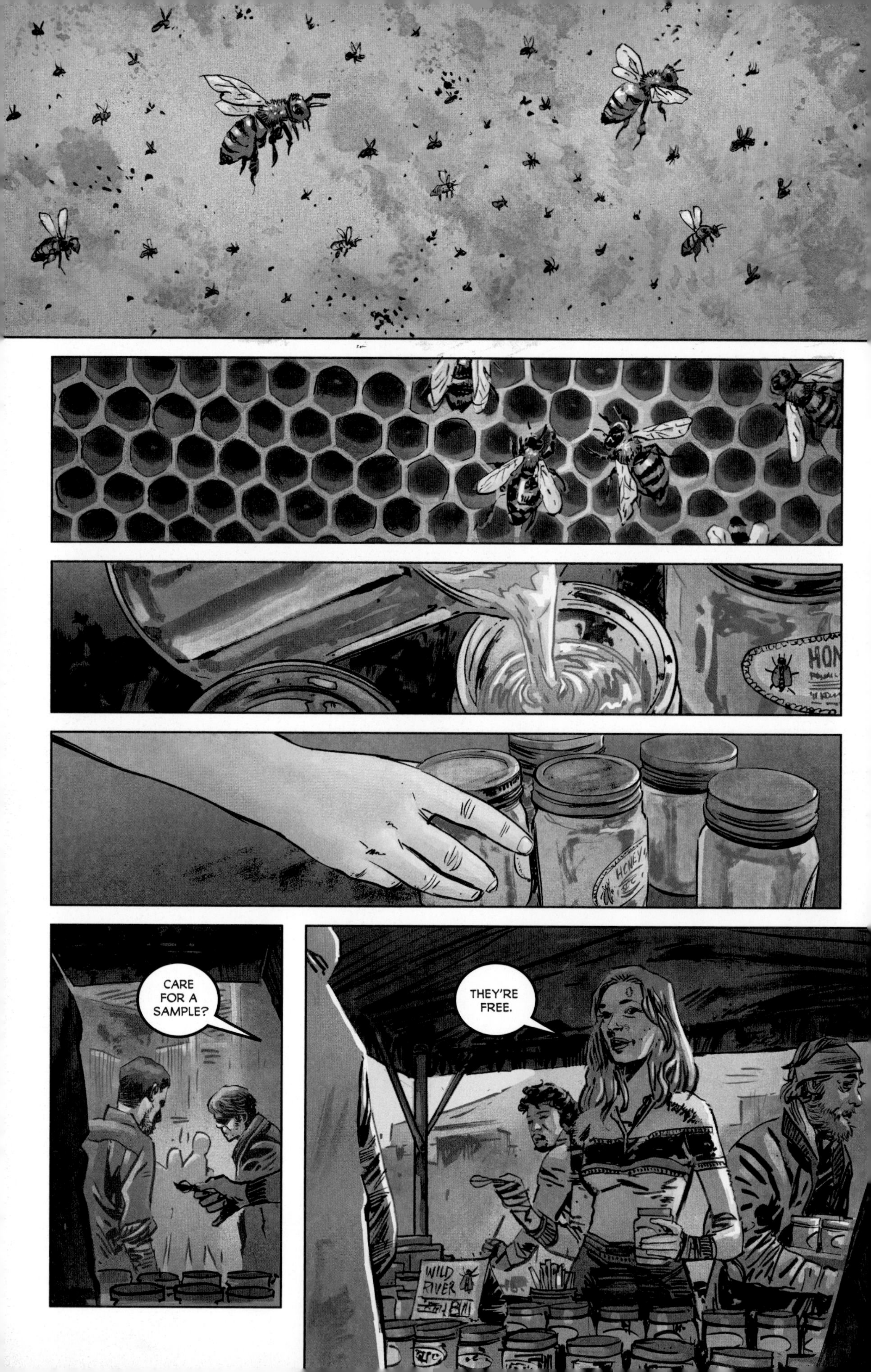
HONEY
CARE FOR A SAMPLE?
THEY'RE FREE.
WILD RIVER

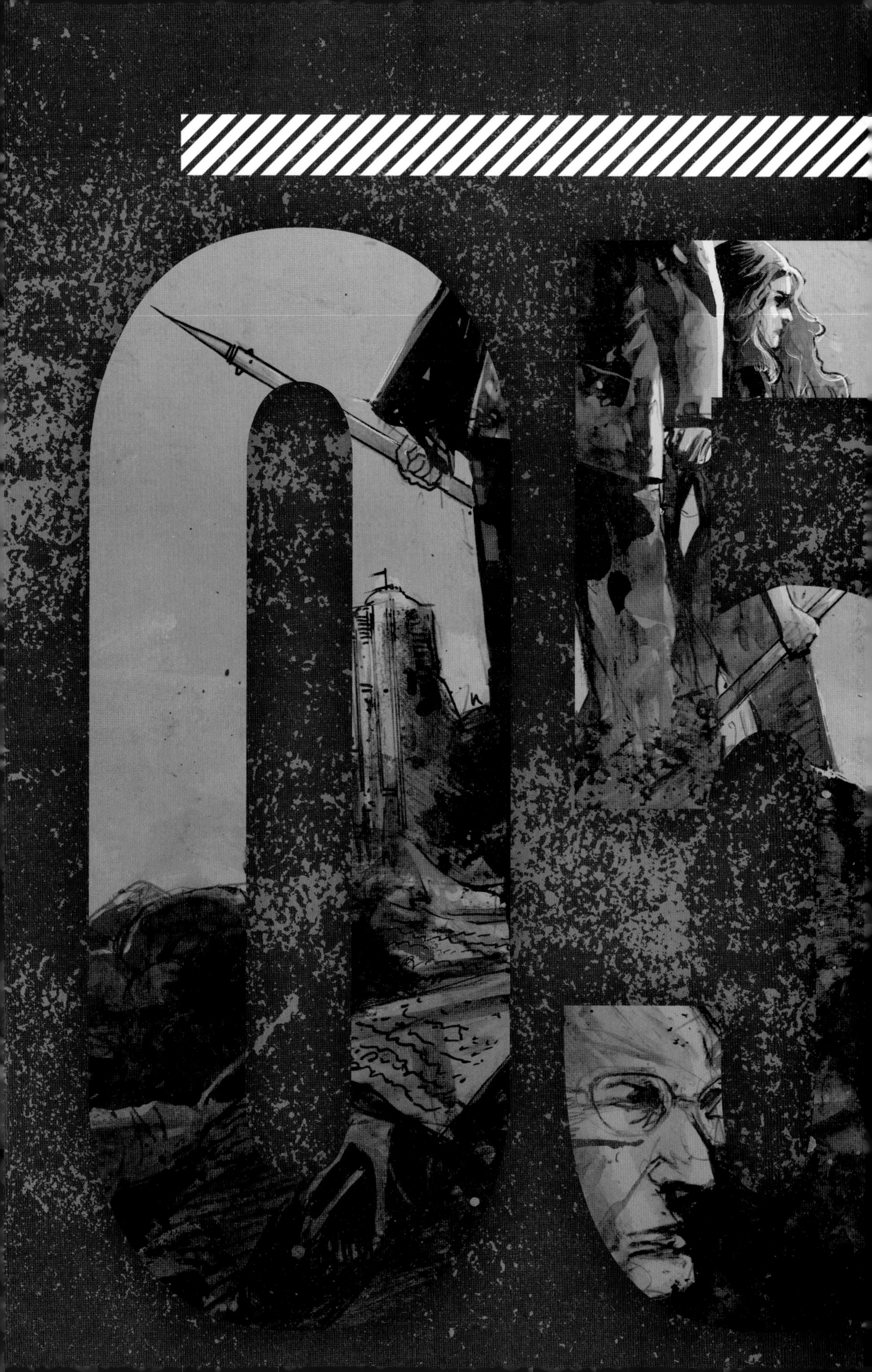

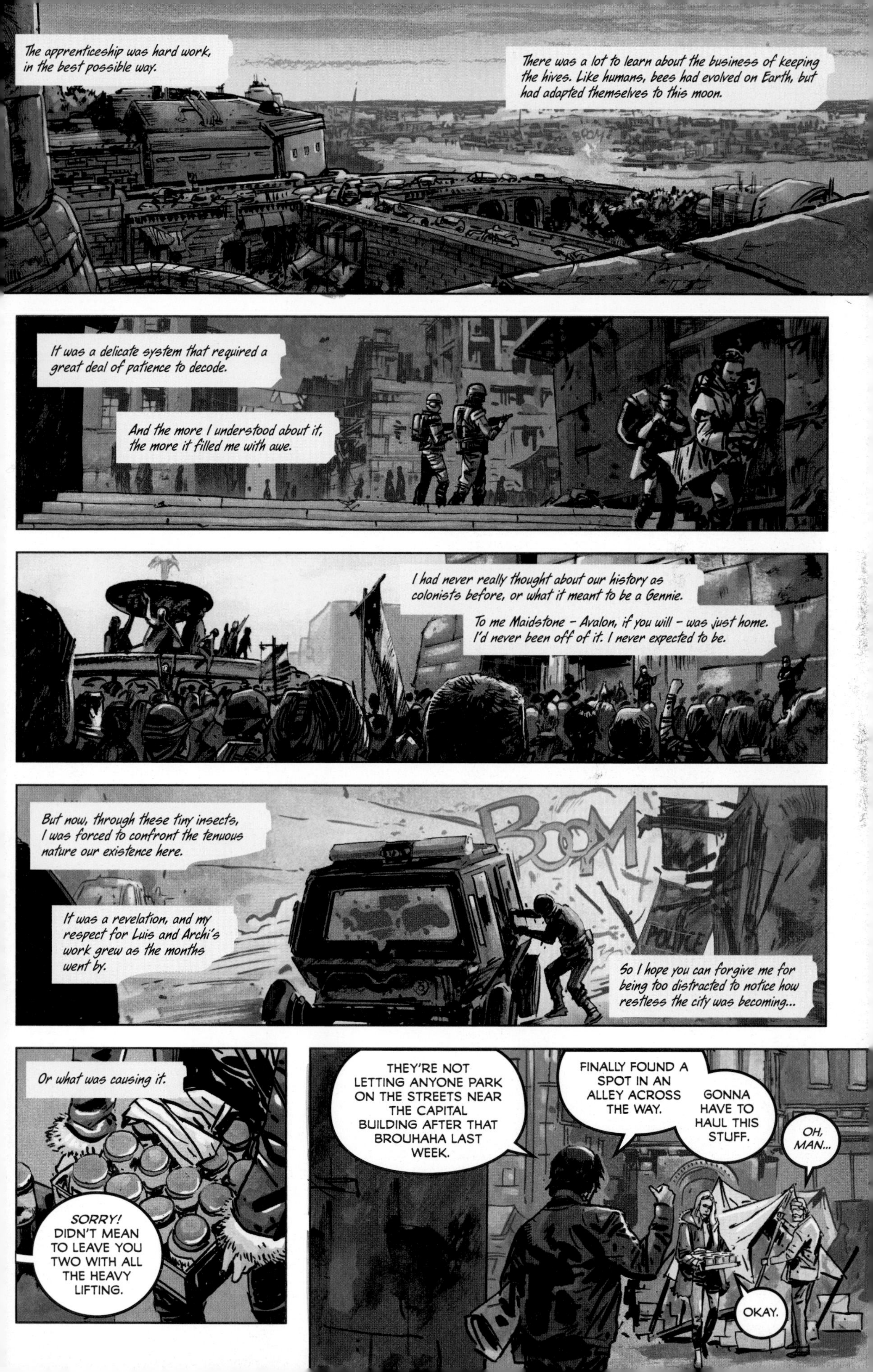
The apprenticeship was hard work, in the best possible way.
There was a lot to learn about the business of keeping the hives. Like humans, bees had evolved on Earth, but had adapted themselves to this moon.
It was a delicate system that required a great deal of patience to decode.
And the more I understood about it, the more it filled me with awe.
I had never really thought about our history as colonists before, or what it meant to be a Gennie.
To me Maidstone – Avalon, if you will – was just home. I'd never been off of it. I never expected to be.
But now, through these tiny insects, I was forced to confront the tenuous nature our existence here.
BOOM
It was a revelation, and my respect for Luis and Archi's work grew as the months went by.
POLICE
So I hope you can forgive me for being too distracted to notice how restless the city was becoming...
Or what was causing it.
SORRY! DIDN'T MEAN TO LEAVE YOU TWO WITH ALL THE HEAVY LIFTING.
THEY'RE NOT LETTING ANYONE PARK ON THE STREETS NEAR THE CAPITAL BUILDING AFTER THAT BROUHAHA LAST WEEK.
FINALLY FOUND A SPOT IN AN ALLEY ACROSS THE WAY.
GONNA HAVE TO HAUL THIS STUFF.
OH, MAN...
OKAY.

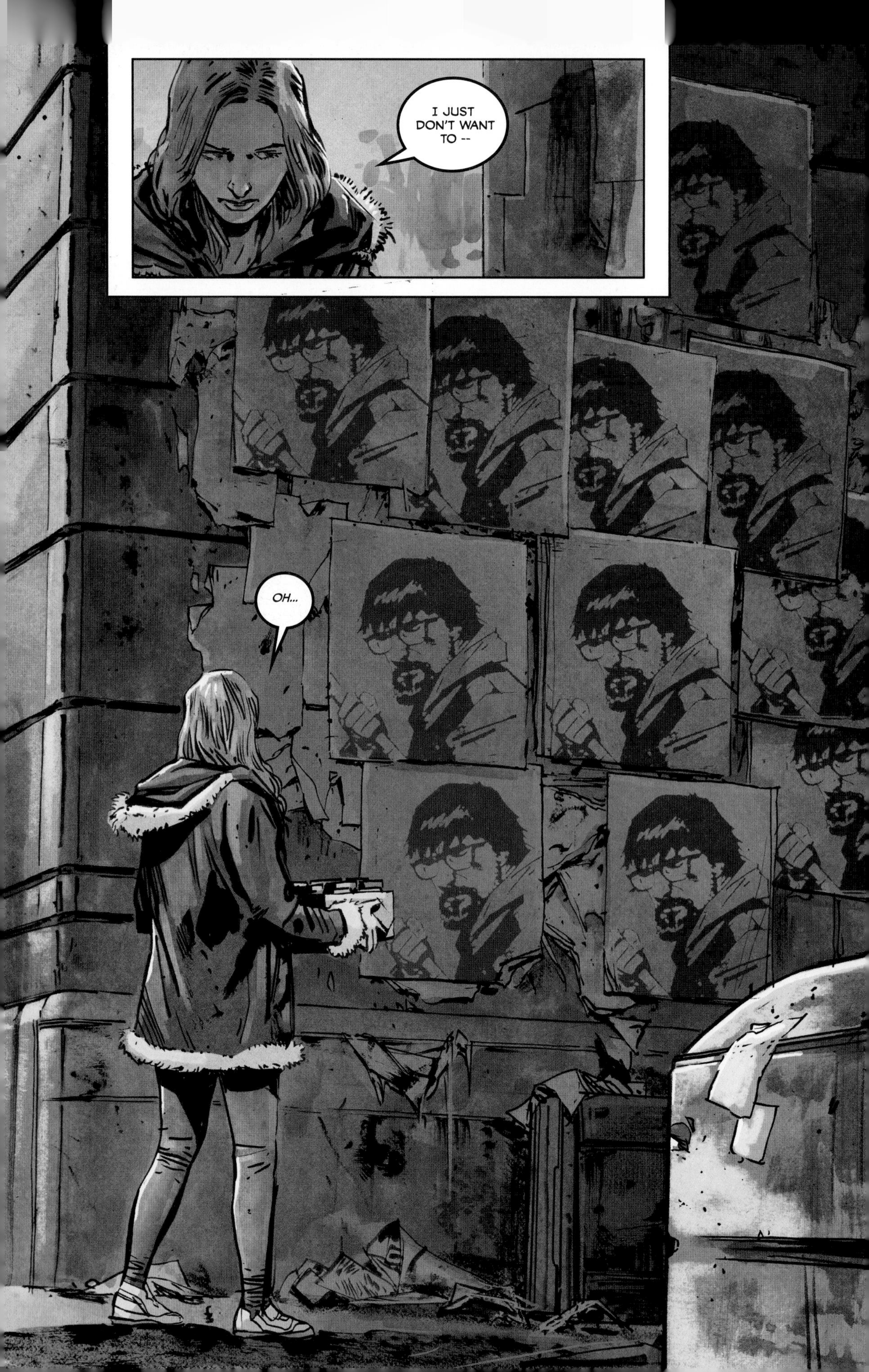
I JUST DON'T WANT TO --
OH...

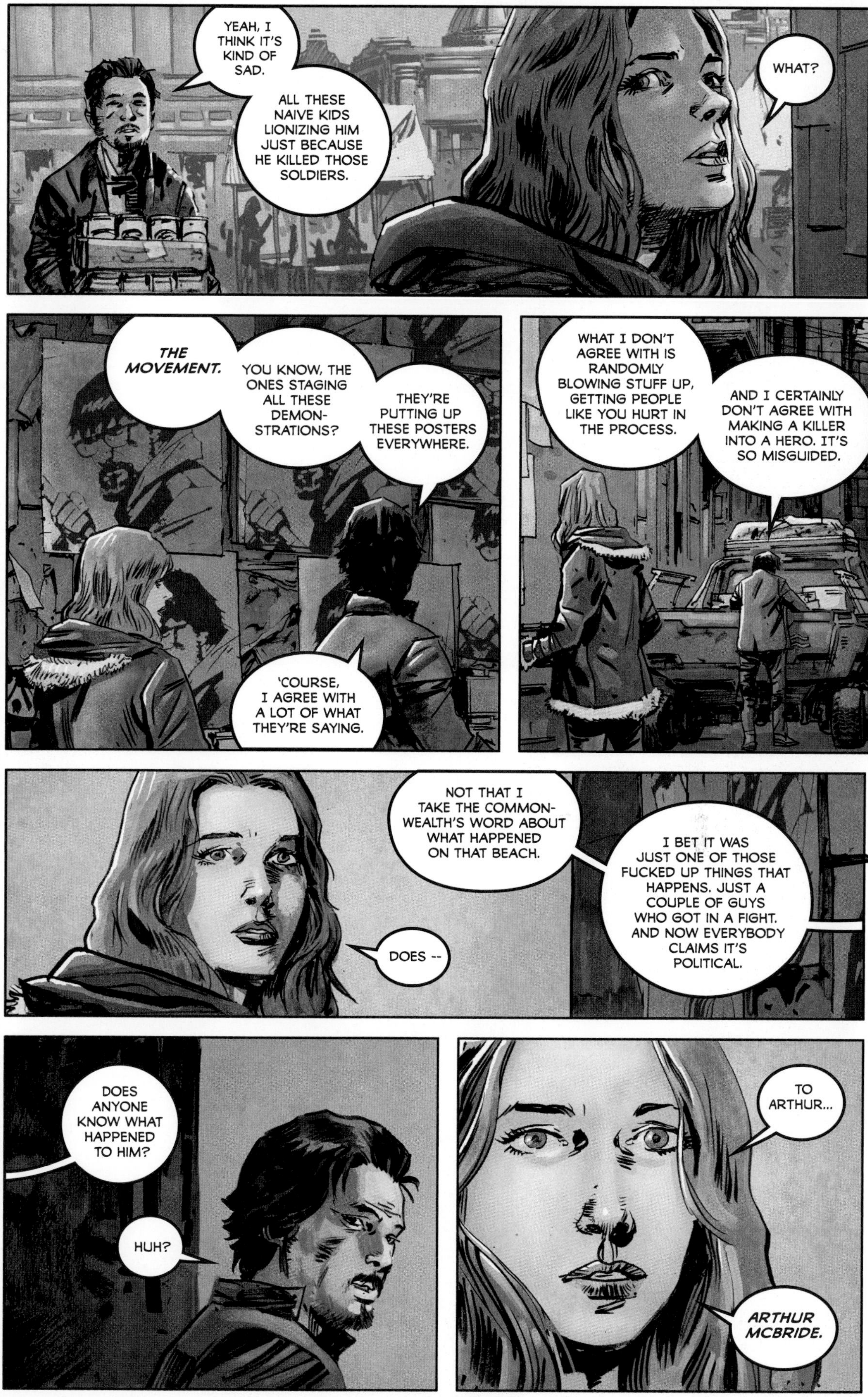
YEAH, I THINK IT'S KIND OF SAD.
ALL THESE NAIVE KIDS LIONIZING HIM JUST BECAUSE HE KILLED THOSE SOLDIERS.
WHAT?
THE MOVEMENT.
YOU KNOW, THE ONES STAGING ALL THESE DEMON-STRATIONS?
THEY'RE PUTTING UP THESE POSTERS EVERYWHERE.
'COURSE, I AGREE WITH A LOT OF WHAT THEY'RE SAYING.
WHAT I DON'T AGREE WITH IS RANDOMLY BLOWING STUFF UP, GETTING PEOPLE LIKE YOU HURT IN THE PROCESS.
AND I CERTAINLY DON'T AGREE WITH MAKING A KILLER INTO A HERO. IT'S SO MISGUIDED.
NOT THAT I TAKE THE COMMON-WEALTH'S WORD ABOUT WHAT HAPPENED ON THAT BEACH.
I BET IT WAS JUST ONE OF THOSE FUCKED UP THINGS THAT HAPPENS. JUST A COUPLE OF GUYS WHO GOT IN A FIGHT. AND NOW EVERYBODY CLAIMS IT'S POLITICAL.
DOES --
DOES ANYONE KNOW WHAT HAPPENED TO HIM?
HUH?
TO ARTHUR...
ARTHUR MCBRIDE.

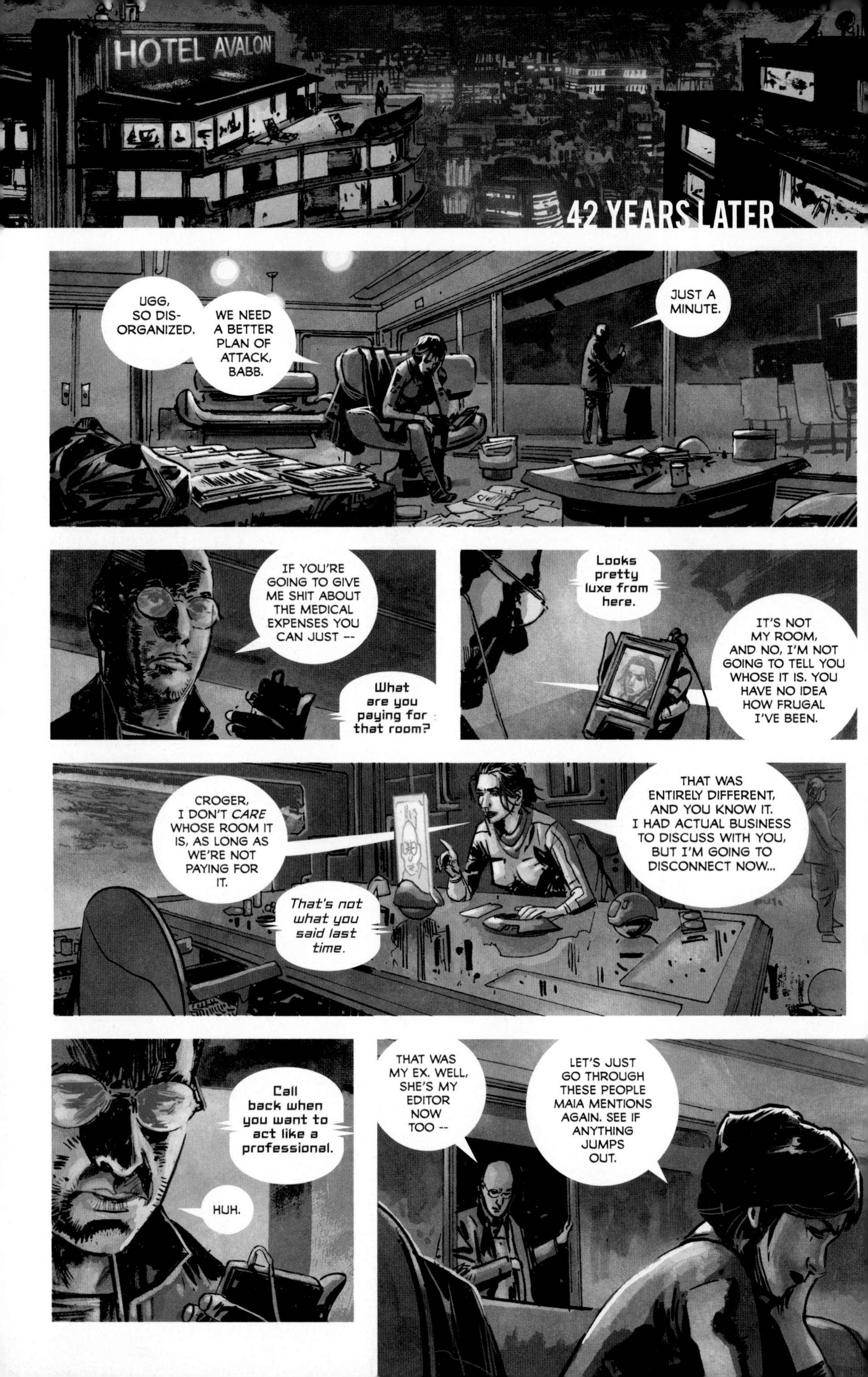
HOTEL AVALON
42 YEARS LATER
UGG, SO DIS-ORGANIZED.
WE NEED A BETTER PLAN OF ATTACK, BABB.
JUST A MINUTE.
IF YOU'RE GOING TO GIVE ME SHIT ABOUT THE MEDICAL EXPENSES YOU CAN JUST --
What are you paying for that room?
Looks pretty luxe from here.
IT'S NOT MY ROOM, AND NO, I'M NOT GOING TO TELL YOU WHOSE IT IS. YOU HAVE NO IDEA HOW FRUGAL I'VE BEEN.
CROGER, I DON'T *CARE* WHOSE ROOM IT IS, AS LONG AS WE'RE NOT PAYING FOR IT.
That's not what you said last time.
THAT WAS ENTIRELY DIFFERENT, AND YOU KNOW IT. I HAD ACTUAL BUSINESS TO DISCUSS WITH YOU, BUT I'M GOING TO DISCONNECT NOW...
Call back when you want to act like a professional.
HUH.
THAT WAS MY EX. WELL, SHE'S MY EDITOR NOW TOO --
LET'S JUST GO THROUGH THESE PEOPLE MAIA MENTIONS AGAIN. SEE IF ANYTHING JUMPS OUT.

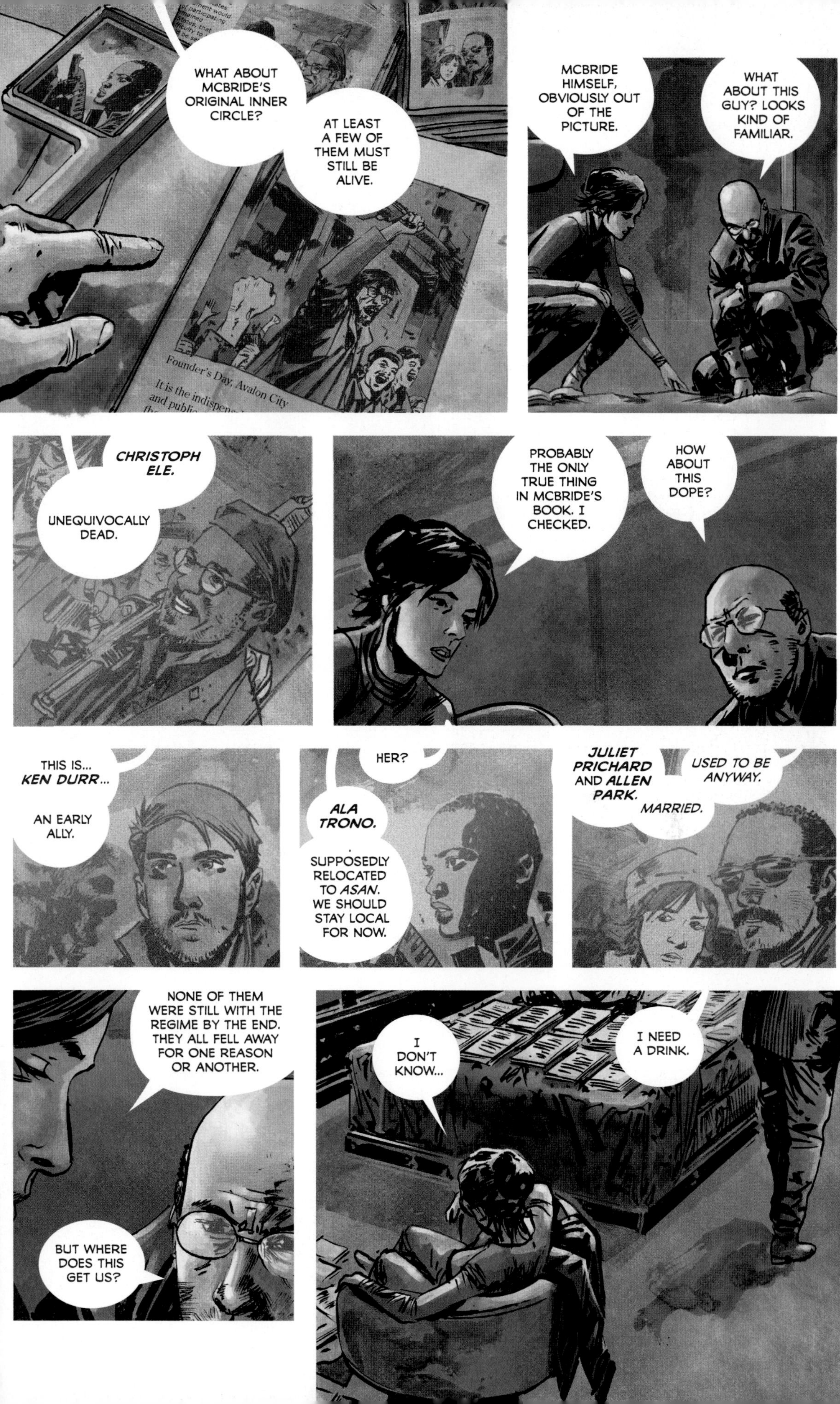
WHAT ABOUT MCBRIDE'S ORIGINAL INNER CIRCLE?
AT LEAST A FEW OF THEM MUST STILL BE ALIVE.
Founder's Day, Avalon City
MCBRIDE HIMSELF, OBVIOUSLY OUT OF THE PICTURE.
WHAT ABOUT THIS GUY? LOOKS KIND OF FAMILIAR.
CHRISTOPH ELE.
UNEQUIVOCALLY DEAD.
PROBABLY THE ONLY TRUE THING IN MCBRIDE'S BOOK. I CHECKED.
HOW ABOUT THIS DOPE?
THIS IS... ***KEN DURR***...
AN EARLY ALLY.
HER?
ALA TRONO.
SUPPOSEDLY RELOCATED TO *ASAN*. WE SHOULD STAY LOCAL FOR NOW.
JULIET PRICHARD AND ***ALLEN PARK.***
MARRIED.
USED TO BE ANYWAY.
NONE OF THEM WERE STILL WITH THE REGIME BY THE END. THEY ALL FELL AWAY FOR ONE REASON OR ANOTHER.
BUT WHERE DOES THIS GET US?
I DON'T KNOW...
I NEED A DRINK.

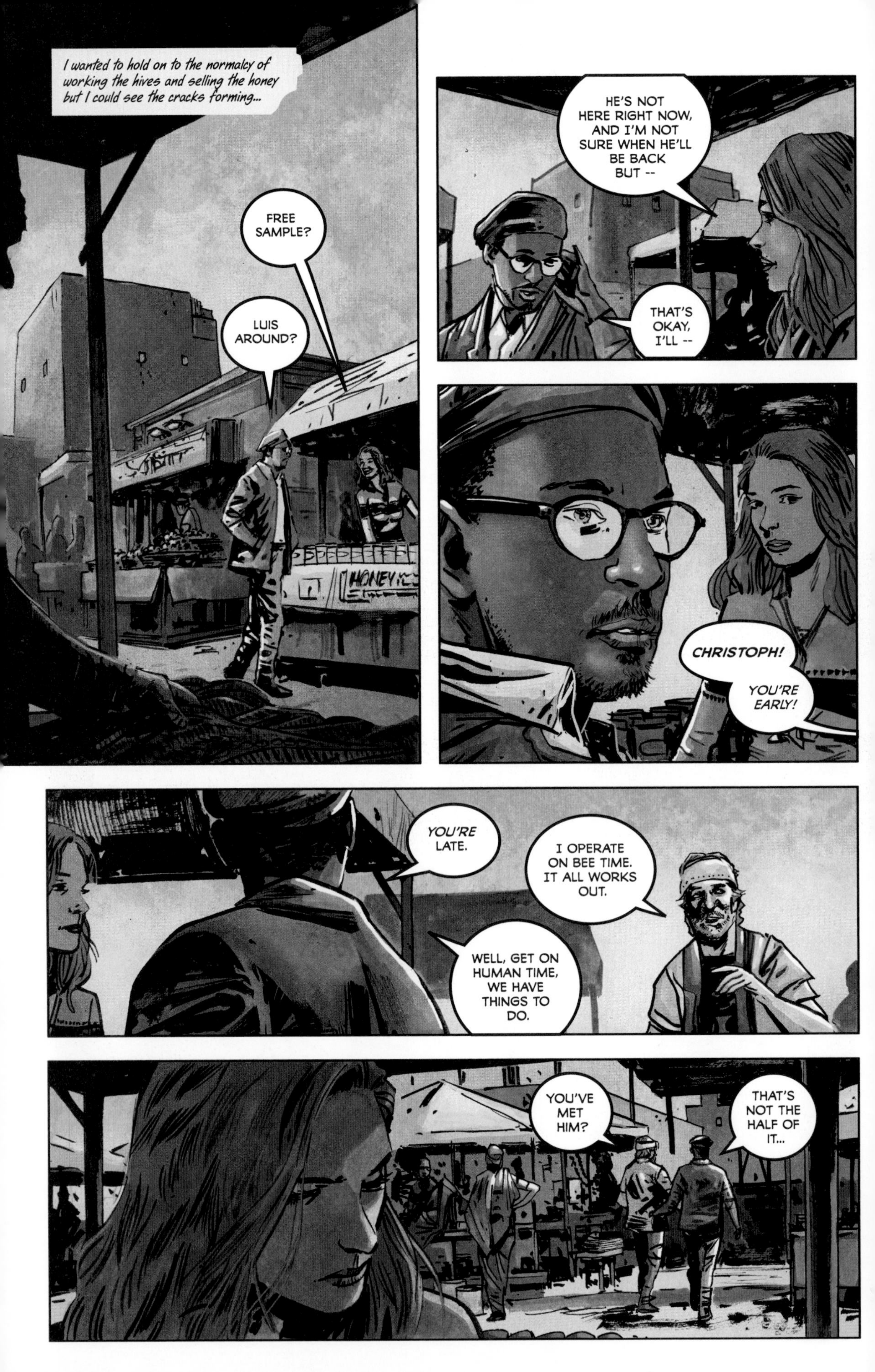
I wanted to hold on to the normalcy of working the hives and selling the honey but I could see the cracks forming...
LUIS AROUND?
FREE SAMPLE?
HONEY
HE'S NOT HERE RIGHT NOW, AND I'M NOT SURE WHEN HE'LL BE BACK BUT --
THAT'S OKAY, I'LL --
CHRISTOPH!
YOU'RE EARLY!
YOU'RE LATE.
I OPERATE ON BEE TIME. IT ALL WORKS OUT.
WELL, GET ON HUMAN TIME, WE HAVE THINGS TO DO.
YOU'VE MET HIM?
THAT'S NOT THE HALF OF IT...

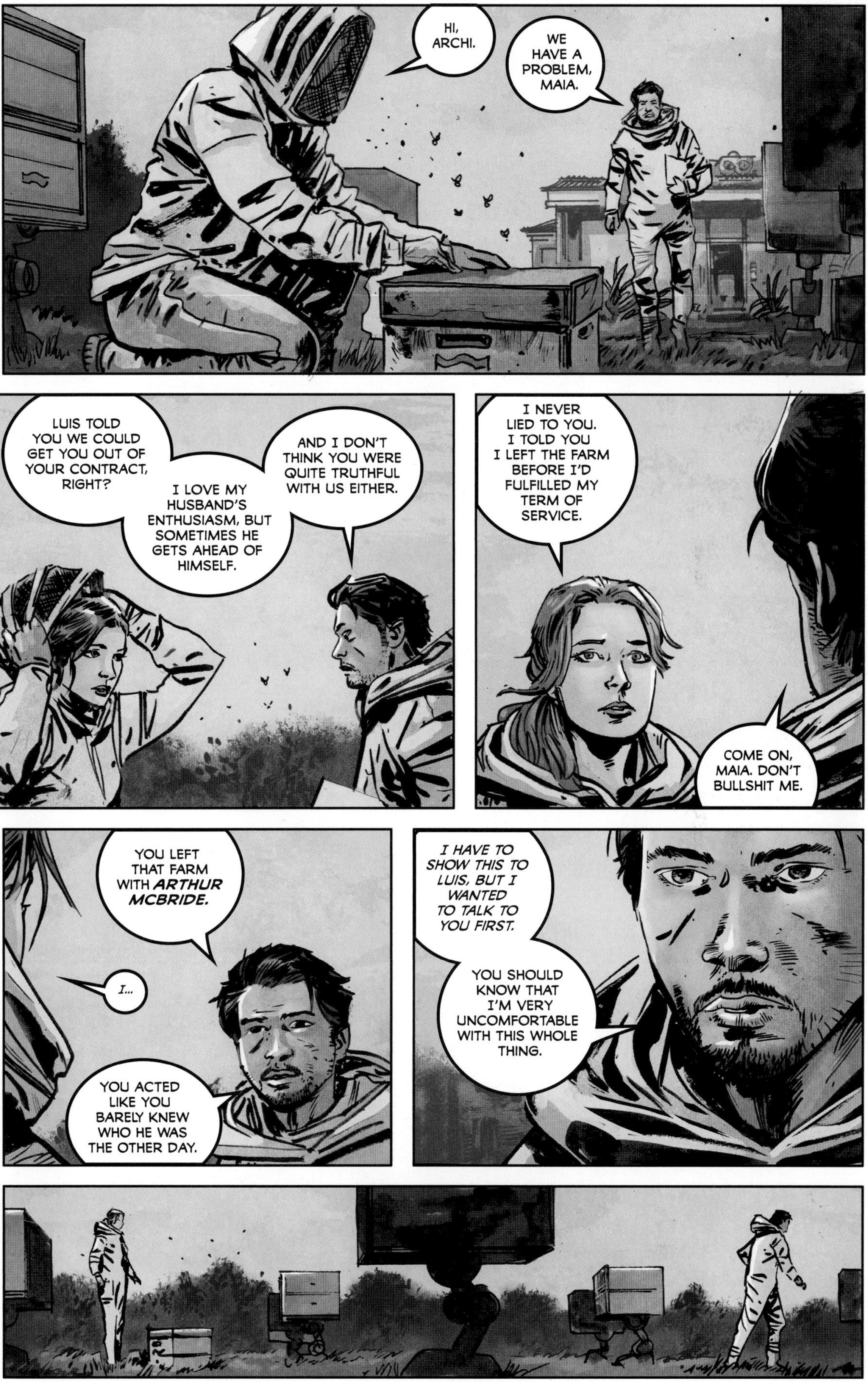
HI, ARCHI.
WE HAVE A PROBLEM, MAIA.
LUIS TOLD YOU WE COULD GET YOU OUT OF YOUR CONTRACT, RIGHT?
I LOVE MY HUSBAND'S ENTHUSIASM, BUT SOMETIMES HE GETS AHEAD OF HIMSELF.
AND I DON'T THINK YOU WERE QUITE TRUTHFUL WITH US EITHER.
I NEVER LIED TO YOU. I TOLD YOU I LEFT THE FARM BEFORE I'D FULFILLED MY TERM OF SERVICE.
COME ON, MAIA. DON'T BULLSHIT ME.
YOU LEFT THAT FARM WITH *ARTHUR MCBRIDE.*
I...
YOU ACTED LIKE YOU BARELY KNEW WHO HE WAS THE OTHER DAY.
I HAVE TO SHOW THIS TO LUIS, BUT I WANTED TO TALK TO YOU FIRST.
YOU SHOULD KNOW THAT I'M VERY UNCOMFORTABLE WITH THIS WHOLE THING.

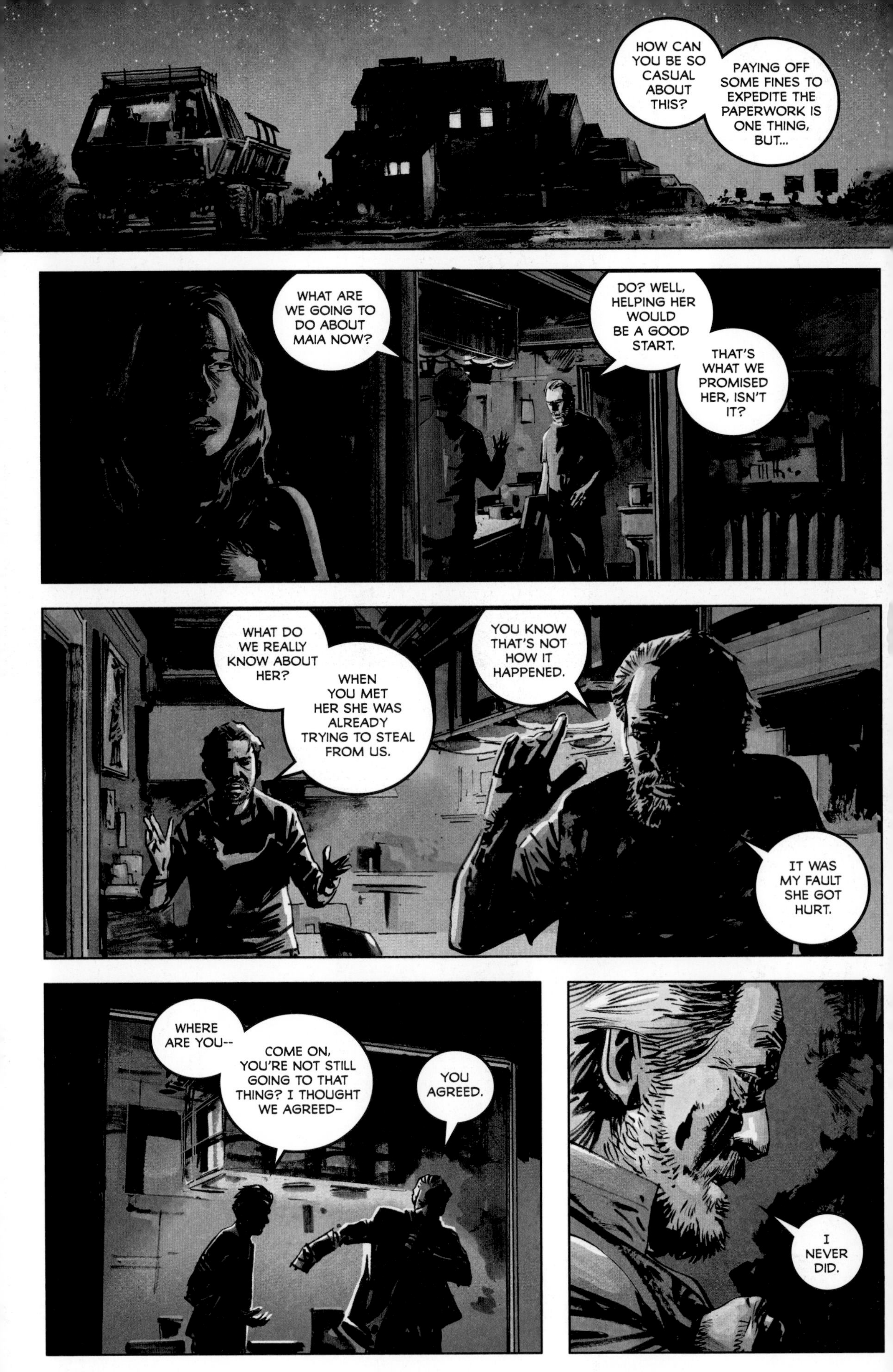
HOW CAN YOU BE SO CASUAL ABOUT THIS?
PAYING OFF SOME FINES TO EXPEDITE THE PAPERWORK IS ONE THING, BUT...
WHAT ARE WE GOING TO DO ABOUT MAIA NOW?
DO? WELL, HELPING HER WOULD BE A GOOD START.
THAT'S WHAT WE PROMISED HER, ISN'T IT?
WHAT DO WE REALLY KNOW ABOUT HER?
WHEN YOU MET HER SHE WAS ALREADY TRYING TO STEAL FROM US.
YOU KNOW THAT'S NOT HOW IT HAPPENED.
IT WAS MY FAULT SHE GOT HURT.
WHERE ARE YOU--
COME ON, YOU'RE NOT STILL GOING TO THAT THING? I THOUGHT WE AGREED–
YOU AGREED.
I NEVER DID.

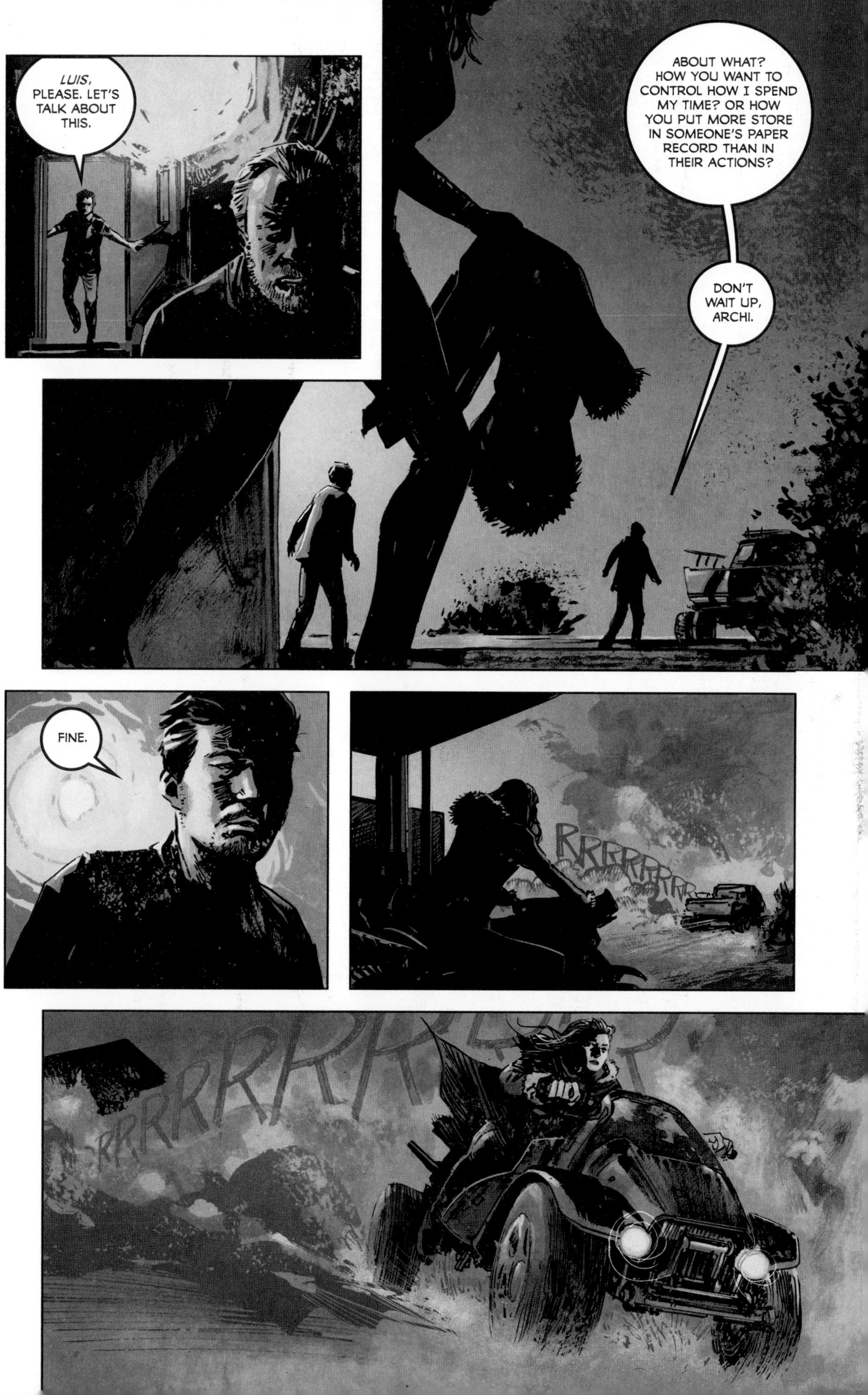
LUIS, PLEASE. LET'S TALK ABOUT THIS.
ABOUT WHAT? HOW YOU WANT TO CONTROL HOW I SPEND MY TIME? OR HOW YOU PUT MORE STORE IN SOMEONE'S PAPER RECORD THAN IN THEIR ACTIONS?
DON'T WAIT UP, ARCHI.
FINE.

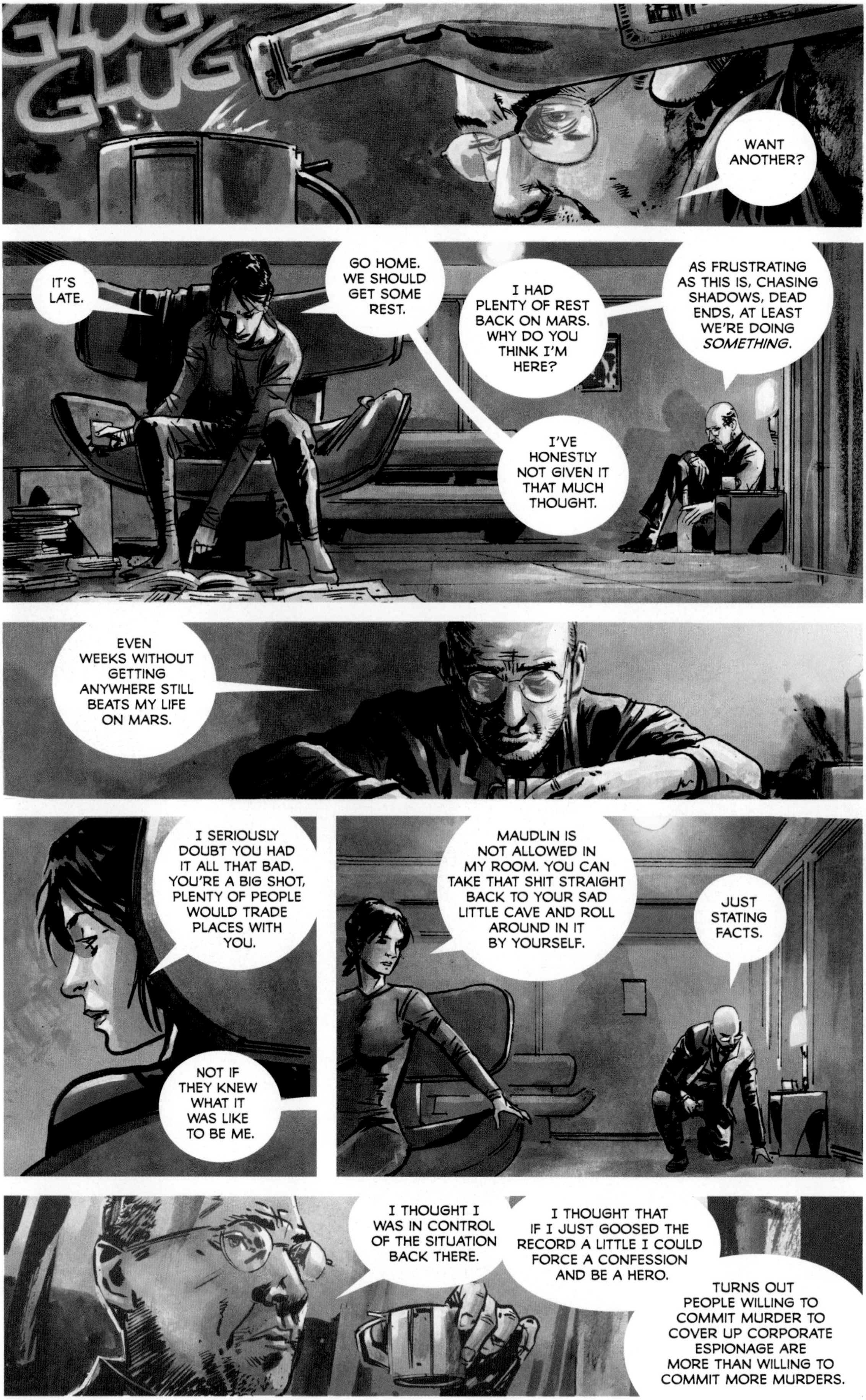
GLUG GLUG
WANT ANOTHER?
IT'S LATE.
GO HOME. WE SHOULD GET SOME REST.
I HAD PLENTY OF REST BACK ON MARS. WHY DO YOU THINK I'M HERE?
AS FRUSTRATING AS THIS IS, CHASING SHADOWS, DEAD ENDS, AT LEAST WE'RE DOING *SOMETHING*.
I'VE HONESTLY NOT GIVEN IT THAT MUCH THOUGHT.
EVEN WEEKS WITHOUT GETTING ANYWHERE STILL BEATS MY LIFE ON MARS.
I SERIOUSLY DOUBT YOU HAD IT ALL THAT BAD. YOU'RE A BIG SHOT, PLENTY OF PEOPLE WOULD TRADE PLACES WITH YOU.
NOT IF THEY KNEW WHAT IT WAS LIKE TO BE ME.
MAUDLIN IS NOT ALLOWED IN MY ROOM. YOU CAN TAKE THAT SHIT STRAIGHT BACK TO YOUR SAD LITTLE CAVE AND ROLL AROUND IN IT BY YOURSELF.
JUST STATING FACTS.
I THOUGHT I WAS IN CONTROL OF THE SITUATION BACK THERE.
I THOUGHT THAT IF I JUST GOOSED THE RECORD A LITTLE I COULD FORCE A CONFESSION AND BE A HERO.
TURNS OUT PEOPLE WILLING TO COMMIT MURDER TO COVER UP CORPORATE ESPIONAGE ARE MORE THAN WILLING TO COMMIT MORE MURDERS.

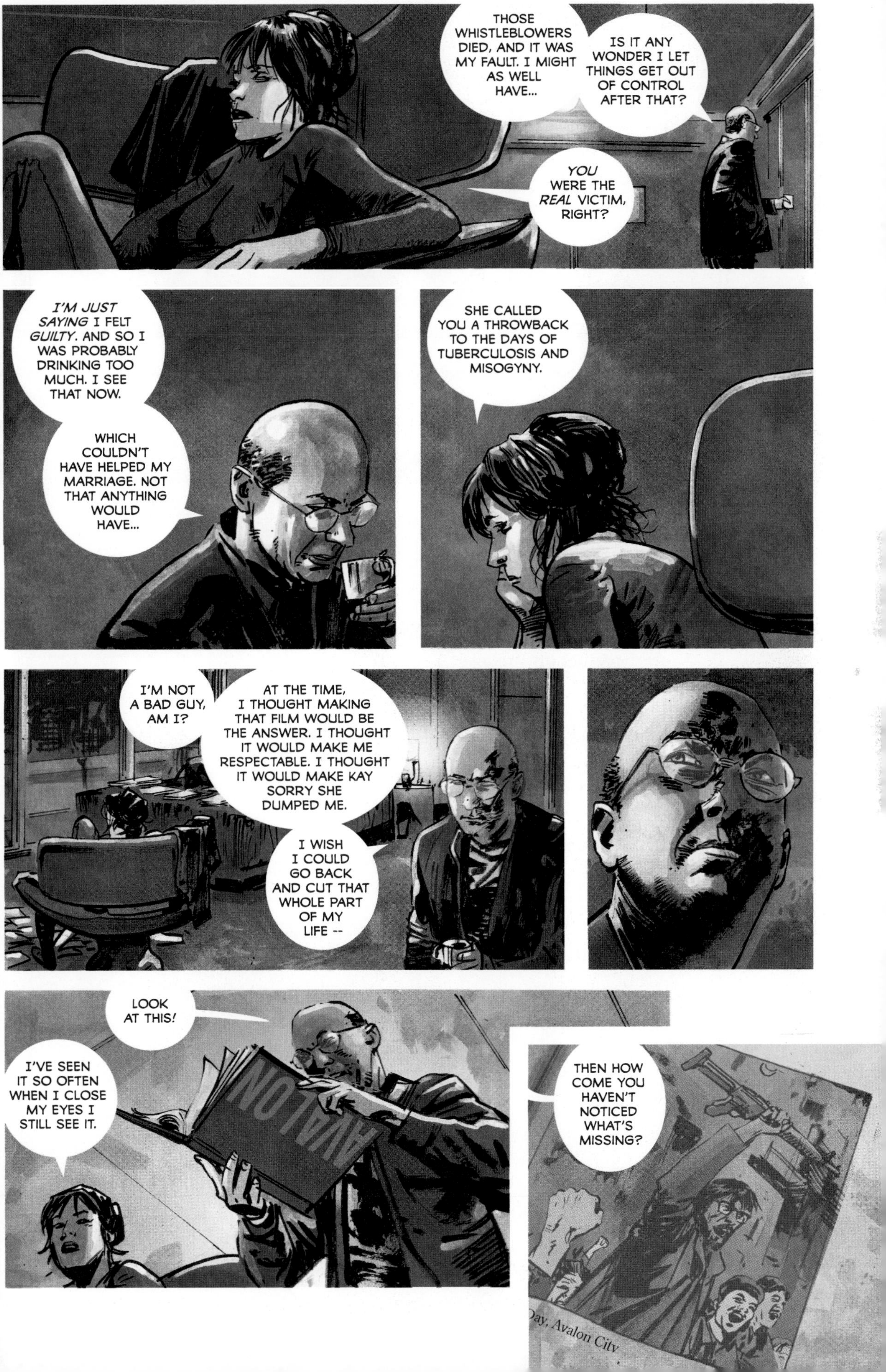
THOSE WHISTLEBLOWERS DIED, AND IT WAS MY FAULT. I MIGHT AS WELL HAVE...
IS IT ANY WONDER I LET THINGS GET OUT OF CONTROL AFTER THAT?
YOU WERE THE *REAL* VICTIM, RIGHT?
I'M JUST SAYING I FELT *GUILTY*. AND SO I WAS PROBABLY DRINKING TOO MUCH. I SEE THAT NOW.
WHICH COULDN'T HAVE HELPED MY MARRIAGE. NOT THAT ANYTHING WOULD HAVE...
SHE CALLED YOU A THROWBACK TO THE DAYS OF TUBERCULOSIS AND MISOGYNY.
I'M NOT A BAD GUY, AM I?
AT THE TIME, I THOUGHT MAKING THAT FILM WOULD BE THE ANSWER. I THOUGHT IT WOULD MAKE ME RESPECTABLE. I THOUGHT IT WOULD MAKE KAY SORRY SHE DUMPED ME.
I WISH I COULD GO BACK AND CUT THAT WHOLE PART OF MY LIFE --
LOOK AT THIS!
AVALON
I'VE SEEN IT SO OFTEN WHEN I CLOSE MY EYES I STILL SEE IT.
THEN HOW COME YOU HAVEN'T NOTICED WHAT'S MISSING?
Day, Avalon City

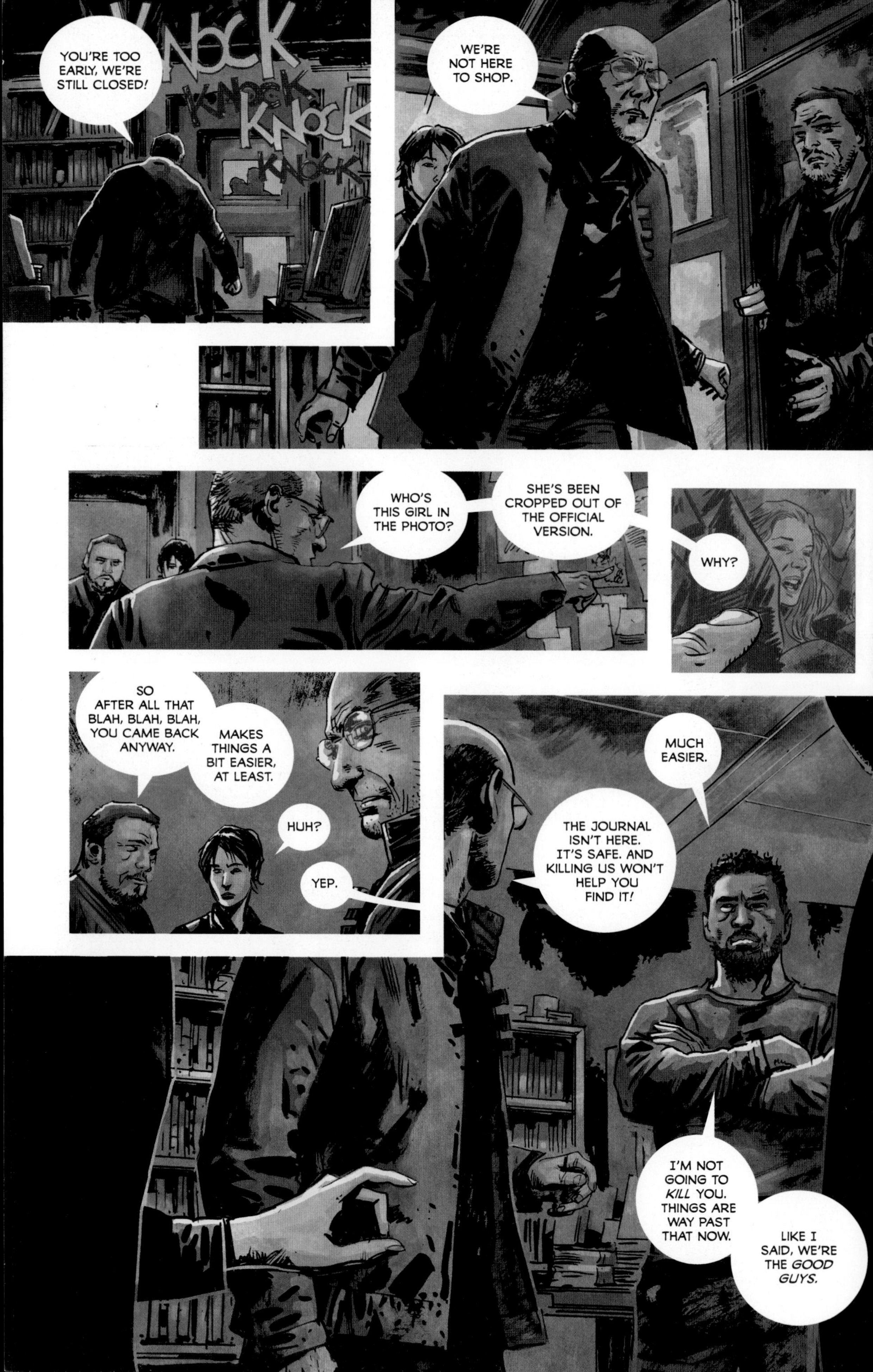
KNOCK
YOU'RE TOO EARLY, WE'RE STILL CLOSED!
KNOCK
KNOCK
KNOCK
WE'RE NOT HERE TO SHOP.
WHO'S THIS GIRL IN THE PHOTO?
SHE'S BEEN CROPPED OUT OF THE OFFICIAL VERSION.
WHY?
SO AFTER ALL THAT BLAH, BLAH, BLAH, YOU CAME BACK ANYWAY.
MAKES THINGS A BIT EASIER, AT LEAST.
HUH?
YEP.
MUCH EASIER.
THE JOURNAL ISN'T HERE. IT'S SAFE. AND KILLING US WON'T HELP YOU FIND IT!
I'M NOT GOING TO *KILL* YOU. THINGS ARE WAY PAST THAT NOW.
LIKE I SAID, WE'RE THE *GOOD GUYS.*

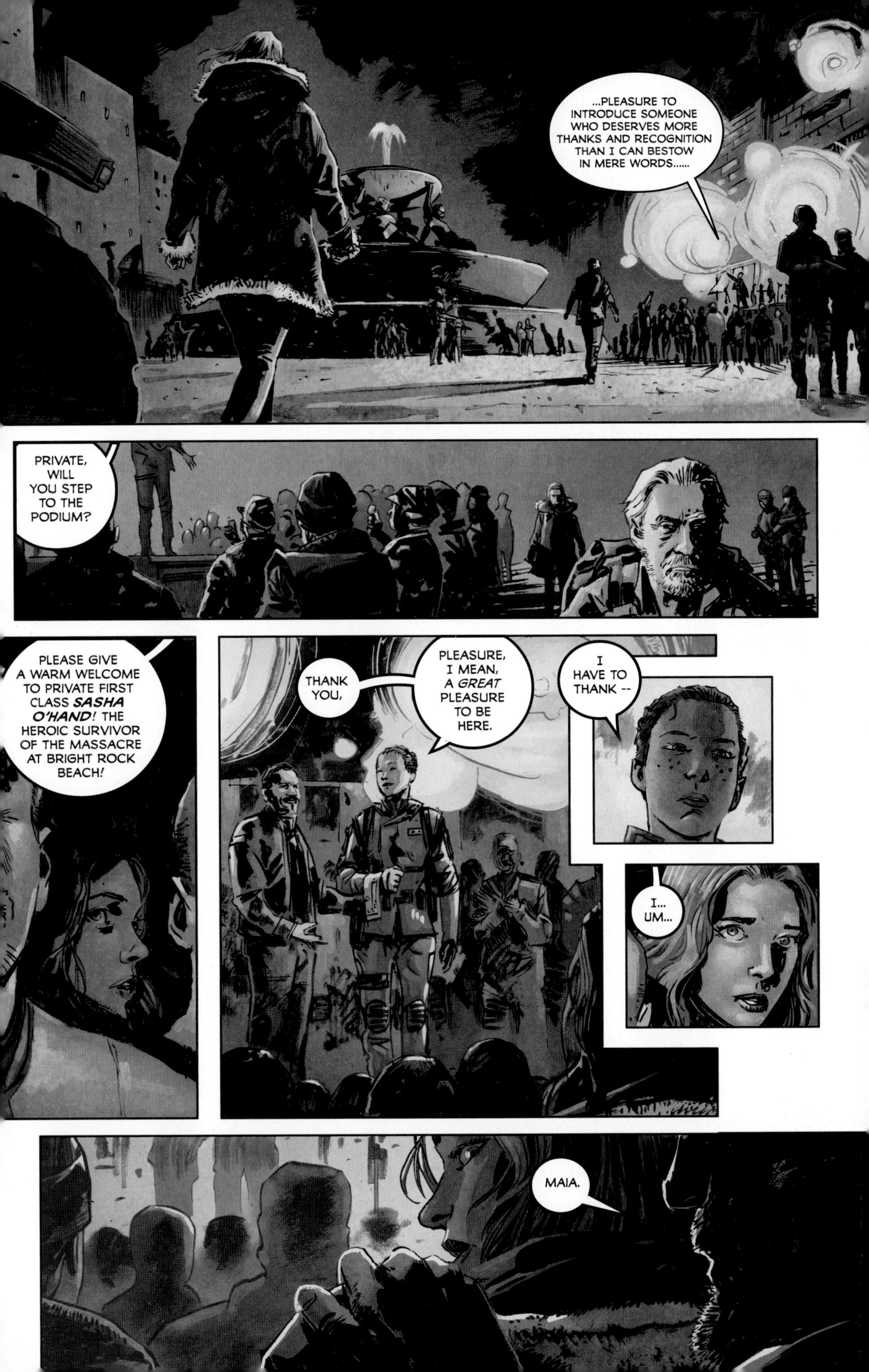
...PLEASURE TO INTRODUCE SOMEONE WHO DESERVES MORE THANKS AND RECOGNITION THAN I CAN BESTOW IN MERE WORDS......
PRIVATE, WILL YOU STEP TO THE PODIUM?
PLEASE GIVE A WARM WELCOME TO PRIVATE FIRST CLASS ***SASHA O'HAND!*** THE HEROIC SURVIVOR OF THE MASSACRE AT BRIGHT ROCK BEACH!
THANK YOU,
PLEASURE, I MEAN, A *GREAT* PLEASURE TO BE HERE.
I HAVE TO THANK --
I... UM...
MAIA.

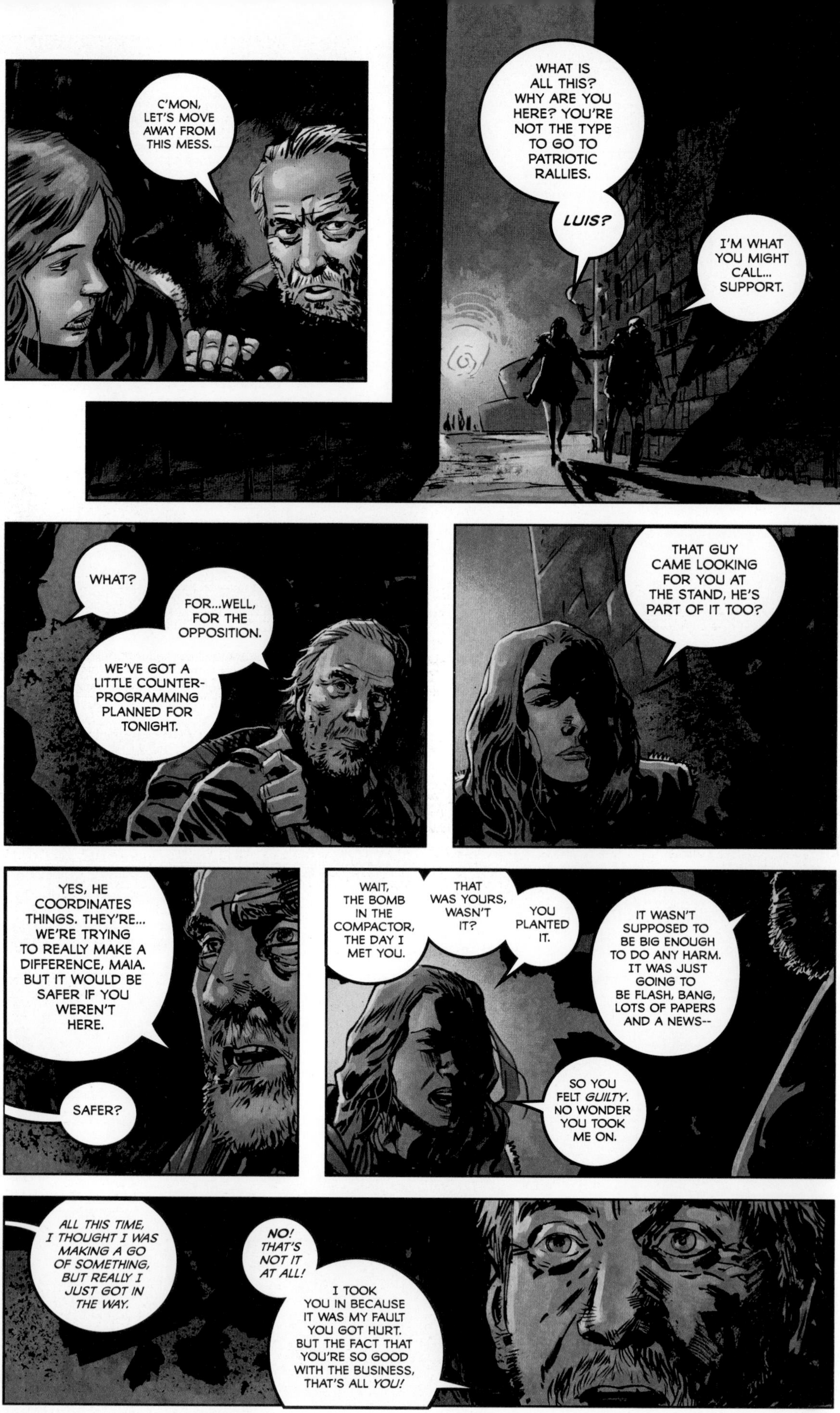
C'MON, LET'S MOVE AWAY FROM THIS MESS.
WHAT IS ALL THIS? WHY ARE YOU HERE? YOU'RE NOT THE TYPE TO GO TO PATRIOTIC RALLIES.
LUIS?
I'M WHAT YOU MIGHT CALL... SUPPORT.
WHAT?
FOR...WELL, FOR THE OPPOSITION.
WE'VE GOT A LITTLE COUNTER-PROGRAMMING PLANNED FOR TONIGHT.
THAT GUY CAME LOOKING FOR YOU AT THE STAND, HE'S PART OF IT TOO?
YES, HE COORDINATES THINGS. THEY'RE... WE'RE TRYING TO REALLY MAKE A DIFFERENCE, MAIA. BUT IT WOULD BE SAFER IF YOU WEREN'T HERE.
SAFER?
WAIT, THE BOMB IN THE COMPACTOR, THE DAY I MET YOU.
THAT WAS YOURS, WASN'T IT?
YOU PLANTED IT.
IT WASN'T SUPPOSED TO BE BIG ENOUGH TO DO ANY HARM. IT WAS JUST GOING TO BE FLASH, BANG, LOTS OF PAPERS AND A NEWS--
SO YOU FELT *GUILTY*. NO WONDER YOU TOOK ME ON.
ALL THIS TIME, I THOUGHT I WAS MAKING A GO OF SOMETHING, BUT REALLY I JUST GOT IN THE WAY.
NO! *THAT'S NOT IT AT ALL!*
I TOOK YOU IN BECAUSE IT WAS MY FAULT YOU GOT HURT. BUT THE FACT THAT YOU'RE SO GOOD WITH THE BUSINESS, THAT'S ALL *YOU!*

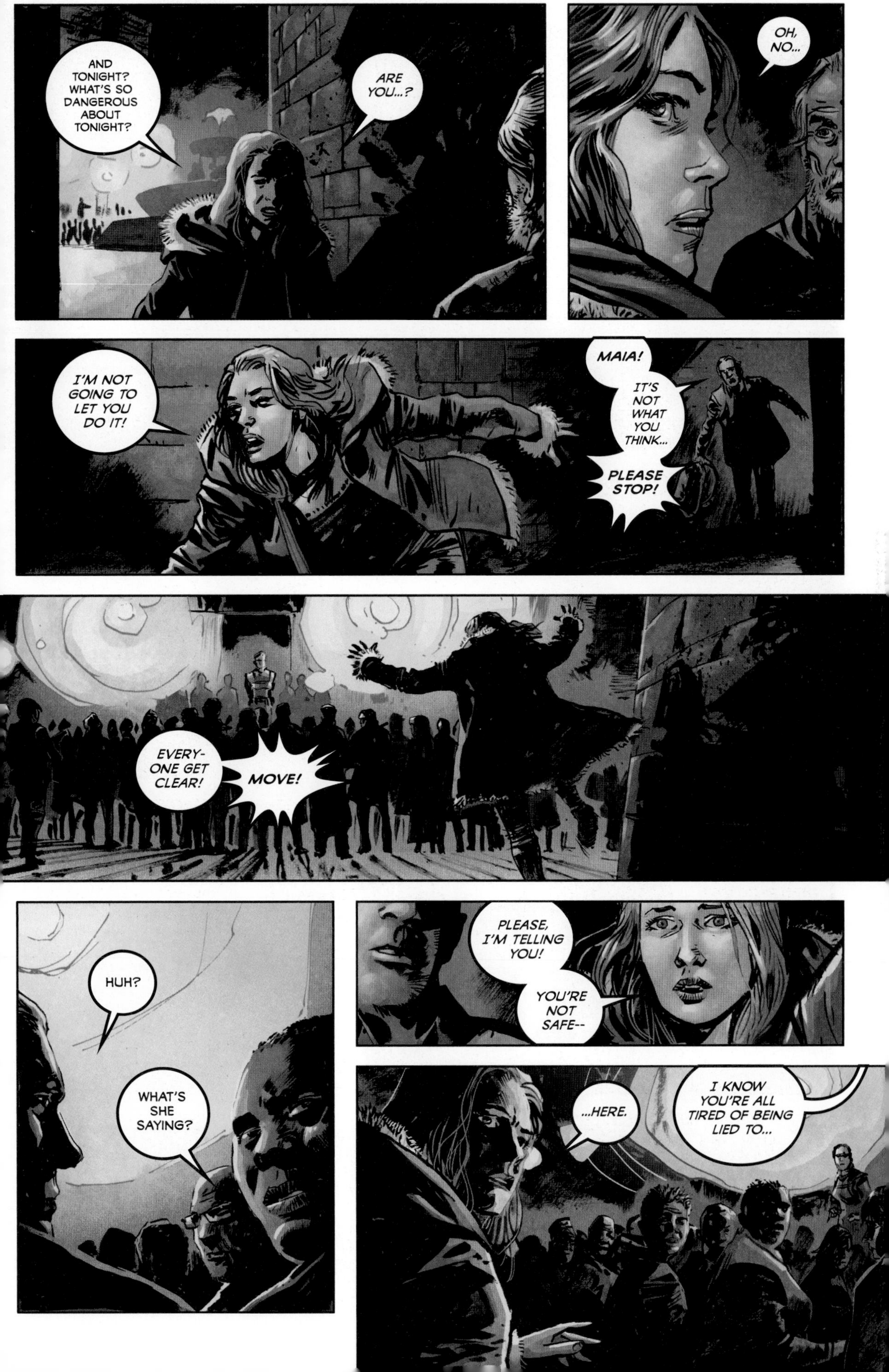
AND TONIGHT? WHAT'S SO DANGEROUS ABOUT TONIGHT?
ARE YOU...?
OH, NO...
I'M NOT GOING TO LET YOU DO IT!
MAIA!
IT'S NOT WHAT YOU THINK...
PLEASE STOP!
EVERY-ONE GET CLEAR!
MOVE!
HUH?
WHAT'S SHE SAYING?
PLEASE, I'M TELLING YOU!
YOU'RE NOT SAFE--
...HERE.
I KNOW YOU'RE ALL TIRED OF BEING LIED TO...

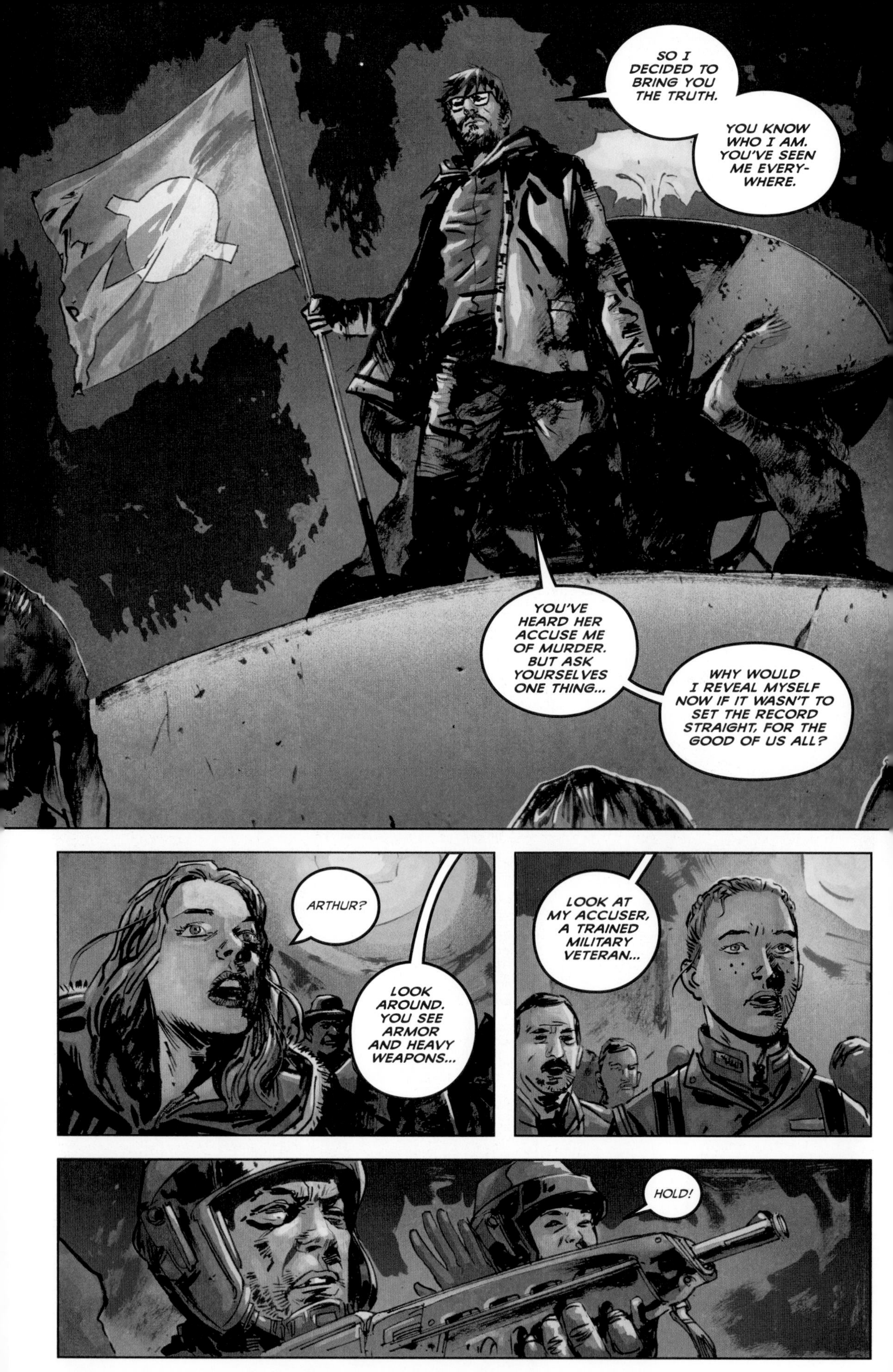
SO I DECIDED TO BRING YOU THE TRUTH.
YOU KNOW WHO I AM. YOU'VE SEEN ME EVERY-WHERE.
YOU'VE HEARD HER ACCUSE ME OF MURDER. BUT ASK YOURSELVES ONE THING...
WHY WOULD I REVEAL MYSELF NOW IF IT WASN'T TO SET THE RECORD STRAIGHT, FOR THE GOOD OF US ALL?
ARTHUR?
LOOK AROUND. YOU SEE ARMOR AND HEAVY WEAPONS...
LOOK AT MY ACCUSER, A TRAINED MILITARY VETERAN...
HOLD!

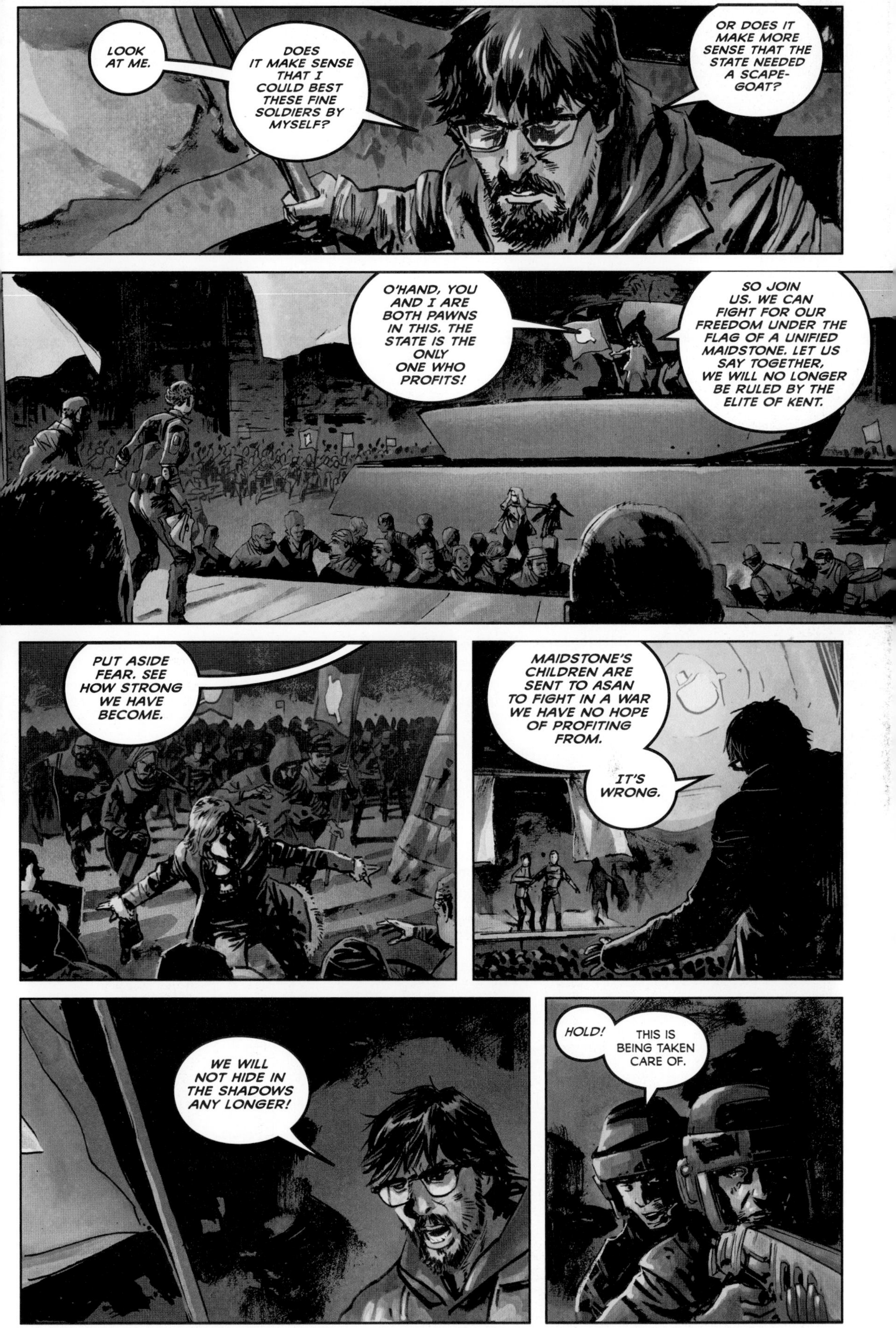
LOOK AT ME.
DOES IT MAKE SENSE THAT I COULD BEST THESE FINE SOLDIERS BY MYSELF?
OR DOES IT MAKE MORE SENSE THAT THE STATE NEEDED A SCAPE-GOAT?
O'HAND, YOU AND I ARE BOTH PAWNS IN THIS. THE STATE IS THE ONLY ONE WHO PROFITS!
SO JOIN US. WE CAN FIGHT FOR OUR FREEDOM UNDER THE FLAG OF A UNIFIED MAIDSTONE. LET US SAY TOGETHER, WE WILL NO LONGER BE RULED BY THE ELITE OF KENT.
PUT ASIDE FEAR. SEE HOW STRONG WE HAVE BECOME.
MAIDSTONE'S CHILDREN ARE SENT TO ASAN TO FIGHT IN A WAR WE HAVE NO HOPE OF PROFITING FROM.
IT'S WRONG.
WE WILL NOT HIDE IN THE SHADOWS ANY LONGER!
HOLD!
THIS IS BEING TAKEN CARE OF.

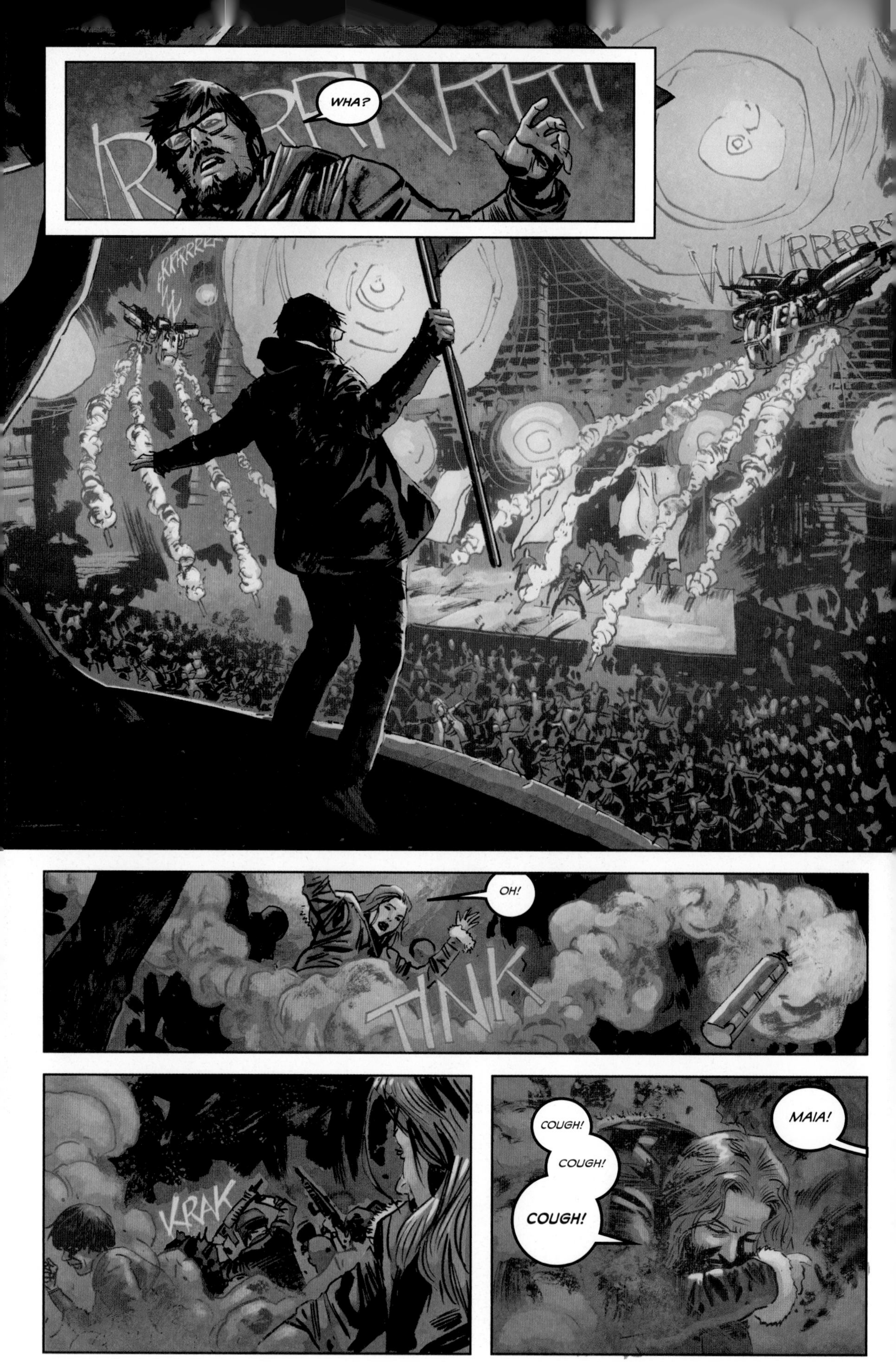
WHA?
OH!
TINK
VRAK
COUGH!
COUGH!
COUGH!
MAIA!

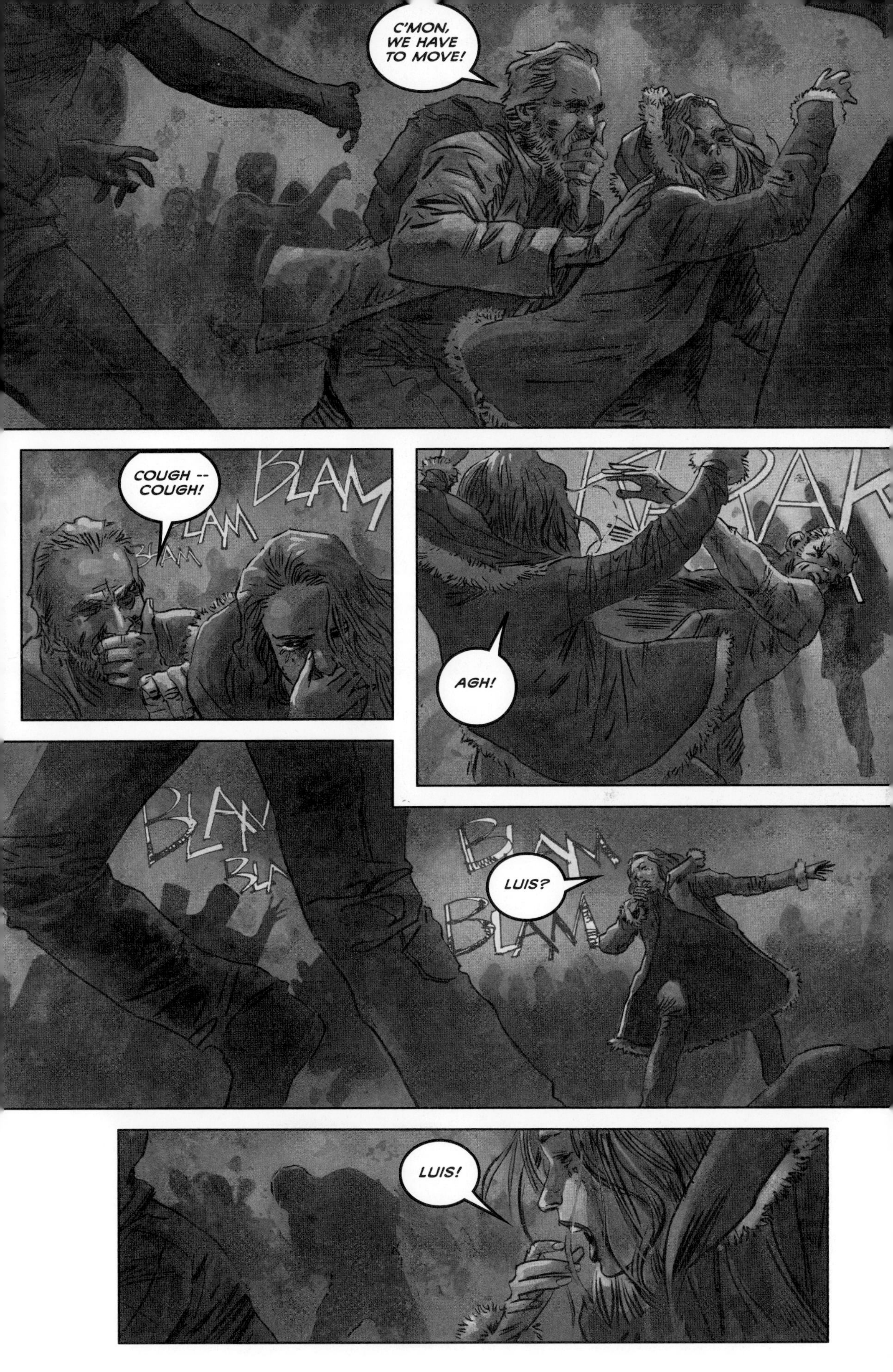
C'MON, WE HAVE TO MOVE!
COUGH -- COUGH!
BLAM
BLAM
BLAM
BRAK
AGH!
BLAM
BLAM
BLAM
LUIS?
BLAM
LUIS!

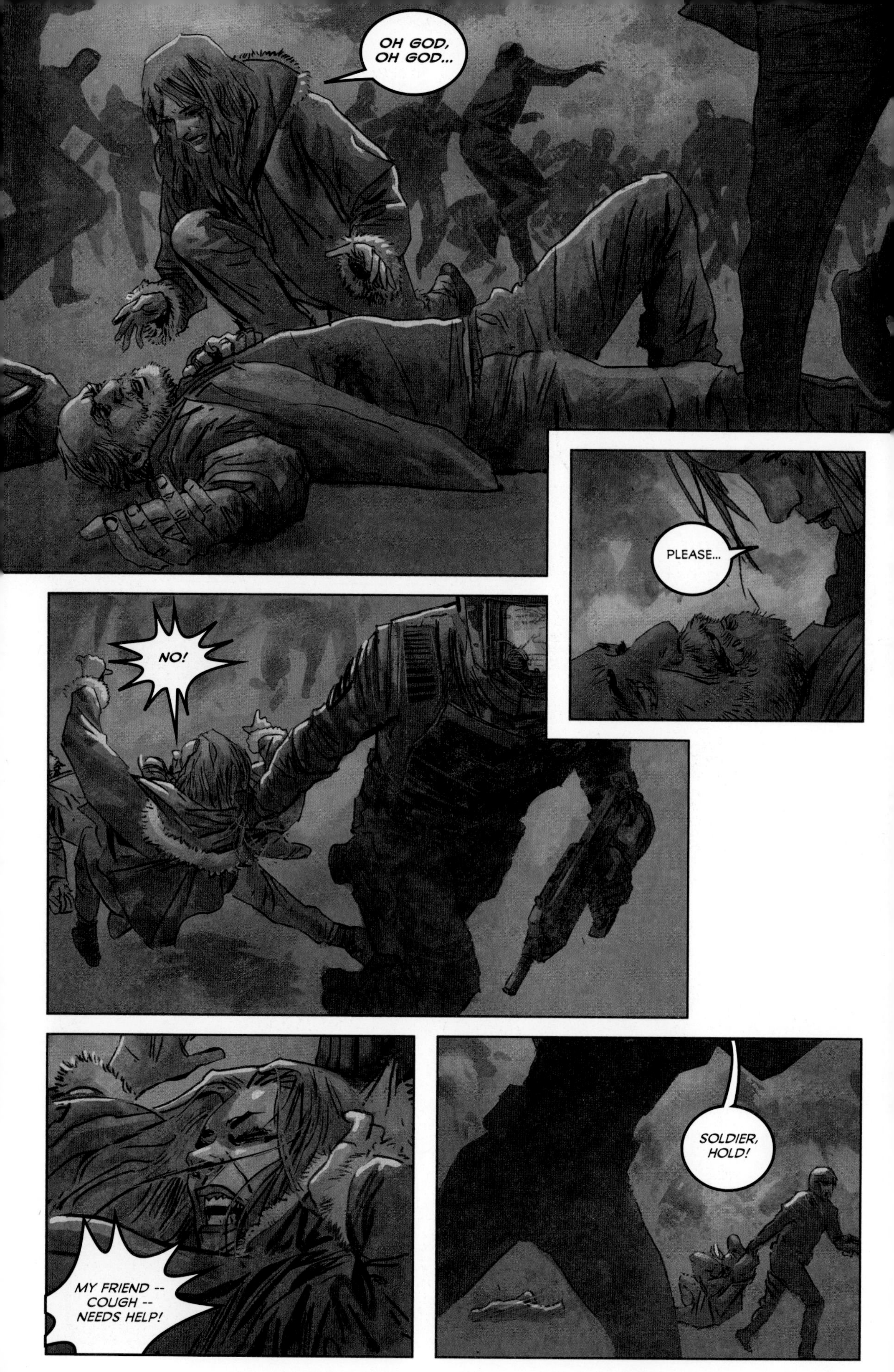
OH GOD,
OH GOD...
PLEASE...
NO!
MY FRIEND -- COUGH -- NEEDS HELP!
SOLDIER, HOLD!

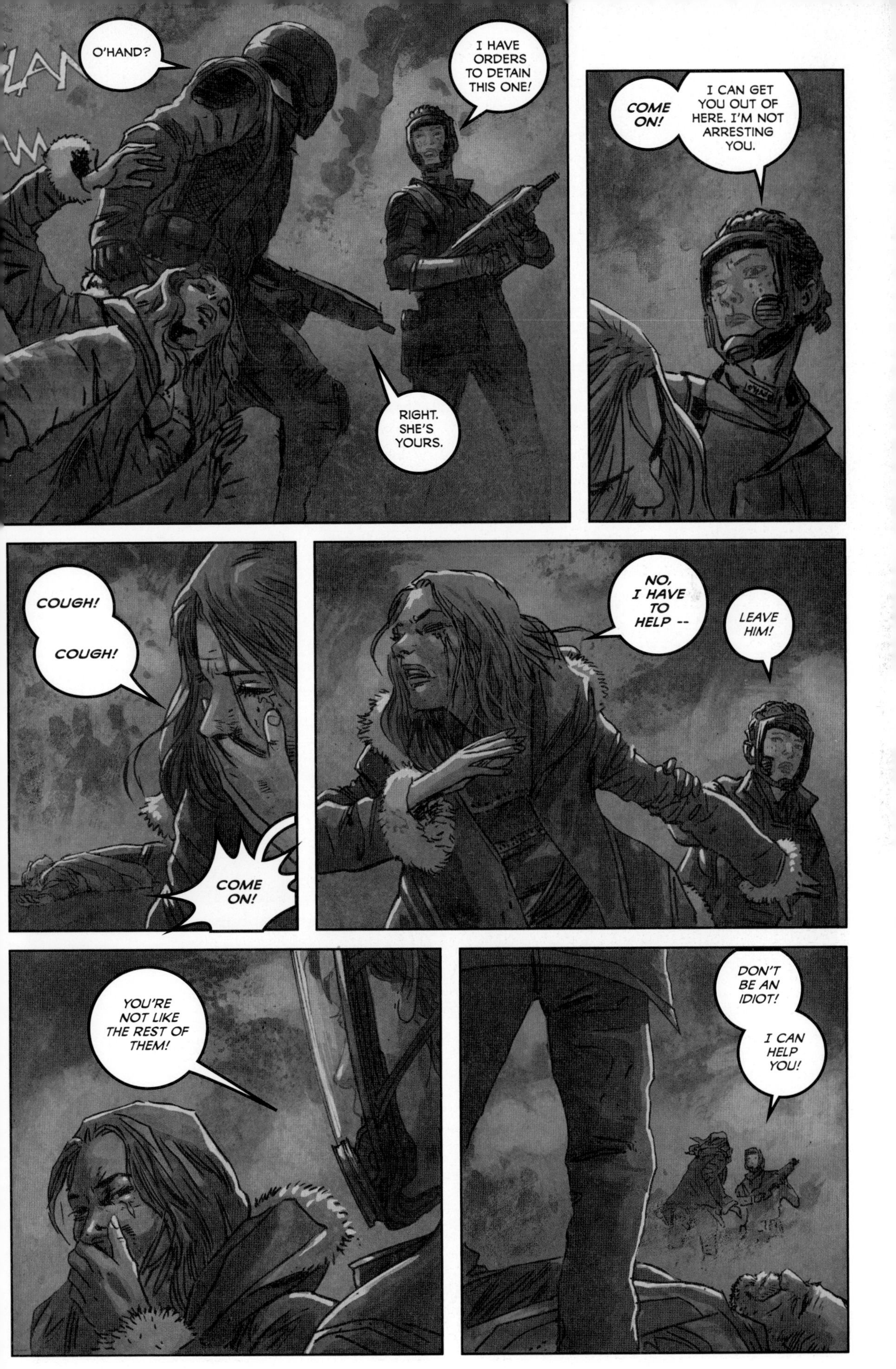
O'HAND?
I HAVE ORDERS TO DETAIN THIS ONE!
RIGHT. SHE'S YOURS.
COME ON!
I CAN GET YOU OUT OF HERE. I'M NOT ARRESTING YOU.
COUGH!
COUGH!
COME ON!
NO, I HAVE TO HELP --
LEAVE HIM!
YOU'RE NOT LIKE THE REST OF THEM!
DON'T BE AN IDIOT!
I CAN HELP YOU!

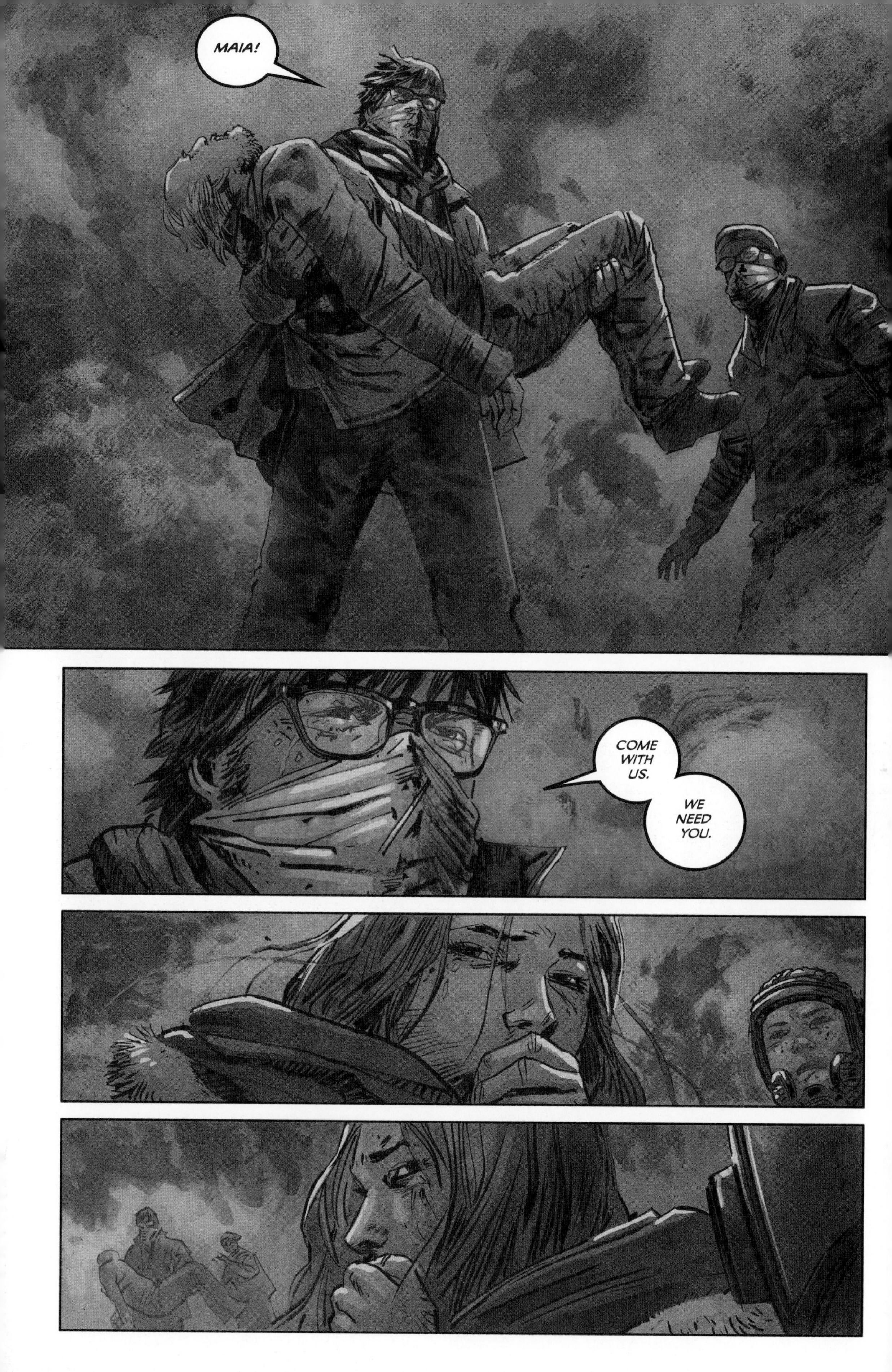
MAIA!
COME WITH US.
WE NEED YOU.

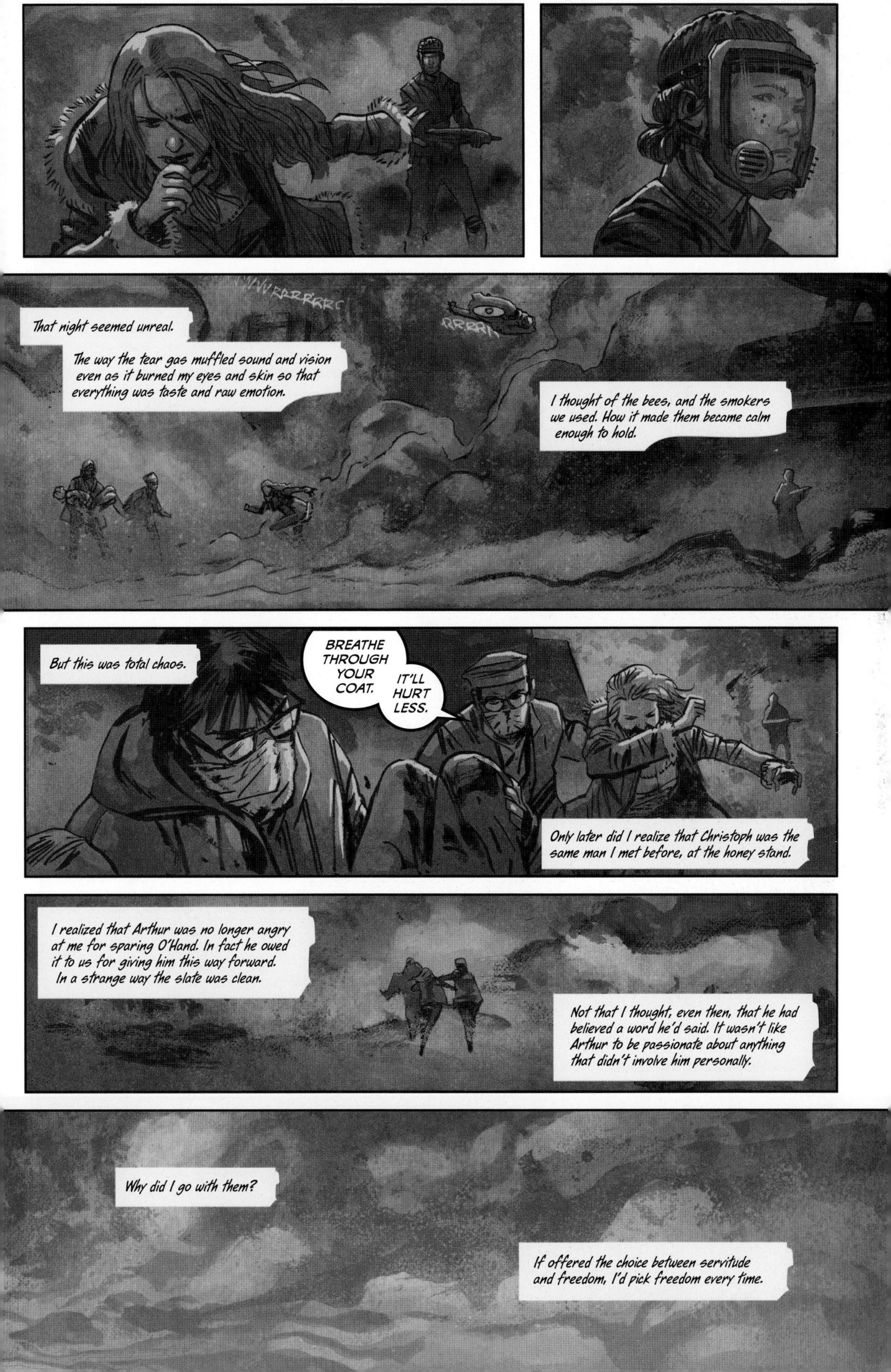
That night seemed unreal.
The way the tear gas muffled sound and vision even as it burned my eyes and skin so that everything was taste and raw emotion.
I thought of the bees, and the smokers we used. How it made them became calm enough to hold.
But this was total chaos.
BREATHE THROUGH YOUR COAT.
IT'LL HURT LESS.
Only later did I realize that Christoph was the same man I met before, at the honey stand.
I realized that Arthur was no longer angry at me for sparing O'Hand. In fact he owed it to us for giving him this way forward. In a strange way the slate was clean.
Not that I thought, even then, that he had believed a word he'd said. It wasn't like Arthur to be passionate about anything that didn't involve him personally.
Why did I go with them?
If offered the choice between servitude and freedom, I'd pick freedom every time.

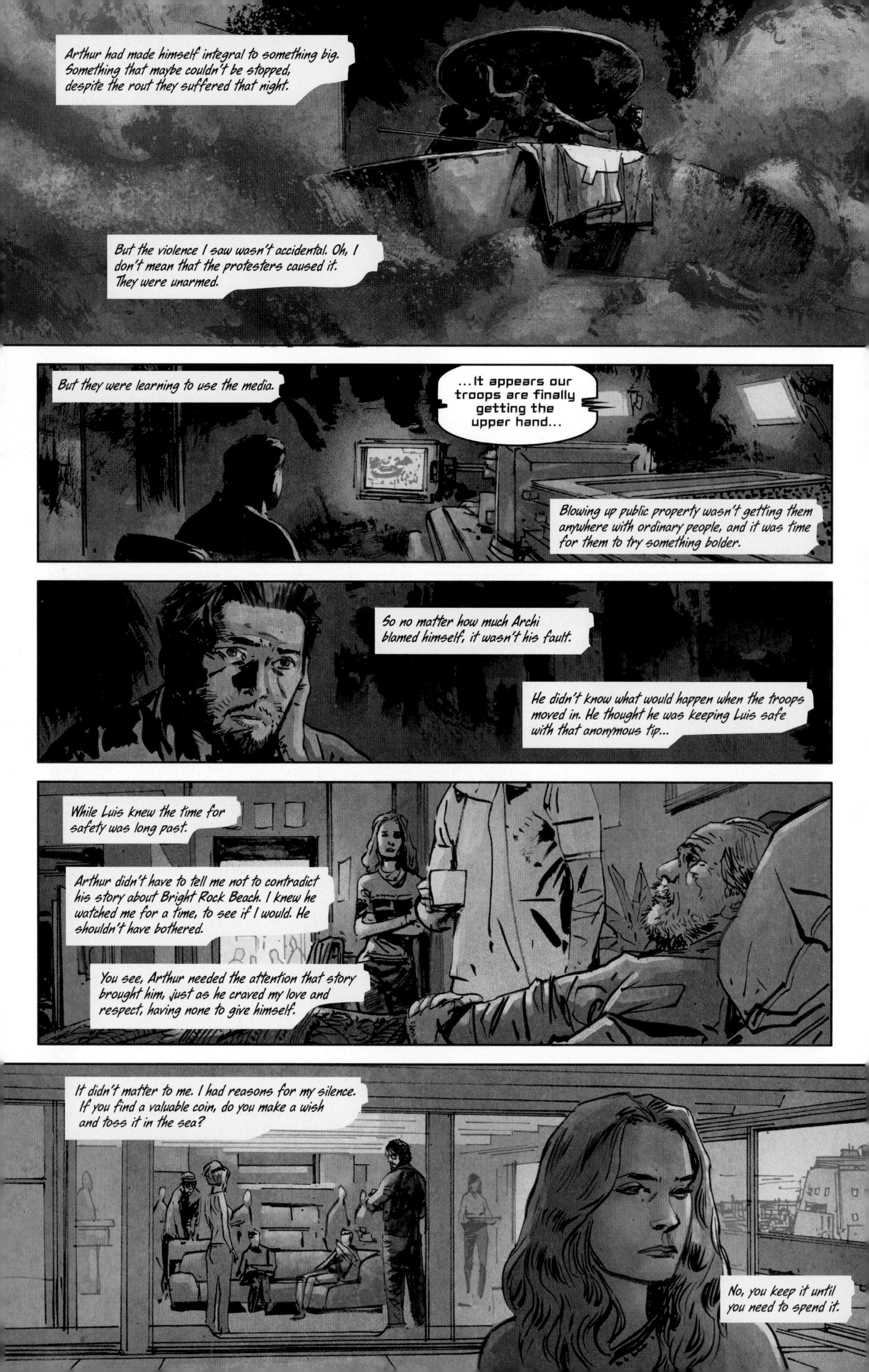
Arthur had made himself integral to something big. Something that maybe couldn't be stopped, despite the rout they suffered that night.
But the violence I saw wasn't accidental. Oh, I don't mean that the protesters caused it. They were unarmed.
But they were learning to use the media.
...It appears our troops are finally getting the upper hand...
Blowing up public property wasn't getting them anywhere with ordinary people, and it was time for them to try something bolder.
So no matter how much Archi blamed himself, it wasn't his fault.
He didn't know what would happen when the troops moved in. He thought he was keeping Luis safe with that anonymous tip...
While Luis knew the time for safety was long past.
Arthur didn't have to tell me not to contradict his story about Bright Rock Beach. I knew he watched me for a time, to see if I would. He shouldn't have bothered.
You see, Arthur needed the attention that story brought him, just as he craved my love and respect, having none to give himself.
It didn't matter to me. I had reasons for my silence. If you find a valuable coin, do you make a wish and toss it in the sea?
No, you keep it until you need to spend it.

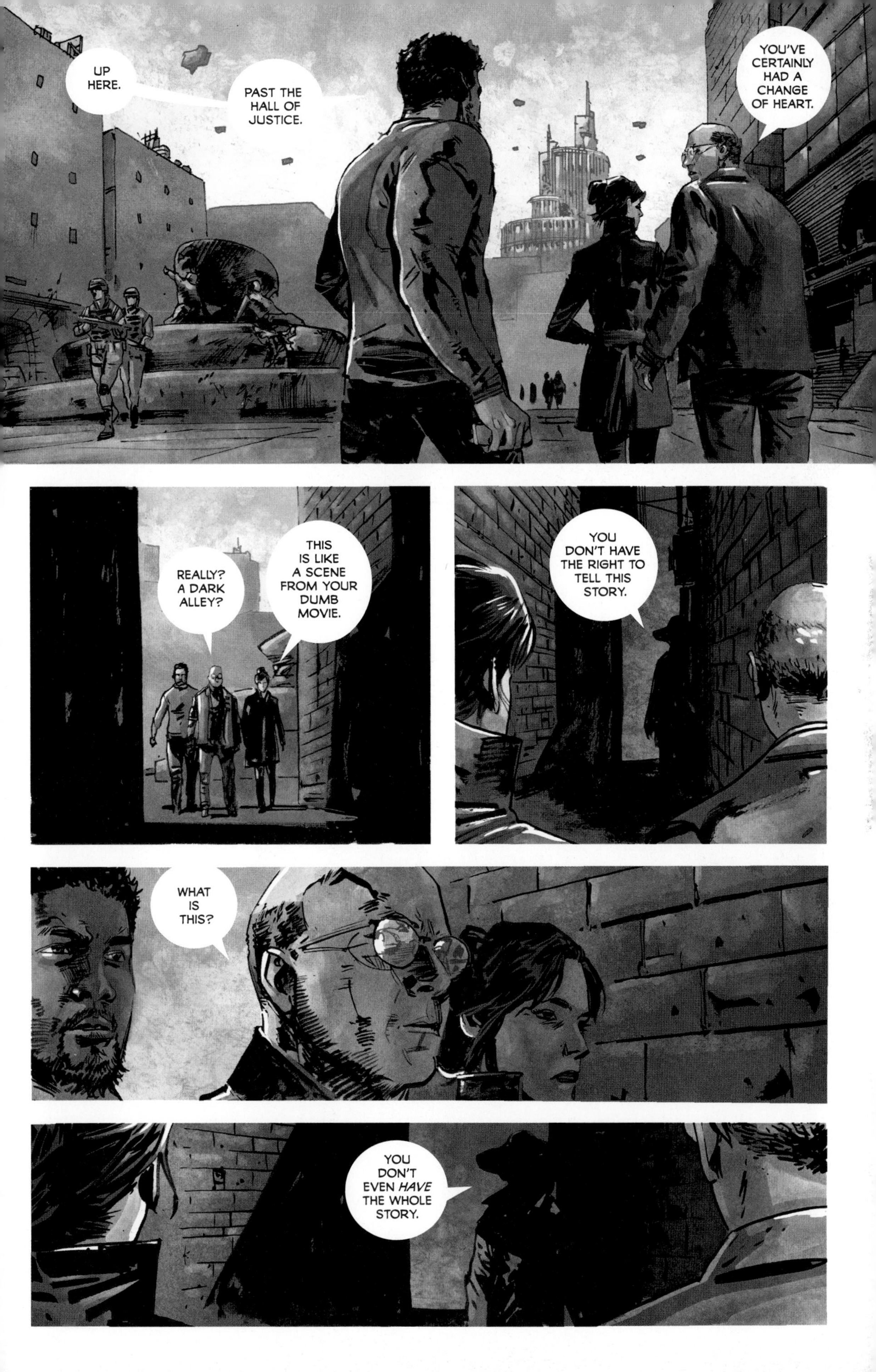
UP HERE.
PAST THE HALL OF JUSTICE.
YOU'VE CERTAINLY HAD A CHANGE OF HEART.
REALLY? A DARK ALLEY?
THIS IS LIKE A SCENE FROM YOUR DUMB MOVIE.
YOU DON'T HAVE THE RIGHT TO TELL THIS STORY.
WHAT IS THIS?
YOU DON'T EVEN *HAVE* THE WHOLE STORY.

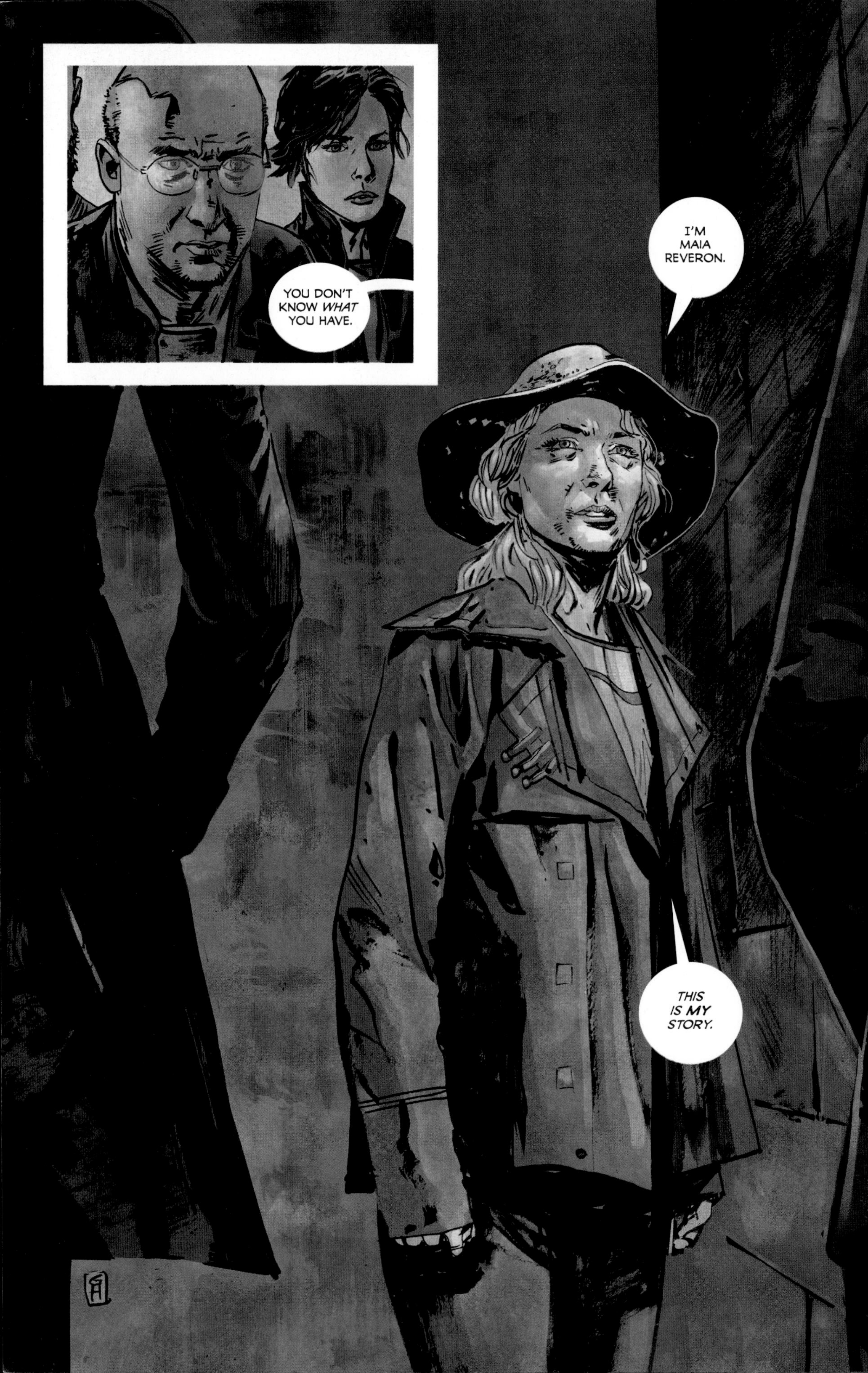
YOU DON'T KNOW *WHAT* YOU HAVE.
I'M MAIA REVERON.
THIS IS ***MY*** *STORY.*

END OF
CHAPTER
01

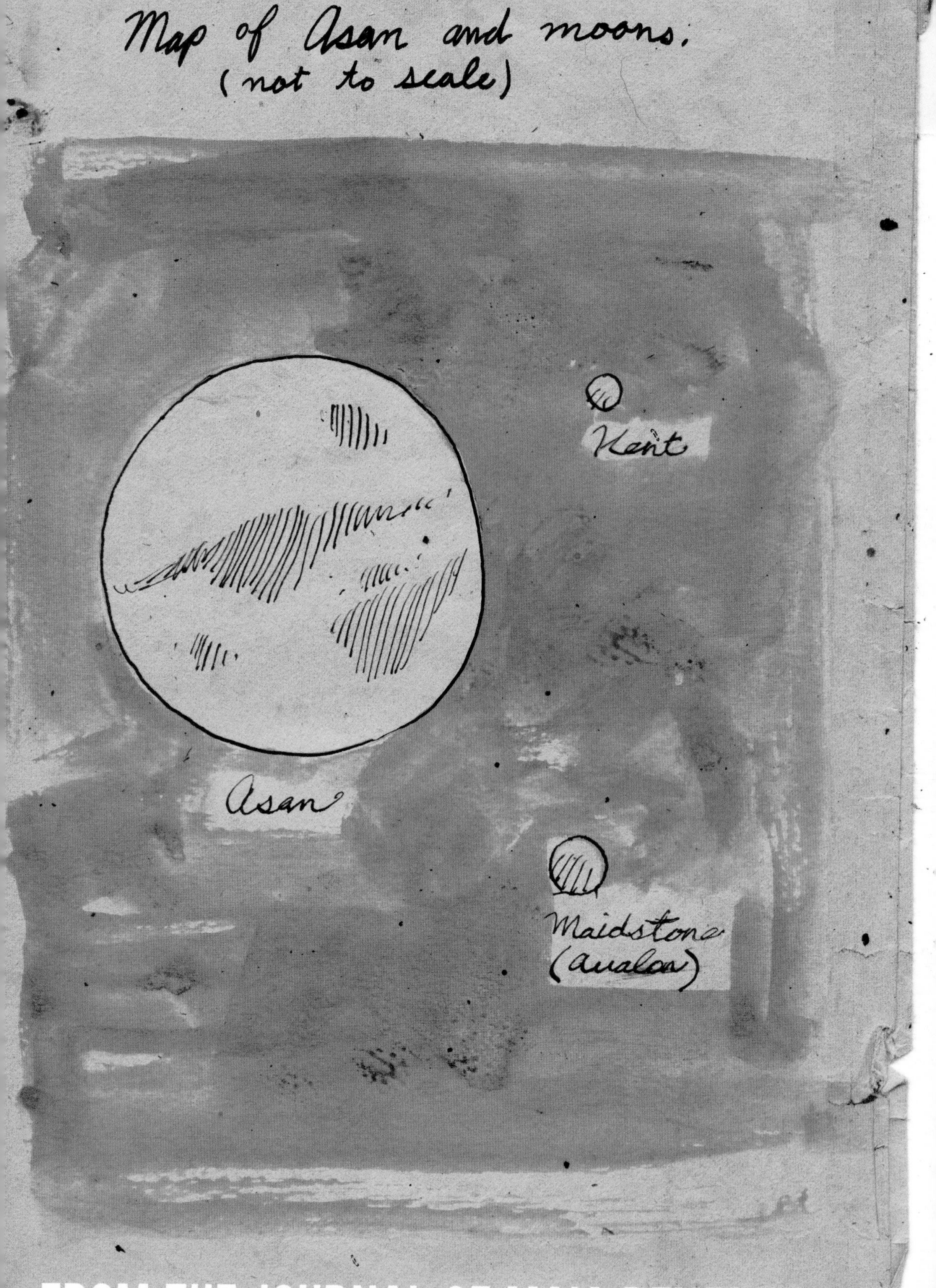
Map of Asan and moons.
(not to scale)
Kent
Asan
Maidstone
(avalon)

FROM THE JOURNAL OF MAIA REVERON

The Social Insect

BY CORINNA BECHKO

"For where's the State beneath the Firmament That doth excell the Bees for Government?"– Du Bartas

The St. Helena giant earwig became extinct just last year, but barely made the news. Insects are disappearing from our world at an alarming rate, but if the same thing happens to bees, the ramifications are enormous.

We tend to think of bees as pollinators and producers of honey. We may associate them with hard work and industry. Their communal lifestyle fascinates us with its implications for emergent complexity. But we tend to forget the ways that bees, and beekeeping, have directly changed our history.

The oldest records of gathering honey date to around 7,000 BCE, in the form of cave paintings in Africa and Spain. A few seem to show untroubled people in the midst of a swarm, leading some archaeologists to believe that humans had already mastered the use of smoke as a calming agent by that ancient date.

Later, artificial beehives were built from clay and straw, fashioned to mimic the hollow trees and crevices that bees naturally utilize. Once captive, a sharp eye was needed to learn how best to maximize honey production. This "nectar" was highly valued, said to be the food of the gods on Mount Olympus in Greek mythology, and cherished by the Mayans. For thousands of years, before the cultivation of sugarcane, it was among a tiny handful of sweeteners and usually the only one readily available.

But bees are of value in another way too. Despite the close watch kept by their caretakers, much of their society remained hidden. What was observable seemed well-regulated, purposeful, and civilized. Soon a tradition sprang up equating bees with politics, and beehives with tiny utopias. Workers behaved communally, sacrificing themselves if necessary. Their ruler was a benevolent queen. Never harsh or unfair, she too existed merely to enrich her nation. There were lessons here for commoners laboring to support the top-heavy societies that balanced on their backs. It's no accident that bees are among the oldest symbols of the French monarchy, a subtle reminder of how royalty fits into the natural order.

But there was another side to this lesson, one that many human workers took away instead. Bees "revolt against fraudulent management" wrote Lucius Columella in the first century ACE, warning beekeepers that they must practice "perfect honesty." Much later, the beehive (in the form of a "skep") was used as a potent symbol during the American Revolution, even appearing on money issued by the American Republican Congress in 1779. Here the imagery was meant to suggest inalienable rights, a theme and symbol used, ironically, by the French a few years later for a similar purpose.

Social responsibility. Communalism. Rule by divine right. Revolution. Big ideas, but through it all bees continue to pollinate our crops and produce our honey. Some believe that the extinction of bees will lead to an economic collapse unlike any other. Hopefully humanity will be able to dodge that particular bullet, allowing our entwined societies to continue far into the future.

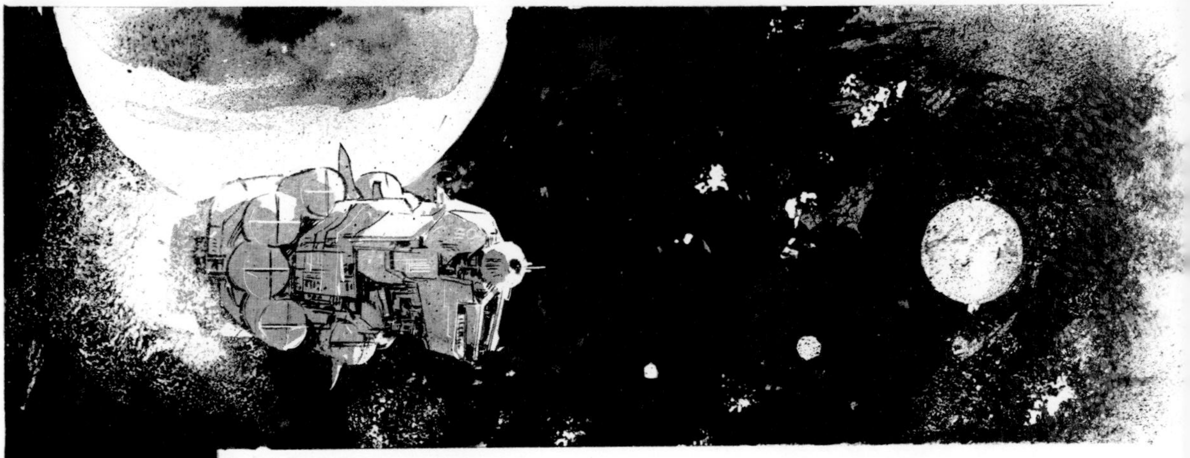

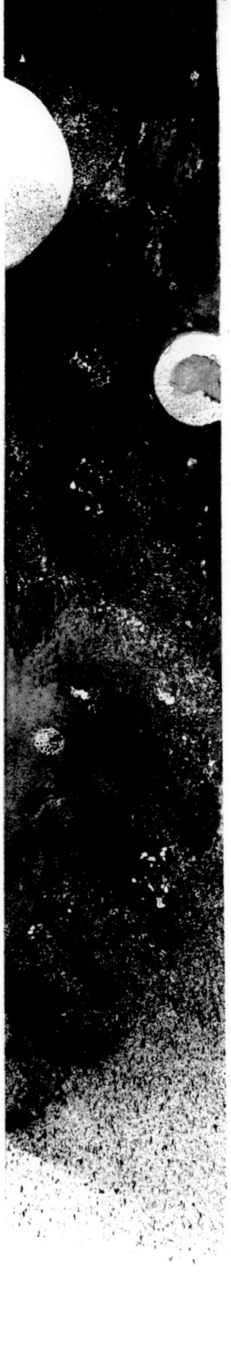

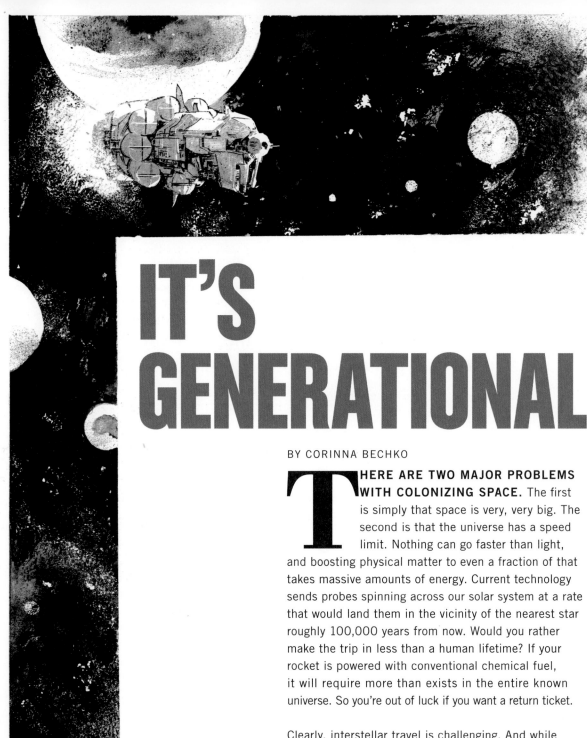

IT'S GENERATIONAL

BY CORINNA BECHKO

THERE ARE TWO MAJOR PROBLEMS WITH COLONIZING SPACE. The first is simply that space is very, very big. The second is that the universe has a speed limit. Nothing can go faster than light, and boosting physical matter to even a fraction of that takes massive amounts of energy. Current technology sends probes spinning across our solar system at a rate that would land them in the vicinity of the nearest star roughly 100,000 years from now. Would you rather make the trip in less than a human lifetime? If your rocket is powered with conventional chemical fuel, it will require more than exists in the entire known universe. So you're out of luck if you want a return ticket.

Clearly, interstellar travel is challenging. And while it's safe to say that we won't be building a ship with extra-solar capabilities within the next few years, there are already plans underway for a launch by the twenty-second century. That is, if a few nagging details can be worked out ahead of time.

At first glance, a reliable propulsion system might seem to be the largest hurdle. But there are a surprising number of detailed designs that should work to keep an enormous ship not only moving, but accelerating.

Fusion, for example, provides something on the order of a million times the energy that a similar amount of chemical fuel would yield. A more pressing problem then becomes one of deceleration. When traveling at 10% the speed of light it would be easy to fly right past the target system without even realizing it. Slowing down takes time, and even more fuel.

But in many ways the most intractable problems are familiar ones. If the ship is meant to colonize another world instead of robotically explore it, it will have to carry people as part of its payload. And people don't always do what you expect them to.

The solution seems clear: pick the best candidates, subject them to massive amounts of screening, and educate them thoroughly on what to expect. This is roughly how we pick astronauts currently, so why mess with success? Like most things involving interstellar travel, it's not that easy. The distance between star systems is so gargantuan that even at a significant fraction of light speed it will take multiple human lifespans to reach the closest viable destination. Suddenly, this ship becomes an ark with a breeding population of humans on board along with all of the ecology and technology necessary to not only sustain them but to preserve their culture. Sure, you might like to go into space knowing you'll never see the Earth again. But what about your grandson? The ethical implications alone are staggering.

A working government would also have to be preserved over a span that rivals the length of time the United States has existed. The population of such a ship would have to be at least several thousand to ensure its survival against disease, inbreeding, and pure bad luck. And forget using every spare centimeter for living quarters, food production, and machinery. Many generation ship designs call instead for excess room that would only be exploited as a "relief valve" when a disgruntled minority needed a place to call their own. A feature like that might just circumvent a ship-wide war.

Other problems include the unknown consequences of such a long space voyage. Even with massive radiation shielding, artificial gravity, and a huge complement of plants and animals, would the humans that emerged in the new star system still be the equivalent of humans left back on Earth? Genetic drift is a major driver of evolution in small populations, and immune systems can only adapt to what they are presented with. Disease would be a real concern not only on board, but also as new ships arrive at the destination with different sets of microbes to set loose, each massively mutated from what they started out as at home.

Does all of this make interstellar travel impossible? Of course not. Humans are highly resilient and adaptable. They have the unique ability to conceive of a future different from their current experience and work towards it. Generation ships will test humanity's limits, but chances are good that we are up to the task.

The distance between star systems is so gargantuan that even at a significant fraction of light speed it will take multiple human life spans to reach the closest viable destination.

To learn a lot more about how a generation ship might actually work, visit ***icarusinterstellar.org****, a nonprofit dedicated to achieving interstellar flight within the next one hundred years.*

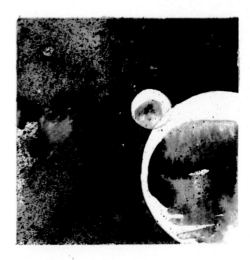

COVERS

BY GABRIEL **HARDMAN**
AND JORDAN **BOYD**

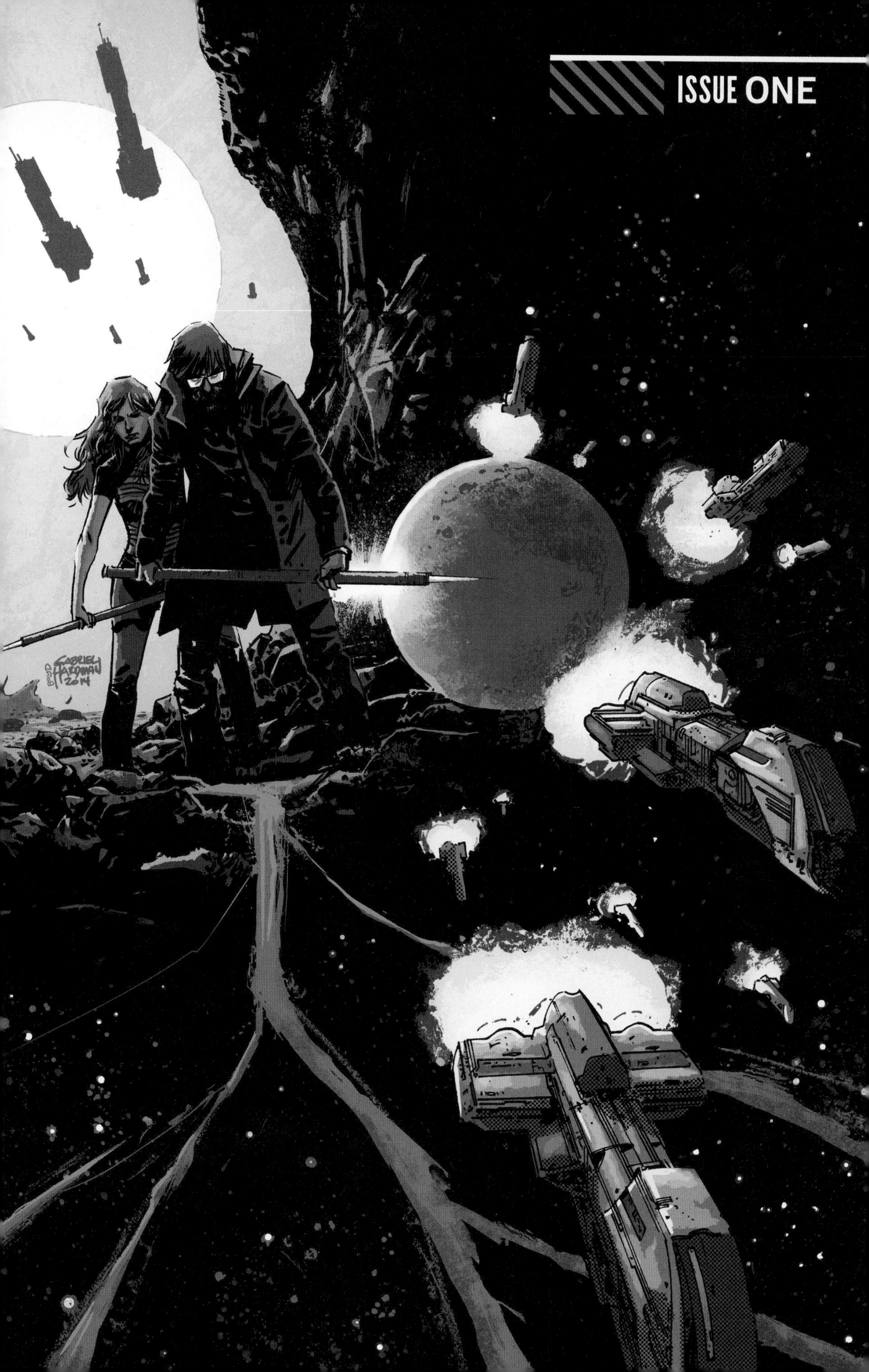
ISSUE ONE
GABRIEL HARDMAN 2014

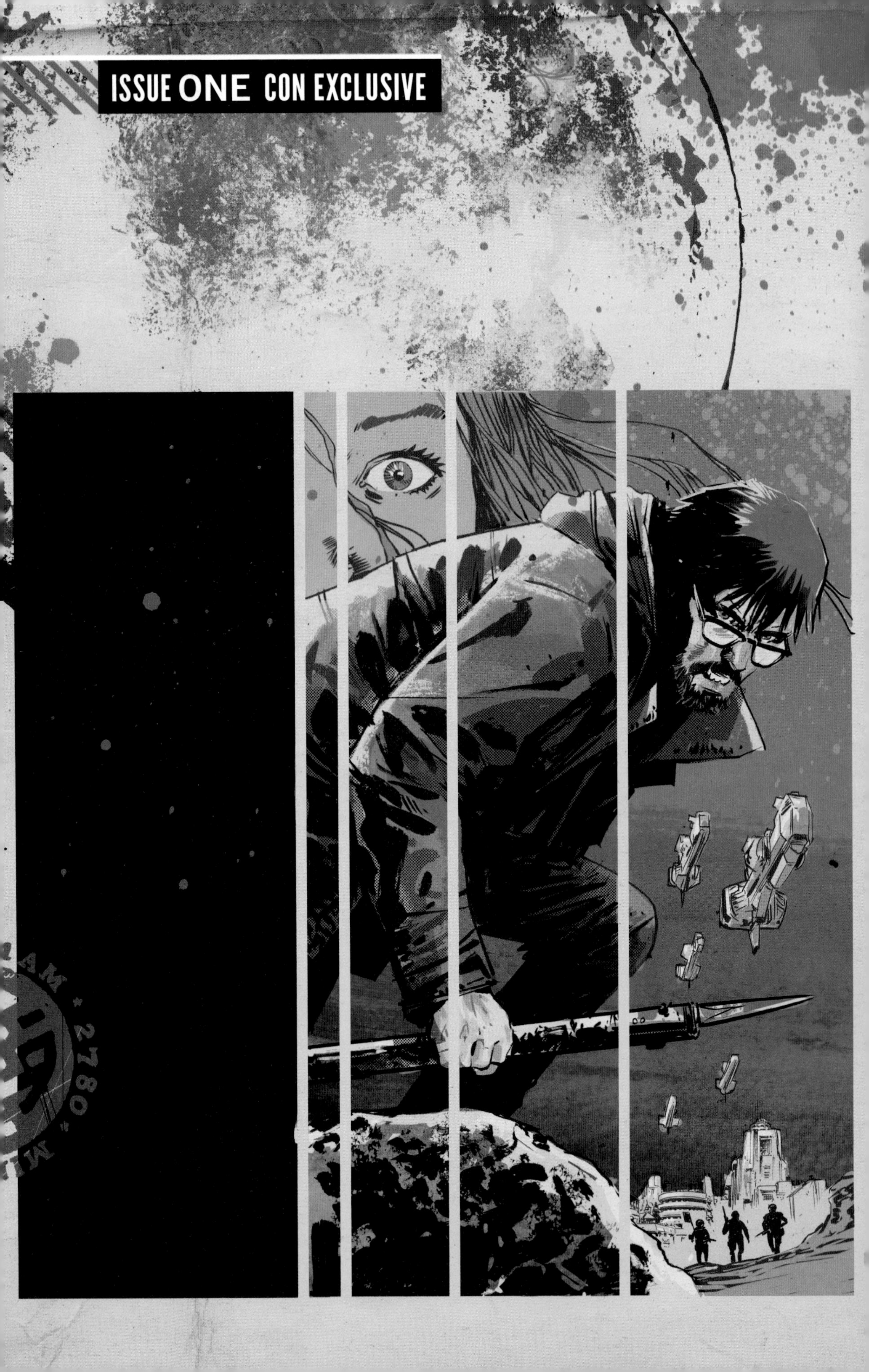
ISSUE ONE CON EXCLUSIVE

ISSUE TWO

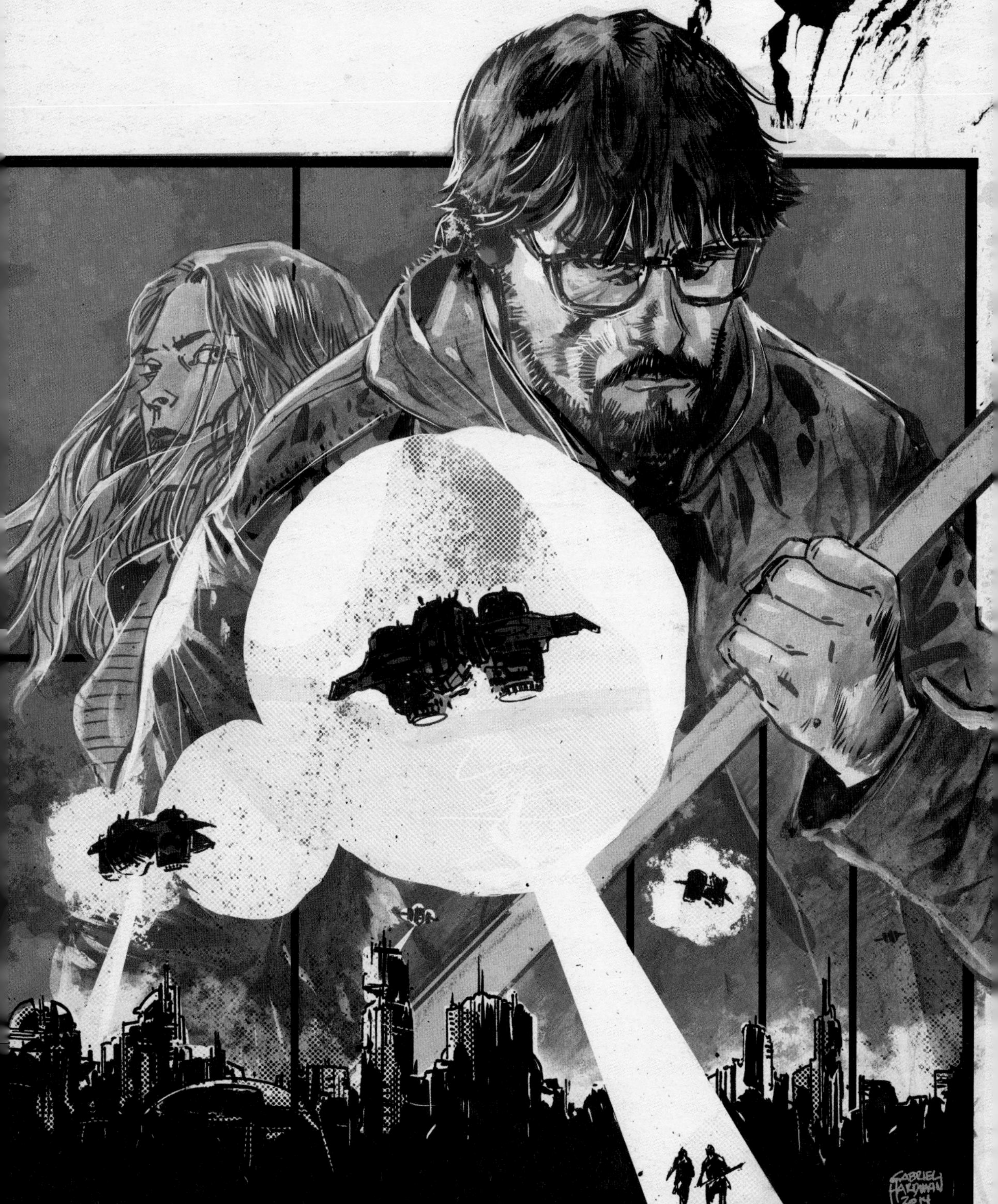
GABRIEL HARDMAN 2014

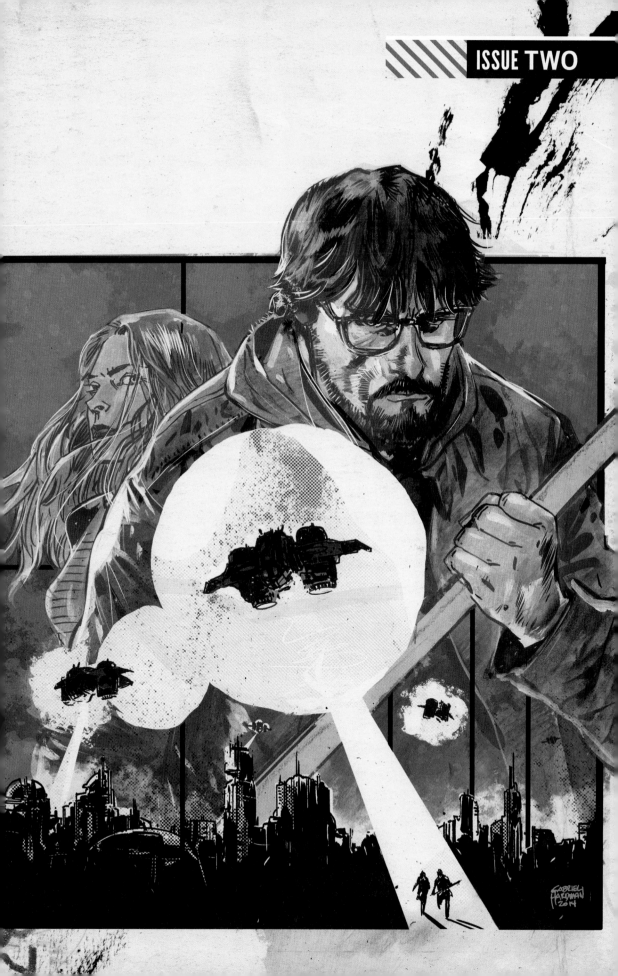

ISSUE THREE

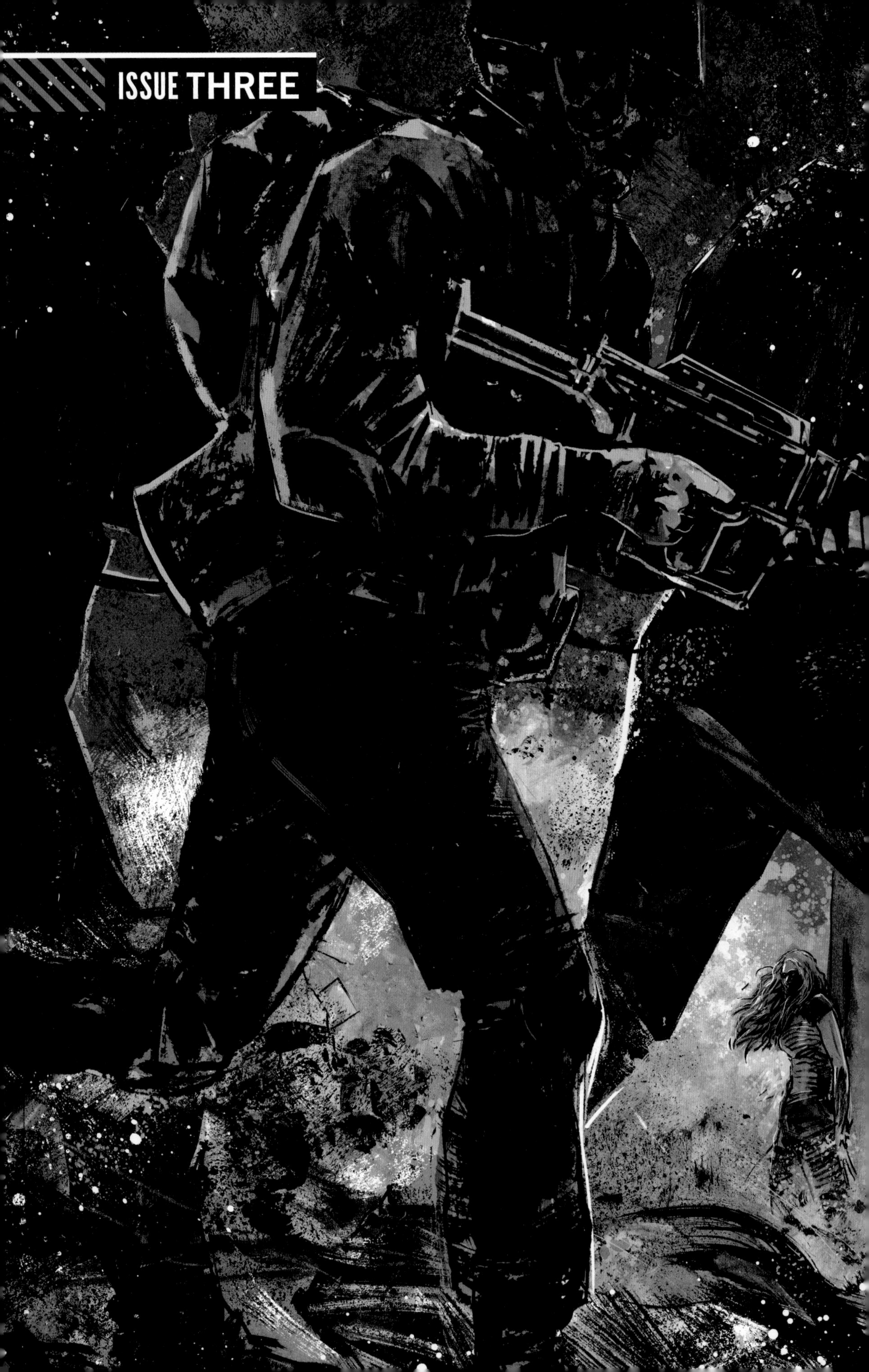

ISSUE FOUR

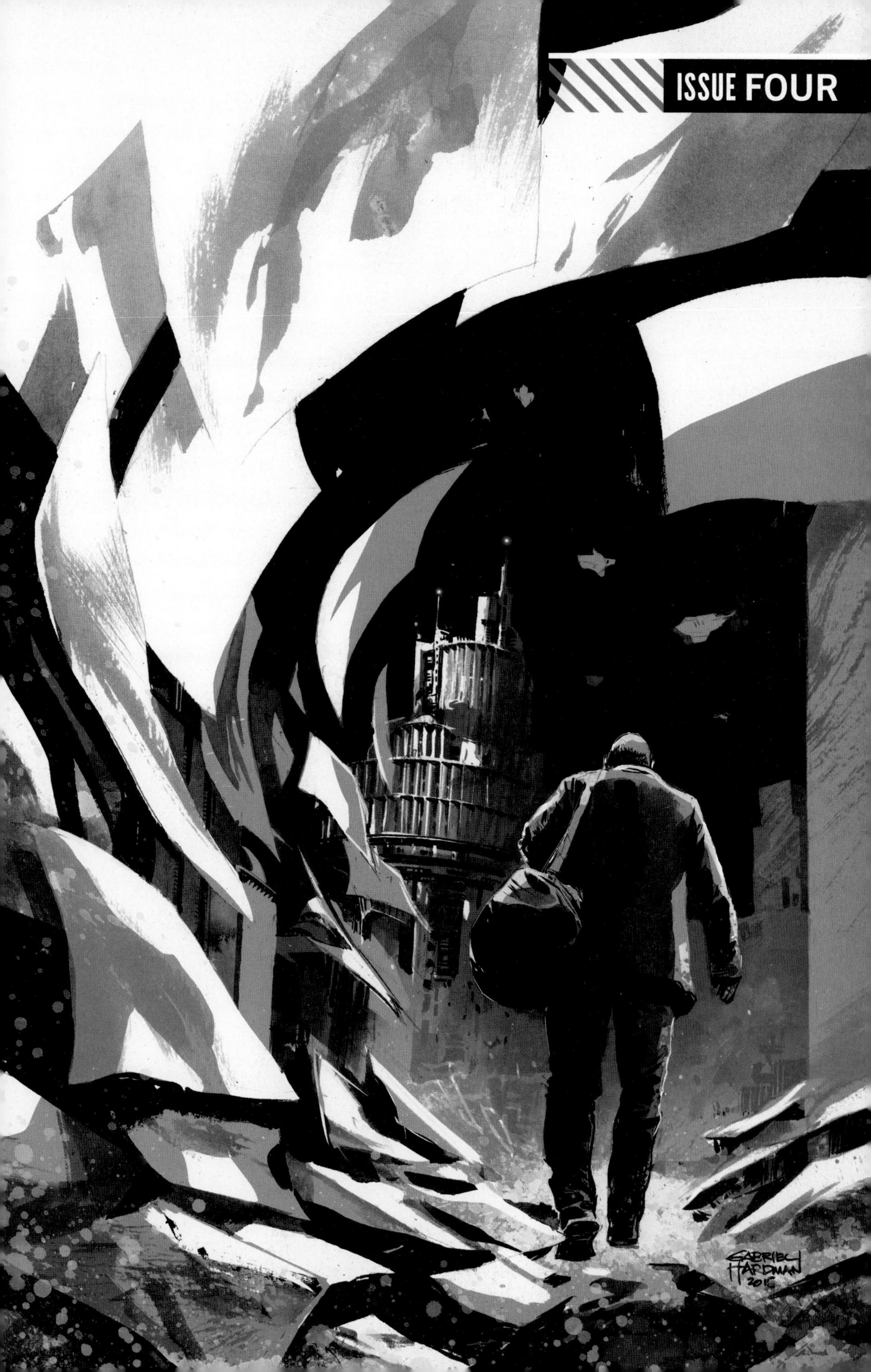
GABRIEL HARDMAN 2015

ISSUE FIVE

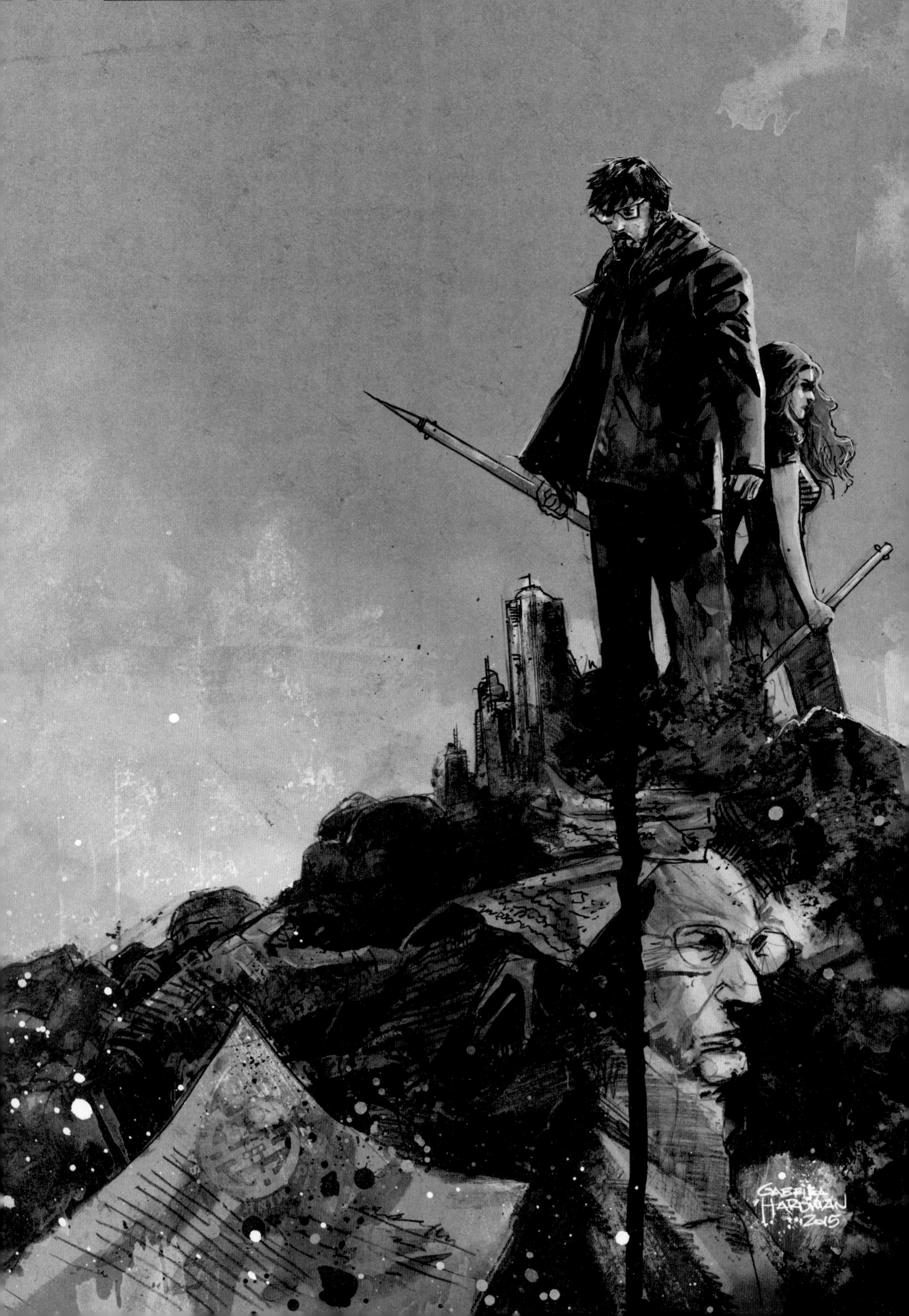
GABRIEL HARDMAN 2015

GABRIEL HARDMAN is the writer/artist of *Kinski,* published digitally by Monkeybrain Comics and collected in print by Image Comics. He also co-wrote (with Corinna Bechko) and drew *Savage Hulk* for Marvel Comics, *Sensation Comics* for DC Comics, *Star Wars: Legacy* for Dark Horse Comics, and *Planet Of The Apes* for Boom! Studios. He has drawn *Hulk, Secret Avengers* and *Agents of Atlas* for Marvel as well as the OGN *Heathentown* for Image/Shadowline. He's worked as a storyboard artist on movies such as *Interstellar, Inception, Tropic Thunder,* and *X2.* He lives with his wife, writer Corinna Bechko in Los Angeles.

gabrielhardman.tumblr.com   @gabrielhardman

CORINNA BECHKO has been writing comics since her horror graphic novel *Heathentown* was published by Image/Shadowline in 2009. Since then she has worked for numerous publishers including Marvel, DC, Boom!, Dynamite, and Dark Horse on titles that include *Aliens/Vampirella* and *Lara Croft and the Frozen Omen,* as well as co-writing *Star Wars: Legacy Volume II, Savage Hulk,* and *Sensation Comics featuring Wonder Woman.* She is a zoologist by training and shares her home with co-creator/husband Gabriel Hardman, three cats, a lovebird, a farm dog, and a fancy street rabbit.

corinnabechko.tumblr.com   @corinnabechko

JORDAN BOYD

Despite nearly flunking kindergarten for his exclusive use of black crayons, Jordan has moved on to become an increasingly prolific comic book colorist. Some of his most recent credits include *Planet Hulk* and *Ant-Man* for Marvel, and *Deadly Class* for Image. He and his family reside in Norman, OK.

boydcolors.tumblr.com   @jordantboyd

DYLAN TODD is an art director and graphic designer. You might have seen his work on comics like *Sacrifice, Five Ghosts, Edison Rex, POP,* or *Avengers A.I.* Sometimes he writes comics and sometimes he writes about comics. Despite the fact that they don't show up in pictures, he actually does have eyebrows. His life's ambition is to meet an actual ewok.

bigredrobot.net   @bigredrobot

ALSO BY THE AUTHORS

HEATHENTOWN
WRITTEN BY CORINNA BECHKO
ART BY GABRIEL HARDMAN

When Anna travels deep within the Florida Everglades to attend her closest friend's funeral she finds herself in an eerie, small town where death might not be the end. To discover the truth she unearths a coffin, starting a chain reaction and bringing an ancient malevolence into the town bent on Anna's destruction!

"An unorthodox horror story, equal parts hidden worlds, lost love and mammoths, Heathentown is that rarest of things—a genuinely unusual take on the undead... Bechko and Hardman are a perfectly matched team as Hardman's beautiful, highly cinematic art captures the excitement and complex emotions of Bechko's memorable and nuanced story."
–Publishers Weekly

FROM IMAGE COMICS/SHADOWLINE

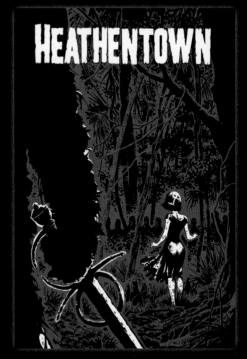

KINSKI
WRITTEN AND DRAWN BY GABRIEL HARDMAN

Kinski. The story of a boy and his dog. Only the boy is a traveling salesman and the dog doesn't belong to him.

Joe's self-styled mission to save a puppy from its neglectful owners escalates into a righteous crusade in this quirky crime thriller written and drawn by Gabriel Hardman (*Hulk, Heathentown, Planet of the Apes*).

"Hardman...creates a tense atmosphere that makes *Kinski* the *Breaking Bad* of dognapping tales." –A.V. Club

"[Gabriel] Hardman doesn't waste one line here, and the work is strong, iconic, and just plain awesome...This one is a true winner. You need this comic."–Bag and Board

FROM IMAGE COMICS

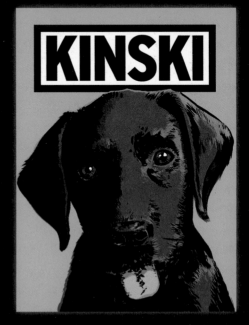